I0667112

This is a work of fiction. Any names or characters, businesses or places, events or incidents, are either fictitious or used in a fictitious manner. Any resemblance to actual persons, living or dead, or actual events is purely coincidental.

Cover Photo by Wayne Wood

ISBN-13: 978-0692840450 (City on a Hill)
ISBN-10:0692840451

The Homestead

Chapter 1
May 1966

*Be sober, be vigilant; because your adversary, the devil, like a
roaring lion walketh about, seeking whom he may devour.*
(1 Peter 5:8)

If you had ever had the hairs on the nape of your neck
stand up or felt an unexplained chill race down your spine, if you
had ever had the sensation you weren't alone in an empty room,
you knew what it was like to spend a night in the Felder House.
The house stood as a monument to its builder, Jonathan Felder,
for more than a century.

No one had lived there for years. It stood vacant and
decaying but not empty. The walls were said to vibrate with a life,
an evil energy, of its own. As locals were fond of saying, it
"stood a head taller" than the other houses in Delphi. It stood a
somber guardian over the town's secrets, and daring anyone to
tell.

The town called it "The Felder Place;" the Baumers
would nickname it "The Homestead." Roger and Rose Baumer
would find the old two-story house by accident.

Roger was a career soldier on leave prior to a year's tour
in Korea. Rose and their two children, Roger Jr., sixteen, and
Danny, twelve, were preparing themselves to spend another year
alone in St. Louis. On one afternoon the couple had left their
children to play with their cousins and had taken a drive to get
away from grandparents, kids, and numerous. Roger headed
north on Highway 70, leaving the congestion of the metropolitan
sprawl of the greater St. Louis area into the vast wheat and
cornfields of rural Illinois.

The car almost drove itself as Rose snuggled next to her
husband and gazed out at the broad expanse which was
swallowing them. One felt so small out here, she thought,
remembering how pioneers had crossed these plains more than a
hundred years before. She tried to imagine how they must have

2

felt taking days to cover the ground their vehicle would in an hour.

She read the exit signs as they flew past - Maryville, Troy, Marine... Roger pulled the car onto an exit ramp.

"Where're we going?" Rose asked lazily as Roger deftly maneuvered a sharp curve.

"I dunno, Willa Rose." Roger said absently, using Rose's full name affectionately, not taking his eyes off the road, "I just got tired of the highway. Let's explore."

"We need to watch the time..." Rose began with a note of warning in her voice. "You know how Mom is about supper."

"Yes, I know how your Mom is about supper. Look, this may be the last chance we have to be alone for a long time. I'm going to make the most of it."

The countryside was getting hilly now. Roger let the car cling to the road as he took every curve, dip and rise as fast as he could safely. He was dreading the coming separation. After all, he'd only been back from Nam a year, and he was leaving his family alone again. He had tried to get an assignment to a station they could follow him to such as Germany. Department of the Army had refused to allow him to get his orders changed. They needed helicopter pilots in Korea. It could have been worse, he reflected philosophically. He could be on his way to his third tour in Nam, where helicopter pilots were needed even more.

He drew Rose closer to him and risked a glance down at her. It was hard to believe they had been married almost seventeen years. In the early afternoon sun, she didn't look much different from the girl he had married. He was filled with a fresh outpouring of love for his wife. It happened every so often. There were times when he'd catch himself taking her for granted, thinking he was getting bored, maybe. Then, he'd catch himself looking at her and getting lost in her green eyes all over again, or melting at her smile.

He watched her hair flying in the breeze from the open window. The sun's rays would catch her hair, causing it to throw off a reddish brown glow. He thought of the years they had spent together, regretting the separations, and feeling amazement at the love that gave her the patience to tolerate the hardships of being an Army wife. He caught himself falling in love with her all over again.

She looked up into his eyes and smiled, "Gotcha!" she whispered. *How can she read my thoughts?*

The Homestead

Rose gazed into the eyes of her husband. It hadn't been easy, these years. There had been their shares of ups and downs, particularly in the beginning, but it had been worth it. She knew she could have searched the whole world and wouldn't have found another man as good as he, and many who were much worse.

She regretted the conditions under which they had been married and wished it could have been different. Her parents, Harold and Emily MacCrae, had been devastated. From the first they had opposed the relationship. Her father listed the objections – first Roger was four years older than she, and second he was a Catholic. Harold was a holiness preacher.

For the first time in her life, Rose disobeyed her parents and saw Roger secretly. She found herself lying: telling her parents she was with girlfriends, or at one school function or another. She hated herself for it but saw no other choice.

One of the ladies in the church had seen her getting in a car with Roger and broke her neck calling up her father to tell him that his daughter was going out with "that Catholic boy."

"I don't know what's gotten into that girl, Emily!" There was a pause, as though he were thinking. "No, I know what's gotten into her – lust for that Baumer boy!"

When his parents found out, the reaction had been just as drastic.

She physically shook herself. *Such morbid thoughts on such a beautiful day,* she scolded herself. She literally shook the morbid mood and the bad memories, as she had a thousand times over the years, and took note of her surroundings.

They were entering a small town now. A water tower, which dominated the skyline, announced the name, Delphi. *A dead little place*, Roger reflected as he drove through its deserted streets.

There was something about the town that depressed Roger. He was driving aimlessly now with no real destination. He just let the car choose its own route, turning right at this intersection, left at another. There was an incongruity about each street, which made him uneasy. On this street there would be one or two nice little houses, freshly painted, with neatly trimmed lawns next door to shanties that looked as if they had been transported off the pages of *Tobacco Road.* It was a nice summer day, but the streets were strangely deserted. So far he hadn't recalled seeing one living being outside. There was - for want of a better word- a *spirit* about the town, a spirit of despondency. It was as if the entire town had lost its hope.

He looked over at Rose again; she was gazing out her window absently, apparently lost in thought. Suddenly, as if she realized he was watching her, she turned. Their eyes met for a moment. Roger checked for traffic, and leaned over toward her.

He was about to give her a quick kiss when she sat straight up in her seat and shouted, "Oh look!"

"What?" Roger said, startled by her exclamation. He had almost driven the car off the road. "What is it?"

"Stop the car, quick!"

"What is it?" Roger slammed on the brakes.

"Look at that house!" Rose said, pointing. Roger slowly turned his head to where she was pointing.

"What hou- oh, you've got to be kidding!" he said as he saw what had caught her attention. "Is *that* what you almost got us killed over?" he asked in disbelief.

Rose jumped out of the car and ran across the street to get a closer look.

"It's *beautiful*!" she said.

"Honey, it's falling apart!"

"Look at it!" she said.

Roger crossed the street and put his arm around her shoulders, "I am, baby, I am!"

Roger studied the house with a practiced eye. He had learned that the smallest item out of place could be a matter of life and death. It didn't take too close a look to see the problems with the house.

It was a large two-story white frame house sitting on the corner. Roger didn't know a whole lot about architecture, but he figured this house was at least one hundred years old. It looked every day of its age. It was suffering from a severe case of neglect. Weeds had grown up around the house to the eves of the first story windows. Someone had installed aluminum siding. It was still in pretty good condition, but the window frames appeared to have not been painted in years and all of them needed caulking. Roger could only imagine what the inside of the house looked like.

"I know," Rose said. "It needs work... but the foundation looks to be good." She began wading through the weeds to look through a window. Roger watched her for a moment, then shrugged his shoulders and followed.

"Be careful, Baby," he warned. "There might be all kinds of snakes in this grass- they- "Rose wasn't paying attention to him. She had reached a window. She was working the palm of her hand against a pane, trying to rub away the grime and peer in.

"Honey..." Roger began almost pleadingly, "We'd better get on the road..."

"In a minute," Rose said, moving to another window and peering inside. "Oooooh look!" she squealed, "Come here, quick!"

"What now?"

"Look! Hardwood floors!"

"Swell. How can you tell with all the dirt?"

Rose made a face, "Don't be such a sourpuss!"

Roger grinned as he tried to peer through the window, "*You* were the one talking about getting back to Mom's in time for dinner..."

Rose was gone again. Roger looked up, just in time to catch her rounding the corner.

"Rose! Be careful, after all we don't know... great!" he looked skyward, "Why is it I see this one coming from a mile away and feel powerless to stop it?"

At that moment he heard Rose squeal from somewhere around the corner. His heart leaped as a thousand visions of tragedy swept through his mind, he rushed around the house, "Rose!"

He turned the corner and didn't know whether to be relieved or angry at what he saw, Rose was standing, excited at the edge of the yard. "It's for sale!" She pointed to a sign.

"Surprise!" Roger said, rolling his eyes. "I wonder what kind of fool would want to get rid of a magnificent palace like this?" Roger didn't understand it; he had never seen his wife so excited about anything like this before.

"Could we call the real estate man?"

"Honey...

"We've talked about buying a place."

"Yeah, but..."

"I bet we could get it cheap..."

Roger looked at the rear of the house; if anything, it was even worse from the rear. The back porch was rotted, there appeared to be an opening for a well. He could picture Danny falling in there. *Cheap. Any price would be too much.*

6

"We've been saving for a house for years. You've got your bonds..."

"I know..." Roger drawled, "But I was thinking we'd find someplace outside of Ft. Rucker... someplace livable...where the winters are warm..."

"What would be the harm in talking to the real estate agent?" She came over to him and put her arms around his waist. She looked up at him, making the most of her big green eyes. He looked down at her, how could he ever say no to her? She asked for so little.

He looked at the house again, trying to see it through her eyes "Is it that important to you?"

"What harm is it in asking?"

"None." he conceded. *But why do I get this feeling it won't stop there?* "What is it about this place that has you so excited?"

"I don't know," she answered, "there's just something about it, it feels like home to me. You know, being a preacher's kid and Army wife, I've never really had any place I could call home."

"I know, babe." he tried to avoid her eyes, "Well, it won't hurt to call."

"Oh Roger!" She squealed, wrapping her arms around his neck and jumping in his arms, "I love you so!" She hit the ground running, heading to the car, "Let's find a phone!"

"All right, all right. One of these days your green eyes aren't going to work..." Roger turned around and started to follow her. He made it to the front yard when he stopped dead in his tracks and turned quickly.

"What's wrong?" Rose called happily from the car.

"I don't know," Roger said thoughtfully, staring at the upstairs front windows. "I just got the feeling someone walked on my grave. 'Like we're being watched."

"Probably the neighbors..."

"No." Roger said firmly, crossing the street, "Not the neighbors, it was like someone was up there," he pointed to the upstairs front windows.

"Honey, you've had too many tours in Nam."

One's too many, he thought. "Maybe," Roger said, starting the car. He looked at the upstairs windows again. They were empty, but Roger could swear there was someone up there watching him.

The Homestead

Tom Hartzog studied the couple sitting across from him a moment. He contemplated showing them other properties, then thought better of it.

"It sounds like you're asking about the old Felder place," he said dubiously. He reached behind him and found a portfolio. He placed it opened on the desk in front of him facing so Roger and Rose could see the photograph. He watched as they both looked at the picture and nodded to each other.

"That's it," Roger said. "Is it still available?"

Tom stifled a laugh.

"Mister -er- Baumer?" he paused while Roger nodded, "Mr. Baumer, that place has been available for almost five years." He let that sink in. He'd been in real estate ten years; the Felder place had been the hardest property ever for him to sell- and he was selling property in an area that had been depressed since the mines closed down fifteen years before. He decided to play it straight with them.

"It's a mess really." He leaned forward in his seat, placing his elbows on his desk, and brought his fingertips together in front of his face, "That piece of property, that house, has been in the Felder family since the 1800s. Then, oh - was it fifty-two or fifty-three? I forget now- anyway, Johnny Felder, who'd inherited the place from his aunt, was giving Fred Grambling, the current owner, a ride home from a tavern in New Hauptstadt one night when the car they were driving ran off the road. Grambling sued ol' Johnny and won the only thing of value Johnny had to his name - the house. The folks in Delphi didn't appreciate Grambling suing his buddy when the guy was doing him a favor. Poor old Fred had to leave town. He put the house up for sale. The place has been empty ever since. Are you really serious about buying the place?" Tom asked again.

"Yes," Roger said, almost defensively, "What's the problem here?"

"Well," Tom drawled, "No real problem. It's just that it's an old place and it's going to take a lot of work to get it even livable, not to mention a lot of money..."

Roger was wondering what was going on here. First, there had been the reaction of the secretary who answered the phone when he called the number on the real estate sign. She had treated him like he was a prank caller when he got specific about which property he was talking about. Now this guy was acting, well, weird! Did he want to sell the place, or not?

"Isn't that our worry?" Roger asked impatiently, even while he was wondering at his irritation. After all, he didn't want the place anyway.

"I suppose so," Tom said, trying to smooth things over. "Don't get me wrong. I was raised in Delphi. I remember when I was a kid and Old Miss Felder lived there; it was the showplace of the town. But she's been dead fifteen years. Johnny moved in there. For a while, things were okay, but he lost it after his wife committed suicide. He started drinking. Then he began doing things to the place - well, I guess we can drive over there and let you see for yourself." He checked his watch, "It's four-thirty. I guess we have time for you to take a look at the place before dark."

He held the door open for Roger and Rose, "I just want to make sure I'm honest so no one can say later I wasn't upfront if the deal goes through…"

Tom's office was in Glen Haven, the county seat, and a twenty-mile drive from Delphi. Tom talked them into making the drive in his car, a decision Roger regretted immediately. Rose was in the back while Roger rode "shotgun." Tom chatted sociably, explaining that while Delphi had an elementary school servicing grades K through 8, high school kids rode buses to Glen Haven High School. Tom began regaling them with stories of the long bus rides to and from school, occasionally interrupting himself to point out a place of interest.

The Baumers listened politely. Rose was anticipating touring the house. Roger was contemplating the time they would lose riding all the way back to Glen Haven with Tom to get their car and the drive back to Belleville. Roger glanced back at Rose. He hadn't seen her this excited in years. He wondered what it was about that place that had her so excited. It was moving too fast for his taste. He didn't like making big decisions too quickly. Well, they hadn't signed any papers yet. There was no commitment. Not yet.

They finally reached the house. As Tom fiddled with the locks on the front door, stiff from lack of use, Roger noticed the front door, which appeared to date to the previous century. The upper half was a smoked or frosted glass portrait of a young lady, delicately done. She appeared to be staring out at the world invitingly, with a knowing little Mona Lisa.smile. Roger found himself staring at her, wondering if this had been a real woman or was the product of the artist/craftsman's imagination.

"They don't even make windows like that anymore!" Rose said, noting Roger's interest.

"Much less houses like this!" Roger quipped, evoking another face from Rose.

"I've been told old Doc Felder had that done. It's supposed to be his daughter." Tom said as he jiggled the key in the lock. "Here we are!" Tom exclaimed triumphantly as the door allowed itself to be unlocked and opened. They found themselves in a large front room. Roger estimated at least twenty-five by twenty-five feet. The ceilings were about twelve feet high.

"This place would be the devil to heat in the winter..." Roger mused, getting another face from Rose.

"Look at this woodwork!" Rose oohed. She was at one of the windows admiring the delicate hand-carved sashes.

"Someone must have really loved this place." Roger admitted.

"The Felders had controlling interest in the mines," Tom offered. "Along with the Baumholders – they were all interrelated by marriage- they were the richest family in town. They've come down a bit since the mines closed right after the war. They still carry a lot of clout in the area and own most of the desirable properties in Delphi. Doc Felder spared no expense building this place, I'm told."

"Look at the wallpaper, Roger!" Rose exclaimed, fingering a strip, which was peeling from the wall, "It feels like cloth!"

"It is." Tom said, "They don't even make wallpaper like that anymore."

"It's a shame we can't save it!" Rose said sadly.

"If we get the place," Roger said, "and that's a mighty big 'if. We're going to have to completely strip and redo all these walls, not to mention sand and re-varnish these floors. How big is this place?"

"There are only eight rooms in the house, not counting the walk-in cupboard and the bathroom, but they're all about this size."

"That's a lot of work," Roger said. "I only have a little over three weeks left on my leave. We'd have to close the deal on the house-"

"That'd be no problem, Mr. Baumer. Mr. Grambling has been trying to get rid of this place for years. Things are kind of informal in Glen Haven and I know everyone. We can close the house, at least to the point where you could move in and begin work, in a day or two."

Roger looked at Tom reproachfully. "Thanks," he said dryly.

Tom grinned sheepishly, "Well, let's see the rest of the place." Tom took them into the next room, which opened directly from the parlor. It had its own door opening onto one of the four corner porches. "This used to be Doc Felder's study. Here," he said moving to and opening a solid door on the far side of the room, "is where Johnny was going to put his bathroom."

The Baumers peered inside a small room, about six by ten, which was completely empty.

"Miss Felder had never installed an indoor toilet. As you can see, Johnny closed in one of the corner porches to create a new room. He was working on this when Grambling sued him."

"Okay, let's see... scrape, repaint or paper all the walls; sand and refinish all the floors; install bathroom..."

Rose gave Roger a not-so-friendly nudge with her elbow.

"What's behind that door?" Rose asked, changing the subject.

"Johnny made that the furnace room. I'd best show you that from the kitchen."

Tom led them back the way they came, back through the study, straight across the parlor, and through the opposite door into the largest room they had seen thus far. This was in a little better shape than the others, and was made to look even larger by a bay window, which protruded from the southern wall of the house. Even Roger had to admit he was impressed, in spite of the deterioration evident all around. What remained of elegantly expensive wallpaper covered the bottom half of the walls; this was framed by intricately carved chair railing and floorboards. The top half of the walls were covered with a fine velvet covering, inlaid with delicate designs. The decor approached gaudy, but drew back before going over the edge. The elegance was ruined by a kitchen sink on the east wall of the room and gas pipes sticking out of the southeast corner. There was an outside door on the west wall. On the north wall were three doorways, one of which they had used to enter the room, the entrance to the stairwell was in the center. Roger looked through the third door and couldn't believe what he saw.

"This used to be the dining room," Tom explained, "until

The Homestead

Johnny installed the furnace and moved the sink and stove hookups in here." Tom saw Roger heading toward the furnace room door, "I think that's part of Johnny's revenge.

"When Johnny lost the house, Grambling made a big stink about how he had removed several valuable fixtures from the house when he moved out. Grambling threatened to sue Johnny again for contempt of court if he didn't replace them. One of the things he said Johnny removed was the furnace. It came down to Grambling getting a court order making Johnny install a furnace.

"The school was in the process of installing a new furnace at the time. Johnny went down and bid on their old furnace and won. He cut out the kitchen floor to make room and installed it in here. Someone told me he was laughing about it at Klinghoff's in New Haupstadt that Grambling ought to be satisfied, there was enough furnace there to prepare him for his next home." Tom chuckled at that.

"It's a mess." Roger said.

"I can't argue with you there." Tom said, looking at the big iron metallic gray monster, which sat on the concrete sub floor of the kitchen. Heating ducts rose from the top of the furnace like the tendrils on Medusa's head. It was a coal furnace and its door hung open, giving Roger the impression of a gaping mouth. Roger could see where the floor had once been, jagged edges of the old floor still stuck out from around the wall, peeking out from beneath the floor molding like teeth. There were about six inches of water standing on the floor. With the concrete sub-floor (Roger wondered about that, had Johnny done it to install the furnace?) meeting the foundation, the room was like the bottom of a swimming pool, catching water from openings in the foundation. Tadpoles darted to and fro in the stagnant broth. Roger felt a tinge of sadness as he surveyed the sight. Like the rest of the house it had once been a nice room.

"There's a sump pump on the far side of the room over there." Tom offered, "All you have to do is flip that switch and it'll drain nicely. You have to do that when it rains..."

"That's nice."

"Do you want to see the upstairs?"

Roger looked at Rose, "Is it really necessary?" In his mind the furnace room was a deal breaker.

"Roger..." Rose pleaded.

"'Might as well take the full tour," Roger said with a note

of resignation in his voice.

As they went up the stairs, Roger felt a bit claustrophobic at first; it was a closed stairway. His vision had always been of the broad open staircase with a banister and open balcony from which the lord of the house could look down upon the front door. This stairway opened upstairs to a nice sized landing, which was above the furnace room. There were two windows facing west, from which one could get a glimpse of the backyard and part of main street Delphi. Wonderful.

Directly across from the top of the stairs was a bedroom, its windows faced north. Roger figured they were directly above the old study. He glanced around, if this room and the landing were any indication, the upstairs was definitely in better shape than the downstairs. He looked at the wallpaper. Except for fading from age and a few water spots, it was in pretty good condition.

"I guess you'd call this the master bedroom," Tom explained. Outside, the shadows were lengthening, signaling the setting of the sun behind the trees. Roger noticed Tom seemed to be in a hurry now.

"Look at how big it is, Roger!" Rose exclaimed.

"Yeah, great." Roger said, "It's getting late, honey." They had spent too long here; it was getting to be late afternoon. He wanted to get back to Belleville. Rose's parents would be worrying.

"There's not a whole lot left to see folks. We do want to get out of here before it gets dark. If you'll follow me, we'll show you the other two bedrooms."

They crossed the short hall into the middle, or east bedroom. If one was coming up the steps he or she would have had to have made an immediate one hundred and eighty degree turn to the right to enter it. This room was directly above the parlor and was the parlor's full size.

"A closet." It was the first Roger recalled seeing in the house. It didn't match the rest of the house. Roger opened one of the doors to a large walk-in closet. When the house was originally built, the entrance from the hallway had not been flush with the wall. There had been a section of room, which extended back behind the door. Someone had formed the closet by walling that section in so the south wall of the room was flush with the door.

"Yes," Tom said, "it's the only one in the house. As you

13

can see, it was added later. From what I can tell of the old houses I've been in around here, they weren't much for closets. They used wardrobes and dressers a lot." The light from outside dimmed appreciably. Agitated, Tom moved across the room quickly to the door to the south bedroom and opened it.

"This is the south bedroom, it used to be Old Miss Feldman's room," Tom said. "I remember when I was a kid I used to walk by on that street down there. You could see her in the window most times, just staring out. Everyone said she was a bit touched."

Tom looked at the couple, "Well, that's the tour, what do you think?"

"We'll have to think about it..." Roger said, avoiding his wife's pleading eyes.

"Let me tell you," Tom said with a confiding manner as he ushered the Baumers toward the stairs, "Grambling's eager to get this off his hands. The lawsuit has finished him in the town. At first he thought someone in town would pick it up, perhaps one of the Felders, but they refuse to buy the house because they believe it's theirs in the first place. Then he thought it would make a great tax write off, but he's in trouble with the IRS over some of his other deductions. His car business failed a few years back; there was talk about him not paying off notes on trade-ins, who knows?

"Anyway, he's been asking ten thousand for this place. He knows he'll never get it. I can give it to you for five."

"Five thousand dollars?" Roger said, looking around disbelievingly. Rose almost squealed.

They were outside now and Tom visibly relaxed. "The land alone is worth almost that. You've got almost an acre on this lot," he continued. "I know the house looks pretty bad, but most of this is just cosmetic. Other than the furnace room, all you need is a lot of water and a couple buckets of paint. As far as the bathroom's concerned, I think I can get him to throw that in. As I said, he's desperate for cash and needs to unload this."

"Let me think about this."

"Here's my card. Let's get back to the office, " Tom said, glancing warily at the sky. "It's getting late."

That night, as Roger and Rose lay in bed at her parent's house, they discussed the house.

"I hate leaving you for a year in that dump," he said.

14

"It won't be a dump for long, just let me move in there and get to work."

"I don't know..."

"Listen, Roger, how much money do we have saved up?"

Roger thought a moment. He counted the savings bonds his parents had been making him invest in since he was a kid on his paper route. There was the savings account at his hometown bank, and then there was the money Rose had managed to scrape together out of the household expenses. They had been a rare military family to manage to actually save money through all the moves and separations. "I figure we have about fifteen thousand saved."

"Honey, we can buy the house, spend another five thousand or so to paint and repair it, and still have money left over," she said. "We'll have a house of our own, paid for – a home to come to. You're going to be retiring in a few years. Won't it be nice to have a place to go?"

Roger looked at her squarely, "Yes, but I was thinking of some place warm..." He paused, "You really want this place, don't you?"

She nodded, "Yes, I do, Roger."

"Why?"

"I don't know. For some reason I feel like it's home. I haven't felt that way about a house in years."

"All right then. I'll call the guy in the morning."

Chapter 2
June 1966

"Behold, I send you forth as sheep in the midst of wolves; be
ye, therefore, wise as serpents, and harmless as doves.
(Mt. 10:16)

Roger carefully tooled his brush around the inside corner of the window frame, trying to avoid hitting the glass pane. He dabbed at a spot that had spattered on the glass and leaned back on his ladder - not too far- to get a better perspective on his work. He frowned as he saw an irregular mark on the wet surface. A bug of some sort had landed and gotten stuck. He took his brush and worked at the spot, finally prying the insect loose from the hardening surface. He wiped what was left of it on his rag. He dipped his paint in his bucket and smoothed out the spot where the bug had been with a fresh coat of paint. Looking at his work again, he smiled, satisfied. He didn't consider himself a perfectionist, at least, not any more, but he strove for excellence in everything he did. Rose always said it was the soldier in him.

He began climbing down the ladder. One more window left and he'd be through. He still had four days left on his leave to enjoy the new house. If that were possible, he thought. Tom Hartzog had been true to his word in getting the deal to close. In a matter of days, all the preliminary paperwork on transfer of deed and title had been accomplished. All they were waiting on now was the official deed to come back from Springfield. Roger figured that was one of the advantages of small town living.

The following two and a half weeks after the sale had been a flurry of activity, cleaning up the place in preparation for the renovations. Roger had insisted that first priority be made in making the house livable for the winter. He knew Rose had thousands of ideas about redecorating and adding on to the place. They would have to wait until the basic repairs were done. After the house had been "washed," Rose's brother-in-law, a professional carpenter came in to help. He had been a godsend, even though he charged union scale for his help. Roger smiled wryly at the thought. But still, his professional knowledge had saved days, perhaps a week or more, in paneling the downstairs

16

rooms and patching the plaster upstairs. The floors looked beautiful now, the hardwood renewed by sanding and fresh coats of varnish and lacquer. A plumber had come in and installed the bathroom and septic tank. The house had an indoor toilet for the first time in its history. The family had made a small ceremony of burning down the old outhouse. Several of the townspeople had driven by to gawk at the spectacle. Roger hated to admit it, but the dump was starting to look like a joint.

He had spent the last three days re-caulking and painting the windows. All he lacked was the last of the twin windows on the east bedroom and he'd be done with everything he could do before leaving.

Rose was inside with the kids unpacking. They had moved their furniture in a few days before. They'd had it in storage in Kansas, his last duty station, expecting to get it out when they moved to their next post. Last night had been their first night in the new house. The kids had been excited at having their own house instead of an Army housing unit or staying in a rented apartment. They had joined in with the work with an enthusiasm that surprised both their parents. Roger had been surprised at how much help the boys had been. Maybe Rose had been right about this place.

He could hear their dog, Ginger, barking. Another good point about the house, he reflected the kids got to keep their dog. *It's bad enough I have to go overseas without them losing their pet.*

He frowned as he moved the ladder over a foot or two to paint; he didn't like the furnace room the way it was. He hadn't trusted the old coal furnace to heat the house through the cold Illinois winters. He'd had a heating expert over to check it out. The guy said the unit might be a dinosaur, but it was a healthy dinosaur, and could be expected to last at least the winter. A new furnace would run over a thousand dollars and Roger didn't want to completely exhaust his savings. Then there was the time hack. Roger only had so many days, and he wanted to take time to enjoy his family before he left them. Roger figured he would have the furnace replaced next summer when he came home from Korea. *It gives me something to look forward to, ha! ha!*

Roger put his foot on the rung to test the ladder's footing and was about to begin his climb when something flitted across the corner of his right line of vision. He jerked his head swiftly around to see what it was, but there was nothing there. He swore under his breath, though he was not normally a profane man. That was the second or third time that had happened. He'd been shaving that morning when he thought he caught sight of a mouse running across the bathroom floor out of the corner of his eye. When he turned to look - nothing.

Then, later on, he'd been coming down the steps when he thought he saw a small animal or something flit between his feet. He'd almost fallen down the steps trying to avoid whatever it was, but again, when he looked squarely at where he'd seen the -what? Object? Animal? There was nothing. He wondered if he were going crazy.

He didn't mention any of this to Rose of course. She'd tell him he was combat happy.

He resumed his climb. Reaching the window, he began to organize his equipment. He hung the bent clothes hanger he used to hang his paint bucket on a rung on the ladder. He reached down and pulled his brush out of his pocket. Rose was going to give him a fit over the paint stains on his blue jeans. Well, what did she expect?

He dipped his brush and turned to the window to begin. As he looked up, a face staring out the window startled him so that he almost lost his balance on the ladder. His foot slipped on the rung as he wobbled and struggled to stay on the ladder. He dropped his brush and grabbed for anything to hold. His left hand slipped through the rungs, while his right got a grip on the top rung. The ladder pulled away from the wall. For an eternity, it seemed he hung there motionless in midair, balancing. He found himself staring down at the ground almost twenty feet below. He was tempted to let go and take his chances with a freefall. He knew if he went down with the ladder he would be slapped against the ground, or worse. The car was parked nearby.

"Dear, Sweet Jesus," he muttered, "Lord help me."

Finally, he was able to exert enough weight to bring the ladder against the wall again. It landed with a thud.

Roger hung there for a moment, clinging to the ladder as if for dear life, hearing his heart pounding in his ears, feeling the sickening sensation of fear in the pit of his stomach. What had it been he'd seen? A face? He looked at the window, nothing.

He thought about it, shaking his head as if to physically remove the confusion there. His entire body was quivering with fear. *Whose face?*

It was an awful face, contorted as if screaming out in

18

torment. It was no human face. No, nothing human ever had a face like that, though it was humanistic. He thought hard. It was like flesh stretched over a skull. That was it!

Hold on, Roger, he thought, *you're letting your imagination get the better of you. It had to be a reflection.*

"Dad?" a voice came from inside the house. Roger looked up; it was Danny inside the window, peering out. "Are you okay?"

Relief poured over Roger. It was Danny. "DANNY!" he screamed, his relief turning to rage, "I want to see you in the kitchen young man, now!"

Roger flew down the ladder and ran into the house. He entered the kitchen to see Rose standing with a protective arm around a frightened Danny, "What's going on?" she demanded.

"He almost killed me, that's all!" Roger accused.

"How?"

"I had just climbed up the ladder to finish his window. I look up and there he is staring out at me making a face. He startled me so bad I almost fell off the ladder. I could have been killed."

Rose didn't know whether to laugh or not. She had a picture in her mind of Danny sticking his tongue out at his father and of Roger hanging from the top of the ladder. The whole thing was so childish and silly. At the same time though, she realized the seriousness of what might have happened. She also looked into her husband's eyes and knew better than to laugh. She fought a smile.

"Well, honey, he's just a kid and kids do things like that. He didn't think."

Roger looked down at Danny's frightened face, and softened, "Next time think Son, okay? How'd you feel if I'd been hurt?"

"Apologize to your dad." Rose said.

"I'm sorry, Dad." Danny said with tears welling in his eyes.

"Okay," Roger said, "Give me a hug."

Danny came over and put his arms around his father's waist. Roger gave him a bone- crushing squeeze, "Next time be more careful, okay?"

Danny nodded.

"Well, I'd better go finish up." Roger said sheepishly, leaving the room.

19

Rose looked over at Danny, "Well?"

"Mom, I don't know what he's talking about. I came into my room and looked out the window and there's Dad hanging on the ladder in the air. I was about to yell for you when he slammed into the side of the house. All I did was ask him if he was okay, and he started yelling at me."

"Well," Rose said thoughtfully, "your Dad had just had a scare; he was just letting off some steam. 'Remember how it was the last time he came home from Nam?"

Danny nodded.

"It'll be okay. Go on and play. And stay out of that window for awhile."

That night Danny lay in bed staring at the shadow of the oak tree cast on the wall by the corner street lamp. He was picking out shapes in the shadows. Here, he could see an elephant, there, a car. He didn't know if he liked the new house or not. *That looks like an atom bomb* explosion. All day long, whenever he was alone in the house, he had felt as though someone were watching him. He had turned around several times to try and catch someone sneaking around behind him. Of course, there'd be no one there. *There's a tank.*

He had thought about telling Mom about it, but thought better of it. He didn't want everyone thinking he was like Roggie. Roggie was always seeing ghosts or hearing weird things. One time Roggie claimed he saw a glowing face on his wall. That had been at Ft. Polk, Louisiana. Mom and Dad had rented an old house outside of Leesville. Roggie claimed he could hear the rattling of chains in the night. One time in Alabama his father had spent several nights in Roggie's room to see if he saw the floating flame Roggie claimed to see every night. Mom and Dad humored Roggie, but he knew they thought he was flaky. Danny wondered if Roggie was going to see any ghosts here. Probably, he always did.

Danny felt a chill creep through his body. The shadow on his wall had changed. Where there had once been a black tangle of branches a new figure had been added. Danny studied it curiously for a moment, then realizing what he was looking at, he wanted to scream, *No, no, don't scream! Mom and Dad will think you're flaky! It's just shadows, that's all, just shadows.*

He squeezed his eyes shut for a moment then looked at the shadow again. No, it was there, the shadow of a man hanging

from the oak tree outside. *'Gotta look outside, gotta check, make
sure.*

No! No! Don't look, it'll get you!
What'll get me? I gotta look.

Slowly, carefully, Danny pulled the covers back from him
and crawled to the window at the foot of the bed. Swallowing
hard, he pulled back the drapes and the sheer curtains his mother
had hung there that afternoon. He peered through the window at
the street lamp.

'Nothing but branches. There, see?

Danny looked back to the wall. The body was gone.
Weird.

He lay back down in his bed and covered his head with
his blanket. *I'm not going to like living here.*

The next morning at breakfast Danny was contemplating
telling his mother about the shadow when Roggie came down the
steps into the kitchen.

"Mom," Roggie began.

Here it comes, Danny thought. *There's that whiny tone
he always gets when something's wrong...*

"What is it baby?" Rose asked without looking up from
the sausages she was frying.

"I had the weirdest thing happen to me last night..."

Oh boy, Danny thought, *the one time I've got something
weird to tell and Roggie has to beat me to the punch.* Danny
watched his mother. *She's good at pretending she doesn't know
what's coming.*

"Oh really?" she asked. *There's the voice, she knows
Roggie's getting weird!*

"I woke up in the middle of the night last night. It felt
like somebody was holding me down. I couldn't move."

"Oh really?" Rose asked, breaking an egg into the skillet.

"Mom," Roggie pleaded, "Are you paying attention to
me?"

"Yes dear," Rose said, reaching for another egg, "You
said you felt someone holding you down last night. What
happened after that?"

"Nothing. All of a sudden whatever it was let go."

"Did you take your asthma medicine?"

"It wasn't my asthma. I haven't needed my asthma
medicine in years! Mom, could you take me seriously?"

21

"I am taking you seriously, Roggie. You tell me you woke up last night feeling someone was holding you down. It passed, nothing else happened. What am I supposed to do about it?"

"Well, you could act like you cared more."

"Honey, sometimes when you wake up in the middle of the night, weird things happen with your equilibrium. Sometimes, you can still be dreaming and not realize it. If it happens again, then we'll look into it, okay?"

"All right." Roggie mumbled, "No one takes me seriously around this house."

"Get serious and we'll take you serious, Roggie!" Danny quipped.

"Who asked you, twerp?"

"The boogey man who held you down, freak!"

"All right, you two knock it off!" Roger came down the steps. Rose took him his coffee; he gave her his customary morning hug and kiss, tousled Danny's hair and made a feint at Roggie's chin. "What's the fuss about?"

"Roggie's seeing ghosts again!" Danny said, rolling his eyes.

"I didn't see anything! It held me down!" Roggie was embarrassed now, "I wish I hadn't said anything now."

"Well, that's not a good attitude," Roger said. "If there's a problem we need to know."

Danny began pointing to his head, making circular motions with his finger and crossing his eyes. Roger caught him. He didn't miss much, "All right, knock it off troop or I'll be making motions with your heinie!"

Still, he was amused at Danny's antics. Danny knew just what to do to crack him up. He tried to hide his amusement, but knew he was failing. He glanced furtively at Roggie; he knew if his older son saw his amusement he'd misconstrue it as taking sides.

"You all think I'm crazy!" Roggie said reproachfully.

"No, sport, that's not true." Roger said, regaining his composure, "I think some folks are just more sensitive to things than others. Let's see if it happens again, okay?"

"That's what Mom says."

"Your Mom's a genius."

"Yeah," Danny said, finishing the punch line which had been used a million times, Rose and even Roggie joined in, "Look

22

who she married."

"It's about time this family became enlightened!" Roger exclaimed with mock pride, "What about your night, trooper?" Roger turned to Danny. "Everything okay?"

"No problem, 'slept like a baby, Dad." Danny took a sip of his milk. There was no way he was going to tell them about the hanging man now.

That evening, as she lay in bed, Rose worried over Roggie. It seemed to her she had worried over Roggie for one reason or another since she knew he was coming. She had fought to keep him from being adopted out of her hands while she carried him. She had fought to keep him after his birth.

She had hoped to escape her past by moving across the river to St. Louis. She was wrong. Her parents, worried over her living alone in St. Louis while Roger was overseas, were constantly coming across the river to "check" on her. Interfere was more how she termed it. She would come home from work, worn out from a long day. She'd be carrying Roggie in one arm and trying to balance her purse, and whatever else she was carrying with the other. She remembered the dread she'd feel when she'd find her parents waiting in the stairwell outside her apartment.

Inevitably, an argument would start over her inability to care for the baby and work full time. One time, after she had taken the offer of some of her co-workers of a ride home, her parents had threatened to go to the authorities and have custody of Roggie taken from her. Her friends had stopped off on the way home for a drink. She had been forced to go into the bar with them, though she'd only sipped a soda. She'd come home with the smell of cigarette smoke all over her. Her mother called her a harlot. What made it worse was that her mother had done it in front of her friends.

Then she went in to work one morning to discover that her father and mother had been in to speak with her supervisor, Mrs. Humboldt, about their concerns for her. During the course of their talk, they had, of course, let Mrs. Humboldt know how she had been pregnant when she and Roger were married. She lost her job. Of course, her parents' revelations never entered into the discussion over the reasons for her dismissal. She was told she had done a good job and would be given a good recommendation. The office was just overstaffed and she was the last one hired.

The Homestead

They had to let her go.

To make matters worse, her parents were waiting for her when she got home to tell her to come home. After all, there was no way she could support herself and Roggie now.

"I've still got my allotment from Roger," she answered.

"You know you can't live on that," Harold said.

"Come home where you belong, Rosie," Emily pleaded, "where we can take care of you."

The anger that had been simmering beneath the surface since the early afternoon came seething out of her now. She glared at her parents with a hatred she had never before felt for anyone. How dare they come here after what they had done? The fact that she knew they were, in their own misguided way, trying to look out for her seemed to infuriate her more.

"Let me make this perfectly clear, Mother, Father," she hissed. "Before I live under your roof, I will sell myself on the street to feed my baby! And before I let you take him home and screw him up the way you've done me, I'll kill you both!"

Her eyes met her father's for an instant and he backed down. "Let's leave, Emily. We've done enough here," he said sadly. Rose watched her parents as they walked down the steps. Harold reached the bottom step and turned around. He looked up at his daughter, who was glaring down at him through tear stained eyes. He started to speak and thought better of it. He opened the door to the street and helped his wife out.

Things didn't get much better when Roger came home from Korea, either. He spent the last six months of his enlistment at the Army Depot in Granite City. He took his discharge when his time was up and got a job working at a steel mill in Granite City. But he was miserable in his work. He had learned to love the Army during his stint. The only reason he hadn't re-enlisted was for his family's sake. He was afraid the nomadic life of a soldier, the separations, and the hardships, wouldn't be fair to his wife and child.

His attitude brightened when he was picked up for a civil service job at the Army Depot in Granite City. He hoped that working at the Army Depot, close to the Army, would somehow make civilian life easier. It only made it worse.

However, with Roger home, Rose now not only had to deal with her parents, but Roger's. The Baumers had made no effort to contact Rose or see little Roggie while Roger was in Korea. Now that Roger was home, they were there all the time.

Rose got tired of the comments about his dark hair and hearing how they missed Little Roggie's first two years. Like it was her fault! She had called them several times; they never returned her calls. Now they were trying to make her look bad in front of Roger.

What really bothered Rose was that neither of Roger's parents seemed willing to recognize the fact that their son was an adult, a decorated combat veteran with a family. They still treated him like a child. They tried to run every facet of his life, even down to which type of car he should drive. They tried to run Rose's life, too.

One day they were over at the house visiting; Roger was at work. Rose left the room to put Roggie to bed for his nap. When she came back into the room she found the Baumers re-arranging the furniture.

"We thought it would look better this way," Mrs. Baumer said authoritatively. Rose told Roger later she really chewed her tongue on that one to keep the trouble down. And then there were the circumstances of their marriage. It seemed that every visit, every gathering, every conversation, Mrs. Baumer had to make a comment about her being pregnant when they got married.

There were more hassles with her parents. With Roger's return, she had tried to mend the fences between them. If they saw that she and Roger were happy together and could make a "go" of their marriage, maybe they'd accept him. They never did. They blamed him for ruining their daughter's life just as Roger's parents blamed Rose for ruining his life. Their parents appeared to hate each other for giving birth to the source of their sorrows.

In short, life was miserable. It was Rose who suggested Roger re-enlist to get away from the constant conflict. Perhaps, if they could get completely away from everyone they could have a normal life. Also, the less Roggie stayed around the family, the less chance they'd have to hurt him with distortions about their marriage and his birth. She intended to tell him the story one day, in the right way, when she felt he was ready. She knew if she stayed around St. Louis, someone in one of the families would break their necks telling him. They'd make it sound dirty.

Her plan had almost worked, too. Until a few years before, when her mother had told him the family version of the story. Roger was doing his first tour in Vietnam. Rose and the kids were staying in a rental house a few miles from her parents' house. Rose had come down with a severe kidney infection.

The Homestead

She'd required hospitalization. Her parents had offered to take care of the kids.

While the kids were there, Emily got out the family photo albums and began going through them with the boys. Roggie was about twelve, Danny, eight. In the course of looking at the pictures, Roggie noticed there were no wedding pictures of his parents as there were with his aunts and uncles.

"Where's Mom and Dad's wedding pictures, Grandma?" he asked.

"We don't have any, honey." Emily said sadly.

"Why not?"

"It's because your parents weren't married properly."

"What do you mean, Grandma?" Roggie asked.

That's when Roggie learned more about the facts of life than he cared to and that his parents hadn't been legally married when he was conceived. He still didn't understand everything his grandmother told him though. He decided to go to his mother after she returned home from the hospital for answers.

Rose and Roggie were sitting up one Saturday night watching TV. Danny had fallen asleep on the rug on the floor. Both had been silent, in their own thoughts. Rose was worrying over her husband thousands of miles away. Roggie working out in his mind a question that struck at his very identity. "Am I a bastard?"

Rose almost fainted when she heard the question. She feared the worst. It took her a moment to regain her composure, "What-why do you ask?"

"Well, Grandma told me if I'd been born a few days later I'd have been one."

"Did she tell you it was her fault?" Rose fought the rage that was threatening to overwhelm her and regained control. Even Danny, now awake, seemed afraid of his mother.

She took a deep breath, "None of your grandparents wanted your daddy and me to get married." She sighed again, "They thought we were too young to get married and they didn't like that we went to different churches so we ran off and got married secretly right before your daddy joined the Army the first time.

"We went over to Missouri where the age was different; there was a preacher your daddy had heard about down south who liked to see young people get married so he didn't pay much attention to paperwork. We made it look like my parents gave

26

permission and we got married – thinking once we did that there wouldn't be anything else our folks could do to keep us apart.

"Boy, were we wrong."

Rose tried to explain what happened next in a way that wouldn't make Roggie – or Danny, who by now was fully awake and listening eagerly to a "good" story (and Rose figured he'd better hear it sooner than later) – hate his grandparents.

Police found the couple in a motel room outside St Louis where they had gone to spend their "honeymoon" night. They were taken to the local sheriff's office and held until their parents arrived. There was a great deal of talk about charges being pressed against Roger – who was now eighteen – for contributing to the delinquency of a minor. Rose's parents even talked about having him arrested under the Mann Act because he had taken Rose across State lines.

The local sheriff wasn't unsympathetic to the youngsters and spoke with both sets of parents. In the end, reason prevailed and all talk of prosecution stopped. Roger was going off to the Army soon – that would keep them apart.

The marriage wasn't legal, but her parents went through annulment procedures anyway – just to be sure.

Roger went off into the Army and everyone thought the problem was solved. Time and distance would end the passion; Roger and Rose were willing to wait until she was of legal age to marry.

Then she discovered she was pregnant when Roger was in Korea.

Eventually, she managed to explain to her sons that with the help of the Army they were able to get married before Roggie was born. Roggie would be almost two years old before he would see his daddy.

She had stayed away from her family for three years after that. Considering that most of the time they were stationed in Germany it wasn't too hard. Then her mother had come down with a terrible case of pneumonia and she was called home to see her. A truce had been called and Emily had gotten better.

The damage to Roggie had been done. She noticed as time went by his entire personality began to change. He became less confident, more dependent on her. She had tried to talk it over with Roger, but he told her he was probably going through a phase and would grow out of it.

It had now been over four years ago and he appeared to be getting worse. They went through this ghost thing with him with every move. She had no doubt the periodic disruption of moving around was hard on the kids. Add to that the stress of having their father going off for a year at a time and not knowing whether or not he'd come back. She knew many kids from otherwise stable backgrounds who had problems with being Army brats. But a kid with Roggie's baggage, deserved or not…

He always seemed so sad, so lost. He would try to be a clown, a joker. He had a great sense of humor. Rose saw through the act, though, as only a mother could. She saw the pain behind the jokes and wisecracks. But try as she might she knew she didn't have the first clue as to what was really going on inside his head – in his spirit.

Maybe having a home would stabilize him. She hoped it wasn't too late. She didn't know what it was about this place, the Felder House. *We'll change that. It's the Baumer Place now.* It was a mess, she knew, but she loved it. It was like she had come home.

Roger left three days later. The family drove him to Lambert Field in St. Louis to see him off. As usual, Rose gave her final goodbye hugs and kisses before he boarded the plane. She never wanted to see the takeoff. She held her tears until she was alone in her bedroom. She tried to keep a strong face for her "men."

As she lay across her bed weeping softly, she felt a soothing presence sweep over her, almost like a hand caressing her shoulders. She felt a warmth flood through her she hadn't experienced since a child praying to God in her father's church.

She knew everything, somehow, was going to be all right.

Life went on. Soon, she was developing a pattern to her new life in Delphi. Without realizing it, she agreed with Roger that Delphi was a sad little town. Main Street, a block away from the house, ran about a mile from one end of Delphi proper to the other. There was a four-block strip that served as downtown, two rows of storefronts facing each other across what, at first glance, was a rather substantial street for such a small town. Then one noticed most of the buildings were vacant.

Entering what passed for a business district from the house there was the town's filling station, "Ralph's" a franchise of one of the minor national oil companies. It was on the same block as the house, on the direct opposite corner. It would be on the left. Across the street from that (on your right) was the town's funeral parlor. There was the only grocery store in town – family owned – Clevenger's Super Mart (on the right). She discovered in spite of the monopoly she could do fairly well buying odds and ends there to get through the week, or to the end of the month. She decided she could do better for the bulk of her groceries by making the fifty-mile trip to Scott Air Force Base Commissary once or twice a month.

Across from Ralph's gas station was the Mason Hall; behind the Mason Hall was the American Legion Post. Traveling on down Main Street, one crossed Green Street. On the left was Spanky's Grill, that passed for the town's restaurant. After passing a vacant lot on the right, one saw Lil's Bowling Alley, which was the big gathering spot for the town's youths on Friday and Saturday nights. After that, there was a row of vacant stores, unkempt and deteriorating on the left side of the street. On the right, a row of vacant lots, until one reached John Wahlberg's Auto Body Shop which was across the street from the post office. After the Post Office, the only business was Schofield's Hardware on the right, just before the tracks.

On the other side of the tracks was "Hickory," the "rough" part of town. No one knew where it got its name.

The folks at Delphi were typical Midwesterners, cordial, but standoffish until they knew you better. Rose knew from experience it might take two or three generations to be accepted as a true local in town. At the same time, she knew if they passed whatever character test the townsfolk decided applied, they would be accepted as homegrown. Still, it seemed as though the people in town were watching them expectantly, waiting for something to happen.

There were the knowing looks at the grocery store, the questions from - was it Nita? - Clevenger when she checked out. "How are you all enjoying the Felder House, Mrs. Baumer?"

Rose would wonder at the smile on the woman's face, she would notice how whoever happened to be in the store would appear to pause in their activity to hear her reply. It wasn't obvious, and often Rose would scold herself for being too suspicious. Still, she couldn't help but feel the people in town were watching her and the boys.

The kids had already made several friends. Roger had been gone a week when a bunch of twelve or thirteen year olds showed up on bicycles at the door one morning. Rose saw them as they rode up into the yard. There had to be at least ten of them.

There was a knock on the door. Rose answered it to see a tow-headed boy with a freckled face standing sheepishly at the door, obviously appointed the designated spokesman for the group of youngsters straddling their bicycles in the street, "Excuse me, ma'am, I'm Randy Hoffer... I -uh-we were wondering if your son would like to go swimming with us. He has a bike, doesn't he?"

"Yes, where do you go swimming around here?"

"We got lots of places," the boy said. "There're creeks all over here. This year, though, we're going over to Falling Springs. Ma'am." he added.

After a few more questions, she felt she could find the place. She let Danny go. She stood on the front porch as she watched him ride off with his newfound friends and sighed, Kids bounce back so quickly. She glanced back up to the south bedroom where she heard the strains of Roggie's radio.

That was the day the tree fell.

Rose was cooking dinner when it happened. Roggie was in the old doctor's study, which had been converted to the living room, watching TV. Rose heard a loud crack followed by an equally loud squeaking noise. Then a crash, as the tree fell into the yard. It's top branches scraped the roof of the front porch.

Rose had frozen a moment at the noise. Realizing what the noise was, she ran into the dining room (the old parlor) for safety in case the tree penetrated the outer wall of the house. Roggie came running from the living room, "Mom! What was that! Are you okay?"

"Yes, yes! The tree fell." she said, pointing toward the front door. They left through the kitchen entrance and walked around the house to the front. It was hard to see how much damage had been done, as the tree's branches obscured the house.

It was the tree on the corner. Roggie walked to the trunk and whistled softly, "It could have been worse, Mom. If it had been the tree outside my window, we'd have lost the house..."

"What on earth are we going to do now?" Rose said helplessly.

"Are you folks okay?"

Rose looked over to where the voice was coming to see a short, heavyset man standing in the middle of the intersection. She had noticed him several times before, standing in the yard across the intersection, staring at the house.

"We're all right." Rose said, "I don't know about our tree or our house though."

"I know some guys who'll clear this out for you; they probably won't charge you much considering they can use the tree for fire wood."

"That would be nice, Mr.-"

"Thompson, Frank Thompson," the man said drawing closer and holding out his hand. They shook. "I'm your neighbor. I live across the street there." He took a look at the tree, "Well, let's take a look at this and see what's going on."

Thompson disappeared into the branches. Rose could hear him rustling around, "It doesn't look like too much damage. One of the branches has broken your railing, but I don't think it's major."

He reappeared out of the brush, "I'll call those guys up and see if they can get out here. The Renfrow brothers."

At about that time Danny came riding up with his buddies, "Wow Mom! What happened?"

"What do you think, kid?" Roggie sneered.

"I'm glad it's the weird tree!" Danny said.

What did he mean by "weird" tree? Rose wondered.

"Would you like me to get this taken care of?" Thompson offered.

"Yes, please," Rose said, gratefully.

Thompson ran off to his house to call the Renfrow brothers. It didn't take them long; they were at work within half an hour. By dark all that was left of the once mighty oak were a few branches and a carpet of leaves. Rose figured the boys could take care of that in the morning.

Frank Thompson came by after the Renfrows left.

"I can't thank you enough for all the help you've given me today."

"Don't mention it. That's what neighbors are for. Did they do a good job?"

"Yes, as a matter of fact, they even put a brace to hold the porch roof up until I can get it fixed properly."

"Good. By the way, I haven't noticed your husband around lately. Is he all right?"

"I hope so," she said. She noticed the puzzled look on his face, "He's an Army helicopter pilot. He'll be in Korea for a year."

"Oh," Frank said thoughtfully, "it must be tough on a young woman, being alone all that time with two young boys."

"You learn to get by. And it seems there are always friends to help."

"Well, if you need anything- *anything* - don't hesitate to call." he paused a moment, "Well, I'd better get going. My wife'll wonder what's taking me so long. Remember, call if you need anything."

"Thanks."

They watched him amble off to his house and his wife, who was watching anxiously from their front porch.

"Boy, Mom, he was coming on to you." It was Roggie.

"Oh, Roggie! He was just being nice."

"I'm serious, Mom, he was eyeing you up and down. You'd better watch out. Do you think he'd be so nice to you if you weren't such a fox?"

Rose laughed at the idea of her being a "fox."

"I'm just glad Dad wasn't here to see him drooling over you."

"Your dad doesn't have anything to worry about from Frank Thompson."

"Watch him anyway," Roggie said, going inside the house.

That night, as she lay in bed waiting to fall asleep, Rose thought about Roggie's warning. *Here we go on another hardship tour. Every guy in town will think I'm easy prey because I'm alone. I don't care what people have said about me, I've only known one man in my life; I only want to know one man.*

She tried to take her mind off the subject. She thought of how the kids had gotten such a kick out of watching the Renfrow brothers argue as they sawed up the tree. She didn't even mind their profanity so much as they cursed each other. Roggie had commented the guys had to be smart in spite of appearances to think up some of the names they called one another.

She thought it odd, though, what the older one said – was it Cary? Gary. When she paid them, Gary Renfrow gave her a funny look, "Ma'am, if you don't mind my askin', are you really going to try and live in this dump?"

She was taken back by the directness of his question. No, it wasn't that, she corrected herself; it was something in his tone.

"Yes," she answered with what she hoped was firmness. "We are."

The two men shook their heads, "Good luck to you, Ma'am."

In the middle bedroom, Danny was trying to ignore the shadows of the branches of the tree that was no longer there being cast on the closet doors by the corner streetlamp.

Chapter 3
August 1966

And the Lord said, "Simon, Simon, Behold, Satan hath desired to
have you, that he may sift you as wheat.
(Luke 22:31)

Danny lay on his bedroom floor. Spread out before him on the carpet was his representation of the Battle of Gettysburg. He had used his bedspread to re-create Little and Big Round Tops. A spare Army blanket from the closet served as Cemetery Ridge. About one hundred light blue figures from his Civil War Set served as the Army of the Potomac, settled in the folds in the blankets waiting for the hundred or so light gray figures he had painstakingly set up in formation as Lee's Army of Northern Virginia. In the front of his "rebel army" stood one of his favorite figures, the Confederate general, charging with pistol and sword in hand, raised to urge his troops on. It was his "Armistead" figure.

Toy soldiers were Danny's love and these were his favorites. Ever since his sixth Christmas when he found the gigantic Civil War set under the Christmas tree he'd had a love affair both with toy soldiers and the history behind them. He had carried them with him on every move since that Christmas. Other toys might be given or thrown away or put in storage when it was time to move, but his Civil War set went with him.

One of the things he liked most about the house was its large rooms. Before, he'd never had the space to really set his soldiers up the way he wanted. Forget small skirmishes, Danny was a general at heart; he loved grand battle scenes. He had been working for hours that morning setting his figures out. He had a book on the subject lying open beside him so he could set up each "unit" representing real units with as much historical accuracy as possible with his resources. He just hoped Rose wouldn't come in and raise Cain about the blankets on the floor until he was finished.

He was about to move "Pettigrew's Division" forward onto Bloody Angle when he heard a car door slam outside in front. He paused to peek curiously out the window. He saw a

34

large blue Dodge parked in front, behind Rose's station wagon. He immediately recognized the figure getting out of the car. His face transformed from curiosity to one of joy, "Uncle Brew!"

He leapt to his feet and ran down the stairs, forgetting he was a bare year away from being a teenager, "Mom! It's Uncle Brew!" Danny flew through the kitchen, into the dining room and out the front door. Brew was limping up the sidewalk to the house. Danny caught him as he stepped on the porch, hugging him enthusiastically, "Hey, Uncle Brew!"

"Hey, Dighty Dan!" Brew said in a gravelly voice, chuckling at his own humor.

"I'm getting too old for that!"

"What?" Brew asked in mock consternation.

"Dighty Dan?"

"Stop it!"

"Diaper Dan, with the bottle in his hand!"

"Oh Brew!" Rose was at the door grinning, "I don't know which of you two is the littlest." Brew just chuckled.

"How's it going, Rose?"

"Where've you been?"

"Oh, around," he said casually. "I didn't even know you were in town until a few days ago. I heard you were staying with your folks. I called up and asked where you were, but you know how your Mom and Dad are."

"I know how Mom and Dad are," Rose said flatly.

"I did get that you'd bought a place up here, so's I finally got the time to drive up. I found a nice little tavern in New Haupstadt, started talking to some of the guys; most of 'em are from Delphi- what are you doing living in a dry county anyway? Youse guys are real celebrities around here, did you know that? They've got a pool going, 'betting to see how long youse guys stay here. They must really be hard up for entertainment…

"The long shot gave you a month. I bet one day over the long shot – I win anything over the longest bet. I know youse guys are tough."

"It's nice to know we're performing a public service, keeping the guys at Kopf's entertained." Rose remarked wryly.

"Listen, Rosie," Brew said with a conspiratorial wink, "I'll keep tabs on the pool. You help me win; I'll split the pot with you."

"I always wanted my own business."

"Anyway," he changed the subject. "They gave me good directions. I had no problem finding the place."

"It's good to see you, Brew," Rose said, hugging his neck, "Come on in."

They went inside. As they entered the kitchen, Roggie was just coming down the stairs, "Hey, Uncle Brew! How're you doing?"

"'Gettin' by, gettin' by." Brew said, taking a seat at the kitchen table.

Uncle Brew. He now hauled beer for a major brewery in St. Louis, hence his nickname. He was also known to have an enormous affection for his company's product. After all, he'd say, he had to demonstrate loyalty to his company, didn't he? It was his custom to drink at least one beer at every stop on his route.

He really wasn't Rose's uncle; at least not by blood. The truth of the matter was that he had been married to one of Rose's mother's cousins some years ago. The marriage had ended in divorce due to his incessant drinking, and everyone in the family except Rose ostracized him.

Rose admitted he was by any definition an alcoholic. He was legally drunk by lunchtime every day, though his supervisor would tell you he could do more work drunk than two drivers half his age could do stone sober - and do it better. And his background was a bit questionable. The family spoke of rumors of his mob involvement back during prohibition. Rose thought it was uncanny how he managed to know just about everyone who was anyone in the greater St. Louis area, and how much respect a lowly beer truck driver commanded from those who knew him. Rose wasn't quite sure of his influence on the children; but she knew he loved the kids, and what was more, they loved - no adored - him.

She led him through the house on a guided tour. It had been six months since she had last seen him. That had been when he had driven out to Kansas to visit with them. He hadn't appeared to have aged a day since the first day she met him years before, though she noticed as she led him upstairs he took the steps a little slower.

The truth was, she tolerated Brew's idiosyncrasies because he had always been there for her.

She couldn't look at him without remembering how he had found her in the winter of 1951. She'd been a young mother,

36

almost on the streets unemployed, facing the choices of either freezing with her child (Roger's allotment as a private wasn't enough to pay rent and other expenses plus feed and clothe her baby), or having to subject themselves to what she considered her parent's cruel authority.

She had been out of work almost a month. It appeared there were no jobs available where the word hadn't gotten out about her past. Her parents were well known in certain religious circles. It seemed the only places she could think of to look for work were filled with people who knew and respected them. St. Louis suddenly appeared to be a small town. She had taken her last few dollars to buy food and milk for Roggie. She didn't know what she was going to eat.

Her rent was due the next day; Roger's allotment wasn't due for another two. Her landlady had been visited by her parents and was siding with them. She had made it plain it wouldn't take too much for her to put Rose and Roggie on the street. Then she'd have to go back home to her parents, who would take care of her and her baby. She had been sitting at her kitchen table in her apartment praying and hoping God would listen to her prayers when she heard a knock at the door.

"Who is it?" she asked apprehensively. So far that week everyone who had visited her had brought trouble and bad news.

"It's me, Brew," came the voice from the hall.

"Brew?" she had to think. She hadn't seen him in years, since before his divorce.

"Yeah," he said, a bit impatiently, "I used to be married to your Cousin Doris."

"Oh yes," she had said, still reluctant to open the door for him, "What do you want?"

"I guess I want to stand out here in the hallway all night."

"Oh, I'm sorry!" Rose said, beginning to undo the locks on the door, "I try to be careful-" She finally opened the door a crack to peer at the elderly man standing in the hall outside.

"Yeah, I know, sweetie," Brew said as soothingly as his voice would allow. "A young girl alone in the city and all."

"How-how did you find me?"

"Oh, I heard what happened between you and your family. Me and Doris still communicate occasionally. Then I heard what happened at your job and all. It's a pretty crappy deal if you ask me, and I figured I'd check to see how you're

37

doing."

  Rose didn't know what to say. She'd remembered seeing him at a few family gatherings. She'd heard her parents talk about him, but never anything good. She'd been fairly innocent back in 1951, but she'd learned enough to wonder whether he had any ulterior motives.

  At that time, Roggie began to cry in the bedroom; Rose got up to see about him. She cradled her son in her arms and brought him out. She went through a balancing act as she tried to hold him in one arm and prepare his formula with her free hand.

  Brew watched this performance with some amusement for a moment before rising out of his seat, "Why don't you let me help?" he said, reaching for the baby.

  "That's okay," Rose said, "I've gotten used to this, I can do it myself..."

  "Sure you can," Brew said agreeably, "but why should you if you've got help?"

  Brew took the infant from her arms and cuddled him with an amazing skill, which betrayed experience. He looked down and cooed at little Roger, "It's been a long time since I held one this small," he said wistfully.

  "So, have you had any luck with your job hunting?" he asked while pretending to swoop down and bite Roggie's nose off. Roggie was just old enough to appreciate his antics; he cooed and giggled.

  "No." Rose answered relaxing. Brew appeared harmless, it was good to have a sympathetic ear, "I guess I'm a scarlet woman..."

  "Nonsense, little girl," Brew said with disgust. "You and Roger just went about things the wrong way from what I hear. That's all. Now you're trying to do the right thing by it. The least those holy rollers can do is let you alone so's you can get your life straightened out!"

  Roggie's bottle was ready, Rose went over to take him so she could feed him, "Here," Brew said, reaching out, "let me." He took the bottle from her hand and stuck it gently in the baby's mouth. Rose sat down tiredly across the table and watched him rock softly back and forth. Roggie's eyes began to close. "I've got a knack for this, "he whispered, "I think it's the beer on my breath, it knocks them out." He laughed softly at his joke, a soft, "heh, heh, heh." She grinned at him. In spite of all the terrible things she'd heard about him from the family, in spite of her own unease at being alone with him in the apartment, he was winning her over.

"Oh my!" she said, rising up straight in her chair, her eyes widening, she almost woke the baby, "I've been rude! Do you want any coffee or something else to drink?"

"Coffee'd be nice, if you have any." he said. "Don't make any special on my account."

"I think I have some left over from breakfast," she said, going to the stove and shaking the pot. "There may be a cup left."

"That's fine."

"I don't know how good it'll taste; it's sat there all day."

"That just gives it strength!" Brew said with a chuckle. "There's a place I stop at over in Florissant that has coffee you have to chip off with a fork before you can drink it; it's so strong, heh, heh, heh."

She turned the burner on the stove to heat the coffee and pulled a cup out of the cabinet. She sat back down while the coffee warmed.

"If you don't mind, I'll call around to a few friends and see if I can't maybe find an opening somewhere for you. St. Louis is a place you can always find work; you just have to know where to look and who to see."

"Thanks," she said, meaning it.

"The baby's asleep."

She took Roggie from Brew's arms and carried him into the bedroom. As she laid him in his crib, she heard the opening and closing of cabinet doors, "Brew?"

"Just lookin' for cream and sugar for my coffee!"

"I'm sorry, we're out!"

"That's okay. I normally drink it black anyway."

She thought she heard the refrigerator door open. She went into the kitchen to see him closing the freezer door, embarrassed to be caught snooping.

"I've always been fascinated with these things," he said, "When I was a kid, well you remember the ice boxes - these things are neat." He wasn't a very good liar, she noted, which was a plus for his honesty, "Well, I've taken enough of your time, I'd better be going."

"But you've barely touched your coffee-"

Brew made a wry face, looked at his cup, and downed it in one gulp. He made a face at the bitter taste, gasping as he swallowed, "Now, that's a cup of coffee!" he exclaimed. He started toward the door, "If it's all right with you, I'll stop by tomorrow evening and let you know if I've found anything for you."

"Sure," she said.

"Take care and give that baby a hug for me!" With that he had left.

She had been sorry to see him go. She hadn't realized how lonely she was. His had been the first truly kind voice she'd heard since- she couldn't remember.

She saw his coffee cup and saucer left on the table and moved to put them in the sink. As she picked them up she noticed something folded on the table beneath. She put down the saucer and picked it up, unfolding it. She caught her breath when she saw what it was, a hundred dollar bill!

She looked at the door and felt the urge to call him back. I can't take this money. Why I barely know him. What if he wanted something in return? She had bitten her lip, torn by her need and her pride. Well, he hasn't asked anything of me, and I certainly haven't asked anything of him. I **was** praying, she reasoned, what if he was the answer to my prayer? She giggled at that thought, Brew? An answer to her prayers? God does work in mysterious ways... and her rent was due tomorrow.

The next morning, she went to her landlady's apartment to pay her rent.

"It's already been paid," Mrs. Saur said, primly.

Rose was shocked, "Who-"

"Your gentleman friend stopped by last night. He said he was your uncle..." she acted as though she didn't believe it. She stared at Rose as she might stare at a glob of a nasty substance on a freshly cleaned window.

Rose tried to explain, "We're related by marriage-"

"Whatever you say!" Mrs. Sauer said with a hint of disdain, "Your private life is none of my business so long as you keep it out of my house. If he stays the night, you're out!"

Rose was too shocked and stunned at the implications of Mrs. Sauer's words to reply quickly. She was just about to retort when Mrs. Sauer closed the door in her face, leaving her standing in the hall, flushed with anger, tears of frustration in her eyes. She turned and stormed up the steps to her apartment to keep Mrs. Sauer from seeing her cry.

That evening Brew was at the door with several bags of groceries in his arms.

"I was wondering," he said sheepishly, when she opened the door. "It's been ages since I had a home cooked meal. Would you mind fixing me one?"

Rose paused a moment, wondering whether or not to let him in. It was obvious from her encounter with Mrs. Sauer that gossip was already starting. Her anger rose up again, How dare those busybodies gossip! We've done nothing wrong! My goodness, he wasn't here even an hour; how can they construe something dirty out of that? And he's twice my age, he's old enough to be my father. The more she thought about it, the angrier she grew, "Come on in, Uncle Brew! I'll be glad to fix you dinner!" she said, loudly enough, she hoped, for the whole building to hear.

"Goodness, Uncle Brew," she said as she unloaded the groceries, "you've got at least a week's supply of food in here!" It was hard to keep her mouth from watering as she surveyed the goodies in the bags. There were vegetables, canned and fresh, ground beef, roast, part of a ham, a frying hen, bread, rolls, eggs, cheese, milk, flour, some things she hadn't seen since she'd left home. She reached in the last bag and pulled out two wrapped T-bone steaks! She was on the verge of tears. For the last week she had been eating bologna sandwiches.

"Well, I didn't know what you were in the mood to cook so I brought a little bit of everything," he said. "I figured what you didn't cook tonight you can eat later. I can't take it home with me, I got no place to cook or keep it in my room."

After they had finished their steak dinner, Brew sat back in his chair, "I just knew you could cook when I looked at you! Your husband's a lucky man!"

Rose thought of Roger, so far away. In his last letter he had described how cold it was getting in Korea. I've never even cooked a meal for him. Oh, Lord, please don't let him die before I've cooked a meal for him!

"Hey, honey, don't look so sad." Brew said comfortingly. "He'll be home before you know it. Youse'll be thinking about these days and laughing about 'em."

Rose looked at him gratefully. She found it strange. Usually she was reserved around people she didn't know well. Brew was different. She was already beginning to love him like an uncle. She had been thinking about him all day, trying to remember him from her childhood. Things were coming back. She remembered how funny she used to think he was at family

41

get- togethers. *She remembered how he seemed to love the children. She remembered when his daughter died of leukemia. It had been shortly after that the family began whispering about his drinking. That was followed by the scandal of his and Doris' divorce.*

"I've got good news for ya!" Brew said. "I did some asking around at the union hall and they need a new receptionist there. I mentioned you. I said you'd add some class to the joint. They said come on in. You can start work tomorrow if you want to. Just show up sometime."

"I don't know..." she said, "I had to give my sitter up when I lost my job. I might not be able to get her back."

Brew showed some frustration at this, "Do ya want to work or don't ya?"

"Well, yes..."

"Then don't worry about it." He reached in his pocket and produced a slip of paper, "Here's the address. 'You know where Cheauteu Avenue is?" She nodded. "Good. There's the address of a good sitter who comes highly recommended. Her house is right on the way. Show up sometime tomorrow morning. Tell 'em you're my niece. They'll take care of you."

"Brew, I don't know how I'll ever repay you for all this."

Brew made another of his faces, which would become familiar to her over the years, "You don't have to repay family!"

"I've got to go now," he said. "We wouldn't want you to lose this place because I stayed too late," he smiled at her surprise. "I talked with old Mrs. Saurkraut downstairs. I explained everything nice for her. I don't think she'll give you any more grief. Imagine some perverts with their dirty minds thinking an ugly old mug like me could make time with a gorgeous young babe like you!"

With that, he left. It had been like that now for years. Brew had always been there when he was needed. He never asked anything in return. It seemed enough that the family loved him and considered him one of their own.

When Roger came home from Korea it didn't take long for the two to become fast friends. It seemed Brew had always been in the family.

When Roger went back in the Army, he'd had to work his way up through the ranks again. There were some tough times. It seemed Brew always knew when to show up to have Rose cook him dinner. When Rose was finally able to follow Roger on his tours, Brew would spend his vacations visiting the family wherever they were. Roger always took comfort in knowing Rose had someone around to protect her when he was on a hardship tour without her.

Rose called him their guardian angel. Roger couldn't help but think God had some strange angels. Still, Brew always came through in a pinch.

Now he sat at the table sipping coffee, chewing on a cigar that had gone out and looked around, "Not bad, Rosie. 'Needs a little more work, but not bad."

"You should have seen it when we first bought it. I wish we had pictures. Are you going to stay for dinner?"

"Oh, I might if the menu and price's right," he chuckled again.

Now Rose and Brew sat on the front porch listening to the music that came softly from the town's annual Homecoming celebration at the town park several blocks away. The boys had left the house several hours before, their allowances augmented with a generous contribution from Brew.

Roggie had a "hot" date that night with Renee Grossman, a girl he'd met shortly after coming to town. Renee's younger brother, Billy, had become one of Danny's best friends. Already, Roggie was talking marriage - at seventeen.

Rose shook this off. Roggie was in love with love, and desperate to marry every girl he ever dated.

Rose checked her watch. It was nine-thirty. She had told the kids to be home by ten. They had protested the "early" curfew but Rose had stood her groud. After all, the fair closed at eleven and even though Delphi was a small town there was nothing good that happened after ten o'clock anyway.

Brew sighed, "Well, Rose, I gotta go. It's a long drive back to Collinsville. Tell the kids I said goodbye, okay?"

"You don't have to go, Brew. The kids will be sorry they missed you. You could always sack out on the couch."

"I gotta get back, Rose, maybe some other night. I'll tell you what; I haven't had any of your sauerbrauten in a long time. What if I brought up the fixin's tomorrow?"

Rose heaved a sigh and smiled, "Sure, Brew, that sounds fine."

She watched the old man drive off before turning to go

43

inside. She had barely closed the door when Roggie burst in behind her.

"Mom, there's all kinds of crazy stuff going on at the cemetery! The guys want to spend the night in the cemetery to check it out- can I go?"

"Wait a minute, what kind of 'crazy stuff' is going on at the cemetery?" For all she knew there could be a maniac out there.

"Lights, Mrs. Baumer." A tow-headed boy, she recognized as Ronnie Allsup, spoke up. He had a rough reputation, she understood, but he'd always been polite to her. As long as he behaved he would be welcome in her home. Rose knew about bad reputations. "There's all kinds of weird lights 'been seen out at the cemetery."

"Yeah," Roggie agreed. "A bunch of us guys want to go out and check them out."

"What do you mean, 'check them out?'" Rose asked, skeptical.

"Well, ma'am," another boy, Jerry Ferrell, spoke up for the first time. "We thought we'd take our sleeping bags out to the cemetery and spend the night- see what happens."

"Yeah, Mom, maybe we'll see a real ghost!"

"Can I go, too?" It was Danny.

Rose looked at her two sons, who were returning the gaze with eager eyes. She noted the pleading look in her older son's eyes. She realized he would rather leave his little brother home on this trip, "You stay with me, Hotshot; one ghost chaser in the family's enough for one night."

She watched sympathetically as her youngest son sullenly plodded into the house. She'd make it up to him later, somehow.

"That's okay," he said as he opened the door, "you don't have to go all the way to the cemetery to find ghosts anyway..." He disappeared inside.

She smiled and shook her head. *Sour grapes.*

"Thanks, Mom!" Roggie said, gratefully, and was off.

It was one-thirty when the boys returned. Rose hadn't retired yet. She couldn't rest easy when one of her boys was out. Somehow, she had known they wouldn't make it through the night.

She had expected excitement on the boy's face when they returned. After all, they'd been out on an adventure. She didn't count on the terror she saw on Ronnie and Jerry's faces; she was confounded by the total impassivity reflected on Roggie's as they burst into the kitchen.

"What on- what on earth happened?" she asked, alarmed.

"M-m-Mrs. Baumer- I never seen anything like it!" Ronnie finally blurted out.

"What?"

"Lights!" Jerry exclaimed, breathlessly, "Dozens of lights! All over the cemetery, coming out of the graves!"

"I never seen anything like it!" Ronnie repeated, a bit calmer now. He was shaking his head as though he couldn't believe his memories.

"What lights? Where? You boys had better tell me what happened."

The boys looked at each other for a moment. Finally, Jerry began, "Well, Ma'am, we got up to the cemetery okay? We parked the car at the foot of the hill, down by McGilly's pond. We walked up the rest of the way. We didn't want to disturb anyone – or anything. So, we got up there and took a look around, you know? We were making sure there wasn't anyone hanging around there playing a trick" He paused.

"Go on," Rose prompted.

"Well, we had laid out our sleeping bags on the ground, over by Terry Newcomb's grave." Rose felt a twinge, Terry was a Delphi boy who'd recently been buried; Delphi's first casualty of the Vietnam War.

"We were just getting settled," Ronnie continued, breaking the silence.

"Then it happened."

"What happened?"

"The light!"

"What light?"

"There was a light over by Old Miss Felder's grave."

"Yeah, we went over to investigate it."

"Rog got there first." Rog?

"And then 'boom!' There were all kinds of light, almost like fireworks, coming from the graves."

"I didn't see nothing." It was the first time Roggie had spoken since coming home.

"Rog, you were surrounded!" Jerry said, disbelievingly. "You had to see something."

"I didn't see nothing."

45

"Well, they were all around him, Mrs. Baumer! I saw 'em, Jerry saw 'em!"

"Yeah, I saw 'em!"

Rose was perplexed. She didn't know whether to laugh at the looks of sincerity on their faces, or be concerned. She studied Roggie, he sat there, impassive, aware of what was being said, but totally oblivious to its relevance.

"What did they look like?"

"Well, at first, I thought it was like fireworks. But they began to look more like straight beams."

Pillars! Jerry said. They looked like pillars of lights! But there was something in each of them!"

"Yeah," Ronnie said, remembering. "There was like a brighter spot in the middle, almost like someone was inside them!"

"I don't remember anything," Roggie said.

"They were all around you! I thought you were a goner."

"Ain't nobody ever been hurt by lights! Jerry said scornfully.

"What if they were men from Mars?"

"Men from Mars don't look that way!"

"How do you know?"

I saw a movie!"

"That's swell! How do you know the movie was right?"

"That wasn't men from Mars! They were ghosts, I tell you!"

Rose shook her head and tried to keep from smiling. She pondered whether or not to tell them Frank Thompson had told her earlier that evening that the lights were caused by car headlights reflected from the road beside the cemetery. *Let them enjoy their fantasy.* She didn't have the heart to spoil their tale.

What Rose didn't know was there had been no cars on the road that night.

A little later, Danny got out of bed to go to the bathroom. Music filtered through the door to Roggie's bedroom. The Rolling Stones were belting out "Satisfaction" from the radio. Roggie had started leaving his radio on all night about a week after moving into the house.

Danny dreaded the long walk through the house to the bathroom. It was so far to go down the steps and through the entire house to get to the bathroom. He'd be glad when Dad came

46

home next summer and put in the second bathroom upstairs, as he'd promised.

Well, he thought, *Ya gotta go, ya gotta go!*

He stumbled to the door of his bedroom and turned to go down the steps. He was about halfway down when he saw a man appear in the kitchen at the foot of the steps and begin to climb them.

Who's he? I don't know him.

Danny noticed he was dressed strangely. The man didn't even appear to notice Danny; he was intent on getting up the stairs. When the two met, Danny politely flattened himself against the wall to let the man by and continued on his way.

He was washing his hands, preparing to go back to bed when he felt a chill rush through him. *Did I just see what I thought I saw? Could I really see through that guy?* He fought nausea, his heart beating rapidly now as he opened the bathroom door to the living room, half-expecting to see something out there waiting to pounce on him.

He reached the entrance to the dining room. Warily, he peeked around the doorway; he heaved a sigh of relief. *Nothing. Good.*

He crossed the dining room to the kitchen, again, peeking through the door before continuing up the stairs. He could only breathe normally again once he was back in his bedroom. *Maybe I was dreaming. That was it; I was half asleep, the lights playing through the windows... I'll wake up in the morning; it'll be all right.* He crawled into bed and closed his eyes to avoid looking at the shadow on the wall. It was going to be hard to go to sleep.

From the next room, it sounded like Roggie had turned the volume up on his radio; what was with that guy, anyway? How could he sleep in the middle of all that noise?

Rose wiped the last smear from the window and studied her work with justified pride. It was brilliantly clean, she reflected. It had been a little more than three weeks since Roger had left for Korea. He would be shocked to see at how much had been done to improve the house. The windows alone were a testimony to her determination and hard work. There had been layer upon layer of dirt and crud crusted on the panes when they moved in. Now, Rose marveled at how they sparkled in the morning sun.

She found washing the windows was relaxing to her.

47

The Homestead

There'd been a big argument that morning between Danny and Roggie- Rog. She caught herself; he'd announced a few days ago he wanted to be called Rog, now. Roggie was a kid's name. She sighed and returned her thoughts to the argument.

Danny had wakened that morning and discovered that one of his favorite soldiers, the "Armistead" figure, was gone from his battle setup in his bedroom.

He'd come downstairs asking Rose if she'd seen it, claiming he'd looked "everywhere" for it. When he asked Rog if he'd seen it, Rog had blown up defensively, accusing Danny of accusing him of taking it.

"I wasn't accusing you, Roggie," Danny had angrily retorted. He refused to, as he stated, bow to his brother's "whims of identity crisis." Rose wondered where he came up with some of his "stuff." "But now that you mention it- you were complaining about having to step over my stuff to get to your room!"

"You little punk! If you picked your cra-"

"Roggie- Rog!" she'd interrupted, "Watch your mouth, young man! Danny wasn't accusing you; you had no reason to fly off the handle."

"There you go again, taking his side!" he left the house, slamming the door behind him before she could reply. She realized she was going to have to deal with that problem when he finally cooled off and made it home.

She moved on to her favorite chore, cleaning *the* window. The frosted glass pane on the "front" door of the house. How she loved that window. How often had she stopped and stared at the girl in the picture, wondering who the girl was, or whether it really was the portrait of a real person, or the fantasy of the artist/craftsman who rendered it.

She sprayed some of her vinegar/water mixture on the glass and began polishing in small circular motions, all the while studying every feature on the glass, as had become her habit. She wondered at the portrait. Usually the girl in the glass seemed so sad. This morning, if Rose hadn't known better, she'd swear the portrait wore a pleased look on its face. *I must have drunk too much coffee today.*

It was weird, she thought, how the girl's eyes always seemed to follow you everywhere you went in the room. Today, as she wiped the glass, her eyes had peered into the girl's, she had gotten the distinct impression those eyes were looking back.

48

Each time, she quickly glanced away, as if to break some awful spell that was being cast over her. She chided herself for being silly and went back to work.

She dipped her rag back into the bucket and put it to the glass for a final wash and started. She could swear the expression on the image had changed; the girl was now actually smiling at her!

That's it, Rose Baumer! No more household work for you today, the fumes are starting to get to you!

A few days before school started, Danny heard Roggie coming up the stairway and hid behind the door to his bedroom. When Roggie came through the door, Danny grabbed him from behind and shouted, "Boo!"

Roggie turned around and would have hurt Danny if he'd gotten hold of him. Danny flew down the steps, Roggie close behind.

Rose had been in the kitchen writing a letter to Roger when the commotion broke out. She looked up in time to see Danny fly over the last several steps and land in the middle of the kitchen floor, barely missing the table.

"I'll kill you, you little brat!"

"What's going on here?" Rose demanded.

"I was playing a joke and Roggie doesn't have a sense of humor!"

"I'll show you my sense of humor, punk! I'll beat your stinking head in!"

"You'd better watch your mouth, Mr. Baumer!" Rose said, getting between Rog and Danny, "If there's going to be any fighting done around here, I'll be doing it!" *I'm beginning to sound like Roger now.*

"Danny," she turned around to see Danny crouching behind her as though for protection, a devilish smile on his face, "that was a stupid thing to do! You know Rog isn't feeling well; that isn't funny to scare him."

"All right." Danny said, "I'm sorry Roggie, I was just playing around."

"Yeah, right," Roggie said hatefully, "Do it again and I don't care what Mom says I'll nail you!"

"All right, young man, that'll be enough out of you. I don't care what he's done or how bad you feel, the day you think you can openly defy my authority is the day you can pack your

49

bags and leave! The door swings both ways; don't let it hit you on your butt on your way out!

"You're always taking his side against mine, protecting him!" Roggie protested.

"That's in your head. I've skinned him more than once over you!"

"Well, all I gotta say is he better stay outa my stuff!"

"What now?" Rose asked. This was getting to be too much.

"Every morning, I wake up to find he's been in my drawers messing them up."

"Rog," Rose said with a hint of exasperation, "How can you tell if he's been in your drawers?"

"I'm serious, Mom. He moves things around. He moved my entire sock drawer from the dresser to the chest-of-drawers. 'Stuff like that. I find my underwear in my drawer for my personal stuff and my personal stuff is scattered all over."

"Danny-" Rose said sternly, turning again to her second son.

"Mom," Danny said, as contritely as possible. "I don't know what he's talking about, I never touched his drawers... I wish I'd thought of it though, " his voice trailed off with a giggle, which was stifled by a sharp look from Rose.

"I can't get into his room anyway, Mom. He's always got it locked, remember?"

"That's right, Rog," Rose said, "*I* can't even get in there, which needs to change."

"I only started locking it after he started messing with things! He must be picking the lock or something."

"Oh *please*, Roger Stephen!"

"I don't know how you're doing it, buddy," he said threateningly, "but when I catch you you've had it!"

"Oh I'm soooo scared, Roggie!" Danny said as Roggie walked upstairs, "Remember, you're the lover of the family, not the fighter!"

Roggie walked up the stairs muttering what seemed to Rose to be obscenities. She started to call him down on it but decided it would wait. She turned to Danny again.

"What did you mean by that crack?"

"Aw, nothin', you know how he's always chasin' girls and I'm always getting into fights."

She stared at Danny for a moment, thoughtfully, *What*

50

does he know that he's not telling me.

"Mom," Danny said seriously; Rose thought for a moment it was as if he knew what she was thinking and was interrupting her intentionally. "I haven't been in Rog's room in a month."

Chapter 4
July 1967

So Saul died for his transgression, which he committed against the Lord, even the word of the Lord, which he kept not, and also for the asking counsel of one that had a familiar spirit, to inquire of her, and inquired not of the Lord; therefore, he slew him, and turned the kingdom unto David, the son of Jesse.
(I Chronicles: 13 & 14)

Rose sat at the kitchen table, her back to the outside door, writing a letter to Roggie. *Rog,* she corrected herself.

No, I don't care what he wants to be called; I can still call him Roggie to myself if I want to. He can call himself anything he wants; he'll always be Roggie to me...

It seemed to her she was spending a great deal of her life writing her men in uniform. *Men,* she thought, *it seemed like yesterday I was changing his diapers. Now he's at Ft. Sill, at Artillery School. Where has the time gone?*

Indeed, she could hear the sound of Roger working outside trying to clear a clogged septic tank line. It was hard to believe Roger had finished his tour and was home from Korea. It was hard to believe they had lived in the "Homestead" a year. It was harder to believe they had survived their first year here.

Now, Roger was home. They had the place to themselves. Roggie had just finished basic training. Danny was off at a summer youth retreat sponsored by one of the local churches. It was the first time she could remember being alone with her husband in years. All the bad memories of the past year seemed lost in the far distant past now.

She couldn't remember a more terrible winter than the one they had just spent. Any military wife will tell you things always seem to go wrong when the husband is away. Cars break down, kids get in trouble at school, and the bank begins bouncing checks - everything that can go wrong, goes wrong. Never had Rose had a year like the one past.

It had started with Ginger. It was late September when Ginger disappeared. It was Roggie who first noticed; it was his job to feed her. He asked her if she'd seen Ginger lately, she hadn't eaten her food in a few days. Danny chimed in he hadn't seen her. Rose concluded she was probably in season and would be returning soon with a blessing. Let her have this litter, but she was going to be spayed as soon as possible.

When Ginger didn't return immediately, Rose began to worry, though she didn't let on in front of the kids. She began to prowl the streets in her station wagon looking for the dog. Then, one Friday night, Ginger returned.

It was late; everyone in the house was sound asleep when the most terrible racket of howling, barking, and growling Rose had ever heard, awakened them. It was coming from the front of the house. Rose ran into Danny's bedroom to get a look at the front yard through his windows. Danny was already awake staring outside. The noise, she noticed was even louder in here.

"What's going on?" she asked.

"Look, Mom," Danny said, pointing out the window, "Have you ever seen more dogs in one place in all your life?"

Rose peered through the window. The front lawn was illuminated by the street lamp on the corner. "Oh, my Lord..."

There appeared to be dozens, even a hundred or more, dogs of every breed and size in her front yard, they were barking, howling, fighting, scratching, yelping, and everything else dogs do-in her front yard!

"Roggie!" Rose yelled, "Rog!"

No answer, all she could hear was music blaring from behind the door. She knocked-pounded on the door," Roger Baumer wake up now!" To Danny, "No wonder he couldn't hear all the racket outside; that music's so loud..."

Finally, the door cracked open and a sleepy face appeared. Rose was taken back by the stench emanating from the room. Rose pushed the door open and switched on the light. The sight that met her eyes disgusted her. Unbelievable filth.

"Look at this mess!" she screamed, struggling to be heard over the radio blaring full blast from his dresser. She gestured around at piles of dirty clothes and scraps of half-eaten snacks taken into the room, "We'll deal with this later. Right now, we've got an emergency. Both of you downstairs!"

Rose ran through Danny's room back into hers, she opened up her wardrobe and pulled out Roger's twelve-gauge pump action shotgun. She grabbed a box of shells and hurried down the steps, loading as she went. The boys were in the kitchen already, peering out through the window over the sink, at the spectacle in the front yard.

"Get the mop bucket and my large kettles out and fill them with water!"

"What're you going to do?" Roggie asked.

"I think Ginger's back. We've got to get her in the house before they kill her!"

"Where'd all these dogs come from?" Danny asked.

"It looks like from every corner of the state." Roggie answered, digging out pots and pans from the cabinets under the sink.

Rose used a chair to climb up on the sink to get a better look at the front door from the kitchen window. She saw a cluster of dogs in the corner, by the door crawling over each other, fighting and snarling and whatnot. She shuddered when she thought their Ginger was probably on the bottom of that pile.

"Danny!" she shouted, "Go upstairs and get those old bunk bed sheets out of the closet. We're going to need them to wrap Ginger in."

Danny nodded and was off.

"What're we going to do?" Roggie asked standing ready. For the first time in weeks, Rose believed she saw a glimpse of the old Roggie there.

"I'm going to open the door and give those mutts a couple of blasts with rock salt to scatter them. I want you and Danny standing by with the cold water. There's a pile of dogs in the corner by the door. When I blast and stand aside, you and Danny empty the cold water on the pile of dogs. That should get them off Ginger long enough for me to get her inside, got it?" Danny was back with the sheets. Both boys nodded.

"Ready?" Again, nods.

"Okay, let's go."

Rose led the way into the dining room, the boys followed with their water. Rose paused for a minute, "Ready?" one last time, again nods. "Here goes!"

She pulled the door open, leveling her shotgun. She was about to squeeze off a round when, "Blast it!" the screen door was in the way! She glanced down the street. All was quiet. *Why haven't the neighbors been bothered?*

She looked down at the writhing mass of dogs in the corner, the noise was deafening with the door opened, *To heck with the screen door!*

Rose let loose with two rounds of rock salt, not caring

what she hit. The dogs on the outer fringes of the pile, where the salt was landing, scattered, howling and wailing with agony. Only the group in the corner was left, "NOW, BOYS!"

Roggie and Danny tossed their loads with precision on target. The water was sufficiently cold enough, coming through the pipes in the Illinois autumn, to shock the animals. More yelps and howls, more scattered. Rose caught a glimpse of what might be Ginger on the floor of the porch. She reached down and grabbed her. A dog that looked like a beagle mix snarled at her as she began to pull Ginger in; Rose swore at the dog and punched him in the jaw with her fist. A German shepherd lunged at her as she got her dog in the doorsill. Rose was surprised and relieved to see a broom come down flat on his head stunning him enough for her to get Ginger in the door.

"Got 'im!" Danny shouted triumphantly.

Another shotgun blast nearly deafened her, but scattered the rest of the dogs, at least temporarily. Roggie pumped another round in the chamber and slammed the door shut. They could hear the scratching of animals and pounding against the door as it closed.

"Whew!" Roggie said, "That was close."

"You'd better believe it!" Rose said, "Let's get Ginger in the kitchen so we can get a look at her. Danny, turn the light on, will you baby?"

It wasn't a pretty sight. Rose took a deep breath as she unwrapped the sheet that covered Ginger. Roggie gagged, Danny stared in stunned silence. She had been deeply gashed in several places, probably from other dogs fighting over her. Blood and other fluids had mingled to make her a sticky mess.

"Poor little baby," Rose murmured, with tears in her eyes, "poor little baby."

"Is she going to make it?" Roggie asked, choking.

"I really don't know, baby. She's in pretty bad shape. We-" she was interrupted by the noise of dogs fighting and growling beneath the floor, "Oh no! They're under the house; they'll tear up the heat ducts!"

Now the sounds came from the furnace room, there was pounding against the furnace room door as animals literally threw themselves against the door in an effort to break it down and get to Ginger.

"Boys," Rose said, "you stay here while I make sure that bathroom door is completely shut." Rose ran through the dining room. She hadn't gotten far when she heard noises come from within the walls, "They're in the ventilation shaft!"

She looked and saw the air intake vent screen break from the wall. A mid-sized dog of undetermined breed stuck his head into the room snarling. "No you don't!" Rose snarled, uttering more oaths she'd have to apologize for later. She was enraged now. *How dare these mutts invade my home?* She grabbed the broom, left by the door and started swinging, beating the dog back.

"Kids! I need help!"

Roggie took one look at what was happening and moved. He ran to the huge china cabinet next to the duct and began pushing it along the wall to cover the duct. "Help me, Danny!"

Danny joined in pushing while Rose kept the dogs at bay with her broom. Every time a head peeked through it was met with a heavy blow. "If I wasn't worried about loosing our heating ducts," she said, breathlessly, "I'd just cut loose with double-ott buck and let the owners come and pick up their mongrels!"

Rose looked at the dining room wall clock; it was three a.m. According to the clock by her bed, it had been one-thirty a.m. when she was wakened. She had a feeling, listening to the noises coming from beneath the house and in the furnace room; the night wasn't about to be over.

"We're going to have to get her out of here or they'll kill her or tear up the house trying to get her. Or do both." Roggie said anxiously.

"I know." Rose said, "the question is, how do we get her past those dogs outside?"

"We can call the cops." Danny suggested hopefully. The looks he got from his mother and brother, let him know the uselessness of that suggestion. Delphi didn't have any law enforcement of its own. They relied on county sheriff's deputies who cruised through the town occasionally on their patrols. It would usually take hours for them to respond to a call because they hated to come to Delphi.

"We can call Uncle Brew," Roggie suggested.

Rose listened to the turmoil outside. There were dogs on the front porch, clawing at the dining room door trying to get in, leaping up at the front kitchen window, clawing and scratching. She could see and hear dogs at the bay windows trying to climb up; she could hear dogs on the back porch, trying to batter their way through the door; the sounds of dogs fighting and snarling came from the furnace room. From beneath the house came the sounds of dogs whining, growling, and banging against the heating ducts. She knew it was a matter of time until they broke in. She hated to admit it, but she was scared. No, she was terrified.

She was reluctant to call Brew except in an emergency, but this certainly classified as an emergency. She looked at the faces of her two boys, kneeling beside poor little Ginger, caressing her, avoiding her ghastly injuries, not mindful of the filth that covered her, looking up to her for answers she wasn't sure she had, for courage she felt was waning.

"Yes!" she said finally, "I'll call Brew!"

She walked over to the wall where the telephone was and picked up the phone. She hesitated. *Even if I can get up with him it'll be a couple of hours before he can get up here. Can we hold out until then?*

Meanwhile, on the other side of the room, Ginger opened her eyes and looked up at Roggie and Danny sadly. With her last ounce of strength, she lifted her head and licked Roggie's hand. Then she shuddered and was still. Rose, at the phone paused in her dialing; it was quiet around the house.

"Mom, don't bother," Roggie said sobbing, "Ginger's dead."

Rose remembered looking over at the family dog. She fought back tears as she remembered the little brown and black fur ball Roger had brought home one day after work. He had saved her from the pound. One of the guys in his unit had a dog that had given birth to a litter he couldn't keep. He'd come down on orders. Ginger hadn't even been weaned yet, they'd bottle fed her for three weeks. They'd had her over three years, the longest they'd ever been able to keep a pet, with Roger's constant transfers. They'd even figured they'd be able to take her on their next overseas tour as long as it was a place that allowed dogs to be brought in. Now she was gone.

So too, it seemed, were the hounds of hell that had killed her.

Rose peeked outside one of the bay windows.

Nothing.

She peered down the street for a sign of retreating animals, not a dog in sight.

Odd.

"Roggie," she said, "Check the furnace room. Be careful

now, don't let anything in."

Roggie cracked the door, "Nothing, Mom."

"I wonder where they all went?"

"I'm just glad they're gone!"

The boys had buried Ginger out back. Danny had fashioned a small cross out of two boards nailed together. He'd even read the 23rd Psalm over her.

She paused in her reflections. She looked for the six-month-old German shepherd puppy that had been playing on the floor. Rose hadn't wanted another dog after Ginger. Roggie had brought him home about a month after Ginger's death. He had opened up the shoe box he'd carried him home in and peeled away the newspapers stuffed in the box to insulate him from the winter's cold. She saw those big brown eyes staring out of a black ball of fur and she had to admit her heart melted. When Danny came down and saw the puppy, she knew she'd lost the war.

The kids named him Fritz, after one of their favorite professional wrestlers. He'd grown on her.

She worried where he might be off to, what mischief he might be in. *Forget about it now, Rose, he's probably taking a nap.*

She could hear Roger out in the yard talking to someone. It was an animated conversation, though she couldn't make out what they were saying or the voice (voices?) of the person (people?) to whom Roger was speaking.

Then she was back to reflecting on their first winter in the house. After the dogs came the accident. Rose had gotten bored sitting around the house all day and had enrolled in a special course they were offering at the State hospital over in Springfield. It was a long drive, more than sixty miles one-way, but she figured it was worth it. It was a yearlong course. When she finished, she would have her GED and be a licensed practical nurse. This was worth two year's college credit, she'd learned. When she heard of the program she believed it to be too good to pass up. After one finished the course, they could either pay the State back by working at the hospital another three years for great pay or pay the tuition. She'd talked to Roger on the phone about it. They had both agreed they could swing the tuition so she could follow him to his next assignment. Roger had thought it was a great idea for her to attend the course. After all, the kids were at the age now they didn't need her to be home all day, and she could get an outside interest.

"That's great! When I retire you can support me," he had joked.

With the long hours and the long drive, though, it meant her often getting home late in the evening and spending most of her remaining time in the evenings cramming for the next test. This was a cram course. Tests were frequent and hard. She was surprised to find she could carry a high "B" average, in spite of the years since she'd been in school and her lack of formal education as compared to some of the other women in the class.

One night, she'd been driving home from the hospital. It was late. She'd had to stay over late to fill in on a ward and the weather was drizzly. She was on the New Haupstadt road, nearing Delphi, just coming on to the quarter-mile drag strip the kids from town used on Friday and Saturday nights. Sometimes, when she came home late on a Friday, the kids would stop her if a race were on. They had walkie-talkies stationed at each end of the road so they could monitor the progress of the race from both ends and keep innocent bystanders from getting killed. Rose had to admire their organization and thoughtfulness; after all, if you've "gotta do it," and there was something in the American teenager that made them think they "hadda do it!" you might as well do it safely. The kids were always polite, too, calling her ma'am or Mrs. Baumer. They'd hold her until they got the signal from the other end the race was over and then, "You can go now, Ma'am." "Sorry for the inconvenience. Have a nice night!" "Tell Rog, I said, 'hi!'"

This evening there was no race. The kids never, to her knowledge, raced in inclement weather. As she rounded the last hairpin curve before the quarter mile, she saw a car off the road, to her left, about thirty feet off the road. Its nose was buried in the thick grass, its taillights glowing eerily in the mist. She saw the skid marks where he'd come off the straightaway and lost control at the curve. She slowed down her car to see if anyone was still in the car or not and whether she needed to stop and help.

Before she could decide, she felt an enormous force hit the tail-end of her car, sending her forward, full force into the steering wheel, bruising her face and jarring her back. Suddenly the car was spinning in circles, out of control. She tried to sit up straight so she could steer out of it, but found the centrifugal force pinned her to the wheel of the car. *Oh Jesus,* she cried out in her

59

mind, *help me Lord, my kids...*

The car spun to a stop, in the middle of the road.

"Gee, lady, are you all right?" there was a face at her window she recognized as Ronnie Allsup. "Geez, Mrs. Baumer! Are you all right?"

"I'm all right. Can you get my door open so I can get out of here?"

"Ma'am, I don't know if I should move you or not. You know what they say about people in car accidents."

"I believe I'm all right." *I'd better check, wiggle toe- do they work? Yep, they work. Finger check -' fingers work? Yep, they work. Turn head-carefully, okay. There'll be some stiffness, pulled tendons, mostly.* She tried the door. It wouldn't open. She started to panic, and then relaxed. *It might help if you unlocked it, Rosie.*

Safely out of her car, she examined the damage. The entire rear end was crumpled up past the rear tires. She shook her head, to be stranded without a vehicle in Delphi. She wondered how long it would take for the insurance company to move to get her a new car. What would she do until then?

"Gee, Mrs. Baumer, you are lucky you aren't hurt!" It was Ronnie.

Blessed is more like it, she reflected.

She noticed the other car for the first time. Its entire front end had been shoved back into the driver's seat. The front door on the driver's side hung open. Toward the rear, undamaged area of the car, a man sat on the ground, his back propped against the rear tire. He appeared to be unconscious.

"Oh, my Lord," Rose gasped heading toward him, "is he- "

"It's Shorty Ferguson.'Looks like he's passed out drunk, ma'am." Ronnie said.

Rose went toward him and examined him for herself. *Sure enough, he smells one hundred proof.* She looked at the car again, then at him and shook her head. *Not even a scratch! What was it Mama always said? 'The Lord takes care of children and fools? Brew always said, 'children and drunks.' He's drunk; I wonder what that makes me?*

It turned out that the car in the ditch had been Ronnie Allsup's. He'd been trying out a new carburetor on the quarter mile and had been unable to slow down enough before he hit the curve. "I reckon I should have tried it the other way – going out of

60

town," he said.

He had walked down to the Hoffer's house about three-quarters of a mile down the road toward town to call for help. He got back to his car just in time to see Shorty, driving home after a prolonged visit at Kopf's in New Haupstadt, turn the curve doing about sixty, and slam on his brakes too late to avoid ramming the rear end of Rose's car. He ran to the accident, thinking the worst. He was relieved to see Shorty, having neatly avoided being skewered by his transmission, open his own door, stagger out of the car and fall flat on his behind, passed out drunk, against his car. He probably wasn't even aware he'd been in an accident.

Rose rode in the cab as Kissinger's wrecker hauled what was left of the family car away. She asked for it to be towed to the house. Her family's Christmas was still in the back. They'd figure what to do with the car later.

The next morning Rose could barely walk. She'd been expecting this. It was a Saturday and she hoped she'd be up and around by Monday or she'd have to call in. She couldn't afford to miss too many days on this program. Then she thought, even if she were feeling better, how'd she get there without a car?

Rog and Danny got up early and began hauling their Christmas presents in from the car in the rain. Rose was surprised to find them all fairly intact. Danny had been delighted to see Rose had gotten him a Louis Marx Co. "Desert Fox" playset. He had, in his most convincing practical manner, suggested that being Christmas was only a few weeks away, and they had already seen their gifts, why didn't they just go ahead and open them?

Rose had firmly held her ground. No, the gifts would be opened at the proper time. All Danny and Roggie had to do was act surprised and pretend they hadn't seen their gifts.

She could smile now, as she reflected on how miserable she had been. She'd had trouble contacting her insurance agent on a Saturday. She'd fretted about what she'd do about Monday until Brew called. He had a friend who owned a car lot. He'd have her a loaner as long as she needed it. Good old Uncle Brew, she thought, her alcoholic guardian angel.

Rose paused in her reflections and wrote a few more lines in her letter, "*Things are normal here at the house. The plumbing in the bathroom is acting up. Your dad is outside digging up the pipes...*"

She could still hear Roger's animated conversation

outside. *If he doesn't stop talking soon, he won't get the job done before dark and we've got to flush that toilet soon!*

She returned to her memories. As if things weren't bad enough, at Christmas a bad winter storm set in. The weatherman said it was the worst blizzard in twenty years. Twelve inches of snow fell on the ground overnight; in places it was drifting to three and four feet. The temperature dropped to below zero at night. The furnace went out in the middle of the night.

When the family awoke one morning to find the house literally freezing, Rose thought Roggie had let the fire in the furnace go out. She rose from her bed, and, shivering, put on her warmest clothes. Still shivering from the chill of getting dressed, she went to check on her kids. She found Danny under a mountain of blankets and covers. He had raided the closet.

She poked the mountain a few times, eliciting a few moans.

"Danny, get up, babe!"

"Why?"

"You've got to go to school!"

"Mom, there ain't going to be no school today. Look at the snow!"

He was right.

"Mom, can I go out and play in it later?"

Rose shook her head. Too cold and messy to go to school, but okay to play in. "We'll see, we've got to see about getting some heat in this house first. Get dressed."

"Mom, it's cold!"

"Sissy!" she teased. She reached on the floor where yesterday's pile of clothes lay amidst her son's version of World War II, picked them up and tossed them on the bed. She watched as Danny's hand reached out from the abyss of his cavern, found the pants, pulled them in like the tongue of a deep sea creature snatching its prey, re-emerging to grab his shirt.

Satisfied that Danny was taken care of, she moved on to Roggie's room. Upon entering, she noted that the room was cleaner than it had been during that awful night Ginger died. Periodic inspections since had ensured that. There was still a faint odor; she couldn't get rid of, like meat that had gone bad. She had tried everything, disinfectant, shampooing the rug, air freshener; nothing completely rid the room of the smell.

Roggie had pulled out the Army sleeping bag his father had given him a few Christmases before. She nudged him,

"Rog."

"Hunh?"

"Did you properly tamp the fire last night before we went to bed."

"Hunh?"

"The furnace, did you properly bank the furnace before you went to bed?"

"Oh, yeah, sure, Mom," came the sleepy reply. "Why?"

"Something's wrong. There's no heat." She patted the lump on the bed, hoping she was hitting the right spot, "Come on, get up, we need to see what's wrong."

She made her way downstairs. She could see her breath. She reached the bottom of the steps; the kitchen was colder than the upstairs. This was unusual; normally the downstairs was nice and warm. It was the upstairs that was always cooler. With the winter, they figured it was partially because of the inadequate duct system. But even in the summer the upstairs was at least ten degrees cooler than the downstairs, particularly in Roggie's room.

She walked over to the sink and turned the faucet. Nothing came out. *Great! The pipes are frozen, and I let them drip last night. I just hope they haven't burst...* She went to the stove to find the pilot lights were still burning. *At least something in this house still works. As long as we have gas.* She turned on all the burners and the oven. *That ought to at least heat up the kitchen, as long as we don't die from asphyxiation.*

She heard the shuffling of Roggie and Danny coming downstairs, bundled up in all their winter clothes, "Good!" she said, "Now we can check on the furnace."

She didn't want to admit it, but since the incident with Ginger, she was a bit nervous about going into the furnace room alone. Before, she hadn't realized how easy it was for an animal to get in there. Now she worried about opening the door and seeing –well, anything - in there.

She hopped down from the kitchen onto the furnace room floor. She could feel the cold of the cement even through her fur-covered slippers. She touched the handle to the furnace door; it was still hot to the touch. She opened it up. There was a nice blanket of hot coals inside.

Roggie had moved over to the blower motor and was flicking the switches. Nothing happened. "'Nothing working here, Mom."

"Danny-" she looked; Danny had anticipated the next

63

move and was already crossing the kitchen to check the fuse box.

"Mom, the fuse is all right!" he called.

"Take it out for a minute." Roggie called, "I'm going to open this motor up and I don't want to be fried."

Roggie fiddled with the eyebolts on the outside of the motor cover a few minutes with his gloved hands without success. Sighing in frustration, he removed his gloves. He winced as the chill hit his hands. It was so cold his hands actually ached from it.

He touched one of the eyebolts and stopped suddenly. He realized he'd made a big mistake, his fingers were frozen to the metal, "Mom, I've got a big problem."

Rose made her way around the furnace to where her son was standing. Seeing him, she immediately realized the problem, "Don't move."

"I'm not!"

She carefully moved to where she could get her face near Roggie's frozen finger. She moved her mouth as close to his fingers as she could without touching metal herself and began to breathe on them. Roggie's face brightened as he realized what she was doing and he too bent down and began to breathe on his fingers. He began to feel his fingers gradually loosen from the metal. Soon he was free, nursing his frost bitten fingers.

"Put them up in your armpits, help them thaw," Rose said, "Wiggle them a bit to get the circulation back. Go on into the kitchen.

"Danny! Get me a pair of pliers!"

With pliers in hand, Rose removed the eyebolts with gloved hands. Carefully taking off the cover plate, she fought back tears, lest they freeze her eyes up. The entire coil to the blower mechanism was burned out.

She went back to the kitchen and picked up the phone to call a repairman and slammed the receiver back down with an oath. The phone was dead. The lines were probably down. There was nothing to do but sit there and wait until they were back up, or they froze to death.

"Well boys," she said after a moment or two, "We may freeze to death, but we don't have to die hungry!"

She sent Danny out with a large pot to gather snow so she'd have water to cook, admonishing him to be careful to get only clean snow. Danny obediently went outside and gathered up all he could, and was back quickly, Rose noted. She didn't figure he'd be making snowmen this time. It was no fun getting cold and wet when you didn't have anywhere to get warm and dry off.

With the oven set at 250 degrees and the oven door open, the kitchen was at least beginning to be less chilly. Rose again hoped they had enough gas to last this crisis through; she'd had the bottle filled the previous week. They still had power. That was good. She flipped on the radio to listen to weather reports.

She idly listened to the list of school closings as she melted the snow Danny had brought in to make a pot of coffee and started cooking breakfast. The radio reports led her to believe every road leading to Delphi was closed until the graders could get to them. That could take some time. All the roads leading to town were secondary, county roads. She figured the major roads such as Illinois 127 and US 40 would be the first objectives. It might be a day or two before they opened the roads to Delphi. *If they could get the phones fixed maybe I can get some help.*

The kids were on their second cup of coffee and Rose was dishing out pancakes when they heard a car drive up outside. *Who on earth is out driving around on a day like this?* She looked out the kitchen window and smiled, *Brew! I might have known!*

He was struggling over a snowdrift, making his way across the yard when he looked up and saw her in the window. He grinned at her, showing off his brand new pair of false teeth, and waved.

She pointed to the front door, letting him know it was okay to use the seldom used entrance. He smiled gratefully and waved again, changing his direction.

"What on earth are you doing out on a day like this!"

"I saw the snow. 'Heard it was worse up here and figured I oughta look in on youse all."

"But Brew, you could have been killed!"

"Not me, no sir. I'm not dying like this. I figure I'll go buying one for the house!"

Rose shook her head disapprovingly, "Come on in here, where it's warm."

They stepped into the kitchen from the dining room and immediately felt the difference. The oven was doing its job. Rose had turned off the burners; they were no longer needed. As long as one stayed in the kitchen they were all right.

Sitting at the kitchen table, Brew grinned widely as Rose brought him a cup of coffee, "They told me all the roads were closed back on Highway 70. The State Trooper told me not even to bother leaving the highway because it was impossible to get to New Hauptstadt, much less Delphi, I'd never get through. I guess I showed them, heh, heh," he took his first sip. "I guess I did the State a favor by breaking open the roads for 'em, eh? I oughta charge 'em!"

Rose had told him about the blower going out and the phones being out. He listened. "What we need to do is get you some heat!"

After finishing his coffee, he took Roggie and Danny over to Paul Schofeld's hardware store. Old Paul had been in business for years. His store was a mess because he never threw anything away. Danny had seen newspapers and magazines dating back fifty years on his shelves, lying beside tools, gaskets, and the items of hardware he stocked. Generations of Schofeld cats roamed the shop freely, sitting on shelves next to power chainsaws or ratchet sets. Roger once commented that he'd hate to see anyone bring a lit match into the place. The kids in town said his house was the same way.

But he knew right where everything was and could find anything you needed in a few minutes. Only Schofeld would have been open on such a day. The kids hadn't been a bit surprised to see him there. When Brew showed up, he listened politely, "Well, I don't know as I can help you with the furnace. You'd have to call up Hanley's over in Glen Haven for that, but I do have a couple old coal stoves I can let you have. They're in my warehouse next door..."

By warehouse, he meant one of the empty storefronts. He led Brew and the boys over there, had a problem opening the door, finally the key turned.

"Be careful," he said as he opened the door, "it's a might messy inside."

Brew gave a sidelong look that made the kids laugh as he followed the old man into the shop. Brew might have had drinking problems, they knew, but he was always immaculate about his person, his car, and his home. He might live in a single room behind a tavern, but it was clean.

Sure enough, they had to make their way through a narrow aisle in the midst of boxes and crates and other varied treasures and trash. Danny, ever the optimist, peered in the darkened building at all the stuff, hoping to see something that might be of value to a twelve year old.

"Here 'tis." the old man finally said. "I thought I had two.

66

I must have sold the other one last year...I believe I did, Freddie Murphy wanted it for his hen house, I believe..."

"How much do you want for it?"

"Oh, I'll take seventy-five dollars for it."

"Sold!" Brew said, reaching into his pocket and pulling out his wallet.

Schofeld, Brew and the kids wrestled the stove on Schofeld's ancient handcart and managed to get the thing in the back of Schofeld's pickup truck. In a few hours the stove was fired up and keeping at least the kitchen warm.

That night, Rose and the kids piled in the same bed with their clothes on and every blanket in the house over them to stay warm. Rose tried to make a game out of their hardship by saying they were living just like the pioneers.

Danny joined in, "Yeah, Mom, we're homesteaders!"

"I guess this must be our homestead!" Roggie said, dourly, and then laughed, "This is our Homestead!"

The name stuck.

It was almost a month before the cold spell broke and the pipes thawed. Rose and the children continued using melted snow for water. She bought a large washtub from Schofeld's hardware and baths were taken in the middle of the kitchen using water heated on the stove. Rose made sure the kitchen windows were well covered during bath time. The outside faucet was the first to thaw, which was a blessing, as the snow was disappearing. Water was hauled inside after dark; Rose was ashamed to let the neighbors know how miserably they were living.

It was almost March before the plumbing in the bathroom thawed. One could forget how precious little things such as a hot shower can be, Rose reflected sitting at the kitchen table. She looked down at her letter and wrote some more, *"I hope this letter reaches you. Send me your address ASAP. Dad said he's glad he made it home for your graduation. He said he was proud of you and wouldn't have missed it if he had to go AWOL. I don't think Danny has taken off the fatigue hat you sent him since he received it. I'll sign off for now, I have to get this in the mail. We love and miss you and are PROUD OF YOU! Love, Mom."*

She folded and sealed the letter in an envelope, wrote the long military address of the Field Artillery School with his serial number as only an Army squaw, with long experience with military addresses can do. She hopped out of her chair. She knew

67

if she got it to Ft. Sill with his serial number it would reach him. She looked at the clock, *Good! It's still only 3:30; I have time to make the afternoon mail pickup.* Outside, she could still hear the animated conversation.

She bounced out on the front porch and was surprised to see Roger busily digging away on his trench. He was alone.

"Who on earth were you talking to?"

"Me?" he asked, looking up a bit indignant, "I've been toiling away here listening to you run at the mouth, trying to figure out who besides Brew it could be!"

"Run at the mouth!" she said indignantly, then noticed the twinkle in his eye. "Well, if I'm not talking and you're not talking- who's talking?"

They both paused and listened. Rose went around to the front of the house to see if there might be anyone there. No, the front was deserted. As a matter of fact, the whole street was deserted. *What else is new?*

"Roger," she said, feeling a small butterfly in her stomach, "could you come inside for a moment?"

She went inside; she could hear the talking much more clearly in the kitchen, yet still not quite clear enough to understand what was being said. Now it sounded like a crowd of voices, all trying to out-talk the others.

Roger came in the house, paused, listening, "Holy-"

"I know," Rose said.

"Who is it?"

"I don't know, there's no one around the house..."

"Upstairs?"

"Who'd be upstairs?"

"I intend to find out," Roger said, heading for the staircase.

"Be careful!"

He looked at her and winked, "Careful's my middle name. I haven't survived a tour in Korea and two in Vietnam by being reckless."

"That's how you won all your medals then," Rose couldn't help teasing, "by playing it safe."

Roger turned and stuck out his tongue at her, "Especially the ones with the little "Vs. on 'em!" He went up the stairs.

As soon as he reached the top step the voices stopped. Rose felt her heart pounding as she heard Roger move through the bedrooms. She wasn't even worried about the mud he was surely tracking through her house. He re-appeared at the top of the steps, his face a portrait of consternation.

"It beats all," he said descending the steps quickly. He reached the bottom, and stepped out into the kitchen. The voices resumed. "Well, I'll be-" he looked at her, "You're the veteran here, what now?"

Rose thought a moment, then her face brightened, "I know!"

She scurried into the dining room and opened up the bottom cabinet of her china cabinet, which the family used to store the games. She pulled out a white box.

Roger, rolled his eyes, "Oh no! Not the *Ouija* Board!"

"I've seen movies and a TV special where they used one of these things to talk to ghosts."

"Is that what you think we're dealing with here- ghosts?

"Who do you think is making that noise?"

"It could be Danny playing with that tape recorder I bought him in Korea."

That gave her pause, "No. I wouldn't put it past him but he's been gone four days. Even he couldn't figure out a way to rig it to play now."

"You're right," he agreed, "but that thing gives me the creeps!" he said, pointing to the board.

"Me too," she said. It had been a Christmas present for the kids from one of the relatives. She forgot which. The kids had gotten bored with it quickly and it went up with the other games. She had been surprised to find they still had it when she unloaded their household goods from storage. But now it might come in handy. "But what harm could it do, and we might learn something."

Roger shrugged and sat down at the table. Rose pulled the wooden board out of the box. There were letters and numbers printed on the face and the words "yes" and "no" in the top corners. She laid it on the kitchen table between them. She dug her hand in the box and found the plastic disc, or *planchette,* and placed it on the board.

Both she and Roger looked around, surprised. The moment she had placed the disc on the board the voices stopped. She shuddered. It was as if whatever was talking was watching them with fascination and expectation.

She grabbed her writing pad and pulled it over on her side of the board.

"What's that for?" Roger asked.

"To record questions and answers, silly!"

"Oh, I'm sorry," he said, "I'm not used to talking with the dead!"

"If you're not serious about this thing it won't work."

"Okay, okay!" he said, straightening up in a bad imitation of a contrite schoolboy, "I'll be good."

"All right, I'll ask the first question."

"*You* can ask them all, my dear, I'm out of practice interviewing spooks- at least the spiritual kind, not the CIA..."

Rose made a face at her husband, and then got serious, "Try to concentrate now."

"Put your hand on the disk." She said.

"Oh," Roger started and complied.

She thought a moment, her eyes closed, "Who are you?"

There was a moment when nothing happened. She was about to repeat the question when the disk began to move. A thrill ran through her as she peered through the clear plastic window to read the letter revealed. She read each letter aloud and rushed to copy it down with her left hand.

"I" it began slowly, moving to "A," then "M." Now, it began to speed up, rushing from letter to letter so fast Rose barely had time to copy them, much less make sense of the words it was forming. There'd be time for that later. The disk moved to "T" and stopped.

They waited a moment to make sure it was the end of the message.

"What does it say?" Roger asked soberly.

Rose picked up the pad and began reading trying to separate the letters into words, "It says, 'I - am- the- ghost- -of-- Christmas past!" she threw her pad across the table as he burst out laughing, "I hope you think you're funny!" Roger ducked the pad and fell on the kitchen floor laughing.

"I'm sorry baby," he said, getting up. "I couldn't resist it-" he stopped abruptly as a loud thud sounded from somewhere upstairs. The voices resumed louder than before; this time with a different tone as if upset, even angry. "All right, all right!" he said, as much to the air as to Rose, "I'll get serious!"

Rose looked over at her husband, for the first time in their life together she could see he was as spooked by something as she was.

Roger retrieved her pad. They sat back down as before.

The voices stopped.

"All right, let's try it again." she looked at Roger, "Concentrate." she knew now she didn't have to worry about his cooperation. She looked at the board, "Who are you?"

This time the board moved smoothly and briskly, *"M"* *"O"* *"L"* *"I"* *"N"* *"A"*.

She read it aloud. "That doesn't make sense."

"Try it again, to make sure."

Again the board spelled out *MOLINA.*

"Let's move on, we can make sense out of it later."

Rose nodded, "What do you want?"

I want my baby.

"Where is your baby?"

Twenty steps north.

"Twenty steps north from where?"

Well.

"From where?"

Well.

"Are you alone?"

No.

"Who is with you?"

Them.

"Who is 'them'?"

Them.

"What do they want?"

Nothing.

Roger and Rose looked at one another across the table.

"Ask again." he whispered.

"What do they want?"

There was a pause; then the disk moved up to the word *"NO."*

They sat back for another moment, pondering the last answer, and then Roger leaned forward, motioning Rose to join.

"Do you intend to hurt anyone?" he asked.

No answer.

"Do you intend to hurt anyone?"

No answer.

They sat back staring across the table at each other. Rose was about to say something when the talking resumed, even louder, as the disk came flying off the board, hitting Roger in the chest.

The disk hit the floor and the room fell silent again.

71

Chapter 5
June 1967

I the Lord thy God am a jealous God, visiting the iniquity of the fathers upon the children unto the third and fourth generation of them that hate me.

(Exodus 20:5)

Rose studied Roger's pale face. She could count on the fingers of one hand the times she had seen her husband afraid, two of them had been in this house.

"Well," he said hoarsely, regaining his composure, "you can't blame this one on me."

Rose read over the notes from the -what would you call it? *I guess it was a séance.* The word had an odd, almost silly drama to it. It was a word you read in an old horror novel or saw in a grade B movie. They took place in the dead of night in spooky rooms with lit candles that blew out. This had occurred in the middle of a sunny summer afternoon at the kitchen table. There were no long black flowing robes worn by the participants. They were in shorts and T-shirts, but it had happened. Roger and she had actually spoken to - what? Ghosts?

From what she remembered of her Bible, she almost laughed at herself. She was still, after all, a preacher's daughter. She knew it was impossible for the dead to come back. She remembered hearing her mother teach about the rich man and Lazarus in Sunday school, how there was a gulf fixed between the living and the dead. She had heard her father preach countless times about it being given to each to die "and then the judgment!"

So what were they dealing with here? She had no earthly idea. She was tempted to call her parents and ask them. She trusted their judgment in spiritual matters and respected their walk with the Lord, even though she didn't believe she could live up to their standards...

"Rosie," she started. It was Roger.

"Are you all right?"

"Yes," she said absently, "I was just thinking."

"Share."

"Well, it doesn't make sense, Roger. None of this makes sense!"

72

"Explain."

"Well, I've been raised to believe it's impossible for the dead to come back before the resurrection."

"So what are we dealing with here, if not ghosts?"

"I don't know, baby."

"*Some*thing moved that disk."

"I know. I know."

"Let's look at what the *Ouija* Board told us. 'See if we can make sense out of that." Roger moved over to the seat at the head of the table, closer to Rose, so they could go over her notes together. "First, that name, Molina, I've never heard of anything like that."

"Neither have I."

"Could it be a misspelling? A mistake?"

"We asked it twice."

"I know!" Roger said, snapping his fingers. "We can check the abstract of the house!"

A title abstract of the deed of a piece of property is a brief history of that property, previous owners, major improvements to the property, easements against the property, etc. If there had been a Molina Felder, perhaps her name might appear somewhere on the abstract.

"Where is it?" Roger asked.

"Upstairs in our bedroom."

They both looked at the door to the staircase, remembering the noises they'd heard up there bare minutes ago.

"I'll go," Roger said, finally. "Where in the bedroom?"

"I don't want you to go alone." Rose said, anxiously. "Not now. I'll go with you."

"We die together, eh?"

A few minutes later, after retrieving the papers without incident, they pored over the history of their house.

"It says here," Rose began to read, "the house was built by Dr. Jonathan Felder in 1848. Dr. Jonathan Edwards Felder, his son, inherited it in 1888. In 1914," here Rose's eyes widened, "*Molina* Phipps Felder inherited the house. She died in 1953 leaving the house to her nephew, Johnny Felder!"

"There she is." Roger said quietly, "She must have been the "Old Miss Felder, Tom what-his-name-"

"Hartzog." Rose offered.

"-Yes, Hartzog was talking about."

73

"What about this other stuff?"

"About the baby and all?"

"Yes."

"I think that'll wait until I pay a visit to Mr. Hartzog and see what he knows about the place. Then, I might pay a visit to the county courthouse and library and see what I can find there."

Rose felt something warm and wet on her bare leg. She jumped out of her seat with a whoop, startling Roger so that he came out of his chair. A furry ball charged out from under the table making and awful yapping noise.

"What on earth?" Roger hoarsely gasped.

"Fritz!" Rose choked out amidst spasms of relieved laughter. She looked at Roger's combat-shocked and confused face and broke out in hoots rolling on the floor, "The puppy!"

"Why, Mr. Baumer," Tom Hartzog exclaimed as Roger walked into his office, holding out his hand, "It's been awhile! I guess you're back from Korea."

"I guess I am." Roger said evenly. He wasn't being unfriendly; he just didn't have time to waste with small talk. He had a mission, and needed information this man might have.

"It doesn't seem like a year, does it?" It had seemed like forever to Roger, "Where does all the time go. Sit down, sit down," Tom sat back down behind his desk, "What can I do for you today? No problems with the house are there?"

This was more than Roger could bear. From the facial expression and tone of voice, he knew that Hartzog knew good and well there was a problem with the house, and he figured Hartzog had a good idea what that problem was.

"Mr. Hartzog, let me cut straight to the point." Roger began, leaning back comfortably in his chair, leaning his elbows on the arm rests of his chair, gazing over his hands which were brought together, touching at the fingertips, "What's wrong with my house?"

"Mr. Baumer," Hartzog began, visibly nervous. He was alone in the room with this man, whom he knew to be a combat veteran, his secretary was on her lunch break, and he didn't like the look in Roger's eyes. He'd never seen eyes so cold, "I was completely honest with you on everything wrong with the house- I pointed out everything that needed repair. You went in with-"

"You left one important detail out," Roger interrupted him. "The house is haunted."

74

"Haunted!" Hartzog let out with a laugh that was a little too loud and too forced to be genuine. Roger knew he'd hit pay dirt, "Be reasonable, Mr. Baumer, we're both sophisticated men".

"And you were scared as hell that day you showed us the house," Roger said calmly, which was more intimidating to Hartzog than if he'd been screaming. "I remember how many times you spoke of getting out of there before dark."

Hartzog had calmed, now. He believed he had an edge, "Mr. Baumer, I don't know what you want, but if you think you can come in here with some crazy allegations about your house and terrorize me with your threats-"

"What threats?" Roger asked, genuinely surprised, "Say one thing I've threatened you with?"

Hartzog was silenced for a moment, "You know... the sheriff of this county is my cousin-"

Roger looked over at Hartzog meaningfully. Hartzog was reminded of a documentary he'd watched one time about sharks. "Are *you* now trying to threaten me?" Roger's voice as he asked the question was so soft, Hartzog had to strain to make out what he was saying.

"Mr. Baumer, if you're trying to scare me-" *I'm succeeding*, Roger thought, it was hard for him to keep a straight face. *I didn't want it this way, Tom, but you called the shots...* He stood up and stretched, never taking his eyes off his prey.

Roger reached over and locked the door. He saw Hartzog wince at that, his eyes widened, darting from side to side looking for an exit. Roger was braced if Hartzog tried something. Hartzog had at least four inches and about seventy-five pounds on him. Roger wasn't the big man Hartzog was, but Roger figured he could take him if he had to. Hartzog was soft. Roger was anything but. Still, he wasn't getting too cocky. There's nothing more dangerous than a trapped coward.

"I was in a chopper crash my last tour in Nam. Shot down by AK fire. I took a pretty nasty blow on the head. They almost grounded me, but I was able to convince the doctors I was fit to fly." He looked at Hartzog for the first time since leaving his chair, "Did you know what a shortage of chopper pilots there is these days in the Army?"

Hartzog was sweating. He shook his head.

"So I fly. I've been told with this head injury and my war record I have what we call a 'license to kill.' I could kill someone; it would be blamed on my head injury. I'd spend what – six

75

months in the psych ward at a VA hospital weaving baskets? Then I'd be home on a pension." He paused meaningfully, "Isn't that something?"

His objective reached, he sat back in his chair, "So what were we talking about? I'm sorry I got so far off the subject. I'm taking up your valuable time."

"We were talking about the house." Hartzog said, breathing for the first time in what seemed an eternity to him. "Mr. Baumer, you have to understand, I'm in a difficult position."

"Yes you are."

"You don't realize how complicated things can be in a small town like Delphi."

"Clue me in," Roger said. "I'm here to learn."

"I told you I'm from Delphi?" Roger nodded. "Fred Grambling's married to my wife's sister. My grandmother was a Felder. You see, I'm caught in the middle here."

Roger nodded sympathetically. He could see Tom's plight. It made no difference to him though.

"So anything I tell you here, you didn't hear it from me, okay?" He looked down at an invisible stain on his lap, "I don't know why I should be so worried, though, geez, you could hear it from anyone..."

"Listen, if you're worried about a lawsuit or anything, don't. I'm not going to sue you for selling us a haunted house." Roger drew in a deep breath, "I have a problem, I need information so I can solve it. If you can help, I'd be grateful."

Hartzog looked up, saw the coldness gone from Roger's eyes, and relaxed a bit. Roger felt better at that; he'd hated doing "the routine" on this guy. He just didn't have time to waste playing games that eventually led to nowhere. He'd watched Hartzog's secretary leave and figured he had at least a half an hour to forty-five minutes during which Hartzog could talk freely. They'd already eaten up ten.

"It's the big family secret," Hartzog began, "though I'm sure just about everybody in Delphi has heard the story in some form or another. It started with Miss Felder, Molina Felder. She must have been about sixteen at the time. The town was having its annual fall harvest festival and homecoming. Jonathan Felder, the second Doc Felder, was Mayor at the time and he hired the best fiddler in this part of Illinois," he paused. "Let me see if I can remember his name. Leon, Leo, Fuller, Folsom, oh- I don't know!"

76

"Go on."

"Well the story goes, he had more than a way with the young ladies and Molina Felder fell head over heels in love with him." Hartzog loved to tell a story and was starting to get into this one. "It's the same old story, you know, Daddy doesn't think the boy's good enough. The daughter rebels and runs away with her lover."

Roger knew all too well.

"Here's where it gets confusing. There are differing versions of the story. One story says Molina disappeared for several weeks. Doc Felder hired detectives to find her. They caught up with her in St. Louis where she and what's-his-name had married. The detectives kidnapped Molina and brought her home. Folsum/Fuller came after her. He was seen in town, then disappeared and was never heard from again.

"The other version goes, he came to get her to elope and was met by Daddy and the town council. Either way he disappeared and no one ever heard from him. Some say he was bought off, which was what he was after in the first place. Some say they beat him up real good and scared him off. Others say they killed him and buried his body someplace on the property."

"No one ever looked?"

"It was Felder property and Felder's town. Besides, who cared anyway? And there's no evidence to suggest these are anything but rumors and tales to scare your kids to sleep at night."

"What do you think?"

"I think Miss Molina was the saddest lady I've ever met." Tom said, remembering. "She never married. She was a bit eccentric though."

"How so?"

"She always carried this baby doll in her arms when she was at the house. She had it wrapped in a blanket. You'd see her in her bedroom over the bay windows from the street, staring out the window at the old oak tree on the corner, rocking that baby doll, just like it was real."

My baby, I want my baby. Roger felt a sadness creep over him.

"Some folks said the fiddler got her pregnant and if so Doc Felder knew how to get rid of it. Others said he let her carry her to full term and sold the baby to gypsies. Still others said he killed the baby.

"After Johnny moved into the house he began talking

77

crazy things over at the tavern in New Hauptstadt. He spoke of Miss Felder like she was still alive. He'd laugh about having to get back to his 'two women.' At first everybody thought he was kidding around. Then folks began to think he was losing it.

"When Johnny lost the place to Fred, the kids began using it as the 'spook house.' You know how kids are with deserted houses. They'd tell stories about seeing Miss Felder in her window, just like when she was alive. There was talk of hearing noises come from the house like a fiddle playing or a baby crying.

"The teenagers pooled their money one time and offered a reward of a hundred dollars to anyone who would spend the night in the house."

Roger leaned forward, intensely interested now. "Were there any takers?"

"One," Hartzog said. He seemed to be actually happy now to have Roger's interest, "Marty Stacy."

"Did he win the bet?"

"No. He came out in the early morning hours. He never would say what it was he saw or what happened, and Marty's not the kind of guy you press, if you know what I mean."

Roger nodded, "You speak of him in present tense. Is he still around?"

"Sure," Tom said. He wondered if he should warn Roger about Marty's reputation for brawling. He thought better of it. It would be interesting to see this guy tangle with Stacy.

He looked across the desk at Roger. There was sadness in his eyes, "I'm sorry for selling you the house, Mr. Baumer. I did everything I reasonably could to discourage you from buying it. I showed you every flaw, but your wife was so in love with it. I still haven't figured that one out.

"You don't know the flak I was catching at home over not being able to sell the place. Mona, my wife, was accusing me of stalling to punish Fred because I'm a Felder and we want the land back in the family. I finally got my wife back when that deal closed."

There was a shaking of the front door handle. Hartzog's secretary was outside, trying to get in. Roger checked his watch, forty-five minutes to the minute. He rose, "Thank you Mr. Hartzog," he said, extending his hand. Hartzog ignored it, his face reddened, evidently remembering his humiliation a few moments before. *Give him that one, Roger; he's earned it,*

78

"You've been a great help to me and my family." Humiliating a man wasn't something he took pride in.

The secretary was knocking on the door now. Roger walked over, unlocked it and held the door for her as she entered. She shifted her stare questioningly from Roger to Hartzog. Roger smiled pleasantly as he stepped outside. He turned back to Hartzog again, "Thanks again, Mr. Hartzog."

"Any time," Hartzog said sullenly.

Roger spent a few hours over at the county library, where he found copies of the defunct Warden *County Clarion* dating back to 1878. To his delight, he discovered that Delphi'd had a weekly paper back then, *The Delphi Oracle*. The papers had been bound in large leather binders. There was one for each year. He turned the yellowed papers carefully as he read, taking notes as he found items of interest.

He was shocked to find that at one time Delphi had been the leading contender for County Seat with a population of more than five thousand and growing. He was looking for a certain item in particular, but couldn't help stopping now and then to read a particularly juicy item, such as the jailhouse explosion in 1910. It appeared two powder monkeys from the mine had objected when the town sheriff had locked them up for disorderly conduct one Saturday night and repaid him by blowing up his jail with him in it. Roger remembered seeing the ruins down the street from the house on the way to the post office. Why hadn't they ever rebuilt it? They hadn't even bothered to clear the lot. Out of curiosity, he searched the stacks for follow up but found no report of anyone ever being arrested, tried, or punished for the crime.

Then he found it, the advertising for the 1908 Annual Fall Festival and Homecoming. Leon Folsom was featured performer for the square dance. He read on a bit, searching through the issues. He found no report of Folsom's disappearance, *not surprising,* but an interesting note in the society column:

> We regret the absence of Miss Molina Felder
> at this year's cotillion due to a prolonged illness
> which has kept her in the care of relatives in St.
> Louis.
>
> Her father, Dr. Jonathan Felder informed
> our office that her health is improving and she
> may be expected to return home and in full health
> any day now.

The Homestead

A prolonged illness? Had she run off with Folsom? Perhaps she'd been sent away to have her baby. It had been so many years, how would one ever find out? *The Ouija Board?* No, he didn't like that thing; there was something about it that gave him an uneasy feeling. It wasn't just the disk flying at him either, he was sure. No, there had to be some other way of confirming what happened.

He closed the book carefully, his work done. Then, on a hunch, he pulled out the volume labeled *1914*. Again, he scanned the fragile pages, searching for -what? He'd know it when he found it. There! The front page headline of the October 21st *Oracle* proclaimed, *"Mayor Jonathan Edwards Felder Dies in Sleep.*

He found the article and scanned it, "death sudden and unexpected... no apparent illness...tragic... only daughter, Molina to inherit house...due to nature of death Sheriff Hatcher is calling for an inquest."

He read the next few weeks' issues and found nothing new. Strange. He replaced the volume on the shelf and went over to the shelf where *The Warden County Clarion* was kept. He pulled out its 1914 volume and went back to his table. As he suspected, the Glen Haven paper was willing to supply a bit more detail than the *Oracle*. What he read confirmed his suspicions. Sheriff Hatcher had evidently suspected foul play. Though the paper didn't come out and say it, Doc Felder's daughter, Molina apparently had the most to gain and, therefore, was the most suspect. The paper alluded to certain rumors, which added vengeance as a motive. But out of respect for journalistic standards of good taste common to small town papers of the time when leading citizens were concerned, the paper refrained from going into details. Sheriff Hatcher, after ordering the inquest, dropped the case without comment, citing lack of evidence. The coroner's report had been ordered sealed by the sheriff's orders. Nothing ever came of the case, no charges were dropped, the official verdict, Jonathan Edwards Felder had died in his sleep of a heart attack.

But, if what he and Rose had learned, coupled with what Tom Hartzog told him were true, the story in between the lines of these articles was a sordid one.

"So, you think, old man Felder got rid of Molina's lover and took her baby from her so she poisoned him in revenge."

80

Rose thought about it.

"Why'd the sheriff let her get away with it?" Roger sat across the table from Rose looking at her expectantly. He'd rushed home from Glen Haven to tell her what he'd learned.

"Maybe he was in on it?" she frowned. "No, If that were the case he'd never made a big deal out of the old man's death in the first place."

"I was thinking he was blackmailed into covering it up."

"Why blackmail? For what?" Rose was confused.

"Think, Baby, if Jonathan Felder had wanted to find his daughter or get rid of Folsom, who would he ask for help? Where would he find detectives to hunt her? It makes sense he'd go to his buddy, the sheriff of the town."

"Yeah," Rose said. She was clearly mulling over the possibilities here, "and if they did kill Folsom, it makes sense the sheriff was in on the cover-up."

"We don't know they killed Folsom, though. It may be likely, but we have no hard evidence."

"Where can we get it though? And what good would it do if we did? We're talking about a fifty year old murder where all the folks involved are dead."

"Maybe not. There's bound to be someone around here who was alive at the time who knows what happened. At the same time, I don't think there's any point in dredging up a scandal that old. Like you said, all the major participants are dead. What I'm after is knowledge so we can fight this-these things whatever they are and wherever they came from. This is our house! We bought and paid for it and you've gone through hell to live here. We're not giving up that easy!"

She looked at her husband with pride; the soldier in him was coming out. He wasn't about to run from a fight.

"There's something I haven't told you." Roger added.

"What?"

"After I left the library I went over to the courthouse to see if the coroner's report might be on file somewhere."

"And?"

"Well, there was a pretty little clerk over there, Sarah Jenkins," he said with a twinkle in his eye at the hint of jealousy he'd stirred. "who was very helpful. Anyway, they keep all the old stuff in a room in the basement. They've really got a nice file system down there-"

"I'll bet." Rose said dryly.

"We were able to find the sealed envelope fairly easy. I was able to convince her that a fifty year old court order didn't have to be followed-"

"I'll bet you were."

"So we opened it."

"And?"

"It was filled with blank papers."

Rose put her hand on her chin, contemplating the implications of what that meant. "Cover-up." she said finally.

"Yep! They were hiding something."

"But what?"

"They killed him," came a voice from the porch. Both Roger and Rose started and turned to see Danny standing on the back porch holding his bags, looking at them through the screen door, "They hung him from that old oak tree that used to be out front." He came inside.

Danny came over and gave his mother a hug. Rose was clearly uneasy. She didn't know how much of this Danny had heard and didn't know how much she wanted him to hear.

Danny walked over to Roger and hugged him. "Hey Trooper!" Roger said. "How long have you been out there?"

"Long enough to know what you're talking about. I'm sorry. I didn't mean to eavesdrop. The bus made it back from camp earlier than I thought and I figured I could walk home in the time it took for you to come pick me up. I came up on the porch and was going to surprise you, then I heard what you were talking about and I decided to listen. I'm sorry again."

"That's okay this time, Troop." Roger said, "What were you saying about someone being hanged?"

"They lynched him right outside." Danny said, pointing to the corner where the oak once stood.

"How do you know that?" Rose asked, skeptical, but she knew her son. Danny wasn't one to exaggerate or lie, at least, not when he was serious.

"I've seen him. At night." Danny saw the shocked expressions on his parents' face and decided he'd better explain. He began telling them about the things he had seen since moving in the house. He also began telling them other things he knew and how he'd learned them.

They heard him out. Rose was shocked that he'd said nothing during all this time. She thought of the terror he must have felt, "Danny," she said tenderly, "Why didn't you say

82

anything to me about any of this?"

"At first I didn't know if I was imagining it or what, you know?"

She nodded.

"Then, I didn't want you all thinking I was flaking out like Roggie did all the time. Then, after the second or third time I ran into someone at night I began to get the idea that they weren't gonna hurt me. I mean, if they'd meant me any harm they'd have done it already. So, I figured ignore them."

Rose looked at her little boy in amazement. At least it was all out in the open now.

"What do we do?" she asked, turning back to Roger.

"I've made an appointment for tomorrow with Father Kraus at St. Vincent's Holy Cross Church in Glen Haven," Roger said. "That's the only Catholic Church in the area."

"What on earth for?"

"I'm going to see if they'll do an exorcism."

"A what?"

"An exorcism. It's a ritual I've heard my family talk about that rids houses and people of ghosts and demons."

Rose nodded, "I remember folks casting out devils at my daddy's church when I was a kid."

"I figure it's worth a shot. My appointment's for 9 a.m.. Do you want to go in with me?"

"I think I'd better, don't you?" Rose thought a moment. "One thing…"

"What?" Roger asked.

"You said someone spent the night in the house?"

"Yes, Marty Stacy."

"Do you think we need to talk to him?"

"Maybe, we'll see. I figure I got to talk to Sarah I'd let you talk to Marty."

That earned him a playful punch in the arm.

Father Kraus was a kindly looking old man, his silvery hair going thin on top. He stood on the short side of average; Roger may have been an inch taller. There were pouches surrounding his blue eyes, which were a bit glassy to Rose. Rose almost giggled a bit, as he reminded her a bit of Brew. *Well, if I had to live celibate, I'd drink too. Watch it Rose*, she chided herself, *your old time Holiness upbringing is showing forth.* At least he'd listened to their story patiently and thoughtfully with his index finger across his mouth and had not laughed at them when Roger brought up exorcism.

He sat a moment, as if lost in thought after Roger finished. Finally, he spoke, "Mister and Mrs. Baumer, I don't know if the Church can help you."

"Why not?" Roger asked.

"Well, first off, we don't do too many exorcisms any more. Usually psychology or medical treatment can remedy most of what was once assumed to be demonic."

"Father," Roger said, a bit irked at the inference, "I can assure you my entire family has not been suffering from psychosis or even group hysteria. We have all experienced these things separate of each other and have only compared notes recently."

"That's well and good," the priest said, "I apologize, I didn't mean to suggest that you all were crazy. It's just- well-difficult. It could take months to accumulate the necessary evidence required to step ahead. Being in the military, you don't have that time. You must understand, we have to be careful for the reputation and witness of the Holy Church. Otherwise, we'd have every lunatic in the country at our doorstep."

"Do you believe in ghosts and the supernatural?"

"I have an open mind on these things. Please, don't conclude I think you're crazy because of what you've experienced in your house. There may be a natural explanation for these phenomena, but that doesn't make them any less upsetting to you."

This answer appeared to make Roger relax a bit. Rose, however, was getting the feeling they were wasting their time here. However, it was Roger's church and she decided she'd let him handle things here. She'd take care of the Protestant side of the house.

"There is a matter which causes me concern that, perhaps, we can deal with here."

"What's that?"

"Your marriage."

Rose got a sickening feeling in the pit of her stomach, *Oh no! Not again.*

"From what you've told me, you were married in a civil ceremony, without the blessings of the Church?"

"Yes." Roger said slowly, he didn't appear to be liking

84

where the conversation was going any more than Rose.

"I am concerned that your relationship, not sanctified by the Holy Sacrament of a Church wedding, could be placing you in danger and open to these attacks by the enemy."

"We tried to get a church wedding, Father." Rose spoke for the first time, "But no one would marry us because of my condition at the time."

"All the more reason for fear, particularly for the children, considering they have been conceived and born in sin-"

"That's it!" Rose said decisively, getting up, "I'm leaving." She turned to Father Kraus, "Father-" she didn't like that title, but what did you call him? Her voice was quivering with emotion, "you don't know what we suffered because of our mistake- for our sin. We have tried our best to make up for what we did wrong. We have tried to be good parents and raise our kids the best we knew how. It seems to me, if we'd had a little more love and forgiveness from the Church instead of your religion, we'd have made a better job of it!"

"My child," Father Kraus began, "we can't undo what was done, but we can change course now."

"Are you telling me, you can give us a church wedding?"

"We can receive a special dispensation-"

"Today Priest! Today!" she said, "I need to feel clean and right with God today!"

"No," he said, looking down, "I'm sorry."

"Are you telling me my kids can receive communion in your church?"

"No, not until-"

"Then goodbye, you can do nothing for me!" she turned to Roger, "I'm leaving!"

"Right!" Roger said.

They were halfway home before either spoke; Roger broke the silence, "Well, it was worth a try."

"It was a good idea," Rose agreed in a comforting tone.

"I don't know, Rosie, maybe we're beyond the pale of God's forgiveness."

"No!" Rose said with a force that surprised her, "If there's one thing I learned from all those years sitting in my daddy's church, it's that *no one* is beyond the pale of God's forgiveness as long as he or she draws a breath!"

There was silence for a while, both of them lost in their own thoughts. Finally, Roger spoke again.

"If that's true and the church teaches it, why don't they practice it?"

"I'll call Mom and Dad when we get home, they used to do something like what we need in their church."

Roger considered that for a moment. *Sure, they've been so much help in the past.* He held his peace; perhaps they'd come through - this once.

Harold answered the phone. Rose didn't know why it was her stomach always tightened when she spoke to him. It never used to be that way, when she was a little girl. Her father had always been a tower of strength and sanctuary then. It hadn't been the same since that night he found out about Roger...

"Willa Rose?" he said softly as he recognized her voice. "How're you doing, honey? We haven't seen you in awhile."

"I've been busy, Daddy, what with the kids and the house and all. Besides, you've never come up to see the house and I've been here a year."

"Well, honey, you know how we don't like to barge in unannounced..."

"Call ahead, Daddy, you know you're always welcome." *This isn't the way I wanted it; the conversation's going off-track.*

"It's tough sweetheart, what with us expanding the sanctuary and we've begun to travel a bit ministering." *Everywhere but here,* Rose thought, bitterly. She caught herself. *That's not going to accomplish anything.*

"Well, Daddy, I've called because I need a big favor."

"What is it, sweetheart?"

From off in the background she heard her mother's voice. "Who're you talking to?"

"Willa Rose," Harold said, holding his hand over the mouthpiece.

"Willa Rose?" Hopefulness in her voice. "Let me speak to her."

"In a minute, Emily, I think she has something important on her mind."

"Well, we can't give her any money, not after we helped Ida and Norville." Emily was whispering to Harold, not realizing her voice was being picked up by the telephone and transmitted over sixty miles to Rose's ear.

Rose's heart sank, "Daddy, tell Momma we don't need your money," she was fighting back anger and disappointment.

86

She hadn't even gotten around to asking and already there were excuses as to why they couldn't help her.

"Let me talk to Willa Rose a minute so I can find out what she wants, will you?" Harold was getting upset, "What do you need, honey?"

"I need you to come pray over our house."

There was a moment of silence on the line.

"Daddy?"

"Yes?"

"Did you hear me?"

"Yes- I heard you. What's going on?"

Rose proceeded to give a brief run-down of the situation. Harold listened intently, in spite of Emily's occasional "What's wrong? What's she saying?" Finally she finished. She waited for a moment while he gathered his thoughts. In her mind's eye she could see his brow furrowed, his lips moving silently as he consulted God on his next move.

"Let me see my calendar. What day is this, Wednesday? Tonight's prayer meeting. I have a meeting of the board tomorrow night; your Mama and I are going down to Kentucky this weekend, 'we've got a weekend revival at your Cousin Verne's church. That'll take us to Monday, we can't cancel that, not enough notice..."*Here we go again, busy saving the world while his children go to hell!*

"How about Tuesday evening?" he said.

"What?" she couldn't believe her ears.

"That's the earliest I can get up there. That'll give me and your Mama time to pray up."

She couldn't believe her ears. "Thank you, Daddy, oh, thank you!"

"It'll be good to see you honey."

"You too."

"Rose," he said seriously now.

"What Daddy."

"You and Roger really need to get straight with the Lord."

She stalled a moment, "I - I know Daddy," she was close to tears now.

"I was wrong about Roger in many ways, he's been a good husband and as fine a father as he can be, lost as he is, and running around the world with the Army. But you've got to get saved for your children's sake as well as your own." *I guess the sermon's the price of the help. But that's the first time he's said he might have been wrong about Roger. Hallelujah for small steps!* "That's all I'll say for now, honey. We'll talk more Tuesday." *I can hardly wait.* "Here's your Mama."

"Willa Rose?"

"Hi Momma."

"What's wrong up there, honey?"

"We're having some problems with the house; we need you and Daddy to pray for us. I guess Daddy will fill you in on the rest."

"Sugar," she said, trying to be as kind as she could, "You and Roger need to be right with the Lord so you can pray for yourself."

"I know, Momma." *Can you tell me how you can do that Momma, when you can't live your sins down? Can you tell me how to approach a Holy God when you feel so dirty?*

She was finally able to hang up the phone. She went outside to tell Roger. She found him in the front yard talking to Ed Fleischmann, the father of Rog's current girlfriend.

Before moving to Delphi, Rog had always been introverted and shy around girls. When he started "going" with Renee Grossman, Rose had been pleased. Renee seemed like a nice girl from a good family. Danny was a good friend with several of her younger brothers. It seemed a good match.

Though Roggie spoke often of marrying Renee, Rose knew they were too young to even think of getting married (even though Rog still seemed to be determined to marry every girl who went out with him more than twice), Rose hoped they could cool their heels long enough and stay together so that one day, when they were both more mature, they might marry.

Then Roggie and Renee broke up. When Rose had tried to speak with Rog about what had happened all he would say as to why he'd broken up with he was, "Her parents didn't want me seeing her any more."

Rose felt a tightening in the pit of her stomach, but shrugged it off. Perhaps it was a good thing at their age. She paused. She sounded a lot like her parents...

The breakup caused Danny some trouble, Danny got into a fistfight with one of Renee's brothers on the way home from school. When Rose pressed Danny as to the exact reason for the trouble, all Danny would say was, "Ask Roggie!" before running upstairs with tears in his eyes.

Later, at the dinner table, Danny had made a jab at his older brother. "The next girlfriend you get, Roggie, make her an only child, I'm running out of friends!"

Rog had risen up as if to hit Danny, which was forbidden. And for the first time in his life, Rose saw Danny ready to fight back against his big brother. There was an anger (dare she say hatred?) in his eyes she'd never seen before. She'd had to physically separate them.

That reminded her of how she had been concerned about the amount of physical contact she had noticed between Roggie and Renee right before the breakup. Even in the presence of the family the two could barely keep their hands off one another.

In Roger's absence she'd sat down one afternoon and had a long talk with Rog about sex and commitment and marriage, reminding him of how much easier her and Roger's life would have been had they waited.

"You mean, if you hadn't had me." Rog had said.

"No, I didn't say that!"

"Well, not exactly, but that's what it would have meant! Any baby you would have had later would not have been me!"

"You don't know that!"

"Oh Mom! Don't give me that Divine Will stuff! It's a matter of biology. It would have been a different egg and a different sperm cell and a different baby! And it wouldn't have been a bastard!"

"You" she said, feeling anger beneath her hurt, "are not a bastard!"

"Why? Because you and Dad got married a few days before I was born? Boy, Mom, you're a bigger hypocrite than Grandpa and Grandma!"

She slapped him. She hated herself as soon as she'd done it, but there was no going back. He'd run out of the house. She spent the evening beating herself over the head for being just like her father, praying to God her son wouldn't make the same mistakes she had.

Rose didn't even realize she was pregnant with Roggie until she was four months along. Her mother was the first to suspect it. Rose let herself smile ruefully at how innocent she had been. When she had started her first menstruation period, she remembered how panicked she had been. She had screamed out for her mother from the bathroom upstairs. Her mother had come

89

running to find her in a mess, sobbing uncontrollably, in terror that she was dying. Her mother had panicked too, at first. Upon realizing what was really going on, she calmed and seemed almost casual about it.

"Oh, honey." She said soothingly, "You've just started your period."

"What?" Rose had asked, perplexed, her sobs calming at her mother's attitude.

"It's part of the curse of Eve," Mama had said. Then she explained about the cycles as she helped Rose clean up and taught her how to handle it. "It's sin, Honey. You're at the age when you've started looking at boys with lust in your heart. That's what brings it on..."

Riding in the car, Rose remembered being fourteen again, thinking of every boy she had looked at in more than a casual way and asking God to forgive her of that lust.

"It's part of being a woman," her mother had told her. "You'll carry it until you start old age. Then you'll stop. You won't be able to bear children any more." Her mother paused, then added, almost as if she were thinking out loud, "Maybe that's when the lust leaves your heart..."

When Rose stopped menstruating, she was frightened at first. Then she remembered what her mother had said about the periods stopping when the lust left. She figured that now that she had Roger and he was gone, she had stopped looking at other boys. God had forgiven her for her lust and for that night.

Danny had come in from outside shortly after Roggie bolted out the door and caught Rose washing vegetables off for dinner. She was singing "Where Could I Go But to the Lord," staring outside the kitchen window at the sky as if hoping God would appear and answer her prayers. He knew from having seen this scene a thousand times before that this was the way his mother prayed. His grandmother had told him once that Rose sang in church as a young girl. He thought of how nice it would be to hear her sing in church one time. He thought of how proud he was of his grandfather, the "Pennycostal Preacher." Rose remembered Danny walking up beside her and putting his arms around her, holding her. She remembered how surprised she had been to realize how tall he was getting to be.

It wasn't long after that, Rog brought up joining the Army.

Rose had been dead set against it at first. Rog was only seventeen years old; he hadn't finished high school yet. He only had a month and a half to go. Couldn't he wait? Rog had insisted he wanted to go now! Why the hurry? Rog couldn't come up with a good reason.

They had him over a barrel, she knew, he needed at least one of their signatures to enlist. Roger was in Korea and she wasn't about to give him hers. She'd called Roger in Korea in tears.

Roger had calmed her a bit, "Honey, tell him to wait until he finishes high school. It's less than six weeks away. He can cool his heels that long."

"But Roger," she pleaded, "there's a *war* on!"

"I know," Roger said dryly. "I've read about it."

"I don't want him going off to fight some nasty little bush war and be killed before he even has a chance to live-"

"Listen," Roger said firmly. "He's my son and I love him too. I don't want to see him die any more than you. But he's no better than me or any other mother's son. If he wants to serve his country, I won't stand in his way. It's the honorable thing to do, *particularly* in wartime; I don't care how useless the war seems to the folks who aren't there!"

"But Roger-" Rose said, breaking into sobs again.

"Listen," Roger had said softly, "even if he waits until he graduates, he doesn't turn eighteen until December, that's seven months. For most MOS's (Military Occupational Specialties) he'll be done with his training before then. They can't send him to Nam until he's eighteen. Chances are they'll send him somewhere in the States or a non-combat overseas duty station. In that case his enlistment will probably expire before they can send him to Nam."

"Unless he re-enlists..."

"Well, that's his choice. There are worse ways to make a living."

"But if he gets stationed Stateside they'll be able to send him off as soon as he turns eighteen, they could put him in a replacement detachment for that long-"

"Yes, and the Viet Cong could invade tomorrow and make San Francisco a suburb of Hanoi." Roger clearly wasn't enjoying this conversation. "Listen, I used to have a couple friends up at DA (Department of the Army), they owe me big time. When Roger enlists, I'll see if they're still up there. I'll call my markers and see if we can't get him sent to Germany."

A weight lifted off Rose's shoulders. "Do you really think you could?"

"I don't like it," Roger replied. "It's not fair to all those other guys' mothers, but I'll see what I can do. That's all I can promise."

Rog graduated on a Friday. On Monday, Rose, Danny, and Brew saw him off at the Mark Building in St. Louis for Ft. Leonard Wood, Missouri. Rose had been hoping he'd get to come home for a week or two and spend time with the family while Roger was in town. Things hadn't worked out. Rog's orders called for him to ship to Ft. Sill immediately for Artillery School. His drill sergeants had let him have six hours to spend with the family after the ceremony. He shipped out to Ft. Sill early the next morning. Rose held out hope that he'd get some time off after Artillery School.

As she watched Roger speaking with Renee's father in the front yard, she had an uneasy feeling. She hadn't seen Renee since Rog shipped off.

She couldn't see Roger's face as his back was to her, but she could tell from Roger's body language that he was braced for trouble. She could see Fleischmann was angry. She could also see his heart was breaking.

She decided she needed to step outside; perhaps, she could diffuse the situation. She went into the dining room, and opened the front door, "Roger?"

"Hi honey," he said, without looking her way, "he was keeping his eyes trained on Fleischmann."

"How're you doing Mr. Fleischmann?" she said.

"Good afternoon, Mrs. Baumer," he said.

She started to ask him about Denise, but something inside stayed her.

"I don't want any trouble, Mr. Baumer," Fleischmann continued, turning back to Roger, "but if that son of yours tries to see my daughter, I'll kill him as sure as I'm standing here." He turned to Rose, "Good day, Ma'am." he said. With that he strode back to his truck and drove off, leaving Roger standing in the front yard staring at the ground.

"Honey," Rose said, coming out onto the porch, "why'd he say something like that?" *What I feared most has come upon me.* "Why'd you let him threaten Rog like that?"

"Honey," Roger said in a shaky voice, "If I were him, I'd

feel the same way."

Roger turned around and walked past her into the house. She started to ask him what the problem was. She looked into his face as he passed and she knew. She didn't know how she knew, but she knew that her worst fears were confirmed. She now knew why he had been in such a hurry to go into the Army.

I shall visit the sins of the fathers unto their children unto the fourth generation.

Chapter 6
June 1967

And when He had called His disciples together He gave them
power against unclean spirits, to cast them out, and to heal all
manner of sickness and all manner of disease.
(Matthew 10:1)

Roggie was on the roof of the house, walking along the crest. Rose, standing in the back yard, watched him anxiously as he danced along the narrow foothold. He deftly tiptoed from the north end of the house to the southern edge, "Watch this, Mom!" he shouted, twirling around and tiptoeing back. He reminded Rose of a tightrope walker, nimbly showing off for a crowd.

"Be careful, Roggie!" she shouted, "the roof's steep!"

"Don't worry, Mom, I've got this thing whipped!" He reached the northern edge of the house and twirled again. As his foot landed on the roof, a shingle broke loose. Rose watched in horror as he fought to regain his footing. It appeared for a split second that he had regained his balance, but his knees buckled from beneath him and he fell.

Rose watched in horror as he fell, "Oh my Lord, Danny," she cried, "It's all over!"

"Golf-zero-niner, this is Bravo-six-one. We've got Victor Charlie crawling all over our doorstep, what is your echo-tango-alpha? Over."

"This is Golf-zero-nine. I'm about zero-three mikes out."

"This is Bravo-six-one. We're marking our location with green smoke, over."

Roger scanned the horizon; off to his right he saw the tiny plume of green drift off in the air current.

"This is Golf-zero-niner; I've got you, hold on! Over."

Roger veered his chopper toward the smoke. Over his headset the chatter of combat intensified as the firefight heated up. Evidently, Charlie was aware of his arrival and wanted to finish off the squad of paratroopers before they could be rescued.

"This is Bravo-six-one. We've got three wounded-" "This is Bravo-zero-six, call for fire-" "Charlie-six-one, we need

94

enfilading fire-" "I say again, coordinates zero-six-niner-five-three-four-three-" "Bravo-zero-six, watch your six, we've got-" "Oh for-we've got wounded!"

Roger nosed his chopper toward the clearing ahead which would act as his LZ, he could hear the "ping!" "ping!" of bullets as they hit the skin of his Huey. Below, he could see what was left of the infantry squad, near the edge of the clearing. They were definitely heavily involved with fending off the enemy. One or two would cease firing long enough to wave, hoping to attract his attention.

He looked down into the jungle below. He could make out the form of an individual here or there moving through the bush. "Charlie," he thought.

"Goldy," he called through his intercom to his door gunner, Goldstein, "Spray that bush below us, it's crawling with Charlie."

"Roger, skipper," came the reply. What did he expect?

"Skipper we're drawing small arms fire!"

"Dust 'em!"

Roger could hear the chatter of the M-60 and feel the vibration of his ship as Goldy began pouring death into the brush below. He was over the LZ now, hovering as he lowered himself to a height where the troops could crawl aboard.

He saw it coming toward him as if in slow motion. He could see the black blur which was the projectile, followed by a thin ribbon of smoke. He even had time to identify it, "Soviet RPG-7" he thought to himself as it streaked toward him.

He swerved to avoid the missile, but felt it glance off his main rotor and explode, before he knew it, he was plummeting to the ground. He struggled with the controls, trying to recover from his fall, but it was no good, there was no response. He watched in helpless horror as the ground rushed toward him.

Roger woke with a start. He was covered in sweat.

The situation was hopeless. He had been running, it seemed, for hours and still his pursuer was behind him. He looked all around him but all he could see was deep, dense, impenetrable jungle on every side. There was no choice but to continue running.

Just ahead, he saw a pinpoint of light. "An escape!" he thought.

The Homestead

If only he could make it before his pursuer caught him. He dared a glance over his shoulder, fearful lest he slow and allow the dark foe to gain on him. He was still there, at a steady trot, pacing him as if there were no hurry.

Ahead, the light was larger now. Danny sped up a bit. He could feel his sides ache from the exertion, but he knew that if he could make it out of the darkness into the light, somehow he would be safe from whoever – whatever – was following him.

Finally he broke free into the open. The jungle was behind him and the night air seemed to be freer, cleaner. He heaved in its cool refreshing draught, almost drunk with giddiness. He had made it to safety!

Then he stopped suddenly, even more terrified than before. For not a step in front of him the ground literally disappeared, revealing a deep chasm, apparently bottomless, its darkness almost sucking him into its clutches.

It was a trap! No wonder he wasn't in a hurry to catch up.

With no choice left but to stand and fight, Danny reeled to face his pursuer, who was even now catching up. All strength left him as he recognized the face leering back at him.

"Roggie!" Danny cried, "You scared me half to death!"

Roggie said nothing. He had stopped and was advancing on Danny menacingly now. The leer on his face now appeared even more evil.

"Man." Danny said, trying to control his voice, "What's wrong with you?"

"Danny," Roggie finally said, "Why did you let me down?"

"Let you down?" Danny asked, confused, "When did I let you down?"

"Why didn't you back me up?"

"What do you mean, Roggie?" Danny asked, though inside he knew.

"Why didn't you tell Mom and Dad the house was after you, too? Why did you let them think I was crazy until it was too late?"

"Roggie I-"

"Look what you've done to me!"

Roggie was close enough now so Danny could see his face clearly in the darkness. What he saw horrified, fascinated, and disgusted him at the same time. This wasn't Roggie. At least

96

it wasn't the Roggie he knew and loved. This was something out of a horror movie, this zombie-like creature advancing toward him. So close now he could actually smell the rotted flesh.

"Roggie I-"

An invisible force yanked him out of the bed. He felt as though he were thrown over someone's shoulder; someone large, someone immensely strong, someone invisible. It carried him through the bedroom door onto the landing and began taking him down the stairs.

Danny was helpless before this force. He tried to struggle, but his strength was gone. His arms were limp with terror. He struggled to scream, but found his throat choked. He tried to swallow, but was unable. He tried to whisper, but again, his voice failed him.

In his panic, something Rose had told him reached him. "Call on Jesus. They have to obey Jesus!" she said, "Whatever you tell them to do in Jesus' Name they must do."

"Je-Je-" he tried, no sound came forth. He breathed heavily, trying to get strength.

"Je-Je-"

He was halfway down the steps, "Je-Je-sus, Je-Je-Je-sus!" he gasped.

"JESUS!"

Danny sat bolt upright in bed. His heart was beating rapidly. He looked around, panicked. There was someone in the doorway. He almost screamed. *Oh, it's Dad! Thank God.*

"Dad?"

Roger jumped at his words.

"Are you all right?"

"Yes, yes," Roger said, absently. "I've just been dreaming."

"So've I." Rose said from the bedroom behind her husband. "How 'bout you, Shug?" She was now in the door. She looked over at Danny, saw his face. "Yep, we've all got it." She looked at the clock on the stand by her bed, 2:30. "Let's all go downstairs and get some chocolate milk."

Downstairs, they sat around the kitchen table, sipping their milk. Each took turns recounting his or her dream while the others listened.

"What do you think?" Rose asked after Danny finished his story.

"I don't know," Roger began. "I've been having dreams

97

like these for years, you know..."

"Was there anything different about this dream?"

Roger thought aloud, "It was so *real*. I could actually smell the cordite from the ammo, the chopper fuel, the fear."

"I've never been so scared in my life, Mom." Danny interjected.

"I'm worried about Roggie," Rose said. "Could this place somehow have gotten to him? It's like there's some sort of curse. First Molina, now Roggie."

"Then there's us." Roger reminded Rose. She looked down at her glass.

"Maybe that's why you were drawn to this place, Mom," Danny said. He had been told about Roggie a few years before, to prevent her family from informing him as they had Roggie. "Maybe the spooks lured you here."

Rose studied Danny's face for a moment to see if he were joking. No, he was serious. *Could she have been lured here?*

"Well," Roger concluded, draining his glass. "We've got two days until your parents come up here. Maybe they can calm whatever it is down."

"What was that?" Rose was straining to hear something.

"I didn't hear any-"

"Shhh!" she motioned impatiently for silence.

Roger cocked his head to hear too. In the corner, Fritz let out with a little moan as he curled up in a protective ball. *What am I listening for? We're all too spooked; it's probably the wind.* Then he heard it, "*Oh Lord, I must be going crazy!*" But it was unmistakable; there was the sound of a baby's crying coming from upstairs in Roggie's room.

The cries became screams, as if the baby were being mishandled. They ceased suddenly, as if muffled or strangled.

"WHAT HAVE YOU DONE WITH MY BABY!" came a woman's scream through the air vent. The scream coursed through the bodies of all at the table. Wrenching sobs filtered through the air vent. Each looked at the others for confirmation of what was heard.

"That's it!" Roger said, getting up, "We're getting a motel..."

"No!" Rose said decisively, "This is our house now! I'm not letting them drive me out."

"But Baby..."

"No!"

Roger looked to Danny for moral support and found none.

"I don't think they're really trying to hurt us, Dad. Maybe they can't hurt us except to scare us into doing something stupid." Danny thought hard on it for a moment. "I don't think they can hurt us unless we let them," he concluded, almost to himself.

Roger mulled it over for a moment in his mind while he studied his son carefully. He was always amazed at how much his children grew during his absences. He realized his son had matured much beyond his thirteen years, "At least we can stay downstairs," he said finally. He began to move toward the stairs.

"Where are you going?"

"Upstairs to get some blankets and pillows."

"Don't go up there, honey..."

"Don't worry," Roger replied with a wink at Danny. " Danny's probably right. They probably can't hurt us, and I don't think they can scare me much more." He hoped he sounded more confident than he felt as he mounted the steps. There was a tangible presence as soon as he crossed the threshold from the kitchen. It grew heavier as he ascended the steps. He also noted a chill in the air as he drew closer to the landing.

It was dark on the steps. The darkness seemed to close in on him, surrounding him, choking him. He put his hand in front of his face and was surprised to be able to see it.

"Dad!"

Roger started, *Danny! I don't know how much more of this my heart will take!* He turned around angrily, about to pounce and was stopped when he saw Danny holding a flashlight out for him. He smiled and stepped down to take the light from his son. *I thought I'd gotten farther than the sixth step,* he thought.

He flipped the light on. The beam cutting through the darkness was comforting, though he still felt the chill and the closeness. When he reached the top step the cold was severe. He could see his breath in the beam of the light.

"Honey!" he shouted, receiving comfort from the sound of his voice, "Where are the extra blankets?"

"In the closet in Danny's room," Rose answered back; there was a quiver in her voice, "Are you all right?"

"It's cold up here!" he answered, "This is weird." *Weird's not the word for it. I feel as though I'm being watched.* It was true. He felt as though he weren't alone up there. He looked around him trying to catch something, anything out of the corner

99

of his eye. *It's as though the house itself were watching me.*

"Dad, do you want me to come up there?"

"No, Babe," Roger called back, "I think I've got it."

Roger turned the corner into Danny's room. It was like walking into a thick damp fog. A fog one couldn't see. Vibrations ran up and down his skin. If Roger hadn't known better he'd have sworn there were things all over him; slimy, filthy things. He shivered, as much from the thought as from the cold. *Run, Roger, run! Run before it gets you!* He was glad there was no one up there with him to see him this way. He didn't even remember being this scared in combat. In his experience in combat, he had always reacted to the situation without thinking. Fear usually set in later, after the fighting was over. He was ashamed to admit it, but all he wanted to do now was run back down to the steps to the light and safety.

The lights! Turn the lights on, dummy! He pointed his beam to the string hanging from the ceiling light. *Old house,* he thought, *as soon as I put the furnace in I'm installing wall switches!*

He pulled the string. Nothing. *Swell, I'm back to the flashlight.*

He turned to the closet. The door was half open. He shined the light inside. He could see clothes hanging. He stepped into the closet. There were the extra blankets, on the shelf to the side of the closet. He stepped half inside the door and reached for the entire stack, scooping them up in his arms. He sniffed the air inside and curled his nose at the odor inside the closed area. It was growing stronger by the second.

It was a familiar stench that permeated all his senses, so strong he could taste it. *What on earth-* he remembered. It was the smell of death. Rotted flesh. His mind flashed back to Korea. He was on Hill 501 the summer of '52. The Chinese had been hitting his company, defending the hill for three days from human wave attacks. Hundreds of dead Chinese soldiers lay strewn across the hillside. In the summer heat, the corpses had begun stinking after the first day. By day three the smell was unbearable. The GIs at the top of the hill were unable to do anything against the stench; every time they left their foxholes to move a body, they became a target for Chinese and North Korean snipers. Some of the men had lost their minds before relief came.

Roger started to back out of the closet and the stench. He had to escape. He was almost out of the closet when he stopped dead in his tracks. There was someone or something behind him; he could feel its hot, fetid breath on the back of his neck. He swung around with the flashlight, dropping the blankets on the floor, hoping to smash whatever it was. He ended up feeling foolish, standing in the middle of Danny's bedroom floor. Alone.

The stench was gone.

That's it for me! Roger gathered up his blankets and ran down the steps.

Rose had never been happier to see her parents than when they showed up at her door that Tuesday evening. It had been agreed they would spend the night. There was no telling how long this night's work might last. It would be asking too much of them to make the long drive back home. Danny had given up his bed to stay in the south bedroom, Roggie's old room, on the single bed in there. Harold and Emily had refused to take Rose and Roger's room, insisting instead on sleeping in Danny's big double bed in the west bedroom.

This had suited Danny just fine. Having heard the final plans, he had been spending days preparing for his grandparents' visit. If they had come chasing ghosts, he'd give them ghosts. His mind had briefly pondered the consequences of his actions, counted the cost, and figured the joy he would experience this evening would be well worth it.

He had visited Paul Schofeld's for the supplies, and had avoided Schofeld's usual third degree as to what he needed the parts for. Schofeld had the habit of asking a customer what the project he or she was working on and then offering advice on parts or tools, which would do the job better. This always annoyed Danny. He would often tell Danny he was asking for the wrong part and refuse to sell the part Danny asked for until he tried the proffered piece.

Danny, trained to be polite, would walk home with Schofeld's piece, and do it the way he was instructed. The fact that Schofeld was usually right without even seeing the item being repaired, somehow served to irk Danny even more, even though he appreciated Schofeld's help.

He had brought home a bag full of pulleys, catches, nuts, bolts, cable anchors, and the prize, a spool of heavy duty, high-test twine. When he finished, he had rigged the closet doors to swing open and shut as he pulled the twine. He had run other lines to the springs on the double bed so that the bed would jiggle when pulled. A string of piano wire would provide hellish noises when he ran a string powdered with rosin across it. All in all, he gleefully reflected, he had prepared a night for Grandma and Grandpa they wouldn't forget.

Harold and Emily listened as Rose and Roger told them all the things that had been occurring in the house since they moved in, occasionally, interrupting with a question. Danny would add a detail here or there. As dinner and the stories ended, they sat back in thought.

"Are they ghosts?" Danny asked.

"Not as the world thinks of ghosts." Harold answered. "The Bible plainly teaches it's impossible for the dead to come back. Jesus told the story of the rich man and Lazarus. He said there was a gulf fixed between the living and the dead..."

"Then what are they?" Rose asked, plaintively.

"I don't rightly know," Harold said softly.

"This is a lot of help," Roger snorted, earning a dirty look from Rose.

"That doesn't mean prayer won't help." Emily said, irritated at Roger's attitude.

"At least they came!" Rose reminded Roger, "That's more than your priest would do."

"Now, now," Harold sensed trouble brewing, "this will get us nowhere. It's what the devil wants-"

"Now we're dealing with the devil!" Roger was amazed, "I don't believe this!"

"Do you have a better explanation?" Harold demanded, "We've come to help."

This calmed Roger, "I'm sorry," he said, "You did come to help and I appreciate that. You've got to understand; this is all so beyond me. I mean, how do you prepare for something like this?"

"I don't think anyone is prepared for spiritual warfare, Roger, not really," Harold replied, "You just deal with it as it comes and leave the rest to Jesus."

"'Kind of like a firefight."

"Well, we don't call it warfare for nothing-" That's when it began.

Every one at the table started out of their seats as every door upstairs slammed shut, starting with the south bedroom, to Danny's bedroom door, ending with the master bedroom door at the head of the stairs. Fritz, who had been dozing at the foot of the steps, jumped up, every hair on his back standing straight, and charged, yelping in terror, out the back screen door.

The back door had barely slammed shut when a rumbling sound, as if someone were rolling a heavy barrel across the floor upstairs literally shook the house as the doors recently slammed shut were thrown open. Danny looked at the faces of the adults; he could see the fear on each of their faces. Strangely enough, he found he wasn't scared. He was disappointed; his plans for the night were ruined. *Couldn't they have been good for one night?*

There were other slamming noises coming from upstairs, not as loud as the doors.

"They're re-arranging our drawers." Danny explained.

Harold opened his Bible, "Let's begin."

Emily nodded.

"Dear Heavenly Father," Harold began, as Emily spoke in a strange, babbling language. "We come before you tonight in the Name of our Lord Jesus Christ, Who died for our sins..." Rose and Roger bowed their heads.

Those tongues give me the creeps, Roger thought as he tried to pray. He could see the curtains sway as if guided by an unknown wind. It appeared as if the prayers were getting whatever it was stirred up even more.

"...We rebuke you unclean spirits in Jesus' Name and command you to leave this house and not return!" Upstairs, something crashed to the floor.

Harold looked over at Emily. "We need to go upstairs," he said solemnly.

Emily nodded back.

"No, Mama, Papa!" Rose pleaded.

"Greater is He that is in me than he that is in the world!" Harold turned to go upstairs, praying as he went, with his wife close behind.

Rose put her arm around Roger, drawing Danny close with her free hand. "I wonder what they want?"

"GET OUT!" the voice was inhuman, cold, evil. Chills ran down Rose's spine as she heard it. She experienced a moment of abject terror she had never before known. She could hear her parents upstairs, praying louder and harder. It occurred to her that it was as if they were caught in a whirlwind. She thought about how much she had loved this house. How she had felt she had a home for the first time since she'd left her parents' home. She thought of all the work she and her family had put into the house.

Now, whatever it was that shared the house with them demanded they leave.

She felt her fear turn to rage. *How dare this-this THING demand I leave my house?*

She started toward the stairs, "Who do you think you are?" she demanded of the ceiling, "How dare you tell me to leave my house?" Upstairs, she could hear her parents praying, contending with whatever it was up there. She could sense the spiritual tumult, which was the house's response to their prayers. She planted herself at the foot of the stairs.

"Listen to me, whatever you are!" she cried shaking her fist at the darkness, "If we can't live here you're darn sure not going to stay! I'll burn this place and salt the ground it stands on, do you hear me!"

There was a loud sound like an explosion and the house grew deathly still, at peace. Rose felt something wet and cold touch her ankle. She jumped with a squeal. She looked down at her assailant and began laughing. It was Fritz, nuzzling her, his tail wagging.

She picked him up, fussing at him in a loving way, "What're you doing here? You scared me! Shame on you..."

Roger and Danny, sitting at the table, looked at one another in disbelief. "Is that it?" Roger asked.

"I don't know," Rose said, fending off attacks from the puppy's tongue. "It's awful quiet up there..." She looked upstairs into the darkness, "Mama? Papa?"

Silence.

"Are they okay?" Danny asked.

"Let me go check on them." Roger volunteered.

"'Want me to go with you?" Danny asked.

"Yeah." Roger said, "Back me up, Trooper."

The two inched their way slowly up the steps, Roger in the lead with a flashlight. The atmosphere this time was much better, cleaner. Roger topped the steps. From around the corner, in Danny's room, he heard soft mumbling noises. He peeked around the corner and saw Harold and Emily on their knees praying softly in those "tongues" of theirs.

Roger started to speak, but thought it best to leave them alone. He went downstairs.

"It's okay," he answered to Rose's anxious eyes, "they're praying."

It was another hour before they came downstairs to find

Rose and Roger sitting at the kitchen table drinking coffee. Danny was in the living room watching television.

For the next several hours they discussed what had happened that evening. In the course of the conversation, they kept trying to steer the subject back to Jesus and getting right with God as the key to spiritual victory. Roger seemed more interested than ever before about their faith, or, as he called it, their "brand of religion." His questions were pointed, valid, not the usual sarcasm to which they had grown accustomed.

They explained to him the need to not only commit his life to Jesus, but to get involved in a local church to help him grow in the Lord as the only way to keep his house clean. He appeared to see the need. Rose was excited about his newfound interest in God. Since he had become convinced his church had rejected him, Roger had shown little or no interest in organized religion.

She knew he still had a profound belief in and reverence for God and the things of God, in spite of his teasing of her and her parents for being "holy rollers," but he rejected the notion of going to a church of any kind. She had dreamed of one day attending church as a family and bringing her children up "in the nurture and admonition" of the Lord. And she did her best, sending them to church at every opportunity, though never attending herself, lest she offend Roger.

Perhaps, God had allowed the things in this house to happen to draw Roger closer to God so they could get right with him, she thought. It would be nice to be in church and feel clean.

That night they all went to bed upstairs and slept well. Whatever had been in the house appeared to be gone.

Chapter 7
August 1969

When the unclean spirit is gone out of a man, he walketh through dry places, seeking rest; and finding none, he saith, I will return unto my house from which I came out. And when he cometh, he findeth it swept and garnished. Then goeth he, and taketh to him seven other spirits more wicked than himself; and they enter in, and dwell there; and the last state of that man is worse than the first.

(Luke 11: 24- 26)

In spite of herself, Rose felt excitement as she turned the final curve on the New Hauptstadt Road. She could see the Delphi water tower now and the town beneath it.

"Well, hotshot," she said to Danny, seated next to her, "we're home."

"It's neat to have a home, Mom." Danny said, he turned to the back seat where Fritz, now full grown, sat with his muzzle out the rear window, which had been cracked open for his benefit, gazing expectantly at the passing scenery, "We're home, boy, any minute now."

Rose agreed. It was hard to believe they had been gone for almost a year and a half. Where had the time gone? In an instant she relived the previous eighteen months.

After her parents had "cleansed" the house, there had been no more "occurrences". Roger finished installing the furnace, with the help of Schoendienst's heating and cooling; laid the linoleum on the furnace room floor and converted the old furnace room into a utility room. Then he took the last week of his leave off to spend "quality" time with Rose and Danny.

They had traveled down to Ft. Sill to visit Rog, and had had it out with him over Renee. She was glad there had been a time for Roger to cool off before he confronted his son. It had been tense as it was. Roger found a nice motel in Lawton, Oklahoma, outside the post. He said he wanted to get something away from the main gate of the fort on Ft. Sill Boulevard. He said he didn't want to have to pay hourly rates.

Rose remembered seeing her son come running across

the parade area outside his barracks in uniform and feeling so proud of him. How much he had grown, matured, even since basic training. When she had visited at Ft. Leonard Wood she noted how awkward he looked in his uniform. Now he wore it naturally. Somewhere in the previous weeks he had become a real soldier. He reminded her of his father so much she was close to tears when she saw him.

Rog had hugged his mother and saluted his father (even though Roger was out of uniform). Rose had seen the twinkle in her husband's eyes as he smartly returned the salute, then hugged his boy.

"How long until you're free?" Rose asked.

"I had fireguard tomorrow night, but I got Sweeney to swap with me so I pull it Sunday night. Unless something comes up, I'm free until Sunday at 1800 hours."

"That was last formation until Monday. I can leave as soon as I change into civvies."

"We brought some of your clothes from home now that you can have them..."

Roger grinned, "I don't think they'll fit any more, Mom."

Rose looked at her boy again. He had gained about thirty pounds since enlisting. She noted they were in all the right places.

"How does the Army do it?" she shook her head, "They make fat boys thin and thin boys into hunks."

"Hey!" Rog said, feigning hurt, "I was *always* a hunk. There's just more hunk!"

"As long as *you* believe it!" Danny interjected for the first time.

"Hey, squirt," Rog said, grabbing Danny and giving him a loving bear hug, "I was wondering when you'd put your dime in."

"It's supposed to be two cents..." Danny corrected.

"No, Danny," Rog came back, "with you it's at least a dime, sometimes a quarter." Rog looked over at his parents, "Let me go change. C'mon Danny, I've got some guys I want you to meet and some things for you. Is that okay Mom? Dad?"

Sure. Roger and Rose watched their two boys walk to Rog's barracks, Rog's arm affectionately around Danny's shoulders. He seemed so assured, at peace with himself. Perhaps, the Army was going to be good for him.

They waited until later, after dinner, at the motel, to talk to Rog.

"Denise's daddy came over to talk to me a couple of weeks ago." Roger began. He was searching for the right words, "He was angry. I didn't even know who he was until he introduced himself, and even then, it took me a few minutes to remember Denise - you remember, I never got to meet her."

Rose was watching Rog's eyes. She noted the fear, which flashed for an instant when Roger had mentioned Denise's father. She saw him gulp. *He knows! Oh, Lord no, he knows!*

"Anyway, he told me you got Denise pregnant and ran off to join the Army, deserting her. He told me if you ever try to approach his daughter again he'll kill you." Roger paused a moment waiting for Rog to reply, studying his face.

Why doesn't he say something? Rose thought, *What can he say? He's guilty.*

"Well?"

"What?"

"What do you have to say about it?"

"What can I say, Dad? It's pretty much true."

Rose saw the anger flash through Roger's face and moved to get between the two of them. Out of the corner of her eye, she noticed Danny move over in reach of Rog. Then she saw Roger regain his composure.

"What do you mean, 'pretty much' true?" he choked.

"It's true; I guess I got Denise pregnant-"

"You guess?"

"Well, she's pregnant and as far as I know I'm the only one-"

"Okay, okay, go on."

"But I didn't desert her. Dad, I wouldn't do that. I went in the Army so I could take care of her and the baby. I'm not even eighteen, Dad, how was I going to get a job to support a family? The Army don't pay a whole bunch, but I figured once I got in I could come home on leave, marry her and we'd make out with separate rations, housing and the medical benefits... just like you and Mom."

Just like you and Mom. The words stung.

"Rog," Roger began, "I was already in the Army when you- er - were conceived. If I'd known I wouldn't have left your Mom the way I did..."

Rog dropped his head, his face flushed. One part of Rose wanted to reach out and hug him close the way she did when he was little, kiss him and tell him it was going to be all right. The other wanted to shake him and slap him in the face for being so stupid.

"I know, Dad," he began, "I feel so stupid now. I guess I panicked. I was only seventeen years old -I still am - I don't even know if I *can* get legally married. I figured once I got in the Army, I could figure out something. At least I could support the baby. I turn eighteen in a few months, we could get married, I'd get her out of Illinois to someplace where no one knew what had happened - like you and Mom." *Again those words. "* I tried to explain everything to Denise. She was upset and accused me of deserting her and all that. I told her as soon as I got my first duty station I'd get leave and come get her. I told her I'd write and come home every chance I got-"

"What happened?" Rose interrupted.

"Her folks found out. The last letter I got from her said her mother had suspected and started snooping around in her dresser. She found some of our letters and read them. The fat hit the fire. She told me her father almost killed her. Her mother saved her by telling him he might cause her to lose the baby. She said he said that would be a blessing." Tears welled in his eyes, "She said her dad said he was going to take care of things but she didn't know what he meant by that. She also warned me he said he was going to kill me if he saw me and warned me to stay away. She told me this was her last letter to me. She'd had to sneak that out through Melanie Wall. I wrote her a couple more times, but my letters all came back to me."

"What did her father do to her after that?"

"I don't know, Mom. I wrote a couple friends in town, they said Denise's disappeared. They don't know where. Her parents said she's gone off to Chicago to visit relatives. Some folks say she's gone to St. Louis to have the baby and adopt it out. Somebody in her family said her dad took her to St. Louis -" Rog's body began to shake as he fought back tears, "to get- to get an abortion..."

"What?" Roger asked flatly. Rose worried at that tone of voice. When Roger was truly enraged, his voice would betray no emotion whatsoever.

"I'm so sorry about this, Dad and Mom." Roger said, the tears flowing. "I wanted to do the right thing, but no one gave me a chance."

"I need to have a talk with that father..." Roger

whispered.

"Roger-"

"That's our grandbaby, too, Rose. We ought to have a say in the matter, I think. We'd raise the kid if it came to it."

"We'll never get the chance." Rose whispered, tears in her eyes.

"I don't know if they got an abortion or not." Rog said hopefully. "They might have adopted it out..."

"We can only hope and pray," Rose said. *I wish I knew for sure.*

But Rose didn't know which would be worse, living with a hope the baby was alive or, knowing.

The memory gave way to others. Rog was now in Germany. Roger had called in some heavy favors to get his orders changed from Ft. Hood, Texas, which Roger called a holding area for fresh meat for Nam. Germany was guaranteed for at least three years or the end of Rog's enlistment, whichever came first. He was safe, Roger assured her, unless he really messed up. Then they'd send him to Nam for sure.

Rog had now been in Germany over a year. He was due home on leave in two weeks. It was a pleasant surprise. He said he had a couple of surprises for the family. Rose felt uneasy about announcements like that where Rog was concerned.

Roger was due home at the end of the month. He was trying to get his orders moved up so he could get home in time to spend some time with Rog. Rose had come home ahead of him to get Danny enrolled in school when it started the next week, rather than enroll in Alabama and withdraw him when the time for the Permanent Change of Station (PCS) occurred. As usual, Roger would fly on ahead of the family and get established in Germany. They would follow around Christmas.

It was tough on Roger, she knew, having to spend so much time alone while waiting for them, but it was better for the kids. She had delayed following him to Ft. Rucker so she could finish her program at the state hospital. That had paid off in a good job at Lyster Army Hospital at Ft. Rucker. She'd already been told that chances were good she'd get a position at 95th General Hospital in Frankfurt when they got settled in.

She pulled the car into her old parking space. She looked at the house. As usual, it appeared to be looking back. It was her imagination, she knew. The house was clean. She and Danny had stayed in the house four months after the night her parents had come over with no further incident. It was merely a quirk in the architecture that made the two windows in the west bedroom look like a pair of eyes.

She wondered when Brew would show up. He knew she was due in.

He had been caretaking for them all this time. At first he had planned to stay in the west bedroom, Danny's old room. Then she received a letter from him saying he was moving a cot into the front room downstairs, something about his gout and the steps.

A few weeks later, he had written her to tell her he was going to have to get his room in Collinsville back. He couldn't make the drive into St. Louis every day. It was getting to him. She had frowned at that. Since when was any drive too long for Brew? He was a truck driver.

She remembered the time he'd come over to the house in Washington Park when Roger was doing his first tour in Nam. They'd been sitting at the table and Rose couldn't figure out what to cook for dinner.

"Why don't we go out for a hamburger?" Brew had asked, "I know a place that serves the best hamburger you ever put in your mouth,'you interested?"

"Sure. Anytime I don't have to cook."

So they loaded the kids into the backseat of Brew's car, he always drove brand new Dodges, and took off down old Highway 3. After they'd been on the two lane road a few hours and had passed numerous towns, Rose began getting concerned, "Where's this place at, Brew?"

"Oh, just ahead, down the road," he said absently. "Believe me, Rose, it's worth the wait."

"This must be some burger."

"It is. It is."

When they drove through Cairo, only stopping so the boys – Rog was about ten at the time, which meant Danny had to be six – could go to the bathroom. Rose asked again, "How far is it, Brew?"

"Just down the road."

"Mom, I'm hungry," came the whines from the back seat.

"Just ahead kids." Brew assured.

They had ended up in Evansville, Indiana. There was a drive-in restaurant on the main drag. Brew proudly ordered up their special, something called the "Monster Deluxe Burger" for everyone. He'd been right; it was the best burger she'd ever tasted. They ate, leaving some of the burger and most of the fries behind.

Then Brew drove the trip back. They arrived home in the wee hours of the morning. Rose was glad it had been Friday and the kids didn't have school. Even though they had slept most of the trip back, they were still worn out. She knew she was. Brew had gone on to work as though nothing had happened.

She smiled at the memory. Roger had written back from Nam he was sorry he'd missed it. He said *he* definitely wouldn't have minded driving to Evansville for a burger.

They still teased Brew about it whenever he mentioned a good place to eat. How far? Can we make it in a day?

Perhaps Brew was getting old. All the drinking was surely taking its toll. Though the last time she'd seen him, he'd come down to Alabama for a visit during his vacation last summer, she had marveled at how little different he looked from that first evening when he appeared at the door of her apartment in St. Louis. She teased him about pickling himself in all the beer he drank. Maybe he'd just gotten lonely for his tavern friends down in Collinsville.

At least the house looked as though it hadn't suffered any in their absence. The lawn was freshly mowed. Brew had hired the Haupt boys to mow it. They were the only ones other than the Grossman boys who did that sort of thing. She saddened at the thought. The Grossman boys were good kids.

She shook the thought off. She cut off the ignition, "We're home, boys."

Danny was out of the car in a shot. He held the seat and he and Fritz bounded around the corner to the back door. They were waiting for her when she finally made it to the back porch.

She fumbled with her keys, finding the key to the back door. She couldn't believe how nervous she was as she tried to fit the key into the lock. What was wrong with her?

Finally the tumblers turned and the door opened. She stepped inside and felt goose bumps run up and down her spine. *Whoa, Rose,* she thought. *Don't get so emotional- But I'm home, home! Not any old Army quarters or house trailer, no apartment – home. Our home, MY home.*

"C'mon Fritz," Danny urged, "Let's check out the bedroom!" He darted upstairs.

Rose walked slowly through the kitchen, taking

everything in, letting her gaze linger on its familiar objects. They had left many things here, at the Homestead, partially for insurance purposes (their policy wouldn't cover a vacant house), partially to protect precious articles. Rose was tired of seeing her articles smashed by careless movers or, worst, stolen by handlers who didn't think there was anything wrong with taking what they wanted because the government would "re-imburse" the owners for anything lost or stolen.

They didn't realize you can't be reimbursed for the memories stored in an otherwise worthless knick-knack, or the chair you rocked your children to sleep in. And the government was great about "depreciation." She remembered an eighty-year-old end table that had gotten broken during their move to Kansas. She'd gotten it from her Aunt Sophie in Kentucky. Sophie had no living children of her own and took to Rose. It had gotten smashed somehow in the move.

When Rose filled out the form to be reimbursed, in the description of the item, she had to list the age of the item broken. The assessor had tried to pay five dollars for the table. After all, the table was old and used. Roger had hit the ceiling over that one, taking it all the way up the chain of command and was on the verge of writing his Congressman before someone got some sense. It was an empty victory. No, three hundred dollars doesn't replace the memories.

Brew had put a card table and chairs in the middle of the kitchen. *I guess we can use them until our things arrive.* Her stove and refrigerator stood in their corners. They weren't needed at Ft. Rucker, each quarters had their own.

She heard a small whimper and felt Fritz's cold nose against her hand. She looked down, "What are you doing here, boy? I thought you'd be upstairs with Danny."

The dog made a partial whining, partial growling sound. *He's trying to talk. Sometimes, it's weird; you can almost make out what he's trying to say.*

"That's okay, Fritz, the place grows on you."

She walked through the downstairs of the house. It appeared so empty, with only an occasional chair here and there; except for her prized antique dining room set in the front room she had left to save from another move. She realized if they had taken all the furniture with them to Alabama, they'd have been cramped in their quarters on post. She smiled at Brew's cot in a corner of the front room. There was a pile of weekend

113

newspapers on the floor beside the cot. It appeared as if he did at least "camp out" at the Homestead on the weekends.

There was much cleaning and dusting to do before the furniture arrived in a few days. She could hear Danny upstairs, digging around in the closet. They'd left many of his things in the house. The Army only allowed them to take so much on a move. Again, she was thankful for the house. Before, Danny would have had to have thrown or given away many of his things.

She remembered particularly one Christmas; they'd already bought everything when Roger came down on orders for Germany. The move was for January. They'd gone ahead and celebrated Christmas, then the boys were forced to decide what they wanted and what they had to give away of their new things. There wasn't enough room to take it all. Now they had a place they could keep everything.

She walked back through the house and started upstairs. She was halfway up before she noticed Fritz had stopped following her. She looked down at him, standing mournfully in the doorway at the foot of the steps.

"C'mon boy, what's the matter with you? 'Too lazy to climb the steps?"

Fritz wagged his tail sadly and whined, as if he were trying to tell her something again.

"Silly boy," she scolded, "come on."

The dog barked anxiously, then a low growling came from his throat. The kind he reserved for prowlers or unwelcome guests. She frowned at this and shook her head. She hadn't seen him behave like this since they'd had the Peeping Tom skulking around Ft. Rucker.

"Well, I'm not going to wait all day for you. Stay there." She turned and moved back up the steps. She could hear Danny in the closet scuffling around inside. She smiled as a mischievous thought crossed her mind. She began to move quietly, tiptoeing around the corner, sneaking up on her son.

The doors to the closets were both opened, she could faintly see from her vantage point slight movement in the darkness inside. She crept slowly toward the door, frightened of making the least noise, lest she alert him to her presence and spoil the fun.

She could see the door now, see inside the closet, but saw no sign of Danny; *He must be deep inside there. I wonder if he's waiting on me?*

Nevertheless, as she moved closer, she thought she could make out his form in the darkness, hunched over as if digging for something on his hands and knees. *One more step and I'll-*

"Mom?" The sound of the voice from behind her almost startled her out of her skin. She wheeled around crazily toward the source.

"*Danny!*" she cried, "*What are you doing over there!*"

Danny looked at her with those big puppy dog eyes, shocked and confused, "I was in Rog's room, digging through some of the boxes when I thought I heard something. I'm sorry Mom, I didn't mean to scare you."

Rose calmed herself down, struggled to get her heartbeat back to normal. *Well, Rosie, the joke's on you. I could swear I saw Danny in that closet. I saw **something** in that closet.* She turned and looked again, she saw a vague out line of a pile of clothes scattered on the floor. Could that have been what she saw? *Probably.*

She could feel Danny's eyes studying her. Why was it she often got the feeling that Danny knew things, was privy to a special knowledge that he kept to himself? It was as if he somehow *knew* or suspected why she'd been so startled by his voice.

They heard the back door open downstairs.

"Rosie?"

It was Brew. She smiled. *Good old Brew.*

"Up here!" she called. She turned to Danny, "Let's go see Uncle Brew."

She exited the bedroom out onto the landing. She saw Brew standing at the foot of the steps waiting, as though hesitant to ascend them. *I suppose his gout must be bothering him.*

"I was over at Kopf's in New Hauptstadt," Brew said as she descended to meet him. "Bill Kroger came in and told me he'd seen your car at the house. I figured I'd better get over here."

Rose hit the foot of the stairs and put her arms around Brew, giving him a big father/daughter hug and a kiss on the cheek.

"How're you doing, old man!"

Brew grinned sheepishly; he always blushed when she showed him affection. "I'm doing. It's better than gettin' done. Heh, heh." He looked around, "I brought these in here to help you get by until your stuff comes."

"Thanks."

115

"How long're youse staying this time?"

"Probably until Christmas. Roger doesn't have to report until the end of September. There's a two to three month wait for housing where we're going. We can move then."

"You're going to leave your furniture here?"

"Yeah," Rose answered with a sigh. "I'm tired of dragging it around getting it torn up for no reason. I figure it'll be safe here."

"Probably," Brew agreed, "ain't nobody in this town going to try and break in this place after dark."

Rose caught something in his voice but let it go. It'd wait. He seemed uneasy. "We'll use government furniture over there; maybe buy some things this tour. I've always wanted one of those big German cabinets- a *schrank*. It'd look nice in this house."

"Sure."

"Rose," Brew said seriously, "are you sure you want to stay in this house?"

"Why not?"

"Well, you know-" he hesitated, "all the stuff-"

"Brew," Rose said, surprised at him. He'd never been superstitious before. "You know Mom and Dad took care of that."

"Yeah," he didn't sound convinced.

"What's eating at you?"

"Nothin'." he brightened and almost ran over to the refrigerator, "Look, I bought youse some groceries." He flung the door open to reveal a well-stocked larder. "There's canned goods in the pantry."

"Brew," Rose put her hands on her hips in mock anger, "you shouldn't have done all this. We've got money."

"I know, Rosie, but it's been a long time since I've had a good home cooked meal-"

"Yeah, I know, and you don't know what I feel like fixing."

"Yeah," he smiled, "You're finally learning."

"Tonight I don't feel like fixing a thing."

"Yeah, you're probably wiped out from the trip. That's okay; we'll scuttle over to Vandalia. They've got a nice restaurant just opened up over there. You can cook some other day."

"Say no more, Brew. You've got me sold. It's better than a trip to Evansville."

116

Two weeks later, Rose, Danny, and Brew stood at Gate A-1 at Lambert Airfield in St. Louis as Rog's plane taxied to the gate. Rose had spent those weeks getting the house in order, papering, painting, cleaning, and finally setting up the furniture and other belongings where she wanted them when they finally come in. The house was better than ever now. It was a place to be proud of.

They'd had heavy rains the previous week and the space beneath the new floor had flooded. Rose and Danny had giggled at the gurgling sound coming from the new heating ducts when the furnace kicked on. Danny plugged in the sump pump and soon the smooth sound of warm air being pumped into the house was heard. She was hoping Roger would have some ideas about keeping water from draining into the house.

The plane stopped. Soon passengers began appearing at the door. Rose craned her neck expectantly, hoping to get a glimpse of Rog. Danny saw him first.

"There he is!"

"Who's that with him?" He was holding the hand of a tiny, blonde haired girl who was gazing warily at her surroundings.

"I don't know."

Rose felt a sick feeling in the pit of her stomach. *One of Rog's surprises.*

Rog saw them, his face brightened and he rushed over, leaving his companion. He hugged Rose first, "Hi Mom! How's it going?"

He turned to Danny, "Hey squirt!" He looked at Danny again, realized Danny was almost his height, "Well, maybe not so much of a squirt anymore." The brothers hugged. Rog turned to Brew, "Hey Brew!" he said, holding his hand out for a shake.

"What's this?" Brew said, "I diapered your butt, kid, gimme a hug!" Brew pulled Rog close to him and gave him a bear hug, "You never get too old to give your parents or me a hug!"

"Okay, okay!" Rog conceded, laughing.

"I suppose this is one of your surprises," Rose said, gesturing to the girl who was shyly approaching from behind Rog.

"Oh yes!" Rog said, reaching back to put his arm around the girl and bringing her up, "This is Uta. We're going to be married."

117

Rose studied the girl a moment as only a boy's mother can do. She had long blonde hair, braided and brought up behind her head in a bun for convenience. She was petite, Rose noticed, but not skinny, well proportioned. *Well,* she thought wryly, *Rog always had a good eye for women.* He looked into her big umber eyes; saw the mixture of hope, intimidation, and innocence and her heart melted.

"Come here, baby." She reached out and folded her into her arms. She felt small spasms through the girl's body as she held her. *My Lord, she's crying.*

"*Entshul-* I'm" the girl struggled to think of the right word, "-sorry."

"Why?" Rose asked, confused, "I get all misty myself sometimes."

Rose noticed Uta's face, saw her strain to catch every phrase, and realized she didn't understand what she was saying, "*Sprechen sie Englische?*" She asked.

"Sure," Uta answered, with a slight smile, "hot dog, hamburger, Coca-Cola."

At this she and Rog both laughed.

"I'm sorry, Mom," Rog explained. "It's a joke between Uta and me. She doesn't speak much English, but she's learning fast."

"But I thought all German kids-"

"They have to take a second language in high school, Mom." Rog interrupted, "Uta's Daddy made her take Spanish because he hates Americans."

Rose took a deep breath. *Here we go again, why can't he ever do things the easy way?*

"Rog, we need to talk-"

At that moment, Brew intervened, much to Rog's relief. "Rose, let's get out of here, this ain't the time or place, okay?"

"You're right."

It was a long ride home. Everyone made small talk, avoiding what was on everyone's mind. *It's normal to bring a girlfriend home to meet the family,* Rose reasoned. *That's no problem. It's normal for her to be nervous; she's in a strange land around a bunch of strangers. But she's scared, terrified. Why?* Rose mulled it over. Was she reading too much into everything? Was she being unfair? She looked at the face in Brew's rearview, *How old can she be? She doesn't look like she's much past fifteen or sixteen.* She could see her son, with his arm draped protectively around her, there was something going on here. She added it all up and didn't like the sum. Not one bit.

They finally pulled in at the house and Rog took Uta up to show her where she'd be sleeping. She'd get the south bedroom, as it had more privacy, until other arrangements could be made. Rog and Danny would share the middle bedroom. Care would have to be taken for Uta to come in and out of the room. But it would work. It was only for three weeks while Rog was home on leave.

Finally, Rog was seated with Rose, Uta, and Brew at the dining room table. Danny was sent upstairs. This was to be an adult conversation, but he knew he could hear everything through the heat vent in the south bedroom.

"Rog," Rose began, "What's going on?"

"Nothing, Mom. Uta and I just want to get married while I'm home on leave."

Everything's wrong, Rose thought.

Brew sat back, chewing on the nub of a cigar, deep in thought.

"Why don't you get married in Germany?" Rose asked, "I mean, I want to be at your marriage and all, but it would seem to me, Uta's parents would want to be there too. It's not like we're not on our way over there ourselves. What's the rush?" Rose feared the answer to the question.

"No," Rog said sadly, fighting back tears. Rose studied her son sadly. He looked like a man, sounded like a man, but was still a little boy inside. With a little boy's tender heart. "They told her if she married me they never wanted to see her again."

Brew finally leaned forward, folded both his hands in front of him on the table, "Rose, if you don't mind my interfering?"

"Brew, how can you interfere? You're family!"

Brew smiled at that. He knew it, but it was nice to hear it said occasionally. "Well then," he began. "Rog, it's pretty plain you're home because you need help. So why don't you cut the crap and tell us what's going on - from the beginning."

"Okay," Rog said, relieved. "I don't want to sound like I'm trying to hide anything. I just didn't know how to break the news to you. I didn't know where to begin." He looked down at Uta, who'd been tensely trying to follow everything. He smiled down at her. Rose fought back tears again. That look. This was the real thing. *"Alles gut, Schatzi."* He said, smiling down at her. She smiled back up at him and then at Rose and Brew.

Rose was usually guarded with her emotions, but she couldn't help it. She was falling in love with this little girl, too. "Go on, honey." she prompted.

"Well, it was before last Christmas," Rog began, "actually in the fall. I was out looking for gifts in town. I was on a back street just off the main square in Hanau when I passed this little hobby shop. I knew there was nothing I could get Danny that he'd love better than some toy soldiers." Now the monthly packages of soldiers made sense to Rose. "And this place had one of the best selections I'd ever seen. So I went in. I saw Uta.

"That's where I bought Danny that big World War II set I got him. I kept going back to see Uta. The next thing you know we're talking-well- as much as we could. She didn't speak any English and my German, well you know how that is- was. But I started studying. It was a couple of months before I got courage to ask her out on a date. Then I had to figure out how to ask.

"But we got it done. The next thing you know, we were seeing each other all the time. She lived in a small town outside of Hanau. When we had a date, she'd spend the night with her girlfriend, whom she worked with in town. I'd pick her up at work and leave her at Frieda's. I knew something was wrong because she never invited me to meet her parents.

"Finally, we'd been dating about six months when she asked me to meet the family. That was when she told me why she hadn't had me over. Her daddy had been in the war, had fought on the western front, against Americans. His entire family had been wiped out in the bombing of Hanau by American bombers and he never forgave us. He wouldn't let her take English in high school. She took Spanish. When she told him she was dating an American GI he hit the ceiling.

"I didn't see her for two weeks, except at work. Even then I had to be careful, because he was picking her up and dropping her off to keep her from me. She went on a hunger strike, " Rog looked down pulled her closer to him, squeezing her shoulder. She looked up at him lovingly. "So I got the invitation. He figured he might as well meet the *schwein* who had so captivated his daughter.

"I showed up at the house. Uta answered the door. She brought me into the den where Mama and Papa were waiting. I reached out to shake his hand and he ignored it! I mean, I'm sitting there with my hand stuck out feeling stupid and he says to Uta, 'I'd rather you brought home a Turk than an American!' Brew, in Germany, that's an insult. For some reason, he hasn't figured out I can understand German pretty good. I mean, he should have known we must have been communicating somehow. And me with a last name like Baumer.

"Uta looks over at me and rolls her eyes. She's expecting a scene. I was playing it cool, pretending not to understand him. All through the evening he's making little digs. Even Uta's mom got mad at him. Finally, after dinner, Uta and I are about to leave. I say goodbye in perfect German, telling him I was sorry he didn't like me, but if he gave me half a chance his opinion might change.

"Mom, he was floored, it was funny, Uta giggled, even Frau Muller, Uta's mother, was smiling. He just stood there with this stunned look on his face, turning beet red." At this point Uta whispered a question in Rog's ear. Rog answered, Uta giggled. "I just told her where I was in the story, sorry.

"Where was I? Oh yes, well, I'd hoped to earn their respect or something. I didn't. Things got worse. Every time we turned around they were doing something to keep Uta from seeing me. There were always lame excuses why she couldn't stay in town. She'd get phone calls telling her there was an emergency or something, just to get home and find out it was all bogus. But German kids are obedient to their parents and she was trying to be a good daughter to them and love me.

"A few months ago they gave her a choice drop me or move out of the house. She moved in with Frieda, but Frieda had a boyfriend living with her already and it wasn't working out, so we got a place..."

Shacking up? Oh, Lord no...

Rog caught the look on her face, "We didn't want to Mom, but it takes so long to marry a German national, all the red tape. Uta couldn't afford an apartment on her own, but with our combined salaries, we did all right, at first. Then Herr Muller found out what was going on and began to stir up trouble for us. First in the village we were living in, then he tried to cause me trouble on base by accusing me of corrupting the morals of a minor-"

"Hold it!" Brew spoke up, "Just how old is Uta."

"She'll be eighteen next month."

"Seven-" Rose gasped.

121

Brew muttered something unintelligible and unrepeatable and had to apologize to Rose.

Rog gulped, "You don't understand, in Germany she's above the age of consent. But her dad figured he could cause me trouble with my chain of command. If she'd been an American girl, maybe. But as long as she was a German citizen and we weren't breaking German laws we were okay. My CO did tell me what I was doing wasn't helping German/American relations. When I told him Herr Muller was just an unreformed Nazi who hated all Americans he lightened up, but told me he couldn't do much to protect me if Herr Muller went higher up. It turned out Uta's daddy was Burgermeister, mayor of his village, and had some clout politically in the area."

Leave it to my son to fall in love with Hitler's daughter, Rose reflected bitterly.

"I figured the only thing to do was to get out of Germany, but I had almost two years left on my tour. There's no way I'd get a transfer unless" he paused and Rose felt that same sickening feeling in the pit of her stomach again, "I volunteered for Nam." *Oh, my dear God, no!* "So I put in my 1049 form requesting a transfer. It didn't take long, of course, to get it approved. It would have taken too long to get our marriage approved in Germany, so we scraped our money together, and bought her a ticket home. She had to fly civilian, of course. We arranged it so I could pick her up in New York after landing in Maguire. And here we are. I need to marry her before I go to Nam."

Rose studied her son sadly. After everything Roger had gone through to ensure his safety, he'd gone off and done something stupid like this. She looked over at the little girl next to her son and wanted to hate her. But she couldn't. It wasn't her fault, really. Rose wanted to cry, but couldn't find tears. She was numb, completely drained of emotion.

"If you're so hot to get married," she finally said dully, "why didn't you just hop a train to Denmark?"

Rog looked at her dumbly, stunned, "What do you mean?"

"Denmark is the Las Vegas of Europe, Son." Rose stated flatly, "You managed to get her a visitor's visa to come to America. Why didn't you check around?"

"I didn't think, Mom."

"That's the smartest thing you've said all night, kid," Brew remarked, getting up to toss his cigar stub in the trash.

The words stung Rog. *Good!* Rose thought angrily. *He needs something to wake him up.*

"I figured all I needed was to get home. Between you, Dad and Brew, you'd help me find a way to clean this mess up. Help me figure out a way to marry Uta before I have to go."

"Swell." Brew sat back down. "What's the hurry to get married?"

"Well," Rog said, "she needs a place to stay. Her parents have completely disowned her. She's got no one in Germany. I figured you'd put her up but she can't stay in America long unless she's married to me."

"Well," Rose said, trying to get hold of her thoughts, her emotions. She felt so dead. "With you out of the picture, at least temporarily, her parents would probably let her come home. You could always bring her here after you got back from Nam."

Rose struggled with the next thought, the one that was pressing in from the back of her mind. "Son," she said, her voice cracking, of all the times for her feelings to come back, "if something should happen to you over there, she's awfully young to be a widow." The tears began to flow now.

"Mom," Rog said, his voice cracking with emotion, "you don't understand. I've got to marry Uta before I go-" he hesitated a second, "she's pregnant."

Chapter 8
August 1970

As a dog returneth to his own vomit, so a fool returneth to his folly.

(Proverbs 26:11)

There was a moment of silence around the table as the weight of Rog's words sank in. Uta had grasped enough of the conversation to know what had been said. Their faces betrayed their reactions. She sat in humiliation, wanting to run but having no place to go.

Rose looked at her son, sitting in his chair like a small child sent to the principal's office in school. *How could I have failed so miserably?* She screamed inside. *This is a **man**? Was this the "father" of at least two children?* Two that she knew of. How many more did he have she didn't know of?

Danny's words, spoken in this room years before, returned to haunt her. *"You're the lover of the family, not the fighter!"* She wanted to scream; she wanted to cry; she wanted to take her son outside and beat him until her strength failed. Then she looked at Uta, sitting alone across the table. Roger having taken his arm from around her and folded his arms across his chest, retreating inside himself. She felt more anger rise in her. *Of all the people who should know better than bring a child into the world this way... You're the one who's always screaming "bastard!" Didn't Denise teach you anything?* She started to speak and caught herself. *This is going to accomplish nothing.*

She saw tears in Uta's eyes. *How humiliated she must be, without family, among strangers in a foreign land.* Rose got up from her seat and walked around to Uta.

Uta looked up at her with eyes that pleaded, *"Es tut mir leid..."*

Rose searched her mind to remember her little bit of German, understood she was saying she was sorry. *Sorry? For what? For being young and in love? For sinning?* How could Rose throw stones? *Let him among you who is without sin cast the first stone. All have sinned and fallen short of the glory of the Lord,* she remembered from somewhere in her childhood.

124

She put her arms out, "*Kommen sie hier...*"she thought, "*Liebchen.*"

Uta rose from her seat and folded in Rose's arms. Rose held her close and stroked her hair, whispering motherly words of comfort – words which would be understood in any language.

Brew had been sitting staring blankly into space, his eyes came back into focus on Rog "Roggie," for once Rog didn't object to his childhood name, "I love you like my own son, but if you don't learn to keep your pants up, I'll neuter you." He looked over at Rose, who was still cradling Uta, "Rosie, you'd better call Roger, see if he can come home early."

Rose went to the phone, still holding Uta, and began dialing.

"Let me see here," Brew began, almost speaking to himself, thinking out loud, "by bringing her home, you may have opened up an even bigger can of worms. She may be legal in Germany, but here she's still a minor." He looked up at Rog, "You could get in trouble messing with her. I don't care how pregnant she is. So whatever you're doing, stop. You'd better hope Mama and Papa in Germany don't find you. They tried to cause you trouble in Germany. They *will* cause you trouble here.

"Then there's the problem of getting you married. I don't know of any State in the Union that'll normally allow a sixteen-year-old girl to get married. Some States will allow a girl who's pregnant to get married, even then they require a parent's signature..." he looked at Rose who was listening on the phone.

"They're paging him." Rose said, "It'll take a few minutes."

"I need to make a few phone calls myself. I've got some friends in the legal profession who can help." He thought it over a minute. "We'll take care of it! If not in Illinois, Missouri." He mulled it over again, "Or wherever we have to go."

"Thanks, Uncle Brew," Rog said, looking up for the first time. "I knew I could depend on you all."

"I'm not doing it for you, kid," Brew said. "I'm doing it for your Mom and Dad, and that little girl there."

"Hello?" Rose's voice boomed across the room. "Hello, Roger? This is Rose... Yes, I guess you can say I am upset... No, I'm all right... Danny's all right... Rog is here...We're all healthy...Listen Roger, we need you home... Yes, there's an emergency... Listen, Roger, please, let me tell you... You keep asking questions... Give me a chance...I'm trying to tell you... I know I sound upset. Let me tell you why... Thanks... Listen, it's Rog...He's here at home... he's got his girlfriend with him...she's pregnant..."

She pulled her ear from the phone as a stream came out of the earpiece. Everyone in the room could hear Roger's voice. Rose allowed him to wind down before she brought the phone back to her ear. "Of course they need to get married. The problem is she's only sixteen-"

Four days later the entire family stood in the office of the Hon. Jefferson C. Hogan, probate judge of St. Jacobs County, Illinois. Brew had told Roger and Rose that he and Hogan went back to the Depression. The judge had figured out a way the two could get married.

"How?" Rose asked as they sat outside the judge's office.

"What does it matter?" Brew asked. "It's a bunch of legal mumbo-jumbo."

"Is it legal?" she asked.

"Do you think a judge would risk his entire career by doing an illegal marriage?" Brew asked. He obviously didn't want to answer too many questions about the proceedings.

"Honey," Roger said putting his arm around her. "Don't look a gift horse in the mouth..."

The judge's secretary, a lady who appeared to be a young fifty, peeked out the door to the judge's office. "Brew? The judge'll see you all now."

"How're you doin' Sue?"

"Okay, how about yourself."

"If it got any better I couldn't stand it."

"Do you have the blood test paperwork?"

Brew looked over at Rog, in his dress uniform, "You got it, sport?"

Rog reached inside his jacket, pulled forth two thin sheets of paper, "Here," he said, giving it to Sue.

"Birth certificates?" she asked.

Rog produced his, but seemed a bit confused, "We don't have Uta's..."

"That's all right," Brew said, "the judge said her passport would serve in this case. She's got it on her, doesn't she?"

Rog whispered something in Uta's ear.

"*Oh, jah!*" Uta said, she dug in her purse and produced the document.

126

"Good. Follow me."

The family followed her through the outer office into the judge's chambers. The judge, a medium built man with thinning gray hair was behind his desk. His solemn face split into a grin as he saw Brew enter the room. He smiled politely as Brew made the introductions, complimenting the women with a polished charm, shaking the hands of the men, complimenting the men in uniform. *A real politician,* Roger thought wryly.

Hogan asked Danny if he too was going to be a soldier.

"Twenty years, thirty if I like it," was the reply.

"Brewski!" he said when the pleasantries were done with. *Brewski?* Rose wondered. *That's a new one on me.* "Why is it the only time we get together is when we need a favor? Marge asks about you all the time!"

Rose was wondering what kind of favors a beer truck driver could do for a judge.

"How's she doing?" Brew asked.

"Fine, fine."

"The kids?"

"They're not kids any more. Joseph's a lawyer now. His oldest, Joe Jr. is in law school. We're getting old, Brew."

"It's all a matter of attitude, Jeff."

There was a knock on the door. Sue entered. "Here's the paperwork, Your Honor."

The kind of favors that would get a judge to "bend the rules to do this marriage... It was obvious the judge was really fond of Brew. She understood that. *But friendship only goes so far...*

"Thanks, Sue." The judge looked over the paperwork, ensuring everything was in order. "Well, everything appears to be in order, all the 'T's crossed and the 'T's dotted... We've got to sign some paperwork. It really doesn't matter, but let's keep everything in order... Brew, you need to sign this one here. It's a court order appointing you legal guardian over Uta..."

Once the paperwork was signed the ceremony took only a few minutes. Roger couldn't help but think his first enlistment in the Army had been more romantic. Still, it was better than his and Rose's wedding. *History repeats itself,* he thought bitterly.

He was now seated in the front seat of Brew's car. Brew was driving. Rose was in the middle of the two men. Rog was sitting behind Brew, with Uta between Danny and him. He looked back at his son. Strangely enough, the uniform now made

127

him look younger and more vulnerable. *History repeats itself,* he thought again. What now? Would the baby inside this girl grow up to make the same mistakes his father had made, the same mistakes his grandfather had made? *How do you break a cycle like this?*

Similar thoughts ran through Rose's mind. They were both so young. How would they make it? She tried to ignore the next thought in her mind. *What if Rog doesn't come back from Nam?* She pushed it aside. *Roger survived Korea and two tours in Nam, my brother Paul survived World War II. Rog'll be okay. I need to get Mama and Papa to pray for him.* What about Mama and Papa? What'll they say when they find out what's happened? *They don't have to know. It's none of their business anyway; they don't have to know when Rog and Uta were married. I just need to tell Rog to keep his mouth shut...*

They said goodbye to their men on a drizzly September morning three weeks later. The two flights were minutes apart, on gates next door to each other. Roger was flying east to JFK; Rog was heading west to San Francisco, from there to Seattle, where he would report to Ft. Lewis, Washington, gateway to the Far East and Vietnam.

The evening before he left, he had sat down and spoken with his parents. He apologized for all the trouble he'd ever caused them. He apologized for ruining their lives.

"How did you ever ruin our lives?" Roger asked.

"If I hadn't been born..."

"What?" Roger interrupted, "Do you think our lives would have been any better if you hadn't been born?"

"Rog," Rose began. "We love you. We have always loved you. Sure, I wish things would have been different in how everything happened, how we were married. But I made a decision all those years ago to have you and to keep you and I have never regretted my decision." Tears welled up in her eyes, "Your father and I made a mistake, but you are not - have never been- a mistake. You are my gift from God. During all those times when your daddy was off in some God forsaken place and I never knew whether or not I was ever going to see him again, the only thing that kept me going was you, and later on Danny."

"Mom-"

"No, Roger Stephen Baumer, you listen to me! Ever since your Grandma filled your head with that crap about how you were born you've been running around on this trip of yours or whatever you want to call it, calling yourself a bastard, thinking there's something wrong with you. I'm sick of it! You are just as good as anyone else and better than most!

"But your life would have been so easier if-"

"If what?" she was wound up, "Get it through your head, Roger, your father and I love you. Have we been miserable all these years? Is that what you think?"

"Well, Dad had to go back into the Army because of me."

"Is that what your really think?" Roger asked, shocked, "That's the first time I've heard that one."

"Grandma MacCrae, said you wouldn't have gotten married if it weren't for me, and then Grandma Baumer once told me one of the reasons she would never come around is she couldn't get over the fact that Dad would have never gone back into the Army if it hadn't been for him trying to escape all the gossip about me."

"Oh, for crying out loud-" Roger blurted out, following that with some other expletives. He always knew the reason he'd been disinherited was because of his marriage to Rose, but this was dirty, to hurt a kid like this for no good reason. He tried to remember the last time Rog had seen his grandparents. He knew it'd had to be right after the bomb Rose's mother dropped on him. They'd been forced to leave Rog with his folks when Danny was in the hospital at Scott AFB with appendicitis. Neither he nor Rose felt right about it at the time but there was still anger over Rose's mom's stunt. His parents had refused at first, and then relented. Now he knew why. *No wonder the kid's so messed up.*

"Listen, Roggie," Roger began. "I went back in the Army because I was miserable being a civilian. I love the Army. Sure, your grandparents weren't helping out - on either side but I did what I did because I thought it was best for me. More importantly, I did it because I thought it was best for my family. Now that you're fixing to have a family you'll understand that. You do what you've got to do to take care of your family."

Roger's voice softened, became husky. "If I've had any regrets, son, it's that I've had to be gone so much - I regret I've missed so much of your childhood. I missed your whole infancy. I'd go off for a year or so. When I leave you're baby talking, I come back you're in the first grade, reading. I leave, you're riding your bicycle, I come back you're driving a car. I regret I wasn't able to be there when my kids were born. I guess it's the price you pay for being a soldier. Maybe, if I had it to do over again..."

"You'd do it all over again," Rose said with a sad smile on her face. "Daddy used to say he believed everyone was called to something, some folks are called to be preachers, some schoolteachers, some doctors, lawyers, farmers, even soldiers. Roger, I believe you were called to be a soldier."

"But you've been alone so much."

"It's the price I've paid for being your wife. The times we've been together have been worth it. They've been good times. I'd rather have the stolen times with you than an entire lifetime with anyone else."

Their eyes met. Rog could see the love between them. Roger suddenly remembered his son.

"Rog, you've been a part of that. You boys are my hope."

"I'm so ashamed; I've fouled up so badly. I've always wanted you to be proud of me."

"Son," Roger said. "I won't lie to you. I've been very disappointed by some of the things you've done. But I've *always* been proud of you. I've always been proud to call you my son."

The two men broke down and embraced. Rose looked on; tears flowing freely down her cheeks. Perhaps, now, Rog could be healed.

Now she watched father and son hug each other one last time before departing to their separate destinations. A loudspeaker overhead announced Rog's flight boarding.

"Well, I guess this is it," Rog's voice was breaking. "Mom..."

They hugged, "Don't be a hero, baby. Keep your head down. Come home to us."

"Don't worry Mom. I'm gonna dig a foxhole and keep digging. The only way they'll find me is by the C-ration cans and the smell."

She had to smile. She looked up at Rog, trying to see the face of the baby she had rocked those lonely nights, the little boy who'd jumped into her lap with some new treasure he'd found in the yard. Then he smiled. There he was. She struggled to be strong, to be brave. She studied his face, trying to memorize every feature, trying to burn them into her mind. She remembered Uta. Roger wasn't hers anymore. Reluctantly, she let him go.

They all tried not to watch as the young couple said their good-byes. Finally, the last call for passengers was announced,

Rog had to break away. He gave Danny a bear hug, "Be good, hotshot," he said, the tears streaming freely now, "Take care of Mom and Uta for me. You're the man of the house."

Danny nodded, looking up at his big brother, in spite of all their feuding, his hero. "No problem. Do me a favor, kill a Cong or two for me, okay?"

"I'll bring you a necklace!"

Danny smiled through his grief, "Yuttah hey!"

"Yuttah hey!" Rog said, his smile turning to grim determination.

Rose froze. Rog had read somewhere that it was Sioux for something like, "It's a good day to die!" It had been Rog and Danny's motto for years, their joke. There was no humor in it today.

Rose broke her custom and watched Rog through the window until he was onboard the aircraft. She watched the Boeing 707 back out of the gate and onto the railway. Then, Roger's flight was announced.

It was time to go through the ordeal again.

The car was silent on the drive home. Brew drove while the women wept, Rose in the front seat, Uta in the back. Danny sat silently in the backseat, trying to think of something to say to make his mother and sister-in-law laugh or forget their sorrow, finally giving up. Sometimes, he was beginning to learn, it was better to remain silent.

It was her mother who discovered the truth. It was on a Sunday morning. Everyone was getting ready for church. Rose was helping with the breakfast dishes. She stretched up to put a serving plate away on a shelf. Emily saw the bulge and all the little signs came together. At first, Emily was angry with herself for ignoring the signs; she had noticed them all. But, then, she asked herself, how could she have known? After all, Rose had shown no interest in any other boy since Roger had gone off to basic training. To her knowledge, she'd had no contact with the boy since that terrible night with Harold.

Emily called Rose aside and took her into the pantry, where they could speak alone.

"Rosie," she said as gently as she could, "who's the father of your child?" Even as she asked her heart dropped. She knew the answer.

Rose didn't know what her mother was talking about at

131

first. She was stunned at the question, *"What child?"* she stammered.

Emily's first reaction was anger. She drew back as if to slap Rose for being so disrespectful. But she looked into her daughter's wide, fear-filled eyes as she drew back to brace herself from the expected blow and saw pure innocence in them.

Her heart softened, she drew her little girl to her and held her, tears filling her eyes. *"My poor innocent baby..."* she cooed. The poor girl really didn't know what was happening to her.

Emily did the best she could to shield her daughter from the consequences of her actions. She talked to Rose and explained to her that she was pregnant and how it happened. Rose now had to face Harold and his anger. She knew Harold was a good man. He loved his six children as much as any man could love his children. She also knew his love for God's holiness and his desire for it. She often warned him that he set his standards too high for anyone, even himself to live up to. She didn't know how he would react, or, what would become of their daughter.

She waited until after church that morning. Rose stayed home. Emily made the excuse that she was sick, which was not actually a lie. After Sunday dinner she took him to his study and told him. His reaction totally surprised her. Instead of anger, when he heard the news, he fell limply back into his overstuffed chair in his study, put his hands over his eyes and wept like a baby. Emily tried to hold him but he was inconsolable. He asked to be left alone.

Rose had been waiting in her room all day for him, dreading his terrible temper. When he finally came to her after Sunday evening service, she was shocked at what she saw. Instead of the proud, dignified man of God she was accustomed to, she saw a broken man. He sat, (collapsed?) on the foot of her bed. It broke her heart to think of how much she had hurt him.

"Papa-" she said softly, her voice quivering with emotion. She reached out her hand to touch him, soothe him, take away some of his pain. She winced as she felt him instinctively draw back from her touch, as though she were impure.

"This doesn't have to be the end of your life, Willa Rose," he whispered.

"We'll send you down to Louisville, to my brother Ben's until you have the baby. After that, we can find a family for it and

adopt it out."

"No!" she almost shouted, shocked at her boldness.

"What do you mean?" Harold asked, surprised not only by her tone to him, but also by her rejection of what seemed to him the only logical course.

"This is my baby, Papa. God gave him to me, and I'm going to keep him!"

"But Willa Rose, you're only sixteen-"

"I know, but this baby belongs to Roger, and, Papa, I love him. If he's killed in Korea this baby will be all I have of him!"

"Honey, you don't know what you're saying- it's better to adopt him out so he'll have a better chance at life than have him labeled a bastard!"

*"He's not what you call him, Papa, and if he was whose fault is that? **Who** had our marriage annulled? He's mine and Roger's child, and we're going to be married and raise him up!"*

Despite their pleadings and threats, nothing was going to change her mind. Finally her parents gave in. Roger's parents were told the news. They reacted by blaming Rose. Harold almost lost his salvation when Mr. Baumer used a term he didn't like in reference to his daughter.

Roger was contacted in Korea, but there was no way the Army was going to release him from a combat zone to get married before the baby was born. Not with the way the war was going at that time. It was Roger's chaplain who came up with a solution; he suggested they do a marriage by proxy. Someone would stand in for Roger in the States so they could be legally married without his presence.

Rose was always thankful for the way the chain of command assisted in getting the necessary paperwork and approval signed and rushed through channels in the midst of major combat operations. It still took some time. Rose's parents refused to sign the papers until she was eighteen. They had held out hope she'd change her mind. When she turned eighteen they had no choice but to sign or have their daughter bear the stigma of bearing a child out of wedlock. Roger and Rose were married by proxy in a civil ceremony. No clergyman would perform the ceremony, in light of her condition. The baby, Roger Jr., Roggie, was born two days after the ceremony, almost three weeks premature.

If Rose had thought her problems were solved she was

wrong. Word of the ordeal leaked out through the prayer groups in her father's church. Even after she and Roger were married, there were the cold stares and whispered remarks when she entered the church. She could handle that. What she couldn't stand was the way they looked at her baby. When she brought Roggie to church, she could see the sneers on the faces of the ladies of the church when she showed them her baby, as if he were dirty. She would bite back her words. Even if she and Roger were sinners, perhaps they were falsely stained forever in their eyes with the sin of fornication, but her baby was pure. He'd done nothing wrong. He couldn't help what his parents had done; he hadn't asked to be born!

She also couldn't stand the heartbroken looks on her parents' faces when they looked at her and Roggie. She'd been forced to quit school when the principal found out that she was pregnant. Sitting at home all day, helping her mother with the housework was driving her crazy. She'd been saving money from Roger's allotments home, after she paid her parents room and board. She had enough finally to get an apartment of her own. Roger had been advanced through the ranks quickly to Sergeant. Though Rose was blissfully unaware of this at the time, this was a sign both of his own natural abilities as a soldier and the savagery of the fighting he was experiencing.

She moved out of her parents' house and across the river to St. Louis. She hoped that in St. Louis no one knew or cared about the circumstances surrounding her marriage and the birth of her son. Perhaps, her new family could start fresh.

If there is one thing a military family learns to do, it is to adapt to changing situations. Rose and Danny welcomed Uta into the family. Rose discovered it was nice to have a "daughter" to do things with, even if they couldn't converse yet. There were other ways to communicate. Rose was amazed at how bright Uta was. She had no doubt she'd be talking in no time, particularly with Danny's help. Danny had found some German language books on a trip to St. Louis. He was using them to help teach her English while learning German himself.

There wasn't much difference in Danny and Uta's age, this had caused Rose some concern at first. She soon realized Danny looked upon the girl as a sister. She also realized his sense of honor would not allow him to think of his brother's wife in any other way. He began addressing her as "Sis."

134

Rose had always said she'd get her girls when her sons married. It had been a prophecy fulfilled. Of course, she wished it could have been different, that Rog and Uta could have waited until they were older to marry. As Brew said one evening, "You play the cards you're dealt."

She began to look forward to their trips to Scott AFB for her check-ups. They'd make a day of it. If it didn't take too long at the doctors they'd go shopping in Belleville or at least visit the PX and Commissary. At the house, Uta was company when Danny was at school. She was anxious to help out in the cleaning and chores. She didn't want to be a burden. Rose almost felt guilty. The girl appeared so grateful to have a place to stay.

Every evening, they all watched the evening news together for news about the war. Rog was in an artillery unit stationed at a firebase in the south. Whenever there was a story from his area they watched closely, hoping to get a glimpse. Every day they went to the post office to check the mail, hoping to hear from either Roger or Rog. On nice days they would walk.

Rog would send his letters to his mother and wife in the same envelope. His letters to Uta in his pidgin German would make her giggle at his syntax and grammar, but they communicated. Danny would help her write him letters in English, except for personal things, which she wrote in a mixture of both. Danny wryly commented one time that he reckoned Rog got the message.

One day Rose and Uta went downtown to Clevenger's to pick up some odds and ends. It was a nice autumn day, not too cold, so they decided to walk. They had just come around from behind Ralph's Service Station when Rose saw her. She was startled at first, hadn't expected to see her. It had been over two years. The last Rose had heard she'd been sent off to St. Louis. Rumors had it she'd been institutionalized. Rose had thought often of her, wondered how she was doing. She had driven by her house several times to catch a glimpse, to make sure she was all right, without success. It had been as though the girl had disappeared. Now Denise Fleischmann was now sitting on the steps of the Mason Hall, her arms folded in front of her, as though cradling something, rocking back and forth.

Rose wanted to cry at the sight. Instinctively she began moving toward her to speak with her, ask her how she was doing, offer help, sympathy, perhaps find out... Then she thought of Uta, now eight months pregnant. The doctors were worrying about her being so small, carrying the baby to term. What if there was a scene? It could throw Uta into labor; she might lose the baby.

Rose was moving Uta across the street, toward the funeral home when Denise saw them, recognized them. It was more an inner knowledge than anything else that told Rose. She could feel Denise's eyes on them as they walked along. Uta didn't appear to notice anything. Good.

"My baby!" a low, raspy, sibilant voice assaulted them from the opposite corner. A chill ran down Rose's spine. Even Uta seemed uneasy now, glancing over at the pathetic, hideous thing sitting on the steps across the street.

"I want my baby!" Denise was rocking more rapidly now, staring, no glaring, at Rose and Uta. The familiar words were like a slap in Rose's face. It was all she could do to keep from glancing in Denise's direction.

No, she told herself. *Don't look over there; don't give her an opening. It's what she wants.*

"The sins of the father are visited upon the sons!"

Rose risked a glance, their eyes met. Rose recoiled, at what she saw there. Whoever was sitting there looked like Denise Fleischmann, but that wasn't Denise Fleischmann speaking. Denise Fleischmann lived no more behind those eyes. It was more than insanity. It was unholy. The eyes stared at Rose and Uta with an unearthly fire that was simultaneously emitting every unclean emotion and desire known to man.

"I want my baby!" it hissed again, rocking even harder.

Rose was now attacked by fear, fear for Uta, for her baby, particularly for the baby.

"Let's go, honey." she whispered. They increased their pace now, walking quickly.

"*Wie-* Who is that?" Uta's English was improving, Rose noted, anything to take her mind off Denise.

But to answer the question, how much should she say? Honesty always was best, but how much honesty?

"One of Roger's old girlfriends."

Uta sadly nodded her understanding. *Good, that's enough for now; I need to speak with Rog about this. She needs to know.*

"How is she -" Uta began, then corrected herself, shaking her head in that funny way as if shaking off her mistake, "What is wrong - *mit*-with her?"

"Crazy, cuckoo," Rose answered, feeling bad at putting it so crudely. At least Uta understood those words.

"Toeffel." Uta muttered to herself.

Toeffel? Rose searched her memory for the word. *Devil!* Another chill hit her. *She may be right.*

They decided to walk the back way home. Rose had wanted to stop at Clevenger's for milk and bread. It could wait; she'd send Danny later. There were letters from both Roger and Rog in the mail. Rose and Uta rushed home to read them.

Rose opened Rog's first, so Uta could read her letter from Rog. She opened her letter from Roger. Things were going well at his new station. He'd been selected as the Division Commander's personal pilot. It was an honor, but required him to be on call. He could handle it though, he said. The long hours by himself in the BOQ's (Bachelor Officer's Quarters) were driving him crazy. He'd gotten his request to change his tour to a short tour (eighteen months instead of three years) approved. Rose could stay at home with Uta until Rog got back. This meant Danny would be able to graduate with his friends in Delphi. That would make him happy.

Then Roger mentioned something she'd only dreamed about. He spoke of retiring after this tour. He'd have his twenty in, had risen as far as he could go as a Warrant Officer Pilot unless he took a commission and became a captain. He said in his letter he was tired of being away from his family. Rose thought about the idea of having her husband home all the time. It was too much to hope for. She looked over to Uta.

"What's up with Rog?"

"He changes his job," she said smiling. "More pay, promotion."

"Good!" Rose said. In the pit of her stomach she didn't feel as happy as she sounded. She'd been an Army squaw too long to be happy about any change that sounded too good. After all, he was in a combat zone. More pay and promotion usually meant more danger.

She unfolded her letter,

Dear Mom,

> *Brace yourself. I've had an opportunity to get into aviation. A letter was posted throughout the division requesting volunteers for door gunners. They've got a shortage of them over here. I talked with the NCOIC of the effort. He told me with my time in service and grade, I'd get an*

137

> *almost immediate promotion to E-5, not to mention*
> *flight pay, which will come in handy. Also, I'll be*
> *OJTing for crew chief. This'll get me out of the*
> *artillery. Maybe I can even get to flight school. That'd*
> *be neat. I'd be following Dad's footsteps. I volunteered.*
>
> *Don't worry, Mom, I know the rumors about*
> *how dangerous the job's supposed to be. My pilot is*
> *Steve Longfellow, who did a tour in Nam as Dad's*
> *co-pilot, he told me he has three tours in and hasn't*
> *lost a crewmember yet. He'll take special care of me,*
> *he says because of Dad...*

Rose put the letter down. She thought of all the names, the faces of the kids who'd served with Roger through the years, who eaten Thanksgiving dinner at the house, who'd become "big brothers" to their children, whose names they had read on the weekly casualty reports in the *Army Times*. Door gunners. Men, kids, who stood in the open doors of the Huey choppers strapped to the "birds" by their safety harnesses, with their M-60 machine guns on their mounts as they zoomed over the dangerous jungles and forests of Vietnam. Their job was providing covering fire for the infantry as they scurried to and from the choppers, fighting off enemy ground forces so the medics could load their wounded on board, or just shooting at and being shot at by the enemy in the forest below as the choppers flew over. They were targets. Charlie knew that on a dust-off chopper, if you killed the door gunner, you've rendered it defenseless. Door gunners had a short life expectancy.

She looked over at her daughter-in-law, who was re-reading the letter for the third time. "Excuse me," she said rising. "I'm going to take a nap - *schlaffen*."

"Okay." Uta said, not looking up from her reading, "I do dinner tonight, okay? I cook German."

"Sure, Sweetie." she said, kissing the girl on the forehead.

Rose walked slowly up the stairs; her feet were extremely heavy somehow. As she threw herself on her bed, her eye caught a picture on the nightstand beside her head. It was a picture from their trip to Alaska when Rog was ten and Danny seven. She and Roger were in the picture. They had been fishing all day and were showing off the day's catch. Danny was holding a channel catfish nearly as big as he. Rog, the day's winner, was holding up

138

a string of three large catfish. She looked at the pride in his eyes, the smile on his face that was a reflection of his father's. She began crying.

Danny was having another nightmare, the same one he'd had several times before. Someone or something was trying to carry him down the steps. Once more he was trying to scream out for help, to call the Name of Jesus. Once more in his dream his vocal cords were paralyzed with fear. He was out on the landing now, he was reaching out trying to grab onto a banister.

"Danny!" Someone was calling from far off.

He tried to answer but couldn't move his mouth; all that came out were terrified gasps.

"Danny! Wake up!"

Now, he was back in bed, but someone was holding him down, almost forcing the wind out of him. He could feel cold hands on his arms, pinning him to the bed. He could feel a heavy weight on his chest; hear whispering all around him.

"Danny! Get up! It's time!" He now recognized the voice; it was his mother. She was downstairs by the heat vent, calling up. "I'm going to have to shake him, I guess," she was talking to someone else, Uta? "You hang on, Sugar, it'll be okay. Danny!"

"Mom!" Danny tried to scream out but he felt an icy hand across his mouth, muffling his voice, at least his voice was working, "In -" he struggled, "*the - Name- of- JESUS!*"

He was free. He sat up in bed, there was a moment where he was disoriented, didn't know where he was and he tried to focus, recognize his surroundings. He was breathing heavily, he struggled to regain control of his breath.

I'm in the south bedroom. He began to calm now, his breathing came easier, and the fear was leaving. He remembered now. They had moved Uta's bedroom downstairs in the north room, the old living room so she wouldn't have to climb the steps and could be downstairs to care for the baby. Danny had moved into the south bedroom, Rog's old room, so he could have more privacy. The middle bedroom was now the guest bedroom and general storage room, as it had the closet.

What a dream, he thought. *These nightmares are getting worse. They're the same, but more intense. Am I going crazy?*

There was a knock on the door, "Danny?" It was Rose.

"Yeah, Mom?"

"You need to get up, honey. Uta's going into labor. We've got to take her to the hospital."

"I'll be right out!" he said, hopping out of bed. He shivered a bit at the chill in the room. The upstairs was still cool, even cold in the winter in spite of the new furnace. He dressed quickly and was downstairs right behind Rose.

Uta was sitting at the table rocking back and forth, obviously in discomfort. Occasionally, she would wince. Danny knew she was going through contractions. Since Uta had come to live with them, he had been studying on pregnancy and delivery. He had even prepared to deliver the baby if need be. That was a possibility. They were driving to Scott Air Force Base, which was over an hour's drive away. They might have to deliver the baby on the road.

They had rehearsed this routine several times. Danny led Uta out the front door helping her keep her footing on the icy sidewalk. He'd taken care to sweep the walk and de-ice every night before dark, in case she might deliver early, but it had snowed, and then rained in the evening. The temperature had dropped later on in the night and the resultant slush had frozen over. *It's going to be a bear driving in this,* Danny thought.

They finally reached the car. Danny got her as comfortable as she could be in the backseat; he arranged the blankets, which had been stored in the car for that purpose, over her, tucking them in around her. He turned to go back into the house to see if Rose needed his help. She was taking a long time.

As he turned he saw movement in the upstairs window. *What's she doing upstairs digging in the closet?*

Uta moaned. Danny turned around, "Are you all right?"

She looked up at him, questioningly, her English had improved remarkably in the few months she'd been living with them as had his German, but in her pain she was having problems concentrating. Danny searched for the right words, "*Sind Sie gut?*" (Are you good (okay)?)

She gave him a sour look through her pain, which almost made him laugh. It was so typically Uta, *"Oh Jah! Ausgeseichnet!"* (Oh yes! Excellent!) She stuck out her tongue at him as another pain hit her.

Danny touched her cheek tenderly, "Oh, Little Mama," he said softly, his nickname for her.

She smiled then, *" Brudder."*

Where's Mom! He thought, he looked up and still saw

movement in the window. "What's she looking for?" he turned to Uta, and said slowly, "I'm going to check on Mom, okay?"

He watched her face to see if she understood, "*Ja*-Yes, quick, please?"

"Yes!" he started toward the house, tried to run, almost slipped, caught himself and slowed down.

"Mom!" he yelled as he went through the front door.

"In here!" Rose answered from the phone in the dining room.

"Mom, what are you doing?" *How'd she get down here so fast?*

"I'm notifying the Red Cross so they can get your Dad and Rog - Yes, that's APO zero- nine- one - six - five..." she paused, listening, "Yes, thank you..." listening, "Well, it doesn't hurt to try, does it? Thank you very much."

She hung up, "Are we ready?"

"Yes, Mom, we're ready." Danny was getting excited now, "Uta's-"

"'Got plenty of time, honey. Her contractions are still about ten minutes apart. She hasn't broken water yet. This is her first baby. We've got plenty of time, but we need to get on the road."

"Do you want me to drive?" Danny asked, "That's how we planned it."

"I know, Sugar, but we didn't know the roads were going to be icy then," she saw Danny's face fall. "You're a good driver but I've got experience. This could be messy. You hold Uta's hand, I'll drive."

"All right, let's go." They made their way to the front door, "What on earth were you looking for upstairs?"

"I wasn't upstairs," Rose said absently. "Hang on, Uta, we're coming!"

Steven Philip Baumer III was born twelve hours later. The doctors pronounced him a perfectly healthy baby, though he came into the world weighing a bare five pounds seven ounces and thirty-three days premature.

It was in the early morning hours before Danny and Rose were able to go home. Both mother and baby were doing fine sleeping. Brew had shown up and he told Rose he'd sit with Uta till morning. There was nothing more to do at the hospital. Go home and rest so they could come back later.

The Homestead

Roger had called at the hospital after the baby was born, spoken with Rose a bit, spoke to Uta, his German was actually pretty good. He'd made her laugh. Then he spoke to Rose. "They won't give me emergency leave for a grandchild," he said. "I could take regular leave... I've got days saved up..."

"I'd love to see you again."

"It's done."

So, Roger was coming home for a couple of weeks. He couldn't get more. REFORGER was kicking off. It was a semi annual training exercise in which thousands of troops from the States traveled to Germany to get familiar with the countryside. It was designed to help prepare them for war in Europe if the Soviets ever attacked. The general needed - wanted- his regular pilot to fly him around the maneuver area and observe progress.

There was still no word from Rog. She hadn't expected any. Not yet. She hoped he could come home.

Danny, weary from the long evening, trudged up the steps. A shower and bed were in order. Up in his bedroom it took him several minutes of searching to find his clean clothes. Someone had gotten in his drawers and completely rearranged them.

Chapter 9
December 1969

And when they shall say unto you, "Seek unto those who hath familiar spirits (mediums), *and unto wizards that peep, and mutter; should not a people seek unto their God? Should they seek for* (on behalf of) *the living to the dead?*
(Isaiah 8:19)

Danny woke with a start. He looked at the alarm clock on the chest of drawers by his bed. Three a.m. exactly, just like every night since Uta brought the baby home two weeks before. He felt tension in the air, as if the house were alive, vibrating, breathing. He'd lived in the house for the last four years off and on. It appeared that whatever it was haunting the place was digging into a new bag of tricks.

He believed he knew why. His mom and dad had reneged on their promise to God. When his grandma and grandpa had prayed over the house, they had promised to rededicate their lives to God. For a while, after they'd moved down to Ft. Rucker, they had visited various churches in the area.

They'd found a Holiness Church and Mom had enjoyed that. Roger didn't seem to mind it too much. He'd always enjoyed Holiness music. Then the pastor discovered Roger was raised a Catholic and began laying on sermons about the "Whore of Babylon" and Papalism, whatever that was. He began making fun of virgin worship and confession. That had turned Roger off. Danny had regretted that. He had enjoyed the Holiness services, in spite of their constant hammering about his hair being too long (it wasn't that long, he thought, only to the collar), and making comments about proper attire for church. (They didn't like his colored shirts, white seemed to be the uniform). Danny had talked to Rose about why they'd had to go on and on. Wouldn't it have been enough to have preached the truth and let God show his father any truth He wanted him to see?

After that, they'd tried another denomination. Rose liked the preaching but, again, when they'd discovered the couple's religious background there were comments about tongues and the usual Catholic cuts.

They had even gone to the Mormon Church for a while.

The Homestead

Danny really thought they were in left field. One of the teachers had turned several colors when Danny had questioned about the angel Joseph Smith saw. When Danny quoted Galatians 1:6 about angels of light preaching other gospels, he was asked to leave the class and report to the bishop so his questions could be answered. That had been an interesting conversation.

Danny had continued his question about Galatians. Then they had moved to Joseph Smith. Danny asked the bishop how fourteen-year-old Joseph could have run through the woods escaping from those bandits carrying all those gold plates.

They left the church soon after.

The bottom line was, whatever the reason, the Baumers gave up on religion. Roger would occasionally attend Catholic mass on post. Rose occasionally would attend the Protestant service, but she'd found little solace there without her husband. Eventually both stopped going. But Danny had continued reading his Bible.

When they returned to the Homestead, he'd found some tracts the teachers had given him at the summer camp he'd attended four years before. Those were interesting.

In his Bible reading he'd read one passage where Jesus taught that when an unclean spirit had gone out of someone, it would sometimes return. If the "house" were empty, it would move back in and bring seven buddies. Danny had grimaced at that. If it were true (and it was in red in his Bible), then the house was really crowded now.

As he lay in his bed, he could feel the tension building in the house. Now he sensed it. The presence. It was downstairs, right below, at the foot of the steps. It was the same every night. *Here we go again.*

The presence was moving. Danny heard the soft *pit-a-pat-a-pit-a-pat* of small feet running up the steps. He could trace its movement up the steps, through the middle bedroom into the middle of his room where it stopped, waiting, in expectation of - *what?* Danny had come to know it well these past two weeks. It would run up the steps, pause in his room a few minutes, then run back down the steps and repeat the process a few minutes later until four-thirty exactly when it would stop and the house would go back to sleep.

"You again," Danny said to it as it stood in the middle of the room, "don't you ever get tired?"

The first few nights of this had freaked him out, he

144

remembered. Then he realized whatever it was wasn't going to physically hurt him. He'd also figured out that for some reason it couldn't hurt him mentally or spiritually either. Not this one, though there were others in the house who'd tried it. So he'd begun treating this one like a rude houseguest, a nuisance you didn't want but who wouldn't leave.

It was gone again, *pit-a-patting* its way down the steps to stop in the dining room downstairs. *This is it!* He thought. *I've got school tomorrow. I need some sleep.*

He closed his door and locked it. *There!   That ought to take care of you...*

He could sense the presence directly beneath him, at the foot of the stairs. *Pit-a-pat-a-pit-a-pat-a.*

Here it comes. He smiled.

Pit-a-pat-a-pit-a-pat. It was directly outside the door. Danny could sense its puzzlement at the obstacle. *How'd you like that?*

The sound of the doorknob being tested, jiggled, almost brought him out of the bed. He fought the goose bumps running up and down his body as the- *thing*- turned the doorknob, softly at first, then its frustration and anger rising, jerking it back and forth, trying to open the door. Danny giggled a little bit; he could feel its frustration. He wanted to stick his tongue out at whatever it was, but fought the urge, it was, after all a childish gesture.

With a loud crash, the door flew open; Danny jumped up, almost out of bed, his heart pounding.

He heard the creak of footsteps across the floor to the middle of the room. Then silence. It had stopped, was waiting, he could feel its satisfaction, its sense of triumph.

"All right." he said to the air, conceding, "You win, I won't lock it anymore."

It was off, running back through the house and down the stairs.

Danny pondered what had just happened. *Maybe we can get used to this, and just live- or whatever - in peace.*

"Danny, are you all right?"

Danny started; it was Rose.

"Yeah, Mom." he covered himself with a blanket; after all he was sixteen years old.

"I heard a loud slam-"

"It was the ghost." Danny explained what had been going on.

145

"Oh my," Rose said softly, "then you've been hearing it, too."

"Yeah, the 'pita-pat' was driving me crazy, half the night, *pitatpatapitapata*. You've been hearing it?"

"Yes, but I keep hearing a *'clump, clump, clump'* like heavy footsteps."

"Maybe we're hearing two different ghosts." Danny thought about what he'd just said. It was the first time anyone in the family had tried to put a name on what was happening. *Ghosts.* Were they really? Could the dead come back? He'd have to research it, find out.

"I wish your father was here..." Rose said sadly. He'd gone back to Germany, his leave over, a few days before.

"Yeah," Danny said wistfully, but Roger was gone, and as Rog was in Nam, it would be up to Danny to protect the family. As he drifted off to sleep, he thought of his brother, *Is this what Rog went through? Is this why he had his radio blasting all night long?*

Over the next few months the family settled into a routine, adjusting to the presence of the baby in the house. Danny adjusted to the sound of footsteps at night, learning to ignore them and sleep on. Again, he had concluded that if whatever it was had any harmful intentions, he would have already been harmed.

Still it was unnerving. It was as though the presence of Stevie, as the baby had been nicknamed to keep all the Rogers straight, had stirred the house up.

Danny would wake some nights to see the form of a female (Molina?) standing at his window, sadly staring out the window. Often he could hear the soft strains of a fiddle playing in the distance. There were nights when he went to bed late he would hear muffled voices from behind the closed door of his bedroom. As soon as he opened it, they would cease.

Then there were the late night visitors, other figures he'd see in his room at night, sometimes staring at him. He thought often about Rog in this room during that first year at the house. He wondered what he had seen and how it had affected him.

Right now, the spooks, spirits, ghosts, whatever, appeared to be harmless, just acting out some drama over and over. He wondered if this could be their hell, having to relive their great sin over and over again. He knew this was unbiblical. The Bible was emphatic on what happened to the dead, there was no coming back. So what was he dealing with?

He often got the idea it was like the old cartoon series about a friendly ghost. It portrayed ghosts as mischievous entities who enjoyed scaring people. He wondered if that was it. Were they dealing with some sort of malevolent entity that got some sort of kick out of scaring people?

Then he came back to Molina, or what appeared to be Molina. He felt nothing but sorrow when she was around. What was her point? He had to know. Knowledge was the key.

He was reading. He poured through his little Bible. He didn't understand much of it yet, but he'd highlighted every passage he thought might be useful to him in his study.

He'd checked out everything the school library had on the supernatural and the occult. The student aides at the library often gave him funny looks as he'd check out another book. One time, to their questioning stares, he answered, "Know your enemy."

He watched every horror movie that came on Channel 11, the independent station from St. Louis. Most of it was junk, he knew. Still every now and then he'd see something that would strike a nerve, he'd go digging through his notes. He'd crosscheck scripture references until he came up with a satisfactory answer to the question nagging him.

They might be harmless, they might not, but he wanted to be ready if they weren't.

One evening he'd come home from school to find Rose and Uta sitting at the kitchen table playing with the *Ouija* board. He was surprised. He had thought the thing had been thrown out years before. Rose told him she found it behind the kitchen sink while cleaning.

They were asking questions about Rog; was he safe? Was he coming home? When? He'd never felt right about the *Ouija* board, but if it made them feel better, what was the harm?

Then he noticed the *Ouija* board sessions were becoming a daily and nightly thing. It was as if the two women had become obsessed with it, depending upon it for daily updates as to the safety of their men. When he asked about it, Rose had laughed it off as a silly game, a harmless diversion, not to be taken seriously.

"What about the disk flying off the table?" Danny asked, "That wasn't harmless."

He went upstairs, began looking through his notes. He went to the drawer where he kept his old tracts and thumbed through them. *Forbidden Practices* he read, that was it.

147

He flopped down on his bed and began reading. He was surprised at how many things most folks considered harmless were actually forbidden by the Bible. He was concerned at how many occult things, things that were becoming popular, had their origins in black magic, witchcraft, and pagan sorceries.

For instance, it was a big fad to wear *Ankhs*, an ancient symbol which was supposed to represent eternal life. An actress had worn one in a popular movie. The next thing you know, young girls, even women were wearing them. What they didn't know was the truth behind the *Ankh*, that in the ancient Middle East, young women earned the right to wear them by losing their virginity as temple prostitutes in the worship of the fertility goddesses. Danny laughed sadly at that one. He'd gotten a big kick out of telling several of the snooty, popular girls at school that their "cool" necklace was really an advertisement that they were whores.

Horoscopes and astrology were forbidden. Many believed the Tower of Babel had been a ziggurat, and was being built so the astrologers of ancient Mesopotamia could see the stars better and get a more "accurate" horoscopic reading. After reading that, the statement in the Bible "so we may reach into the heavens" made more sense. God had destroyed the tower and confused their tongues to keep them from committing a sin. The Bible was very clear we are not to consult the stars and the moon to foresee the future (*as if it actually worked*) but are to depend on God to take care of us a day at a time.

Ouija boards. Danny fought off the shiver on this one. Definitely forbidden. The Book of Leviticus had several passages against seeking those who had "familiar spirits" (he was still looking up that one, but he had a gut feeling it was what they were dealing with in the house). One should not even try to talk to the dead. That had been the final straw for King Saul, he'd learned. King Saul had gone to a witch to get her to conjure up the spirit of Samuel the Prophet, when the real Samuel showed up. Danny wondered at that, then read the story of the rich man and Lazarus in which Jesus said the dead couldn't come back. *Then what are we dealing with? Familiar spirits? What are they?* The spirit of Samuel pronounced God's curse on Saul for this final abomination and he died in battle soon after.

Nope, *Ouija* boards were out, definitely. Mom should have known better, being a preacher's daughter. *Unless she was never taught?* Horoscopes were getting more and more popular;

just about every major newspaper appeared to have them. He wondered how many folks in the local churches read their horoscopes before going off to teach Sunday school.

He had never really liked the *Ouija* board. It gave him the creeps, even if it was supposed to be a toy. Then he read about a new book soon to hit the stands about a little girl who got possessed using a *Ouija* board. He'd looked it up in the Bible and God's prohibitions against talking to the dead made sense. He wasn't trying to be a mean-spirited old guy in heaven, wanting to keep people ignorant. He was trying to protect us from something terrible. *What? Possession? By what? Familiar spirits? What are they? Ghosts? Demons?*

He felt a chill at that one. Again, it made sense. But he'd have to study more, learn more, and know more. *My people are destroyed by lack of knowledge.* He quoted a passage he'd read. Well, that wasn't going to happen to him if he could help it.

Well, he decided. *I need to take action. We have enough problems around here already without Mom and Uta stirring up more.*

Danny could hear the questions filter up from the dining room through the heat vent. The questions were mainly from Rose, occasionally Uta. It was the same old mill each night. *Is Rog all right? Is Roger all right?* - and a dozen other questions. He felt sorry for Mom and Uta. It was tough enough on him, having a brother and father overseas, but the women?

But he had to protect them from themselves. He rose from his bed and went downstairs. The two women barely looked up when he entered the room, the board was spelling out a message and they didn't want to miss a letter.

Out of some absurd sense of courtesy, Danny waited until it was finished.

"Promotion!" Rose read happily. "Rog's going to get a promotion! I hope so, that's why he went in to aviation. Oh Lord, protect my son!"

How can He protect Rog if we're out on this limb? Danny asked himself.

"Mom," he spoke, "I'm really concerned about you and Uta spending so much time on this *Ouija* board. It's-it's" he sought for the right word, "it's unhealthy..."

"Why?" Rose asked, getting defensive. "It's just an innocent game; there's nothing to it." *Here we go again, round and round...*

149

"The Bible forbids trying to communicate with the dead or otherworldly spirits, Mom."

"But we're not-"

"Mom, *who* are you talking to then?"

Uta had been watching the two. She was now at the point she could follow most of the conversation if it didn't get too technical. "Danny," she began softly, "if it brings your mother - and me-" she hesitated, remembering the right word, "comfort, what can be wrong?"

"What profit a man if he gain the world and lose his soul?" *Where did that come from?* "Listen, I don't want to argue. Mom, before Dad and Rog left, they asked me to protect both of you. I'm going to do it." He moved toward the table.

"What are you doing?"

"I'm protecting you, Mom, I love you. I love you, too, Uta."

He grabbed the board and disk. Rose started to rise, "Danny, don't you dare-"

"It's actually my board, Mom. I got it for Christmas five years ago, remember?"

"But you never played with it."

"I know. Now I know why."

"Danny!"

"I hope you'll forgive me later," he said. With that he brought the board up and broke it over his knee.

Rose left her seat and approached Danny threateningly, "You had no right..."

"Maybe not, Mom, but I did what I had to do."

Danny took the board out to the trash. Their trashcan was an old fifty-gallon oil drum with its lid removed. Inside his pocket he had some kitchen matches. It was terribly cold outside, a hostile wind bit into his cheeks. He put the board in the trashcan with the day's garbage. He hadn't burned the trash yet that evening. He was glad; it would act as tinder for the board. Fortunately, it hadn't rained that evening, so the trash was dry. He found yesterday's newspaper and shredded it up. Reaching into his pocket, he produced a kitchen match, struck it against the trashcan, lighting it. He watched the paper ignite, quickly spreading, lapping around the broken board. He wanted to watch it burn, to make sure it was destroyed.

It seemed as if the board didn't want to burn at first. He watched the flames lick around its edges; it appeared the board wasn't even being scorched. Then the board caught all at once, inside the orange and yellow sea of fire that consumed the rest of the day's trash, the board burned an eerie blue and green. He watched it as it was consumed, and as it quickly disintegrated in the cleansing flames he could swear he heard an eerie howling scream all around him. At first he thought it was the wind, but he knew he felt no breeze stinging his cheeks. As a matter of fact the night had suddenly become deathly still.

The next few days were tense. Neither woman spoke much to him. He could see anger, sometimes even hatred in their eyes when he passed. It hurt. But he knew he'd done the right thing. Eventually, the love returned. At one point, Rose hugged him close and told him how much she really loved him and what a special boy he was. He'd been embarrassed, but knew this was her way of apologizing.

Uta worried Danny. She seemed depressed, as if the *Ouija* board had given her a sense of closeness to her husband. Danny had to fight his feelings of compassion for her with a conviction of a higher love. If he was sure the board was dangerous - and he was- then she would have been worse off had he done nothing. He just had to pray that God would take care of Uta. He just wished he knew more about what he was dealing with.

It was midnight on a Sunday night. Danny was sitting up in the living room watching the late night movie. He had school in the morning, but he was waiting for the midnight run with Stevie. Uta had been looking exhausted lately due to a lack of sleep, in spite of Rose and Danny's help.

The baby was four months old and was still waking up every two hours. Rose had been concerned. She felt the baby should be sleeping better by now, perhaps, for four-hour shifts. He'd wake in the night sometimes screaming, as if something were hurting him. Even when he did sleep it was fitfully. The doctors at Scott had checked him out, found nothing physically wrong with him. They said babies all develop at different rates. Some babies developed faster than others in some ways, slower than others in other ways. So far, Stevie was still in the range of normal in most ways, ahead in some, not to worry.

Rose suggested mixing a little cereal, not much, in his formula before he went to bed to help him sleep all night. "It worked with my boys..."

He still woke every two hours. So Danny volunteered this night to stay up for the midnight shift. Uta had gone to bed around eight. Danny watched TV, did some homework, and waited.

At midnight, on schedule, the baby woke, crying. Danny walked into the kitchen, took the baby's bottle out of the refrigerator and set it in the bottle warmer to heat. He walked back through the living room, slowly opened the door to Uta's bedroom, and peeked in.

The baby's bed was on the near wall, the same as the door. Uta's bed was placed between the two north windows; it's foot directly across from the baby bed. There was a about a four foot walkway between the two beds. Uta had placed her dresser on the wall to the right, covering the door to the corner porch. Danny had teased her about being careful of the high crime rate in Delphi.

As he looked at the dresser now, he thought, *I'd be more afraid about what's in this house than what's outside...*

Stevie was whimpering now. He was a good baby, really, Danny thought, *it's a shame he has his days and nights mixed up...*

"Hey there, little buddy," he whispered, "What's your problem?" He looked back at Uta, who'd rolled over, her head buried in the covers, sleeping soundly. He was surprised the baby hadn't wakened her. Usually all he had to do was grunt and she was up checking him out. This was the second bottle run he'd pulled and she hadn't so much as budged. *Maybe she knows I've got it and doesn't have to get up.*

He checked the baby's diaper. Sure enough, he needed changing. He idly wondered why they didn't catheterize infants until they were potty trained. He found the clean diapers on Uta's rocker in the opposite corner of the room. He examined his work proudly. "Now you're ready to eat."

The baby grinned up at his uncle as he picked him up, giving a little gurgling laugh. Danny held him close. "Poor kid; maybe you'll see your daddy some day. Another Baumer generation, proudly serving..."

He carried Stevie into the kitchen, retrieving the bottle, testing it and sticking it in his mouth. Then he sat in the big rocker in the living room watching his movie while the baby fed.

The baby was asleep before the bottle was empty. Danny held him close for another minute, gently patting his back until he heard a soft burp. He put the baby to bed, cut out all the lights, except Uta's nightlight and went upstairs to get some sleep.

At 3:00 a.m. Uta woke to hear her baby crying. She groped for the switch to the lamp on her stand, turning the light on. She looked at her alarm clock, thought it was late for Stevie to be hungry, but she wasn't going to question a good thing.

Sleepily, she went into the kitchen and prepared his bottle, letting him cry. The doctor said it was good for his lungs to let him cry a bit. He was crying louder now. She went back into the bedroom to pick him up, calm him down a bit. He was getting too worked up.

As she picked him up, she noticed he was all wrapped up in his blanket for some reason. Had Danny done that to protect him from the cold? No matter. She sat down in her rocker and began soothing the child, making cooing noises and singing an old German nursery rhyme she'd learned from her mother.

She thought of her mother and her heart hurt. Rose had asked if she wanted her parents notified of the baby's birth. She had said, "No." She'd wanted to notify them. But she'd given Frieda, who'd maintained contact with her parents and who told her news of them, her address in case they ever had shown any evidence of wanting to see her or relenting on their position. They hadn't. Perhaps one day. Now the wounds were too fresh.

She sang the second verse to the rhyme when unseen hands grabbed the baby in her arms and tugged hard. It had caught her by surprise, but she had reacted quickly, instinctively, closing her arms around her baby automatically. Now she was in a terrible tug of war against an unseen entity that was trying to steal her baby.

"You leave my baby alone!" She shouted in German. She repeated the words in English.

The thing pulled even harder. Uta was afraid Stevie would be hurt by the fight. But she refused to let go. She'd heard the stories the family told, but it was hard to believe them, after all, she'd seen nothing in the house.

"I said, leave my baby alone!"

Panicked, her eyes darted around the room, at the ceiling, where in the bedroom above, Rose slept. She called out for help, hoping Rose would hear her. Her eyes darted around again, stopping on the baby's bed. She saw Stevie lying in his bed, sleeping peacefully.

153

"Mein gott!" she cried. What on earth was she holding?

"Here!" she said, letting the bundle go.

It disappeared.

She didn't have time to reflect on what had just happened. In the crib, Stevie was whimpering. She dashed across the room, picked him up and cradled him in her arms. When she was done feeding and changing him, she put him in her bed and slept with her arms around him, protecting him.

The following Saturday morning, Rose came downstairs to find Brew sitting on a dining room chair, reading his paper, chewing on an unlit cigar. She smelled coffee brewing on the stove.

"Hello, Brew," she said. "Make yourself at home."

"Thanks, Rose," he answered. "I might."

It was the usual ritual, she reflected. If she ever woke up on Saturday morning *not* finding Brew in her kitchen or living room, she'd send out a missing persons report.

"I went over to the bakery in Glen Haven and bought some doughnuts." Brew said. Everything normal.

Rose went into the kitchen to pour herself some coffee. "The craziest thing happened to Uta last Sunday," she said, and began to tell him about the baby. Brew listened never taking his face out of the papers.

"Rose," he began, finally putting his paper aside. "Why do you stay here?"

"It's my house. It's home."

"Rose," he was trying to be reasonable. "There are hundreds, thousands of houses for sale in the area that would be just as nice, nicer. Why not sell this place and move?"

Rose thought on her answer a moment before speaking. "First," she began, "do you know of anyone in this area who'd buy this house? It sat empty for how long before we bought it? Second, even if we did manage to sell the place, we'd take a beating. We've tied up all our life savings into fixing this place up. Third, this is *our* home. We've set down roots here. The town has become home to us. Rog's got friends here. Danny's got friends here. Being a preacher's daughter and an Army squaw, I don't think I've ever lived in a house more than three years. We've been here over four years now. I'd like to retire here, have my kids and grandkids come to visit me in my old age. Fourth, Brew, we really don't have any place else to go. You know that

154

better than anyone else. Roger's folks have completely cut us off. My folks blow hot and cold. You're the closest thing to family we have outside of the kids. At least in Delphi, where the folks know us, we've established ourselves a bit. Yes, we come and go, but they remember us from the last time we were in. It's the closest thing to a hometown any of us have ever had. I'm not giving it up. I don't care if all the ghosts or demons in hell come against me. This is my house."

Brew listened to her quietly. He didn't know whether to admire or feel sorry for her, "I wouldn't stay here..."

"I know," Rose said. "You haven't even gone upstairs since we got back from Rucker. What happened to you, Brew?"

Brew thought about it a moment. Rose could see he was turning over in his mind whether or not to tell. Then he thought if he could convince Rose to move out, it'd be worth the embarrassment.

"All right." he said. He looked up and saw Danny coming downstairs. "You know I started out staying in the middle bedroom." Rose nodded. "Everything was quiet for a week or so. Then I started hearing voices from Roggie's room. At first I thought it was the wind. But you know the difference between wind and voices. I knew there was no one in the house so I decided to get out of bed and check what was going on.

"I looked into the other room and Rose, there were at least ten people standing around Roggie's bed. There was someone lying in the bed, struggling. It looked like a girl being held down. When I opened the door, some of the folks turned and looked at me, as if I'd butted in on something...

"So I says, 'Excuse me,' and closed the door.

"I was back in bed before it dawned on me that what I'd seen wasn't normal. It was like I could see right through them! I ain't a superstitious man, but if they weren't ghosts, I don't know what was. At first I was scared, then I figure as long as they stay in there, fine. I can deal with it.

"A couple nights later I'm going downstairs in the middle of the night to the bathroom and I pass this guy on the steps, all dressed up like the turn of the century. He looks at me as I'm going downstairs. I looked into his eyes and he's got no eyeballs! I'm looking into black holes in his face. Now, Rose, you know I ain't no coward, but that was spooky."

"About a week later, I'm lying in bed sleeping and I wake up to see a bunch of them standing around my bed staring at me.

155

The Homestead

That was too much!

"So I decide to stay downstairs from there. Let them have the upstairs. That's okay for about a month. I mean, I can hear them upstairs moving around, but that's okay, as long as they stay upstairs-"

"They didn't?" Rose asked, surprised.

"Nope, I start hearing all kinds of running noises coming from the kitchen and utility room. Then I started hearing the sounds of a baby crying. And screaming, a woman screaming, 'My baby! I want my baby! Where's my baby?'

"Okay, that makes me want to change my clothes, you understand? But I can handle it. Then they started calling out my name in the night, telling me to come upstairs. That's it, I'm outa here!" he shuddered at the memories. "I came back every weekend to check on the place, but I never went upstairs and I never stayed after dark."

"You spend the night now." Rose said.

"Yeah, but I stay downstairs. I figure with you all in the house they've got more targets upstairs and won't bother coming downstairs."

Danny had been staring out the back door window, listening to Brew's story. From the back door, one could look across their backyard, across the adjacent vacant lot, and see Main Street. He watched as John Washburn's ragged pickup truck made its way toward the downtown area. Then, from the opposite direction, he saw a sight that made his blood run cold. *Please, God, don't let it turn here.*

There were tears in his eyes as he saw the *Western Union* van make its left off Main Street and head down the street towards the house. Towards them.

Maybe it'll pass us. Maybe it's for Frank Thompson. He gets lots of telegrams. He hoped, he prayed. *Oh God, let it be for the undertaker.*

The van stopped on the street, in sight of the back porch. He saw the driver stare at the house for a moment, as if confirming the address. *Do you think we have street numbers in Delphi? We don't even have street signs half the time. You've got the wrong address, pal.*

Danny's heart sank as the driver opened the door to his van and got out. He walked up the sidewalk to the house. "Mom," his voice was a croak. "You'd better come here."

The door was open when the deliveryman reached the

porch. He saw the look on the woman standing in the door. It was one he'd seen before, too many times. It was a mixture of grief, resentment, sadness, and hatred. He'd been a telegram deliveryman for twenty years. Since the war started, he found himself hating his job.

"Mrs. Roger Baumer?" he asked.

"There are two Mrs. Roger Baumers in this house." Rose said flatly.

The man looked down at his invoice. "This is for Uta." He pronounced it Yootah.

"Ootah." Rose corrected, fighting back tears. She turned to Danny, softly, "Baby, you'd better get her. She turned back to the deliveryman. "I'll sign for it. I'm his mother."

"Yes ma'am." He brought his clipboard up, "Right here, Ma'am," he said, pointing to the spot.

Rose struggled to see the line through her tears. Images of Rog kept flashing through her mind. His entire life was appearing before her eyes as a tragic slide show. She scribbled her signature and took the cursed envelope from him.

"Thank you, Ma'am," the man said quietly. He started to leave and stopped. She was still watching him, staring at his back, "Ma'am, I'm so sorry..."

"Thank you," Rose said, "Don't worry. You're just doing your job."

Uta was waiting at the table when she went back inside, her brown eyes open in fear. *She knows*, Rose thought. *How is it we always seem to know?*

She gave the paper to Uta, unopened. *It's hers. She's his wife. It's her right.*

Uta stared at the envelope for a moment as if it were a deadly poisonous thing in her hands. Tears welled in her eyes. Danny moved closer, placed a hand on her shoulder. She reached up with her free hand and squeezed gratefully, never taking her terrified eyes off the envelope. *"Nein,"* she said, thrusting the hated thing away from her holding it at arms length for Rose, *"Bitte?"* Please?

Rose stared blankly at her hand. Brew shifted uncomfortably in his chair. She looked at Danny who was watching her face, "I'll do it," he offered gamely.

"No." Rose said, "I will."

She took it. *Strange, even now I'm hoping it will all be a mistake...*

157

The Homestead

But it wasn't, she glanced over all the official jargon, the addresses and dates, reading down to the important part. *We regret to inform you that on April 11, 1970, your husband, Sergeant Roger Steven Baumer, Jr.* - she skimmed past the other information his serial number, unit, etc. to the last line - *was killed in action in the Republic of South Vietnam. The United States Army...*

Rose didn't read any more, she didn't need to. Roggie, her baby, was dead.

Chapter 10
February 1969

The thief cometh not but to steal, kill, and destroy."
(John 10:10)

By the time Roger came home from Korea his son was almost two years old. He cried the first time his father picked him up in his arms. Rose could see the hurt in Roger's eyes as the boy struggled in his father's arms, screaming for his mother.

"He doesn't know you, Roger," she said soothingly. "It'll take time."

She knew the two had never really bonded. She wondered if those two lost years were a gap that couldn't be closed.

It wasn't that Roger wasn't a good father. He was totally devoted to his family. Even when they were separated, he did the best he could to stay in touch with his children, to let them know he was thinking about them. He tried to stay involved in what they were doing, even if it were nothing more than his inclusion of personal notes to each of the boys with each letter to Rose.

It worked with Danny, who with his light brown hair and stocky build was the image of Roger, in personality as well as physically. Roggie was another matter.

Rose reflected sadly that Roggie was doomed almost from the start to feel like an outsider. It wasn't only the circumstances of his birth that made it so. Even his physical appearance made him stand apart in the family. Whereas Rose and Roger were fair complected with light hair reflecting their German and Scots-Irish ancestry, Roggie was dark, with straight black hair. This had caused some comment from Roger's family at first, to which Harold produced a photograph of his grandmother, a full-blooded Choctaw.

There was a wall between Roggie and his father. Their interests were as diverged as day and night. It bothered Roger when Roggie talked to Rose, rather than him. Rose believed it was to Roger's credit that he didn't appear to fault the boy. He marked it to the long absences. Roggie appeared to sense his father's alienation and reacted by moving farther away.

159

Roggie (Danny would always remember him so) was buried in Hillside Cemetery just outside of town. It was the highest point in the area. From the gravesite Danny could look out over the town. He could see the roof of the house from here. Roggie would have liked that.

As the chaplain from the Army Depot read from the 23rd Psalm, Danny studied the faces of his family. Roger was holding up for the sake of his wife. He would fight back the tears welling in his eyes until later, Danny knew. Then he would make an excuse to go for a ride by himself. There, alone in the car he would break down and cry all his tears where no one could see.

Danny was worried about the women. His mother had wept bitterly for days after receiving the telegram. When the body came in she had wanted to see her son. Roger and Danny had been forced to drag her away physically to keep her from opening the coffin.

"Let it go, Rosie," Roger had pleaded. "You don't want to see him."

"I want to see my baby," she had screamed. "I want to kiss him one more time!"

"No, Mama," Danny begged. "Remember him the way he was." Yes. Remember him the way he was. His father had gotten him aside and confided to him how Roggie had died. Roger had almost broken down crying as he told Danny. He'd managed to talk to a friend of his at Ft. Rucker who was in charge of collecting information on all Army air crashes. The final report hadn't been issued yet, but they had a good enough idea of what had happened. The friend had told him, confidentially, that Roggie's chopper had taken a hit from a Soviet made RPG-7 anti-tank missile launcher. Witnesses, grunts on the ground, said they saw the bird spin uncontrollably as it plunged to the ground. They had found Roggie pinned beneath his chopper, his safety harness still attached to his lifeline. Evidently, he'd been thrown from the aircraft by the impact of the blast and he had hung suspended on the end of the harness, thrown around as the bird plummeted. To make matters worse, the chopper caught fire on impact. There wasn't much left of him after that.

Danny had shuddered at the thought of his brother suspended in air, tossed around, and strapped to a falling helicopter. He hoped Roggie had been killed instantly or at least knocked unconscious quickly. He thought it was a horrible way to die, watching his death come at him, looking up and seeing the huge machine as it fell on him.

Now his mother stood staring vacantly ahead. She'd been like this for several days, since the scene at Thompson's funeral parlor. He worried about her. What if she didn't snap out of it?

Uta worried him too. She was standing close to Rose, seeking comfort, which Rose couldn't give. Somehow, though, he sensed there was a sharing of misery that gave each some comfort. He hoped so.

He studied her closely, protectively. Her face was pale and drawn. There were dark rings under her eyes. Her brown eyes, once so alive and sparkling, were dull, lifeless. She seldom spoke except to answer a question, and then it was only one or two words as necessary. Danny was especially worried over the hacking cough she had developed over the past week.

Danny tried not to listen to the chaplain's words. They sounded so empty, so inadequate. What did this man know about his brother? What did he know about how funny Roggie used to be before - before- *before we moved into that house?* What did he know about what Roggie wanted out of life? *Oh well, he's trying.*

Danny looked around at the headstones around him. There were familiar names from the town, Kopf, Schlossman, and Kemp. Then he saw the headstone on another grave, not ten feet from where they were going to lay Rog. *Richard Barrow 2LT, USMC,* he read, *December 5, 1949 - January 1, 1969.* He turned away. It hurt too much. He remembered Richard Barrow as one of Roggie's friends that first year. He was finishing up his senior year at Southern Illinois University in Carbondale, coming home on the weekends. Just about every weekend the gang would stop by the house to get Roggie. They would pass an hour or two just sitting around shooting the breeze with Rose while trying to figure out where to go that night. Often they'd end up spending the evening at the house, joking, cutting up, or playing games. Richard was the Grand Master in chess at SIU. With an IQ so high he wouldn't tell anyone out of embarrassment, he'd accelerated through high school. One night he noticed Danny trying to teach himself chess out of a book. He was using some of his civil war soldiers as pieces.

"Whacha doin' Danny Boy?" he asked.

"Teaching myself to play chess."

"Need some help?"

161

"Sure!"

"Wait here." he ran out to his car and was back in a minute with his portable chess set.

He ran Danny through the basics in a few minutes and gave him a diagram of basic moves. Then they played. Richard took it easy on him for the first few games, letting it play out so he could learn. Then he took to beating Danny in three or four moves, always explaining to him what he'd done wrong to open himself up for defeat. The next time he was at the house he gave Danny a plastic chess set. They spent the rest of the evening playing.

Then Richard graduated. He'd been on an ROTC scholarship and owed the Marines a tour of duty to pay back for his college. He'd stopped by to say goodbye to Rose. That was right before they left for Ft. Rucker. He was killed at Khe Sanh the following winter.

Danny still had the chess set given him by his friend.

Danny thought about the other names and faces. There was Ronnie Allsup, who'd helped Rose the night the car was wrecked. He'd quit high school and been drafted shortly after his eighteenth birthday. He'd volunteered for airborne training and was killed in the Ashau Valley. There were others. So many names from such a little town. Now, Roggie.

The tears he'd been fighting for so long began to stream from his eyes. *God forgive me, but I pray this war lasts long enough for me to get in it. I want to kill some of them. I want to make them pay.*

The chaplain was finished. The twenty-one-gun salute startled him, even though he'd been prepared for it. Taps began to play. The tears flowed freely now. Now the flag was folded and presented to Uta, who didn't even seem to realize where she was. Danny reached over and took it for her. It was over.

They turned. For the first time he noticed the crowd that had come. He saw his grandparents. Even the Baumers had shown up. *So that's what it takes to be accepted in the family,* he thought bitterly. If he was unimpressed by the family show, he was touched by the support of the town. It appeared as if the entire town had turned out. Danny took comfort in that. He had always felt the town considered them outsiders. But now they accepted Roggie as one of their own. He looked at the coffin, waiting for them to leave so it could be lowered into the ground, *Rest, Roggie, you're home at last.*

Off a bit from the crowd he noticed a news crew from one of the St. Louis stations. They were far enough away so as not to be intrusive. It was apparent they were trying to be respectful, but their presence bothered him. He had the military trait of being distrustful of the media – particularly since they had seemed to turn against the war effort, and by association, military personnel in general. *What are they doing here? Vultures!*

The family made their way to Frank Thomas' limo. The American Legion was providing a covered dish dinner for family and friends. Roger supported Rose; Danny supported Uta, as they walked through the headstones.

"Oooooooh, my little baby!" the voice vibrated through Danny's body, sending chills in its wake. *"My baby..."*

Danny looked around in time to see two American Legionnaires guiding Denise Fleischmann off to a waiting vehicle. She struggled with them for a moment, and then noticed Danny watching her. She ceased her struggle and looked him dead in the eye. Then smiled.

Danny looked away quickly, refusing to meet her eyes. There had been nothing warm or wholesome in the smile, in the eyes. It reminded Danny of -what? He thought as he helped Uta into the car. *A serpent?*

That evening they saw Roggie's funeral on the evening news. They'd made it into a tragedy of Vietnam, an anti-war story. It turned out that Roggie was the eleventh young man from Delphi killed in the conflict. This gave Delphi, with around six hundred residents, the dubious honor of having suffered the highest casualty rate, per capita, of the war thus far. The news people couldn't bear to pass this story up.

It opened with the scene, from a distance, of Roggie's flag draped coffin out at the cemetery. There was a pan of the people of the town who turned out to honor his memory. A reporter's voice-over told the basic facts of Roggie's death in Vietnam as his basic training picture flashed on the screen. Danny noted they left out the fact that he was a volunteer whose father was a career soldier.

Switch to scenes of Delphi, the desolate main street, a few churches, the school, with the reporter describing Delphi as the typical Midwestern farming town, population six hundred. Then there were shots of the headstones of some of the other casualties – Robert, Ronnie, Joe Sankie, and Billy Hartzog. The

163

story ended with the reporter standing by Roggie's graveside, probably after the funeral with the town behind him.

"Delphi, Illinois," the reporter intoned. "Your typical midwestern town. Tonight, as another of its young men are laid to rest, killed in a war which continues with no end in sight, certainly the citizens of this town must be asking themselves how long must it continue? How many more of its young men must be sacrificed? What has Delphi done to suffer so much? This is Mark Gainous, WSTP news, in Delphi, Illinois, a town in mourning."

Roger was incensed. He threatened to sue the station and the network for using his family's image and Roggie's name and picture without permission. Rose calmed him down. What was done was done. Let the matter, and Roggie, rest.

Danny was proud of the town. He found out the reporter had tried to interview several folks to get comments for the story. They'd all refused to cooperate. George Koontz's answer to the reporter's question said it all, "We here in Delphi don't air family business to the outside."

Eventually, life had to go on. Roger had to return to Germany. Danny had to return to school. Uta had a baby to raise - alone. Rose tried to carry on and be strong for the rest of the family.

Roger had suggested the family return with him to Germany – get away from the house and the memories it contained. It was what Rose wanted more than anything else in the world. She refused to go. What would Uta, whose immigration status was now confused by the death of her husband, do?

Returning to Germany at this time was out of the question. Perhaps in the summer, she said. Danny would be finished with his school year and, perhaps, Uta would be settled enough to carry on without the family. She would also be eighteen and therefore completely and legally an adult and free of her family's influence. Roger promised to see a JAG officer (Judge Advocate General – military lawyer) and check both the Army regulations and German law and work on some way to get her declared his dependent so she could travel with the family overseas even if they had to pay for her and Stevie's airfare out of their own pockets. She was a military widow, but the Army and the VA might cause some problems if they looked to deeply into

164

her age and the marriage. Brew was calling in some markers to get help on the immigration problems. Again Rose shook her head at the influence the truck driver seemed to have in high places.

In the meantime Rose tried to lose herself in the mundane routine of keeping the family going. Uta still accompanied Rose on her daily walk to the post office. She pushed the baby, bundled up, in a carriage, European style. She insisted the winter air was healthy for the baby. Rose couldn't argue, after all she had seen the German mothers with their babies on the streets in Germany.

The walks were tinged with sadness now. The empty mailbox shouted the family's loss. Even when there was the frequent letter from Roger, its lone presence in the slot seemed to toll the absence of a letter from Roggie. Then there were the letters to Roggie that trickled back from Vietnam marked: "Addressee Unknown."

Rose began leaving Uta outside with the baby so she could retrieve them before Uta saw them. Finally, even that stopped. All their letters had been returned. At least Rose thought so.

Then came the day when a last letter came from Roggie, written a few days before his death. It had been delayed in the mail. Uta had burst into sobs at the sight of the letter. Rose controlled her own emotions, comforting the girl in her arms and leading her and the baby home. Later, after Uta had calmed, she had gone upstairs to her own bedroom and allowed herself her grief.

It was a month since that last letter had arrived. The pain had subsided somewhat, though inwardly Rose sensed it would never completely leave for either of them. And in that shared grief the two women grew closer, bound by their love and grief.

"Mama Rose," Rose sensed Uta was struggling to find the words. She was amazed at how quickly the girl was mastering English. Necessity, she concluded. "I am sorry for the trouble I cause you-"

"Trouble?"

"I know you want to go with Papa Roger," her words were spoken carefully, haltingly, but amazingly clear. "I know you stay here for me."

"Baby," tears clouded Rose's eyes. She drew the girl close to her and gently kissed her hair. She knew Uta understood English better than she could often speak it, but she chose her

165

words carefully. She wanted no misunderstanding. She spoke just as carefully, watching Uta's face to ensure that she understood, "I'm not doing anything I don't want to do. Do you understand?

"Roger and I agreed that it was best for Danny to stay here and graduate with his friends rather than be pulled up again. And you are family now, understand? *Verstehen? Familie. Wir lieben dich.*" Rose held the girl close. Even if she didn't love her she would have to love her. After all, she and her baby were all she had left of her son.

"I want my baby!" Denise Fleischmann's voice brought chills down Rose's spine.

It was over before she knew it. For years Rose would re-live those fateful moments when Denise sprang from behind the Mason Lodge screaming like a demon from hell.

Rose thought how she could have reacted differently to protect Uta from the butcher knife the other girl wielded. Both Nita Clevenger and Brad Renfrow who'd witnessed the attack from Clevenger's Grocery later said they'd been amazed at how fast she'd moved to get between Denise and Uta, managing to disarm the girl in spite of her seeming superhuman strength.

It ended when Denise suddenly gave up, dropped her knife, and ran off behind the Mason Hall. Rose was left angry and afraid, her adrenalin pumping. She looked down at her daughter-in-law, bleeding profusely from three wounds to her abdomen.

"Uta!" She dropped down beside the stricken girl. Her first impulse was to pick her up and carry her home. Then she remembered the baby carriage with Stevie inside. "Oh baby…" she cradled the girl in her arms. From her training she knew the girl wouldn't last long without medical care, she reached up into the carriage and grabbed the spare diapers Uta was always careful to pack and tried to use them as field dressings to the wounds. Inside she knew it was futile.

"Somebody help me!" she screamed. It seemed an eternity had passed since Denise had fled. It was only seconds. Nita Clevenger was at her side offering help.

"Brad, go get Frank Thompson!" Nita screamed.

By now, several people were in the street, attracted by the commotion. Within minutes Frank Thompson's hearse, which doubled for the town's ambulance, had arrived. Frank and another man gingerly lifted Uta on a gurney and placed her in back of the hearse.

166

Rose paused a moment, torn between her grandchild and daughter-in-law.

"Go with your girl, Miz Baumer," Nita said kindly. "I'll take care of the baby til Danny gets home."

Rose nodded and leaped in the hearse/ambulance.

As Frank peeled out sirens blaring, Rose reflected on the morbid jokes Danny and Roggie had made about the hearse doubling as an ambulance, "If you don't make it, it's a straight trip to the graveyard."

Rose clinched her eyes to fight back the tears. *Oh Lord, not Uta, too... Please God...*

"Mama..." Uta's weak voice startled Rose.

"Yes, baby, I'm here."

"*Ich – I – krank-* hurt-"

"I know, Baby. Just hang on." *Twenty miles to Glen Haven. Too far! God, please help us..."*

It was almost midnight; Uta had been in surgery for over five hours. Danny tried to pray, but he didn't know if God heard his prayers. He'd read somewhere that God didn't hear the prayers of sinners. He wondered what his standing was. He'd read and re-read those tracts and several other books. There were "sinner's prayers" in each of them. He'd said them all several times. He still didn't know whether he was saved or not. He'd say the prayer and wait for something to happen. It never did. A friend had said you didn't go by feelings but by faith. But he'd heard his grandfather preach about something called "sanctification" several times.

He'd say the prayer and wait to be sanctified but it didn't take. He'd manage to go along for a day or two without using profanity or thinking any thoughts God wouldn't like. Then he'd slip and curse, or get angry or worse. Wasn't God listening to him? How did you find Him?

He'd run into some Christians one time that were trying to witness to him. They'd asked him if he knew whether he was going to heaven or hell. He had to honestly say he didn't know.

The Christians seemed concerned about that. They seemed to feel they had a way one could know. He asked them how. They led him through the sinner's prayer. He said it but still didn't know. How could you know?

The doctor came out. He looked tired and worn. Without a word, Rose and Danny knew.

"We did the best we could - there was just too much damage... if we could have gotten to her sooner- the loss of blood."

Danny put an arm around his sobbing mother.

"I don't know if it's any comfort to you, but she did wake up before she died."

Danny looked up. He swallowed.

"She said something. It was German. It took me a minute to realize what she said."

"What did she say?"

"One word," he choked back tears. "*Jesus.*"

Two days later Denise Fleischmann was found hanging by her neck from the Raeford Trestle, which spanned Ford Creek, approximately four miles out of town. The death was ruled a suicide.

Uta was laid to rest beside Roggie. A double stone replaced the individual stone that had been ordered. The ceremony had been small, just a few close friends, who'd gotten to know her, Roger, Rose, Danny, and Brew. Harold agreed to perform the ceremony.

"...We don't know what's in a person's heart before they go to meet the Lord. But we know that we serve a gracious God who is merciful and not willing that any should perish. It is quite possible that on that operating table He came down and ministered to her and gave her the chance to receive Jesus into her heart. We can hope.

"We don't know why God allows things like this to happen, this double tragedy of two young lives lost within weeks of one another. We don't know why an infant boy is left an orphan, but let us resolve not to go to hell over a mystery. The ways of God are beyond us. No matter what happens, we must learn to put our trust in Him..."

As Danny listened to his grandfather's words a cold icy anger rose up inside him. *God didn't have anything to do with this, Grandpa. Satan killed Roggie and Uta. Satan and whatever's in that house.* Deep inside his spirit he knew it. He didn't know how he knew it, but he knew it.

"Danny," he started at the unearthly voice assaulting him. It was familiar, but not, somehow, *"Danny!"* He looked at the family, standing around him. *Can they hear the voice, too?* He

didn't know whether he was hearing it with his ears or in his head, *God, I don't know how much more of this I can take...*

"Danny, I'm over here."

He looked, and saw Denise Fleischmann, standing by a grave. He blinked his eyes to make sure he was really seeing her. *This is crazy! She's dead! No, it's not crazy, not any crazier than anything else in this town.*

Then he saw Robert Barrow, standing by his grave, and Ronnie Allsup, and all the others. He closed his eyes. *Lord Jesus, help me, please...*

He opened his eyes. The figures were gone. He glanced furtively at his parents, sitting with their heads bowed as Harold finished the benediction. He was the only one who'd seen them. *Why me?*

Roger was able to extend his leave until school let out a few weeks later. Then they would close up the house. Roger and Rose had decided it would be better for everyone if they got away for awhile, changed locations, left all the memories, and the bad spirits behind. They would go to Germany with Roger. He would extend his tour to an accompanied tour. Danny would graduate from high school in Germany.

Three days before they were due to leave, there was a knock on the door. Rose opened it and was surprised to see Rennee Grossman standing there.

"Mrs. Baumer?" she said, "Remember me? I'm -"

"Sure Rennee," Rose said. "I remember you. It's so nice to see you." Seeing Rennee brought back painful memories of happier times when Roggie was at home. Rennee had been one of Roggie's girlfriends. Before   she caught herself – before Deniece.

"Why don't you come in?" She opened the door and Rennee entered. Rose tried to think. She couldn't be over twenty years old, but she looked older. There were circles under her eyes and she'd put on some weight. Rose had heard she'd married one of the Mathis boys and things weren't working out too well for her.

Rose bade her sit down and poured her a cup of coffee. Situated at the table, she asked. "Now, what can I do for you, honey?"

"I suppose you've heard I've split from Tommy."

"No, I hadn't, I'm sorry..."

"Don't be, it was a mistake in the first place. I married him on the rebound..." she caught herself. The pain returned. She'd heard there had been talk around town about her and Roggie getting back together, then he'd written her and told her he'd found someone else. "Anyway, it was a mistake. I think he only married me so he could- well, you know, then the thrill was gone. I guess I could handle the indifference, but when he started coming home drunk and beating on me that was it. I guess you heard I have a baby."

"No, I haven't."

"He's six months old. Mom's watching him now. That's what I've come here about."

Rose's heart quickened, *When was the last time Roggie was home?* She began counting back months in her head. She rebuked herself.

"We need a place to stay."

"What?" Rose's surprise was audible.

"We can't stay with my mom and dad. It isn't working out. I heard you all were leaving town, I was wondering if you would consider letting me rent the house..."

Is that all? She was so relieved she almost laughed aloud. This was the closest thing to joy she'd felt since the telegram came.

"... I couldn't pay much, at least not until I got on my feet. I just got a job at a store in Glen Haven..."

Rose became alarmed. "Sugar," she began, "I don't know whether this is a good idea or not..." *The poor girl doesn't know what she might be getting herself into* "... It's not that I have any problem with you staying here. You're a good girl. I know you'll take care of the place."

"I'd only need the downstairs," she added meaningfully. Rose studied her. *How much does she know?*

"I need to talk it over with Rog- my husband. Honey, there are things more than rent to consider in this. I wouldn't feel right if something happened to you or your baby."

"Mrs. Baumer," Rennee was on the verge of tears. Rose's heart went out to her, "I've been looking for a place to stay for a month. I need a place close to home so my mom can baby sit. This house is only a block away. I can't afford much. If I promise to keep it up, do repairs..."

"But honey, do you know what you could be letting yourself in for?"

170

"I know about the house, Mrs. Baumer. Everyone in town does. I used to think they were all fairy stories until Roggie," she hesitated, choking with emotion at the memory. "Roggie told me." *Told her what? No, I don't want to know.* "But I figure if I stay downstairs nothing will harm me."

"Are you sure?"

"Ma'am, I don't have much choice."

Rose was still doubtful. *It would be nice to have someone stay at the place, look out for it.* She remembered Brew had tried and failed. If a tough old nut like Brew couldn't stay there alone, what hope had a young girl like Denise? She thought of Roggie and Uta, knew that Danny had some wild theory that the ghosts of the house had somehow caused their deaths. It seemed improbable, but much of what they'd experienced in the house had seemed pretty far-fetched. If something terrible happened to Rennee, Rose didn't think she could bear it.

She looked into Rennee's pleading eyes, saw the hurt, and saw the need there. Maybe if they boarded and locked the upstairs...

"I'll talk to my husband."

"Thank you Mrs. Baumer, so much."

So it had been agreed, Rennee and her baby would stay in the first floor of the house. The door to the stairs was locked and boarded in the hopes that anything upstairs would stay up there. The Baumers left some personal items in trunks in the upstairs bedrooms. Rose felt secure that Rennee wouldn't bother them. Brew promised to stop by and look in on Rennee from time to time, and her parents did live only a block away. Rose hoped for the best.

So Roger, Rose, Danny, and little Stevie took off for New Jersey and Maguire Air Force Base, their port-of-call. They had a week to make it, but Rose didn't want to stay in the house any longer than she had to. They decided to make a vacation out of it, stopping along the way at various historic sites, such as Valley Forge and Gettysburg. A day or two in Philadelphia finished the tour and they put their family car in storage before flying to Germany.

If going to Germany had been meant to help the family get over its loss, it didn't work for Danny. Everything about Germany reminded him of Uta. Every so often he'd hear a female voice and he'd turn hopefully, then remember.

171

The Homestead

She was gone.

He followed news of the war obsessively. One more school year and he'd enlist. He knew Dad would sign. He'd understand. Mom might be a problem.

Until then he doted on little Stevie. It was all he had left of Roggie and Uta. It was strange, he thought, how the boy reminded him of both of them. He would get home from school and take him on long walks. The Germans doted on him. Rose was amazed at how much they loved kids. He was learning to walk now. Danny would often get tearful watching him, wishing his parents could see him, feeling for the little one who would never know them. He wouldn't lack for love, not if his uncle and grandparents had anything to say about it. He had become the center of their universe. If they had become alienated from one another, lost in the shells of their griefs and guilts, they adored this child, and he, in turn, adored them back.

They'd been in country a month when Roger'd received a letter from Brew. At first Roger had been reluctant to open it. Most of Brew's letters were for Rose. He figured there'd been a mistake. He thought about giving it to Rose, then had second thoughts. He was glad he hadn't first given it to Rose when he read its contents:

Dear Roger,

I wrote you to tell you some news you might want to chew on before you give it to Rosie. I went by the house to check on it like I said I would and heard over at Kopf's that Rennee's moved out of the house. I asked why and Kopf told me she's been scared out of her wits. It's all over town. The story goes that one night she heard a knock on the door. When she opened the door she saw Roggie standing there, all mangled up like the crash. A couple of her brothers were there, they saw him too. They say, he said, "Tell Mom I'm home!" He came right in the house and disappeared. Rennee's moved out. There's some nasty talk of burning the house. I thought you ought to know what's going on. I didn't know how Rosie might take it. Sorry to bother you. Let me know if you want me to do anything.
Brew

Burn the house, Roger thought. *It would probably be a favor.* Why'd he ever let his wife talk him into buying that dump in the first place? *Never go against your gut instinct, Baumer,* he rebuked himself. *It has never let you down. Your gut has kept you alive more than once.*

Now they were stuck. A fire would be a blessing. They could collect the insurance. He'd give the land to the town. He could write it off as a tax deduction and buy elsewhere, like the Ft. Rucker area, where he was likely to be stationed until the end of his career if he played his cards right. He'd always liked Alabama's mild winters. The summers were hot, but there was always the beach a few hours away.

He thought of the house, the "Homestead," as they had taken to referring to it. He had to grudgingly admit the house held some good memories, even for him. It had been the last place they had lived together as a complete family. He closed his eyes and pictured his boys chasing each other through the house. He remembered the joy and pride he'd felt that summer, working with his boys to whip the place into shape.

He bit back tears. It happened to him often now. He'd be working out a flight plan, doing pre-flight checks, and he'd flash back to a happier time, playing in the sand at Panama City Beach, horseback riding in Colorado, their white water rafting trip in North Carolina. He'd see Roggie's happy face as he rounded third on his first home run. See Roggie and Danny holding up their catfish in Canada. And the tears would come.

It would pass, he knew. Eventually the scars would heal. But they'd always be there. There was a big chunk torn out of all their lives. He knew it was worse for Rose and Danny because they had lost two people they had loved. He had barely known Uta, but in the eight short months she had been in the family, he knew his family had come to adore her. So he grieved for their loss.

His mind wandered back to the Homestead. Without all the supernatural, crazy junk there, he realized there was nothing but grief associated with the place. How could they ever live there when every corner, every room reminded them of their loss? He was reminded of a conversation he'd had with Danny, shortly after returning with the family to Germany. Danny had insisted the house was possessed by something evil, which was destroying the vulnerable people in the family. He was afraid it would search out each person's weakness eventually and bring about his or her destruction.

Roger had dismissed the idea at first. After all, Danny was overcome by grief; he was looking for someone or something

173

to blame for his sorrow. Now, he wondered. This letter from Brew made him uneasy. Brew wasn't the type to spook easily. Roger didn't know whether or not to believe in ghosts or demons. This letter, though, bothered him, even if the incidents with the *Ouija* board and the closet hadn't worked. He could get away with dismissing many of the weird things that the family claimed to have happened in the house to imagination and a sort of mass hysteria within the family. This couldn't be dismissed so easily.

What if "Roggie" re-appeared when Rose was home?

He had decided. He didn't know how he was going to do it, but he was not going to allow his family to live in that place again.

Six months later they received a message from the Red Cross, which took the matter out of his hands. Rose's father had suffered a stroke. She needed to come home before he died.

Chapter 11
October 1970

In whom the god of this age hath blinded the minds of them who believe not, lest the light of the glorious gospel of Christ, who is the image of God, should shine unto them.
(2 Corinthians 4: 4)

A bitter wind stung the cheeks as the car door opened. An early heavy snow had fallen the day before, leaving a covering more than a foot deep on the ground. The sun had come out for a short time earlier in the day, but had beaten a quick retreat in the face of an overwhelming cloud cover that threatened to dump more moisture of an unpleasant nature on the countryside. The previous day's snow, which had partially melted in the face of the sun, had refrozen, leaving a stiff crust on the top of the blanket and a nasty sheet of black ice on the pavement.

Rose looked up at the house with a mixture of relief and dread. She clutched Stevie close to her, shielding him from the elements. *Will it be all right?* She asked herself. She watched the upstairs windows a moment, looking for any sign of movement, anything unnatural. *It will have to be all right. We've nowhere else to stay.*

She'd spent twenty-four hours getting here. It was difficult traveling alone, with the luggage and the baby, now a toddler who wanted to run everywhere, investigate everything. She wished she had Danny with her, but both she and Roger had decided it was best that Danny stayed in school. With Danny in his Senior Year trying to adjust to a new school, to pull him out for a week or two might adversely affect his grades and keep him from walking across that platform. Besides, with the Lord's blessings, she'd only be home a week or two. Harold would be out of the hospital or- she dared not to think of that. There was no point disrupting his schooling for that.

He'd wanted to come, of course. He felt he had to protect Rose. His mother and father recognized the presence of the entities and were understandably leery of the Homestead now. Danny believed these spirits were of a malevolent nature. He was frustrated at Roger and Rose's apparent inability to recognize the

175

true character of what they were up against. Roger and Rose still saw no connection to Roggie's and Uta's deaths and the chain of supernatural manifestations that occurred in the house. Danny saw a plan, an organized campaign to possess or destroy the members of the family. He would quote Ephesians 5: 12: *We wrestle* (Danny read "war") *not against flesh and blood, but against principalities, against powers, against the rulers of the darkness of this world, and spiritual wickedness in the high places.* (Danny read somewhere that some folks read the original Greek to say "wicked spirits in the heavenly places." That made more sense to him). Danny was convinced that not only were the spirits in the house hostile to his family, but they were organized and possessed of some sort of intelligence. Every move of theirs was calculated to bring forth a desired effect on the family, weaken them in some way so as to gain control somehow. Failing that, the next step was to destroy them, *"the enemy cometh but to steal, kill, and destroy..."* Jesus taught that.

When he tried to speak of these things to his parents, Roger had listened with mild amusement and disbelief. Rose had looked at him with intense concern and only commented, "You've been filling your head with too many horror movies and books about the supernatural."

When he tried to show them what the Bible said about these things the response was, "I know all that's in the Bible but..."

He gave up. Now, all he could to is pray to a God he wasn't quite sure he knew yet to protect his mother and nephew as they returned alone to Satan's den. Rose looked up at the house again and felt a chill run down her spine. *Nowhere else to go,* she thought.

She had taken a flight out of Munich on *Lufthansa*. It had been a seven-hour flight taking the northern route across Greenland. Stevie had, of course, been restless during the whole flight, wanting to run the aisles. A nice German man had been a Godsend. He took up with Stevie, complimented her on how well the boy spoke for a child his age. Rose figured it was from always being around adults. He had kept Stevie entertained for a while. Rose breathed a small prayer of thanks when the boy finally went to sleep. They'd landed at LaGuardia and had to take a cab over to JFK to catch a flight to St. Louis. Brew, of course, had been waiting for them at the airport.

Rose had wanted to go straight to the hospital. As they

moved through the traffic on I-70 to St. Elizabeth's, little Stevie found the switch to Brew's car radio. As the radio blasted, he began fiddling with the tuning knob, releasing a cacophony of noise. Rose reached out to take his hand from the dial, saying "No! No!"

"Leave the kid alone," Brew said, barely taking his eyes of the driving. "He ain't hurtin' nothin'."

Rose looked at Brew as if she'd never seen him before. He'd always been picky about his cars. He'd not even let Roggie and Danny turn the radio on, much less play with the dials.

"Do I need to check your forehead for a fever?" she asked, playfully.

"He ain't hurtin' nothin', Rose," he said, testily, "Like I said. Let him be."

"Listen, Rose," Brew said. "Give your folks my regards when you go up. I don't reckon it'll help your dad's blood pressure to see me. I'll tell you what. Why don't I take Stevie down to the hospital cafeteria and get him somethin' to eat?"

"Thanks, Brew. That would help."

In the hospital room she was relieved to find her father sitting up, looking at his gathered children, face beaming, eyes twinkling with a humor she'd not seen in years. He saw her, his eyes beamed, he started to speak. She could see it was a struggle. She wanted to cry, to see this man, whom she had always regarded as a giant, impregnable, laid so low.

Finally, he got it out, "If I'd known this is what it'd take to get all my kids home, I'd have had a stroke years ago." His speech was slow, slurred, but understandable. She could tell that he, who had made his living speaking, was now taking great pains to be understood. *How's he ever going to preach again?*

She fought a moment to control her emotions. *No tears, not here.*

"Papa," she said working her way through the people crowded in the room to see him; her brothers and sisters, and some of their children, "if you'll let us know you want to see us so badly, we'll come home and save you the trouble!" She leaned over and kissed him on the cheek, taking great care to avoid the IVs and wires running to and fro.

"If you'd told us you were coming in dear, we would have met you at the airport." It was Emily.

"That's all right, Mama," Rose said pleasantly. "I knew you'd be busy with Papa, Brew picked us up."

177

The Homestead

"It's a wonder he's sober enough to see to drive." That came from Norville, Rose's brother-in-law.

Rose felt a flash of anger. Norville was supposed to be a preacher. Howard had vouched for him before the ordination board of the denomination, and then he'd been forced to resign his credentials to avoid a scandal over finances at his church. She wheeled on him. "He's never been too drunk to be there when my family needed him!"

"Rose!" Emily spoke from the other side of the bed, "Your father..."

I didn't start it! She wanted to say. *Of course she'd take his side.* His wife, Ida, was the baby of the family, Emily's favorite and Norville was good at cashing in on it.

"Rose," it was Howard. He struggled to sit up, to speak, "tell Brew I'm grateful he brought my Rosie here."

Oh Daddy! She wanted to throw her arms around him and hug him, as she hadn't done since that night those many years ago. He hadn't called her "my Rosie," in years. She remembered when she was little he'd sing *Ring around the Rosie* while she danced. He'd told her that was her special song. When she went off to school and learned it hadn't been written especially for her, she remembered the hurt when the teacher and other children laughed at her for believing her daddy. She remembered sitting on his lap, crying when she told him how the rest of the class teased her. He'd held her close, told her, "Teachers don't know everything. Whatever she says, it'll always be our special song."

"Thank you, Daddy." she now said, kissing him on the forehead. She rose to see Norville's smirking face. *Smile now, you jerk. One of these days, Mama won't be there to protect you...*

She looked over and saw her older brother, Paul, leaning against the wall. He looked back at her with a knowing smile and winked. She knew he was thinking the same thing. She fought back a grin. *It'll be my hatred of Norville Richards that'll keep me out of heaven,* she thought. *Lord you've got to help me on this one.*

Paul was older than Rose by four years. He had run off to join the Army during World War II and never returned home, preferring to settle on the east coast, where he'd married the sister of an Army buddy and made a good life for himself for awhile. Then came the divorce and he started drifting from place to place. He never stayed anywhere over three years. Rose often wondered if it was the war.

She gave him a sisterly once-over. He was a well-built man. He had always taken care of himself. At five feet, eleven inches, he always looked taller. *How did he manage to look so young for his age?* She asked herself. *The result of never taking life too seriously,* she answered herself. She thought of the gray she'd started finding in her hair and the lines around her eyes. She'd always looked young for her age. Not any longer, she thought sadly.

He nodded his head toward the door. Rose excused herself and stepped into the hall.

"It looks bad, don't it, Sis."

"Not as bad as I thought it would be."

"We almost lost him."

"He looks so old..." the tears, held back began to flow.

"I know," Paul said, his voice choking. "You think your parents are always going to be there, are always going to be rocks you can lean on, rest on, then you wake up one day and - they're old, and you realize they ain't going to be around much longer."

"Are you in town for long?"

"I don't know," he said, "You know me and St. Louis. We've never gotten along too well."

"I know about St. Louis."

"What about you?"

"I don't know. It depends on Papa. I had to leave Danny back in Germany with Roger. He graduates this year. I couldn't just jerk him out of school. He's had enough to go through."

"It's hard to think of Danny all grown up. The last time I saw him was... gee, he couldn't have been over ten. I'm sorry I wasn't able to make it home for Roggie," he said. "By the time Ma caught up with me and told me, it was too late for me to come home in time. I sent flowers..."

"I know, thanks."

"You look tired, Sis."

"I am. I haven't slept in thirty-six hours, other than a nap on the plane. You can figure how it is traveling with a toddler. But I needed to see Papa before I did anything else."

"I think he's going to pull through. It was touch and go for a while. I just happened to be in town when it happened. I'm glad I was there."

"What happened?"

"Didn't they tell you?"

179

"I called from Germany and got on the phone with Norville-they didn't waste any time getting here from Texas, did they?"

"Well, if Papa dies, it's first come first serve..."

"Right. So what happened?"

"I was staying with them. It was the church," Paul said. "There was a fire at the church; the cops think it was arson. Papa got call from some 'Sister Glory Land Way' who lives down the street telling him about it and he drove over there before I could even get out of bed.

"By the time I could get to the church, they were wheeling him out on a gurney. He tried to go into the church, kept babbling something about Roggie, saving Roggie – getting him out of the fire and being sorry. It didn't make sense to me."

Rose felt a sickening feeling in the pit of her stomach, as though someone had punched her hard. The walls, the ceiling, the floor began to whirl around her.

"Sis, are you okay?" Paul moved toward her.

Get control, Rose, she told herself. *This means nothing, the babblings of a stroke victim. He was probably still grieving over Roggie; it was uppermost on his mind. It would be what he would speak about. Nothing to it.*

"I need some sleep."

"Yeah, kid. You look whipped."

"Listen, if you get tired of Norville and company, come on up to the house. We've got plenty of room."

"I just might take you up on that."

She nodded and turned toward the door. "Help me- let me say goodbye to Papa."

She went into the room which was still crowded. *Why don't the nurses run us all out?*

She worked her way past the family to her father's side, "Papa, I've got to go home now. I need to get some rest. I'll be back tomorrow."

"Willa Rose." he whispered and moved his left hand in a jerky motion, beckoning her to move closer. She saw his right hand, drawn in an odd position, paralyzed? She moved close, put her ear next to his lips, "I love you, Willa Rose, my little Rosie. Forgive me."

"Oh Daddy!" she gasped, aware of everyone's attention. "I love you too. We'll talk in the morning."

He nodded weakly. She looked up into the family's

180

questioning looks. "We all might want to leave him rest," she drawled. She thought of what she'd just said, how she'd said it. *Boy, I must be tired. I sound like I just came down from the hills.*

She found Brew with a happy Stevie in the hospital cafeteria. Stevie was digging into a bowl full of ice cream, getting as much on him as in him. Brew was studiously finishing off a cone. Taking a bite, analyzing it as if figuring where his next assault should take place before taking the next.

"Look at you two! I can't leave you alone for a minute. You've ruined his supper!"

"Ice cream's nourishing food, Rose."

"*Ice cream?*"

"Sure, it's got milk, eggs, there was a cherry on top of the sundae. You've got three of the five food groups there."

"I'm going to have to go back to Germany before you ruin him!"

"Aw, Rose, they're only little once. Let'em enjoy it."

Rose had discovered, to no great surprise, that all her brothers and sisters had come home, taking all the available bedrooms the family left in Illinois had to offer. She reflected wryly she *had* invited Paul to stay with her at the house. She didn't know what kind of shape it would be in since Rennee moved out. Brew had mentioned that he could put his cot in Uta's old room if she needed the company. She was grateful for that. The thought of staying alone at the house with the baby, for no matter how short a time, was depressing.

Sadness had swept over her at the mention of Uta. She thought of the small, frail girl, and how she died. Then she thought of Roggie. She saw his face before her again, it was never far away, and fought back the tears. How was she going to react to going back - there?

It was hard to think of the house without the memories of Roggie coming back. She looked at the house now as if it were the first time. She thought of Roggie and Danny that first summer. *We were so happy then - now?* She had no answer. There was still much love in the family, but it was clouded by grief. Even when there was laughter, which had once flowed so freely in the Schneider house, it seemed hollow.

She looked again at the house. For the first time she felt the sensation it was looking back at her the others had experienced. She fought another shiver not caused by the cold.

The Homestead

It's those windows. The windows and the memories...

There was no joy in this homecoming, only sadness. Too much sadness.

"Are you okay Rose?" Brew interrupted the flow of thought. She was grateful.

She sighed, "Yes, just- thinking."

He put an arm around her, a rare show of physical affection. "It'll be okay, Sugar." he gave her a kiss on her forehead. It reminded her of her father years ago. This surprised her. Brew was not one for displays of affection, always careful to not have his motives misconstrued.

"It's cold out here, 'ya think?"

She nodded, tears forming in her eyes.

"We'd better get inside."

Rose nodded. *Welcome home, kids.*

She nodded unconsciously at the picture of the girl in the window. She could almost have sworn it nodded back. She giggled at her imagination. She fiddled with the key in the lock. It was stuck.

"Oh," Brew said, coming forward. "I had all the locks changed when Rennee moved out. You can't be too careful, you know." He gave her a couple keys. "These are copies. I got matching locks all around. One key fits all," he said as he opened the door for her. "Welcome home, Rose."

Rose was amazed and touched. He had brought, or had hired someone to bring, down all the furniture stored upstairs. She'd expected to have to "camp out" with all the furniture locked away in the upstairs bedrooms.

"Welcome home," he said. "I had the Haupt boys help me out."

Rose felt a load lift off her shoulders. She was home.

Rose trembled before the threat of her father's anger. Her parents had always believed in "Spare the rod, hate the child." To find out about this direct disobedience, coupled with lying, was devastating, and all for a Catholic?

She had been sent to her room. She remembered hearing her father rage while her mother prayed loudly.

Then, he stopped ranting. She heard his heavy foot on the stairs. Her heart stopped beating. She was too terrified to look when the door to her bedroom flew open to reveal him standing there, panting heavily, his heavy razor strap in his hand.

182

He raised it above his head and brought it heavily down on her thigh. Her body convulsed in agony as the leather bit into the flesh beneath her thin dress.

Her father beat her methodically, quoting a scripture with each stroke to emphasize the depth of her sins, "Rebellion is as the sin of witchcraft!" "If a man have a stubborn and rebellious son, they shall stone him with stones!" She groveled on the floor, curling her body into a fetal position to present as small a target as possible and protect sensitive areas of her body. The belt continued to fall, each lash of his belt biting into her flesh. She gritted her teeth to keep from screaming out and giving him the satisfaction of hearing her cry. She fought to keep her modesty as her dress would fly up, exposing her, but the belt showed no mercy. When she would reach to pull her clothes into place, her arms and hands would take the blows meant for the exposed body part. She had never felt such agony before. Her humiliation was increased when she lost control of her bodily functions and soiled herself. Still, the beating continued. Each verse became engraved in her memory. To that day she could quote each one.

Then he stopped.

Rose remembered looking up at her father through tear filled eyes as he stood there staring at her blankly. His entire body was shaking with rage, holding the belt in his hand. Then she remembered his eyes focusing, as if realizing for the first time what he had done. He looked down at her, his face beginning to crack with emotion. He turned and fled from the room.

Rose lay on her floor, sobbing, for some time. Eventually, she gathered the strength to go into the bathroom to wash. The wet rag sent daggers of pain through her when it touched the angry red welts over her body. She could see that the skin between the welts was already discoloring into varying shades of blue and purple. Her mother came into the bathroom.

Not a word was spoken as Emily looked over Rose's bruises with a not ungentle gaze. She left for a moment, to return with a jar of ointment, which she applied tenderly to Rose's wounds. When that job was done, Emily sighed, and broke the silence.

"We might as well get on with it, honey," she said with resignation.

Rose was forced to submit to a humiliating examination by her mother and older sisters to ensure she was still "pure." Later on, lying on her bed, fighting the physical and emotional

183

pain and humiliation, she made a vow, to run away so her father would never have the chance to beat her again.

There was a knock at the door, "Willa Rose?" It was her father.

She didn't answer. He entered the room, his head hung low. "Honey, I love you," he said, his voice choking. "I didn't mean-" he began sobbing. "You have never lied to us or disobeyed us before..."

Rose's eyes welled with tears. She wanted to go to him and hug him, but something in her refused. No, she thought. Let him cry as he's made me cry. I want him to hurt. He's right. I've always been the good girl of the family. The one time I disobey this is what I get! I don't deserve this!

"It's hard being a parent," he said. "I just want what's best for you. It's dangerous being a young, beautiful girl these days..."

He's never called me beautiful before. Does he mean it? Or does he just feel guilty? He should!

"I'm just trying to protect you..."

Who's going to protect me from you, Papa? *She almost broke down crying, but pride won out.*

Her father came over to the bed and put a tender hand on her shoulder. She recoiled, almost as much from revulsion as physical pain. He drew his hand back. It was too soon for this, he sensed.

"Maybe one day when you have children, you'll understand. I just pray you can forgive me, Sweetheart." He left her to her bitterness.

Rose let out a shriek and sat up in bed. She gasped for breath as she tried to orient herself. It took her a moment to realize she wasn't in the apartment in Germany. She was home, in Illinois, at the Homestead.

Home.

Funny, since returning from Germany, it didn't seem like home any more. There were too many memories... too much pain...

She shook herself. *Don't go there, Rose, you'll just start crying again.*

She looked over at the tiny form snuggled next to her in bed. Stevie. He had taken to climbing in bed with her at night.

She and Roger had just broken him in to sleeping in his own room. That was in Germany.

She didn't expect Stevie to sleep in a separate bedroom now. Not in this house. But he'd even refused to sleep in the bed Brew had set up in the corner of the master bedroom. It was probably just the change in surroundings she reflected.

Don't go getting too spooky, Rosie.

She was awake now. She looked at the clock on her nightstand. It was 3:00 a.m. *What is it about three in the morning in this house?*

The dream-nightmare disturbed her. She knew it would do no good to try to go back to sleep. Checking Stevie to ensure he was sleeping soundly, she crept down the stairs to the kitchen. Perhaps, some hot chocolate would calm her enough so she could rest.

Shortly thereafter she was sitting at the kitchen table, mulling over the nightmare in her mind. It was the same recurring dream she'd suffered for years; reliving that same awful night when her father discovered she'd been sneaking around seeing Roger. She hadn't had that dream in years. She believed she'd finally been able to get over the trauma, the anger, and the bitterness. Now, here it was again, the dream, the memories, and all the old emotions resurfacing. Tonight, the dream had seemed so real; she could almost feel the bite of the strap against her flesh.

You can forgive but you cannot forget...

Where did that come from? I have forgiven. How can you forget something like that?

But you had forgotten, hadn't you? You'd pushed it to the back of your mind. Out of sight, out of mind...

Until tonight...

She physically shook the thought off as a chill brushed through her. Perhaps, it was the house and the sadness now associated with it. First Roggie's death, then Uta's. She almost wept as she recalled the safety she'd once felt here, the sense of security. Now, it was ruined- soiled, like everything else in her life had been.

She recalled the looks of concern and alarm on Roger and Danny's faces when she told them she was going to have to stay in the Homestead. She thought they were over-reacting. She caught herself wondering sometimes if the family had fallen prey to some sort of mass hysteria, blowing coincidences and otherwise innocent occurrences out of proportion.

She took a sip of her chocolate and frowned at her dull reflection gazing back from the glazed mug.

You can forgive, Rose, but you can't forget. Have you really forgiven?

There it goes again. Why can't I shake this?

She thought of her father again, lying in the hospital bed, a shadow of the man who'd once been. She thought back to that awful night so many years ago, as he looked on her with tears in his eyes.

"Maybe one day when you have children, you'll understand. I just pray you can forgive me, Sweetheart." He left her to her bitterness.

No, papa, I'll never understand how you can beat someone you're supposed to love this way. I will never do this to my children! As for your prayers, save them, you're going to need them for yourself!

Her eyes teared as she thought of that vow. She thought of Roggie. She realized she now understood her papa. She thought of Roggie. If she and Roger had been stricter would he have gotten into the situations he'd gotten into? She had tried to be lenient where her parents had been harsh.

What do you do, God? My parents were strict and pushed me into sin, I was easy and my boy fell into sin! What do you do God?

No one can push you into sin, Rose.

I thought I was doing it right. We were married.

But you lied – were you married?

She started to take another sip of her chocolate, realized it was cold and set the cup down.

You can forgive but you can't forget…

Blessed art thou O God who forgives us our sins and remembers them no more.

You can forgive but you can't forget…

Blessed art thou O God who casts our sins as far from us as the east is from the west.

Rose, I've forgiven you – can you forgive your Father? Can you forgive yourself?

"Oh, Daddy!" The words and tears poured out from her soul, "Forgive me! God forgive me! God, help me forgive my daddy!"

As she wept and the years of bitterness were swept away. As she cried, head down on folded arms she could swear someone had put his arms around her and was holding her close, hugging her, comforting her. She didn't know how long she remained at the table, but when she rose, she knew something was different, she felt as though a burden was lifted from her shoulders. She felt clean for the first time in years.

It was a weary Rose who pulled her car up to the house a few days later. She'd spent most of the afternoon with Harold, who was doing much better. They'd had a good talk. Harold didn't remember a thing about the fire or the stroke, so Rose was left with a big question mark about his remarks about Roggie that night. They would probably never know what happened in that church. She had just walked through the door when she heard the phone ring.

She answered it with dread; lately no news over the phone had been good. "Hello?"

"Hey Sis!" it was Paul. He'd been drinking, "I'm at a place called Kopfs in New Hauptstadt! Everyone knows you here. You and the family are celebrities. Did you know that? Hey, Sis, since when you been hanging out in taverns?" he was teasing.

"The joy of living in small towns, I guess."

"How do I get to your place?"

"I guess I'll have to come get you..." *I probably need to, you sound pretty tight, brother.*

"Don't bother, Sis. Here's Brew! Hey, Brew, old buddy, how's it going!" She could hear Brew's voice in the background. "We'll be there in a few minutes, Sis."

Or hours, or days, with those two when they get together. She hung up. She looked around apprehensively. Where'd Stevie go?

"Stevie?" she began searching for him. Upstairs, she heard a shuffling noise and a child's giggle. *Great! He's climbing the stairs on his own, something else to worry about.*

She ascended the stairs. At the top she saw him outlined by the northern sky, standing in the bedroom window, his hands and face pressed against the glass, staring outside. Her heart began beating rapidly, *O Lord, don't let him fall through!* She didn't know how secure the window was. It had been years since

187

Roger had caulked and repainted the windows. All the dangers flashed through her mind.

She stealthily crept up on the baby in the window, who still stared silently, motionless outside. She feared making a noise, lest, startled, he'd go through the window to his death on the ground below.

She was a few inches away from him. Still he didn't move. She reached out, grabbed him beneath his arms. Quickly, she whisked him away from the window in a circular motion and in a moment of triumph discovered she was holding – nothing.

The baby had disappeared.

She stood in the middle of her bedroom battling a mixture of emotions, confusion, fear, anger. She heard Stevie from downstairs, "Grammaw?"

My baby!

She rushed to the head of the stairs. He was standing at the foot, looking up curiously. He grinned when he saw her. "Grammaw!"

"Where you been, honey?" she asked, not expecting an answer as she ran down the steps. She picked him up in her arms, kissing him, extracting giggles and a mild struggle. She held him close and looked around at the house angrily, "You won't get him! You won't get him!"

It was several hours later when Paul and Brew finally arrived at the house. She'd expected as much. It was the same old story. They decided to stay for one more round. Then two. Then three. Then, who was keeping count any more? Then, they remembered Rose, remembered she'd probably have dinner waiting for them, be angry because they were late.

They were relieved to find she'd already fed Stevie, and was calmly waiting, their dinner warming in the oven for them.

"Spaghetti!" Paul exclaimed happily. "I love your spaghetti!"

"I know," Rose said. "That's why you couldn't wait to get over here for dinner."

"Aw, Sis," Paul said with a mock sadness. "You know how it is..."

"Yeah, Paul, I know how it is." She turned to Brew. "So did you drink the place dry?"

"Naw," Brew said matter-of-factly, slurping a noodle into his mouth. "Excuse me. Naw, we left enough for the others. It was the humane thing to do."

"You'll get the Nobel Prize."

"So, what's eating at you?" Brew asked.

It wasn't a casual question. Rose was surprised, though she shouldn't have been. He'd always been able to read her moods. He was a freak of nature. He could drink enough for two men, but never show it.

"I had an incident."

Brew immediately understood what she was speaking of. Paul was lost.

"This house is haunted." Rose said matter of factly. We've had a lot of freaky things happen here.

"Like what?" Paul asked, interested.

She explained what had just happened to her upstairs. Then she told him of all the stories, the footsteps, the apparitions Danny and Brew had seen, faces in the windows. Paul listened skeptically, interested in the good stories, but doubtful.

"You saw these things?" he asked Brew.

Brew nodded.

"What? You can't take my word for it you've got to ask Brew?"

"In the mouths of two witnesses let every word be established," he said, grinning.

"PKs - always good with the Bible when it's handy. Papa'd be proud."

"He was always quick with a verse in a pinch..." Paul thought a moment. "Which bedroom did you say was the most haunted?"

"I'd have to say the south bedroom, Danny's and Roggie's."

"I want to spend the night there."

"I don't think that's a good idea, Paul."

"Aw c'mon, I want to see the ghosts."

"You might get more than you bargained for, Paul."

"Sis, there ain't much I haven't seen or done. I want to see the ghost, old what's her name, Marina?"

"Molina," Rose corrected. "Remember what Mama said, 'be careful what you wish for...'"

"Hey, if she's good lookin' I'll sleep with her!" he laughed at that. Rose and Brew didn't join in.

"All right, big brother," Rose finally said. "You're too drunk to drive home anyway."

189

The Homestead

Rose woke suddenly. Stevie was sleeping soundly next to her. She looked at her alarm clock. It was three a.m. She could feel it again. The presence. For the first time since her return. At the bottom of the steps. Thick, heavy, as though the house were breathing.

She felt a coldness to the depth of her soul. Whatever it was. It was standing at the foot of the steps. She could feel it as if it was looking up the stairs, ready to begin its old routine. Then she heard the steps begin, slowly plodding up the steps.

A feeling of dread filled her as it reached the top of the steps, and then left as it turned the corner into the middle bedroom. *It's headed toward Paul. Well, brother, you're about to get your wish.*

The steps receded toward the south bedroom and stopped. *The door. He's closed the bedroom door like I told him.* Her senses were alert, tingling. She could hear the jiggling of the doorknob. Now the dread and fear were replaced by hilarity. She knew what was coming next. She wondered if Paul were asleep, passed out, or awake, aware of what was happening.

"All right Sis, Brew," came Paul's voice. "Very funny! I'm scared!"

Wham! The door burst open. Paul was out of bed; old combat instincts aroused, poised, ready to pounce on - nothing.

"Sis?" he whispered. "Brew?"

Silence. He was alone. No, there was something there.

He waited for a moment for something to happen. Finally, he shook the fear off.

"That's what I get for listening to all those ghost stories."

Still, the door had been busted open. He'd have to ask Brew how he rigged that in the morning. Now, it was time to go back to sleep.

He crawled back into bed. He was just about to go back to sleep when he felt a tug at his feet. "What on -" Before he knew it he was on the floor, the bunk bed upturned.

"All right!" he demanded of no one in particular, "Fun is fun, but it's time to knock it off!"

He got up, switched on the light, and peered all around him. He set the bed upright. He didn't know how Rose and Brew were doing this but he was going to get them back in the morning.

He crawled back in the bed. This time, sleep came a little less easy. Again, he began to doze and found himself being thrown on the floor. This time he rolled as he hit the floor, springing to his feet in a combat stance, his head darting this way and that to spot the unseen assailant.

"All right, this is it! Rose! Brew!"

In her bed, Rose was giggling now, trying not to make a noise. He'd asked for it. The house was having fun. She put a protective arm around Stevie, but she knew they were safe for this night, at least. She wondered if Brew, downstairs, was aware of what was going on.

"All right," Paul said. "One more time."

He crawled back into bed. Almost immediately he found himself on the floor again.

"Lady," he pleaded, convinced. "I apologize for everything I said. All I want to do is get some sleep..."

Now he felt a caress on his cheek. Was he really losing it? Then a weight settled in the bed beside him. Something was nestling beside him, caressing him all over. He was almost beginning to enjoy it when he realized there was no one there.

"All right!" he said, jumping up from the bed. "I've had it!" He charged out of the room and ran down the steps. Rose found him the next morning asleep on the sofa.

At breakfast, Paul described what had happened, "Sis, I can't believe you live here."

"Why not? It's home."

"Yeah, but, there's something seriously wrong here."

"This is my home. So far, the ghosts, spirits, whatever have never hurt anyone. You learn to live with it."

"Not me." Paul said, finishing his coffee. "Sis, I hope you won't mind if I never spend the night with you again."

The next Saturday Brew and Rose were sitting at the table; Brew reading his paper, Rose writing letters to Roger and Danny. Stevie was upstairs sleeping.

Rose paused in her writing, and lifted her head, listening, "Did you hear that?" she asked.

"What?" Brew looked up from his paper.

"It sounded like talking, children's voices." She remembered that summer day when it was just Roger and her in the house. She heard Stevie speak now, giggling. There was more than one voice. *Oh, my Lord, Stevie!*

She bolted up the stairs. She was half way up when she heard him squeal with delight. She reached the top of the steps, the door to her bedroom slammed shut. "No! No! You stinking

191

sons-o-" *No! Get hold of yourself, Rose, this isn't the way,* came a voice from inside her.

She stopped pounding on the door, from within she could hear Stevie giggling and talking to someone. Worse, she could hear something talking back.

Rose stepped back from the door. She took a deep breath, said a short prayer. "I command you in the Name of Jesus Christ, open this door -NOW!"

The door swung open.

Rose rushed in, took her baby up in her arms, holding him close. Again, she looked up at the ceiling, the house, "I told you you can't have him!"

A voice in her head spoke, a wild thought? *Yes we will, if we want him.*

Over my dead body! she answered back.

That can be arranged. Came the answering thought.

Was she going crazy? No, she knew better. Danny was right. There was something evil in the house.

She made up her mind. Her father was out of the woods. His doctors were preparing him with physical therapy to go home. There was no real need to stay.

She turned to Brew, who'd overcome his fear of the second floor to follow her. "Brew, I'm getting Stevie out of here today."

Her heart nearly broke when she saw the old man's face. He dropped his head sadly, "I s'pose it's for the best." Was he crying? "Pack up. We'll get you to the airport."

Rose agonized for years if she would have done- could have done anything different. As she and Stevie said goodbye at Lambert, she couldn't have known it was the last time she would see Brew. She wished she'd known how sick he was; she wished he'd told her. Then, it wasn't like Brew to worry anyone with his problems.

She kicked herself for not noticing the sadness in his eyes, even when he picked them up at the airport. Then again, how was she supposed to have noticed? She was up to her neck in her own problems.

As they stood at the gate, Brew hesitated a moment before saying goodbye. "Well," he sighed, "I guess this is it, Rosie."

"Yeah," she hugged his neck, "I'll miss you, Brew."

"I know, I know, but you'd better get back across the pond to your family. I'll be okay."

"Sure you will. You're still coming to visit us this summer, right?"

"Sure, kid. I wouldn't miss it for the world; we still got to visit Munich, right?"

"Right."

The last call for boarders came over the speaker.

Rose's smile faded, "I guess this is it."

"Yeah." He paused, "Hey Rosie."

"What?"

"Tell the family how much I love them."

"They know that, Brew."

"I know they know. Just tell them, huh?"

She looked at him closely. "Sure," she said quietly. She brushed away the feeling that swept her, "Brew, you'd better be careful, you're starting to get sentimental in your old age."

Brew grinned, that was better. "Too many soaps, I guess. Retirement's killing me. You'd better go."

"Yeah," she said, reluctant now to leave but knowing there was really no choice.

"Thanks for everything," he said, turning and walking away. Rose always felt he didn't want her to see him cry.

She watched him for a moment, fighting the sadness. Maybe she did suspect. But she had a plane to board, a husband and son waiting for her, a baby to raise.

Hank Thompson found Brew a few weeks later in the dining room. Noticing Brew's car parked in front of the house for several days, he went to investigate. An autopsy ruled the cause of death as heart failure. It was also revealed Brew was in the advanced stages of stomach cancer. It turned out that Brew had a sister in Chicago. As the official next-of-kin, she handled all the funeral arrangements. By the time she was able to locate and notify Rose, Brew had already been buried in St. Louis.

Chapter 12
July 19, 2009

...Lest Satan should get an advantage over us; for we are not ignorant of his devices.

(2 Corinthians 2:11)

"Pastor," the young man across the desk said sadly, "We don't know what to say. Laurie has never done anything like this before..."

The Reverend Dean Grossman of the Delphi First Holiness World Fellowship Church leaned forward, his elbows on his desk, his eyes kindly studying the couple sitting across from him. They had been members of his church for years. They had been here when he arrived - he thought back, *Could it have been twelve years before?* Had he been there that long? *No – it was fifteen years next month.*

How could he forget the happiest day of his life – to candidate for pastor at the church he'd grown up in and be accepted? There'd been no real reason to move. He was happy. The congregation was happy. *Fifteen years?*

Things had run so smoothly. Delphi's church was stable, no great growth, but no real decline, either. He had his hard core of members who stayed with him no matter what. They were the "church families," the founders and children of the founders who had an investment, a stake in the fellowship, the backbone of the church. Then there were those who came and stayed. They made up for the ones who came and left, or died or moved away to find work elsewhere. There were always the transients. Not many in a town like this, but enough to keep the mixture from totally stagnating.

Fifteen years of pastoring the church, three years before that he'd been Youth Minister. Except for Bible College he'd spent his entire life at the same church. He'd seen splits, arguments over the color of the carpeting, which hymnal to buy, even whether to take up offering at the beginning or end of the service.

Never had he encountered anything like this.

Del and Becky Neustadt had been members of the church

194

since they were children. He had performed their wedding ceremony as one of his first duties as pastor of the church. He had dedicated each of their three children to the Lord, had baptized the two oldest ones, Jennie, fourteen, and Rhonda, twelve. There were problems with their youngest, Laurie, ten.

Alfreda Miller had come to him about a month ago, telling him Laurie had told her Sunday School Class that God was a fairy tale made up by kings years ago to keep the peasants in line.

"Where did you hear such a thing?" Alfreda asked, stunned.

"Johnny."

"Who's Johnny?"

"He's my friend. He's smart!"

"He's a liar."

"No he's not!" Laurie answered back, getting angry, "You're a liar! You're telling all those lies about Jesus and all his disciples about what holy men they were. They were hypocrites! Johnny told me they were all gay!"

"Gay?" Alfreda couldn't believe her ears. Such blasphemies coming from such a young girl.

"Don't you think it's funny all those guys running around the desert without any women?"

"Laurie! You don't know what you're saying! I rebuke you!"

"Pastor," she said later in Dean's office, "I wanted to lay hands on her right there. I didn't know whether to cast the devil out of her or spank her!"

"You did the right thing by sending her out of the class, Alfreda. I'll talk to Del and Becky. We need to find out who this Johnny is..."

He'd gone over to the Neustadt's house, the old Felder Place, that Sunday afternoon. They moved just a block from his parents' home the previous year. That meeting had been inconclusive, unsatisfactory. When the parents brought Laurie down to explain herself, she'd acted totally ignorant of the entire incident, claimed she didn't remember a thing about talking back to Mrs. Miller. She'd actually begun crying when Del pressed the issue.

After she was excused, Dean and the Neustadts stared dumbly at one another.

"What do you make of it, Pastor?" Del finally asked.

195

"I believe she actually doesn't remember anything. She'd probably pass a polygraph test."

"But Miss Alfreda wouldn't lie about such a thing," Becky said, "I've known her since I was a girl. She was my fifth grade Sunday School teacher."

"I know." Dean said finally, "Maybe she was just spouting something she'd heard on television or at school. Let's keep an eye on her and see. This may be an isolated incident. If we make too big a deal of it, we could push her into worse behavior."

It didn't take long. That morning, Cindy, his wife, had been carrying the attendance books and offering from the Sunday school classes to the church office when she heard voices come from one of the vacant classrooms at the end of the hall. There was a strange giggling. Suspecting foul play, she'd investigated, to find Laurie in the corner of the classroom urinating on a Bible.

As he stared across his desk at the Neustadts, he was at a loss for words. He had heard of such things, *read* of such things, but he'd never in all his years encountered such – he searched for the word – *blasphemy*. He shuddered at the thought. This was the realm of Satanists, twisted teenagers looking for kicks, grim, dark robed adults who rejected all that was holy. Not a ten-year-old girl... This was the stuff of horror movies. This was the act of someone- *No, don't go there,* he thought. That flew in the face of everything he'd learned at Bible College. This was a born-again, Holy Ghost filled family. The fellowship's (the WHF never referred to itself as a denomination) doctrine was plain on this. When a person was filled with the Spirit, he or she was sanctified and didn't have to worry about the devil any longer.

"Have you thought of psychological counseling?"

Del looked over to Becky, then replied, "We've been hoping you'd help us in that area, Pastor..."

Dean was taken aback. He hadn't expected this. Of course, as pastor, he'd taken counseling courses at Bible College, even before it became fashionable. He'd attended the occasional seminar held by the fellowship. He could - and did - handle pre-marital counseling, informing young couples of the meaning and importance of their vows, assisting them in understanding the solemnity of what they were about to enter in. He'd mediated between couples who were having problems, helped them get along. He even handled the occasional child who misbehaved in school, tried to teach them how Jesus wanted them to live. This was over his head.

He felt so inadequate. He had spoken to pastors in larger towns and cities, listened to some of the things they encountered. Such encounters made him thankful for Delphi, for his church. Now they wanted him to counsel this girl?

"I don't know," he began carefully. *They have such faith in me, how can I let them down?* "I was thinking she might need some professional help, an expert in this sort of misbehavior."

"Pastor," Becky pleaded. "We've looked. When she first began acting out, when was it?"

"What?"

"You know? When she began using the words?" Becky's frustration was evident.

"What words?" Dean interjected.

"Awful profanity, Pastor." Del answered. "One day, a few months after we moved into the house, she got into a fight with Rhonda over a TV show, some awful show about witches and demons- it's supposed to be a comedy-"

"I know about it," Dean said wearily. He'd helped lead a petition campaign to have it removed from the St. Louis station. All the local stations had picked up on the story, made everyone involved look like the town council at New Salem during the witch trials. He'd told himself that was the last time he'd go out on a limb like that. "Go on."

"Well, when Rhonda told her that we had forbidden them to watch that show, Laurie let out with a string of cuss words - Pastor, I'd never heard some of them before. I had to go to the library and look some of them up. Some of them was in another language."

Dean closed his eyes. *This is worse than I thought. I have to ask,* "Where do you think she learned those words?"

"I asked," Becky answered. "She told me she heard them from Johnny."

"Johnny?" He remembered, "Oh yes, her imaginary friend."

"She started talking about him, playing with him right after we moved in. I didn't think much of it; a lot of kids have imaginary playmates. But..." She paused, thinking, "Things have gotten positively weird with Johnny lately."

How so?

"Well, a few weeks ago, Laurie was playing on the swing set in back. I called her in for lunch; I heard her talking to

197

someone, telling them she'd be right back after lunch. When she came into the house I asked her who she was talking to. She said, 'Johnny,' he was still on the swing. I glanced outside, I don't know, call it curiosity,"

"And?" Del was concerned; this was obviously news to him.

"I had the strangest feeling looking at the swing. It was still swinging, like someone was in it, moving it."

"Could it have been the wind?" Dean asked.

"No, the movement was smooth. It wasn't like it was still swinging after she jumped out. Like I said, it was smooth, and instead of slowing down, it seemed to be moving faster and faster, as if whoever was on it was pumping it up." she looked down at her hands, folded in her lap, "I was afraid, I didn't know why."

Dean felt a growing dread, thoughts were stirring in his mind, memories, long buried, were digging their way out of the tombs in which he had laid them. "Have there been any other strange things?"

"Like what?"

"I don't know," he said. He was trying to find a way to approach the subject, trying to sort through the tangle of images in his mind, "Like strange noises?"

Del and Becky both stared at him. He suddenly felt uncomfortable.

Del spoke, "What kind of noises, Pastor?"

"Footsteps in the night?"

"How'd you know about those?"

Ye shall know the truth... All right, Dean, it's time to face it, you've run long enough.

"Years ago..." he hesitated, how to begin? "My sister lived in this house. I used to stay with her, keep her company. Things happened here."

"Why didn't you warn us if you knew?" Becky asked, tears forming in her eyes.

He dropped his head; he couldn't bear to look her in the eye. "I'm sorry. It was a long time ago... I didn't think - I thought it would be all right, after all these years..."

"So you thought!" Becky was angry now.

"Calm down, now honey-" Del put his arm around her, trying to console her.

"Calm down?" she shrieked, "You can say that when you know what is happening to our daughter and you could have

198

stopped it?"

Dean sat in silence. He was stung by the unfairness of her accusations, though he knew she was speaking out of frustration and fear. Yet, he couldn't help but feel there was some truth to the accusation. Memories were assaulting his mind now. Specters he had fought back for years. He searched for the term, *repressed memories.*

His mind raced back in time to the night he'd been at the house with Rennee. Rennee had been rocking Earl, her baby; there was a knock at the door. They could see the outline of someone standing outside on the porch. Dean rose to answer the door; he flicked the light switch for the porch light. It failed to come on, burned out. He remembered the shock, the disbelief, the horror, at the sight, which greeted him as he opened the front door to see the creature standing on the porch. He backed away from the entrance and it followed him into the house, barely recognizable as having once been human.

Shreds of uniform hung from the horribly scorched figure. It walked into the house and said, with Rog Baumer's voice, "Mom, I'm home, just like I promised!"

That had been the last straw. He remembered the noises that came from the rooms upstairs, the ones that were locked tight. He remembered the footsteps he heard the nights he spent with Rennee, running upstairs all night. He closed his eyes and reopened them as if to erase the thoughts from his mind.

Actually, he now realized, he had pushed the events in this house away from him. He had buried them in a dark recess of his memory where, hopefully, they'd not be disturbed. He had actually forgotten about the apparition in the doorway.

Until now.

For years he'd passed the house and felt uneasy. He remembered Rennee had lived there once. He remembered spending nights there. He remembered Rennee moving out quickly and had actually forgotten why. Now he knew. He couldn't believe what his mind was telling him was true.

He remembered the Halloween night in 1970. He'd been out trick-or-treating with Scotty Thompson, LeRoy Stang, and his younger brother Dale. It had been a good night for the small town. Their bags were bulging with loot. It was late and they were headed for home to get the final tally.

"Hey, look," LeRoy said. "There's a light on at the Felder Place! Let's go check it out."

"Oh, no," Scotty said. "There's no way I'm going to that place on Halloween night…"

"What's the matter, you scared?" LeRoy taunted, "You've been living across the street from the place all your life!"

"Yeah, but I never been in there and I ain't going there now."

"Boy, and your dad's an undertaker-"

"Funeral director," Scotty corrected. "What's that got to do with anything?"

"You ought to be used to dead people-"

"It's my dad that deals with dead bodies- and they stay dead!"

"What about you, Grossman? You ain't said nothing."

Dean remembered the fear that gripped him at being confronted by Stang. "I got nothing to say."

"Are you afraid to go up there?"

"It's probably just Danny's Uncle Brew. Anyway, what have I got to prove? After all, I've spent the night in the house!"

"Yeah, but not for long." LeRoy paused a moment, "If it is Brew, he won't have candy, but he'll give us money! I'm going, whether you sissies come or not."

LeRoy had taken off to the front door of the house, the others following reluctantly. He peered inside through the frosted glass window. He saw Rose's shadow box on the wall opposite. He saw Brew's reflection in the mirror in the shadow box. He knocked on the door.

"This is weird," he said, "the old guy's not moving. He's just sitting at the table in the kitchen, staring straight ahead."

"Knock again, louder." Henry suggested.

"I think we need to get out of here." Dean said, warily. His brother Dale nodded.

"Are you afraid Rog Baumer's going to jump out and shout, 'Boo!' at you?"

"What do you know about it?" Dean was growing angry now.

"Calm down, Grossman, I was just playing…" LeRoy knew when to back off.

"This is weird!" Scotty snorted, his fear being overcome by curiosity. "He's just sitting there ignoring us."

"You stay here and keep knocking, Scotty I'm going around to the dining room window and knock. Maybe he'll hear me then." With that LeRoy was off around the corner of the

200

house.

Henry knocked again, this time louder.

"Be careful," Dale said. "You'll break the glass."

"That'll get his attention!"

"Hey fellas," it was LeRoy from around the corner. "Is he still sitting at the table?"

Scotty peered into the window again, "'Hasn't moved, not even blinked!"

"That's weird!" LeRoy's voice was betraying fear now."' 'Cause there ain't nobody at the table! The room's empty!"

"I'm outa here!" Scotty was across the street and on his own front porch before the others even cleared the yard.

Dean and Dale ran to their houses and only learned LeRoy had made it home safely the next day at school. When they met again, they all swore not to tell a soul about what had happened lest the town think them crazy. Within a week it was all over town there was more weirdness at the Felder Place. It was made worse when Hank Thompson, investigating Henry's story and checking up on the place, found Brew's body on the dining room floor.

How could he have forgotten all this? How could he have pretended it didn't happen? He had visited them in the house, dismissed the bad "vibes" as coming from all the stories. How could he have ignored his own nightmares in the house?

He tried to explain to the Neustadts, hoped they understood what he himself was having problems with. He didn't know if it would be enough, but it was all he could offer. They listened quietly to him and appeared to understand. After he finished, there was a moment of silence while they digested what he'd told them. Then, the question he dreaded and didn't have an answer for was asked.

"What do we do now, Pastor?"

He closed his eyes and searched his mind for an answer. *Lord, tell me what to do now.* He could sense the Neustadts' eyes on him, drawing on his spiritual strength as though he, somehow, was wiser, smarter, more in touch with God than they. He could sense they had about come to the conclusion he hadn't heard their question.

I heard you. I just don't have the answer.

He was about to say those three words, which made him feel so helpless when the answer came. The revelation hit him so hard and clear he almost jumped out of his chair. Del and Becky started.

"I believe I know of someone who can help us," he said. He smiled broadly. *No, I know there's somebody who can help us! Thank you, Lord!* "Let me make some calls and see if I can get up with him. Tomorrow's Monday, give me a couple of days."

Daniel carefully maneuvered the screwdriver past the wires. He placed the end of the tool into the slot in the screw head and began to turn. *Finally!* He'd been working on this light switch for over twenty minutes and, somehow, it wouldn't work. He'd checked it again and again, rewired the switch, traced the line to the circuit box, everything appeared to be fine. He'd flick the switch - nothing. *The Lord has given me many talents and giftings, but electronics isn't one of them.* He thought about it for a moment. *Lord, I sure could use a good electrician in this church...* In his mind's eye he could see his little congregation. *Come to think of it, Lord, I could use a carpenter, mechanic, secretary, accountant, some Sunday School teachers, actually, a full congregation would be nice, too.* Maybe then, he could quit his job and go full time. *Not that I'm complaining, Lord, I know there are seeds being planted here.*

He made what should have been the last turn, his hand slipped, the screwdriver slipped past the screw, connecting with both the positive and negative posts, sparks flared out of the switchbox, and the lights all over the church went out. *Darn it!* He swore, caught himself. He'd almost said something worse. *Watch it, Daniel. There's not as much of the old Daniel dead as there should be.*

"Swell!" he said aloud. "Now I've blown every circuit in the church."

He began to make his weary way through the large room that passed for a sanctuary to the back, where the circuit box was located. There were several small rooms Daniel and his wife, Ruth, hoped to convert into Sunday school classrooms one day. When enough people showed up to justify different classrooms. *That's it, budget or no budget. I'm hiring an electrician to fix this thing, even if I have to take the money out of my own pocket. Lord,* he prayed for the fifty-thousandth time, *If you'd just give me twelve families who were sold out to you, even couples, individuals, what we could accomplish for you!*

He looked at his watch, 4:30 PM – another half hour

before he could eat. He'd been on a dawn to dusk fast for the last week. Ruth had asked him why. He told her he didn't know why. He just felt the Lord wanted him to fast and pray.

"For how long?"

"I don't know," Daniel had replied. "I guess He'll tell me when He wants me to stop."

Now, as he checked his watch, he had the feeling the Lord didn't want him to eat today. *A total fast, Lord?* No answer, just what Daniel called the "gut feeling." *All right.*

"Daniel?" Ruth's voice came from the church "office," a cubbyhole, no bigger than a large walk-in closet, with a desk, phone, and file cabinet.

"In here!" Daniel replied.

"You've got a phone call."

"If it's Harriet, tell her I'll call back." Harriet Ross was one of the regulars who'd been coming to Daniel's Tuesday night Bible study for the past four years. She told Daniel it was her spiritual nourishment and how she survived. She was a regular member at one of the fastest growing churches in the area, but often complained she wasn't being properly fed there. Daniel had asked her why she stayed then.

"Because it's my church. I was one of the founding members. All my friends go there, and there's a great youth program for the kids. And I look forward to the women's meetings..."

So she stayed at the big church, the "in" church, went to Daniel's Bible study on Tuesdays, when there wasn't anything going on at her church, and called Daniel for prayer whenever there was a problem in her life.

He'd felt funny about praying for her the first time she called up for prayer. She was sick and wanted him to pray for healing. He didn't want to be seen as proselytizing. "Have you called your pastor?" he asked.

"Oh, no," she said, as though fearful of the thought.

"Don't you think you should?"

"Well, he's told us from the pulpit we shouldn't have to call anyone up for prayer. We should have enough faith to pray for ourselves to receive healing. One time, he actually said sickness was our own fault because we didn't have enough faith to stay healthy..."

Oh really, Daniel recalled thinking. *I guess he'd never read James' admonition for the elders to pray for the sick or*

203

recalled Job's problems.   Some folks refuse to let the Bible interfere with their religion. He asked the Lord to forgive him for that last thought.   *I shouldn't judge,* though the thought had recurred to him time and time again.

"Besides, I can't call him," she continued.

"Why not?"

"His home number's unlisted."

That's nice, a real servant's heart. Daniel had been told the pastor had recently sold his house and moved into a mansion he'd had built outside of town worth at least a million dollars. Recently, the church had approved of the purchase of a private jet so he could fly to the numerous speaking engagements he was now being invited to. After all, a man who could build a huge church like his was someone worth listening to. At one time, before he'd moved out of town to where his number was a long distance call, Daniel had been receiving calls and counseling at least twenty members of his congregation regularly.   He wondered one time if he should send the guy a bill for doing his job, then rebuked himself for thinking that. *I'm sorry Lord. Those are not his people. They are Yours. Just as I am. I'll minister to them if no one else does.*

Still, he had to fight the bitterness that often threatened to swallow him.

He'd been in the area twenty years, and it had been a constant battle to serve the Lord. To be sure, there had been missteps and mistakes in his zeal in the early days.   He remembered his first church in North Carolina. His faced burned with pain and shame for an instant. He shook it off. He had learned. And he thanked God that He still used him in spite of his failings. It was difficult now to go anywhere in the area and not run into someone who knew him from his ministry. Grateful people were always telling him how God had used him to change their lives. He was thankful for that. But it was still a struggle to just - maintain.

He often wondered on Sunday morning when he walked into the pulpit and saw the nearly empty church, where everyone was. He had his faithful few; there was Edith, who had worn about every pastor in the area out, constantly having to deliver her of demons of fear, insanity, lust, and suicide, which had tormented her family for generations.

She would pester and hound a pastor, calling him at all hours for prayer, depriving him of rest or peace of mind until he could take no more. She had been "shunned" in about every church in the area. Daniel had once quipped he could almost understand why some of the more "successful" pastors kept their home phone numbers unlisted.

Even Daniel and Ruth had been forced to cut her off when she refused to receive their ministrations and advice. Daniel had called her a "revolving door" for demons. Cast one out, she'd let it back in with seven more buddies. He realized Satan was using her to wear out preachers so he could destroy them, as Peter said, "devour" them.

They'd watched her hit rock bottom. It was painful to see, but when she returned, she was prepared to receive the blessings of the Lord. They were able to cast the devils out of her for good. She still struggled, but she was getting better, stronger. One day, Daniel hoped to see her as an effective servant of God, reaching out to those who had been afflicted as she had been. She would be a great weapon in God's army because she had been there, would understand the torment, the helplessness people in bondage experienced.

Then there was Lillian, who'd been referred to them by a Christian psychologist. Lillian had been diagnosed as paranoid-schizophrenic. She was trying to escape a family that had been into Satan worship for at least four generations. As a child they had subjected her to all forms of ritual abuse, preparing her to assume her role as priestess of the coven. She had resisted, and the more she had resisted, the more - things- they had done to her to break her spirit.

When she grew up, she escaped their grasp and had been trying to live a normal life until her breakdown. She'd been referred to a prominent Christian counselor in the area. After three years of counseling, the psychologist, a friend of Ruth's, realized she had gone as far as she could to help Lillian. She prayed about what to do, where to go. Daniel and Ruth's names came to mind. She called Ruth and asked if they'd be willing to meet with Lillian.

What had followed was a massive four day and three night prayer and deliverance session. After that, they drove with Lillian to areas a few miles south of where Daniel and Ruth lived to the places the alleged incidents had happened. Daniel still had goose bumps when he recalled that afternoon.

They had visited an old graveyard far back in a cypress swamp. Animal skulls and bones placed in meaningful patterns attested that powerful spells had been cast over the land, marking it for the demon spirits worshipped there on nights of the full moon and certain "holy" days. Lillian shivered fearfully, glancing now and again at the branches of the trees surrounding them, for she had the gift of actually *seeing* into the spirit world. Daniel and Ruth explained to her that the Bible in 1 Corinthians, Chapter 12 called it *discerning of spirits.* She could see the demons hovering in the trees above. Daniel and Ruth had anointed the land with olive oil, praying in the Spirit all the while, reclaiming the land for Christ. He could sense the anger of the demons gathered, helpless to do anything in the face of the man and woman of God and His Holy Spirit in them. Then, the final blow came, Daniel had taken a decree, written years before by an unknown sister in Christ, read it aloud for the principalities, powers, and the rulers of darkness to hear, reclaiming the land for Jesus.

Daniel could hear their screams of anger and pain in his head as he nailed the decree to the oak tree in the center of the clearing. *It seems there's always an oak tree.*

Lillian had cried out in pain as he did it. She reached down to her ankle, where she'd felt a sharp, burning pain. She pulled up her jeans and checked beneath her sock to find a trickle of blood coming from a tiny wound. It was a deep wound. She produced a straight pin, "Look," she said.

"It's a curse pin." Daniel said, recognizing it. "They probably stuck it in you when you were little, to control you." He explained to their questioning looks, "They curse it, assign a spirit to it. When you displease them, they call on the spirit to punish you. That's probably been where your sickness has come from."

"It's kind of like voodoo." Ruth said, grasping the idea.

"Sort of, only the pin's in you, not a doll." He looked at Lillian, gave her a hug. "Honey, you are now delivered."

As he released her, he saw her eyes gaze wonderingly at the trees around them.

"What do you see now, Sugar?" he asked.

"The demons are gone."

"What do you see now?"

"Angels."

That had been one of the good times. *Fruits of the harvest.* He thought. It is what kept him going. But it seemed that for every Lillian and Edith there were ten failures. There were folks who got delivered and returned, like a dog to its vomit, to the very lifestyles and sins that had gotten them in trouble in the first place. For every Lillian and Edith who stayed and caught the vision, there had been a hundred who came, got fed, or whatever it was they wanted from the ministry and moved on.

Even the Lillians and Ediths weren't ready to minister yet. They were willing but were still too bruised from their experiences to minister to others yet.

Just give me ten who'll stay, Lord. He said again.

There were the Ed's, who had come on Tuesday nights against the will of his wife, who wanted to go to a "real" church. She didn't like all that "holy rolling stuff" either. They'd been meeting in their living room then. They'd been renting a hall in town but couldn't get the owners to give them a lease. Every time they turned around the hall was being rented out from under them for parties and other types of activities. One couldn't grow a ministry under those conditions, so Daniel and Ruth decided to save God's money for better things and hold meetings at home. He remembered hearing how his grandfather had started several churches that way.

That had lasted three years. Finally, after hearing the complaints about having a "real" church with a building, Daniel and Ruth decided to get a building. They had rented a storefront. Ed stopped coming. He told Daniel he was afraid, now that they had a building, his pastor might not understand his coming to the meetings. It was too much like attending another church.

Ed still called for prayer and advice, which Daniel, though irritated, would give.

So they plodded on. Both Daniel and Ruth worked to support both their family and their ministry. Between their three boys and work and the ministry, they had barely had time for sleep.

The finest gold is tried by the hottest fire, he'd remind himself. David was anointed king how many years before he ascended the throne? How long was Joseph in prison? How many years did Abram wander before Isaac was born? How many years did Moses tend sheep? *We've been at it just twenty, O Lord. Just twenty?*

"Daniel!" it was Ruth, interrupting his thoughts.

"Oh. I'm sorry, Babe. I got lost in the ozone."

"That's been happening a lot lately. One of these days you're going to stay lost up there."

"I rebuke that negative confession." he said, jokingly. He

207

reached out and grabbed her around the waist. "I'd rather get lost in your eyes..."

"Knock it off, Romeo!" she said, with a smile, "you've got a call."

"Who is it?" he asked, a bit irritated. He was beginning to hate phones.

"I couldn't catch his name, but he said he was from Illinois. It must be important."

"Illinois." Daniel repeated, his voice a whisper. It was suddenly cold in the room. "I'd better get it."

He almost ran to the office. He picked up the phone, "Hello?"

"Hello, Danny?" the voice sounded familiar, but he couldn't quite place it. It had been a long time since he'd been called "Danny."

"Yes."

"I don't know if you'll remember me, but my name is Dean Grossman."

A smile broke through Daniel's unease. "Sure Dean, we used to call you Deanie!"

"Yes," Dean laughed, a bit embarrassed by the childhood name.

"How's the family doing? I saw Billy at the class reunion a few years back-" Daniel had been amazed to receive the invitation, considering he hadn't graduated from Glen Haven, but in Germany, and hadn't seen any of the old bunch in over twenty-five years. It turned out they'd found his address through his mother, whom they'd found when his parents finally sold the old Homestead several years back.

"Yes," Dean said, "That's how I got your address and number. Billy -er- Bill still had the reunion book."

"Well, it's good to hear from you, Dean. What's up?"

"I don't know if you know this or not, but I'm a minister now. I've been pastor of the WHF church in Delphi for over fifteen years."

"I remember Billy saying something like that."

"Well, I called you because I've got a family with some problems I believe you can help me- them with."

Suddenly Daniel knew why Dean had called. Thoughts and images flooded his mind. *So this is what I've been fasting and praying about, Lord.* "Let me guess," Daniel said, his voice becoming different, serious, "They live in our old house."

208

"Yes." Dean answered, surprised.

"They're having problems with the 'residents' there."

Dean almost laughed at Daniel's term, despite his anxiety, "Yes."

Daniel saw a little girl in his mind's eye, "They're worried about their daughter?"

Dean's astonishment came through the line. "How did you know?"

"Oh," Daniel said with a sigh, "I just know. The Lord has a way of telling me."

"It's amazing." Dean said, awed.

"It's God." Daniel said, matter-of-factly, "I'm coming up; give me a day or so. Tell the family to move the girl out of the south bedroom." Dean was amazed again but held his peace. "Also, tell them to stop trying to communicate with the demons in the house. That's right," Daniel said, as though reading Dean's mind, "They're not ghosts, or lost spirits, they're demons. Also, one last thing, Dean..."

"What?"

"Tell the father to pray the Blood of Jesus over his family morning, noon, and night, okay?"

"Sure, Daniel." He fumbled for the words. "Daniel?"

"What?"

"Thanks."

"Dean, I have no choice. Listen, I'll call you to give you an idea of when I'll be up there so you can expect me. It'll be good to see you again. Get prayed up. Oh yes, another last thing. Tell them to get rid of that *Ouija* Board."

Daniel hung up the phone. *What to do? Well, I've got to get someone to take over Tuesday service. You never can tell, someone might just drop in. It wouldn't do for the church to be locked up or empty. I'll need someone on standby for Sunday just in case this takes longer than expected. Oh yes! Someone has to take Thursday night at the retirement home.*

He opened his desk file drawer, pulled out a folder, and studied its contents. A mixture of dread and anticipation filled him as once more he pored over every detail. *I'd better take these along, let them know what we're up against. Otherwise, they might not believe me in spite of what they've experienced. Denial. Fear. Religion. Satan's greatest weapons.*

"Ruth?" he called.

"Yes?" she answered from the door behind him, startling

him.

"We need to pack - we're going to Illinois."

"I already did that," she said, smiling smugly. She saw his surprised look. "When you went on your fast, I knew something was up so I figured I'd better be prepared. I just didn't know where."

"Good! Now we've got to-"

"I just got off the phone with Stevie. He said he'd be glad to fill in until you get back."

"What about school?"

"They're on break."

"Good!" he had thought about seeing if Stevie might want to go, but this was better, he might not be ready for the battle in which they were about to be involved. He wondered if he was. This was awful close to home - it *was* home.

"Mom said she'll keep the kids. All we need to do is call our jobs for the time off and we're set."

"Has anyone ever told you you're a good woman?"

"Only men who wanted something from me."

He raised his eyebrows at that, as if thinking it over.

"Have I told you I loved you?" he asked pulling her close to him.

"Not in the last ten minutes or so."

"I'm messing up!" he gave her a kiss.

"Daniel!" she squealed. "What if somebody walked in?"

"I'd die from shock!"

"But-"

"We've got a license to kiss!"

"I'm going to have to pray for you!"

"I'm going to need it." Now he wasn't joking.

Chapter 13
July 21, 2009

They shall put you out of the synagogues; yea, the time cometh, that whosoever killeth you will think that he doeth God a service. And these things will they do unto you because they have not known the Father, nor me.

(John 16:2)

The setting sun cast its amber glow on the western faces of the houses of Delphi. The trees between the cemetery and the town were in their full summer splendor, haloed by the sun's rays. Their leaves reminded Daniel of a golden river flowing through and around the town. He had forgotten how truly beautiful that time of the year was in the Midwest.

He felt a gentle breeze brush against his face. It was warm but not so much as to be uncomfortable. What a contrast to the searing heat they'd been having in the South that year. The sun was setting. When it finally rested behind the western horizon the temperature would drop ten or twenty degrees, change enough to require the wearing of a sweater.

He surveyed the town again. He was avoiding looking at the reason he and Ruth were standing on this lonely, beautiful hill, gathering his courage to read the inscriptions, to see the faces on the picture inlaid in the stone. He could see the high peaked roof of the Homestead, standing out from the newer, lower built houses surrounding it.

The sun's light appeared to shift suddenly, bathing the horizon in a crimson glow. Daniel shivered a bit at the effect. He now turned his gaze to the tombstone. He had only been back to the grave once in the years since Uta's death. That had been at his high school reunion a few years before.

He brought Ruth out here during that visit. He had taken her to the house first. It had been vacant for years. They had picnicked on the north lawn. Daniel recalled the feeling of being watched. He remembered looking up at the north bedroom window and seeing the figure of a woman gazing sadly at the family. He had taken a quick snapshot of the window. The picture was in his briefcase in the car.

The Homestead

Then he brought her to the cemetery. The grief had threatened to overwhelm him. It had surprised him to feel it so strongly after all those years. Both Roggie and Uta's deaths were open wounds on his soul that refused to heal. He had done everything he knew to do to let the Lord bind his wounds, to let him move on. He had asked Jesus to let His Blood wash him clean. The memories of the house still haunted him. He had asked the Lord to show him what it was that kept him from letting go, releasing the burden to Jesus. He looked from the grave to the house, far off. *Maybe that's why I'm here, Lord?*

He looked at the picture on the headstone. Ten years ago, Rose had ordered a new headstone for the graves. The new stone reminded Daniel of his great-grandfather's grave in Kentucky. It had Roggie and Uta's names, their birth dates and dates of death. Roggie's was marked with his unit and the fact he was killed in Vietnam. Above both names, centered on the stone, was the couple's wedding picture.

Daniel squeezed his eyes shut to fight back the tears he knew would come as he was plunged back to that day so many years ago at the courthouse. It was hard for him to think he now had a son older than Roggie had been when he died. Such a waste.

He thought of Roggie's son, Stevie. *He's a good kid, Rog. You'd be proud. He's so proud of you. He served his time just like the rest of the family. He's in Bible College now. I've tried to be there for him, brother. O Lord, how I miss you!*

He felt tender arms around him and realized he'd broken down crying. Ruth held him close in a motherly fashion as he wept his heart out. He struggled to regain control. He could not afford this, not now.

Soon, he was able to gather his emotions; tuck them all away. He straightened up.

"Are you all right?" Ruth asked, staring into his eyes for the true answer.

"Yes." Daniel said, his chest still heaving.

"I don't know that you should be doing this. You're too close to all this…"

"There's no one else to do it."

"Daniel, you're not the only-"

"No, I know there are others who *can* do it," he interrupted. *"but I believe I have to do this thing!* Why else would Dean have thought to call me after all these years? We

212

have to trust the Lord on this one."

"Are you up to it?"

"Yes," he said tenderly, "I have to be." He looked around at the lengthening shadows, "We'd better be going. We have work to do."

They headed toward the car when a headstone caught Daniel's eye. He stopped, stared.

"What is it?"

Daniel shook his head, fighting back new tears. "Nothing, not really," he said. He repeated the name on the tombstone in his mind, *Denise Fleischmann.*

"Daniel," Ruth started again as he started the car, "Are you sure you need to go through this? This is hitting you harder than I thought- than you thought, I expect."

Daniel was getting impatient now, "Listen Ruth, I've said it before; I don't need to have to repeat this over and over. I have to do this thing! I've lived in that house. I know what it does, what the spirits there are capable of doing. There's a little girl down there, an entire family, who needs help. I can't sit back and let the devil take her and no telling who else like he took Roggie, Uta, and Rennee!"

"Denise?" Ruth had never heard about her.

Daniel told her the story, "You were wondering what upset me so much back there as we were leaving. We passed her grave, not fifty feet from Roggie and Uta's."

"I didn't know..."

"No, baby," Daniel said, not unkindly, "you didn't. It's not your fault. I know you're worried and I know you love me." He reached out and stroked her cheek gently with the back of his hand. "I hope I don't have to tell you how much I adore you. But, like I said, we've got to trust God on this one. I have to trust Him on *every* one actually. Where I leave off He takes over. If I'm weak on this one, He'll just be stronger, right?" He paused a moment. "I think I have to do this one for me."

Strange, he thought to himself, *all those years I lived in the house with all the things that happened but I was never really afraid of the place. Now... God has not given us the spirit of fear, but of power and of love and of a sound mind!*

Whose spirit are you walking in, Daniel? Is your armor on tight? Remember, Satan is waiting to devour you in that house.

Greater is He that is in me than he that is in the world!

Yes, Daniel, but is he in you? If so, why are you so afraid?

God has not given me the spirit of fear, but the spirit of adoption, whereby we can cry 'Abba!' Father.

"Oh Daddy," Daniel muttered under his breath. "Help me now."

Delphi First Holiness World Fellowship Church hadn't changed in the almost twenty-seven years since Daniel had last seen it. There'd been no additions to the Sunday school building, no expansion of the sanctuary. *I suppose it should be comfort that some things never change,* Daniel thought wryly. It was certainly true of Delphi. The only real changes to the town were more vacant lots where houses once stood.

Dean was waiting for him. He'd called from that morning from Franklin, Tennessee, where they'd spent the previous night. They could have made the trip in one long day of driving, but had gotten a late start getting out of town. They decided to lay over for the night.

They'd also taken their time getting on the road that morning. It was the first trip without the kids in almost four years. Daniel had teasingly called the trip their "second honeymoon."

"Some honeymoon," Ruth replied. "Besides, we've never had our first honeymoon, unless you call that night at the Holiday Inn in Atlanta a honeymoon."

"You take what you can get, Sweetheart."

It was hard to believe it had been more than twenty years. Daniel had just returned from Nam. He had arrived in country at the tail end of the official U.S. active involvement in the ground war in 1972. He'd served in three different units as units were "redeployed" back to the States or deactivated as part of the withdrawal. Soldiers who had not completed their tours were transferred to remaining units. As more and more units were shipped home, Daniel had fewer options and had actually had to fight to be allowed to finish his tour. One commander thought he was crazy to want to stay when everyone else was fighting for spots on the aircraft home.

He finally had to volunteer for a Special Operations detail to stay. At the end of his tour he volunteered for Special Forces. It was while he was going through Jump School at Ft. Benning he met Ruth. One could say it was love at first sight, though it took more than two years for them to marry.

There was something between them, call it chemistry, call it a spiritual bond. It had been there from the first. He'd met her at a church in Columbus. She'd been singing in the choir. Daniel was impressed with the way she sang. The rest of the choir sounded good, but there was no life to it. Ruth sang with life, to the Lord and no one else.

It wouldn't be until later he would notice how beautiful she was – her light brown hair that revealed a red sheen in the sun, her gray-green eyes that seemed to look at one with an all-knowing love, and her smile. He remembered the first time he had looked deeply into her eyes and drowned in her smile.

There had been a fellowship afterward; Daniel had managed to strike up a conversation. He discovered she worked at the hospital on post. She wanted to be a nurse and was planning on starting her nurses training in the fall. Her father was a retired Command Sergeant Major. She was nineteen and had graduated from high school the year before. Daniel was disappointed to discover she had a boyfriend from the church she had dated through high school who was now stationed in Germany.

They would be friends. It was better that way.

Daniel consoled himself; after all, jump school was only three weeks long. After that, he'd be in the Special Forces course and other schools at Ft. Bragg for at least a year. Who knew when they'd get a chance to see one another again?

During those three weeks, though, they became close. If he could get away from his unit, they'd sit on her front porch and talk. And talk. He could speak to her about things he'd never shared with anyone else. She opened up to him about her plans, goals, and ambitions.

"I've always felt I'd end up a preacher's wife," she said one evening.

"Really?"

"I guess it's not going to happen, though."

"Why not?"

"Jamie, (her boyfriend) doesn't have the call. He's a good Christian, I guess. I mean he never misses church and used to play in the church band, but unless the Lord does a big work, I don't think he has the calling."

Daniel tried not to show his nervousness. "The Call" was a touchy subject for him. He'd felt the call as a senior in high school, but figured if he resisted, it would go away. It did - for a while.

He'd felt it again in basic training, when he knew he needed God more than he'd ever needed Him in his life. He'd gone to the chaplain one Sunday morning after chapel and spoken with him about it. The chaplain had been understanding enough. He told him to fulfill his military commitment; God would use the experience to His glory.

After his tour in Nam, though, God had seemed far away. How could he preach after doing some of the things he'd done? He was just now getting to the point where he believed God was actually listening to his prayers again. He knew enough to know God never left him or forsook him, but it was hard to accept grace and mercy when you felt so dirty.

"Maybe he's running." Daniel suggested. *Like me.*

"No, Danny." she said firmly. She was one of the few people who called him "Danny" since he left Delphi. "I don't think he'll ever have the depth of relationship to preach. I'm not saying he's not saved, mind you, I just think God has him on another track."

"So why're you going to marry him, then?"

"Oh, we dated all through high school. I suppose everyone at church expects it."

Daniel made a face. *That's a sorry reason to get married.* "But do you love him?"

She had to think about it a moment. *Good sign, Danny boy!* "I guess so," she finally said. "I've never dated anyone else." She turned with a coy smile, "unless you count yourself."

"I hardly think sitting on the front porch counts as a date."

"Let's take in a movie then."

He graduated from jump school the next week. Ruth had taken the afternoon off to drive out to Fryar Field and watch him make his qualifying jump. He'd been dropped for pushups for waving at her as he ran off the drop zone to the chute turn-in point.

She'd watched him receive his "blood wings." She winced when the black hat punched the badge into his chest. He got a chance to speak to her as the brand new paratroopers were allowed to visit for a short time with their families who had come to watch them graduate.

"We've got a 'GI' party tonight. I don't know if I'll get a chance to see you before I go."

"I'll wait up. Come by when you get off. That is, if you

216

want to."

Daniel remembered looking into her green eyes. Of course he wanted to.

That night, Daniel was able to slip out of the barracks; he caught the bus into town. He heaved a sigh of relief when he saw the light on in the living room. Walking up the sidewalk, he could see her sitting in an armchair, watching television. He stood in the door watching her for a moment before he knocked.

She looked up and smiled, "I told you I'd wait."

"I know. I take off for Bragg in the morning."

"So soon?"

"Yeah, my class begins in a week. I'll have to inprocess."

"I'll write you."

"You don't have to."

"I know. I want to."

"What about Jamie?"

"Oh, I guess we're through."

Daniel's heart leaped within him. "What happened?"

"I got a letter last week. He says that being he's got another year and a half to do in Germany. He was concerned about me waiting at home alone for him. He's given me permission to go out with other guys if I want to."

"That's bad." Daniel said, not mentioning the fact she'd know she and Jamie were through when they had the talk. People who've been around the Army learn that whenever your loved one gives you permission to run around it means they're running around – or they want to.

"No, that's good," Ruth said, moving toward him.

"Daniel, I've realized something important even before I got the letter. 'Something I'm glad I realized before I made a terrible mistake."

"What's that?"

"I don't really love Jamie anymore. Maybe I never did. We had just grown comfortable together. We might have gotten married. It may have worked. But it wasn't right. Jamie's letter may have been an answered prayer."

There was an awkward silence. Daniel felt obligated to say something at this point. "Why not?"

"Because, silly, I love you," she smiled. "I've only known you two weeks, but I can't picture not being your friend."

"It's going to be tough. The 'Q' Course will last almost a year."

"I know, maybe this is God's way of giving us time. If this is God's will, it will work out. By then we'll know. It will give me a chance to see what you look like with hair."

That was when they shared their first real kiss.

He took a thirty-day leave as soon as he could after he finished his training. His first stop was Columbus, Georgia. He had made up his mind. He loved Ruth, she loved him, and he wanted to spend his life with her. They were married in a small church ceremony. His parents drove up from Ft. Rucker, where Roger was waiting for his retirement papers to come through. They spent their first night as husband and wife in Atlanta, on their way to Fayetteville. Ruth had already managed a transfer to Ft. Bragg and had three days to report to her new job.

Daniel glanced over at his wife as these memories flashed through his mind. It had been a good marriage. He recognized her as a gift from God, even through the rough spots.

He'd never told her about that night in Nam. He was afraid she'd never look at him in the same way again. So he kept it to himself. There were some things you didn't share, couldn't share. No one would understand- unless they'd been there.

So he kept it to himself. Locked up. Another wound that refused to heal. Ruth knew Daniel was keeping something locked up inside. Being an Army brat with a father who'd fought the same demons, she understood no one comes back from combat unchanged. She wished he'd share it with her; sometimes she was hurt he didn't. She loved him enough to wait for him to reveal it in his own time. In the meantime, she prayed over him, asking God to heal his hurts.

He'd found comfort in God. After they settled in at Ft. Bragg, they joined a WHF church and became actively involved with its ministry. The pastor there was a young man who saw something in Daniel even Daniel didn't realize was still there- the Call. Before long, Daniel was teaching Sunday school and leading in the youth ministry (the church couldn't afford a full-time youth pastor).

Years went by. There was a tour in Germany. They returned after three years to pick up where they left off in the church.

Then, in 1981, Daniel'd gotten injured on an operation in Central America. After almost a year of struggling to "come back," Daniel was told he would never be able to jump again. He was given a choice, he could be "reclassified," that is, given another job to do, or he could leave the service on medical retirement.

He and Ruth prayed over their decision. They spoke with their pastor. One afternoon he and his pastor were alone. The discussion of a future in the ministry came up.

"Daniel," the pastor said. "Have you ever felt the call to the ministry?"

Daniel paused, deep in thought. How many times had he felt the pull of God in that direction? As a senior in high school he'd had dreams and visions, but he'd dismissed them. He was going to be a soldier. That was his call. A Christian, perhaps, but a soldier.

That afternoon a chill ran down his spine. He recognized the Holy Spirit's way of telling him this was right. It wasn't like the chills he'd experienced at the Homestead.

He couldn't wait to get home to talk to Ruth to tell the news.

"Ruth," he said almost before he entered the door to their apartment. "Guess what? I've been talking with Pastor Bill and I think the Lord wants me in the ministry when I get out of the Army!"

She smiled at him knowingly, "I was wondering how long it was going to take you to hear God."

"What do you mean?"

"Daniel, I've always known you were called to the ministry."

"I don't get it."

"Don't you remember back at Ft. Benning?" she asked, teasingly. "I told you I always felt called to be a minister's wife. How do you think I knew you were the one for me and not Jamie?"

"You could have told me!" he said, a bit upset at his surprise being ruined.

"Baby, some things you've got to hear for yourself."

The light was still on in the pastor's office. Daniel had known it would be. Such business as he had with Dean Grossman could not be dealt with at home, where small ears could hear and, perhaps, repeat. He checked his watch; it was 8:30 PM. He suddenly felt very tired, as if the weight of the trip, the memories

- his entire life, actually, and the work ahead had all fallen on his shoulders.

Knock it off, Danny, he scolded himself. *"We are not ignorant of Satan's devices."* He rebuked the spirit of fatigue attacking him and asked God for the strength to do what he needed to do. *When I am weak, He is strong.*

There are two excesses one can commit in this type of warfare, he told himself. *One is to ignore Satan and his wiles, the other is to get paranoid about him.* He taught his people to choose their battlegrounds wisely and not fall into Satan's traps. "Be wise as a serpent, gentle as a lamb," the Lord had warned. So he checked himself, asked the Lord to give him the discernment he needed to tell the area he was dealing with; the physical, the mental (or "soulish") realm, or the spiritual. *We don't need to be chasing after wild geese; there are too many real enemies around.*

He was physically tired, he knew. But he also recognized a spirit of fatigue trying to grab him, weaken him, and take his resolve. It was the same spirit, only now stronger, as the one that hit him when he tried to read his Bible or pray. *Anything to interfere with the process.*

He looked over at Ruth, who'd been sitting beside him in the car, praying in the Spirit under her breath. "We need to pray together before we go in," he said.

Chapter 14
July 21, 2009

But if our gospel be hidden it is hidden to them that are lost, in whom the god of this world hath blinded the minds of them who believe not, lest the light of the glorious gospel of Christ, who is the image of God, should shine unto them.
(2 Corinthians 4: 3 & 4)

Daniel thought it was amazing. Except for a few extra pounds and a bit of gray around the temples, Dean Grossman hadn't changed a bit. He'd heard it said somewhere that by the age of fifty one had the face one deserved. Dean must have lived a good life.

They shook hands; both looked at each other, thought of the childhood memories, hugged.

"It's so good to see you, Danny-er- Daniel," Dean said. "I was beginning to get worried..."

"We stopped at the cemetery before coming on in."

Dean nodded sadly, "I always stop by there when I do a funeral. I liked Rog..."

"I appreciate it, Dean." He quickly changed the subject, "Dean, this is my wife, Ruth."

"Nice to meet you," Dean said, taking her hand. "Boy, the Lord blessed you on this one, didn't He?"

"I always thought so," Daniel said, grinning at Ruth's embarrassment.

Introductions finished they took a seat while Dean gave a run-down of Laurie's behavior and the manifestations in the house. Then Dean took the plunge and told Daniel of the night Rog had appeared.

After Dean finished, they sat in silence for several minutes.

"I didn't hear about that," Daniel finally said.

"Rennee told Brew."

"Brew never told us," he thought aloud. "He probably knew how much it would have upset Mom. We never knew exactly why Rennee moved out so fast, though we suspected the house might have had something to do with it." Daniel looked at his watch, "It's - what - Eight-oh-five here?"

Dean nodded.

"Do you think we could go over and meet the Neustadts? I know it's getting late..." He hesitated, "I believe it's important we get over there quickly."

"What is it?" Ruth asked. She knew her husband, knew that when he got this edge to his voice it paid to listen to him.

"I just think we're needed over there. Tonight."

The house appeared little different than it had when he lived there, except someone, the Neustadt's apparently, had painted the trim around the windows a different shade. The trim had been white when he lived there. In the dark, it appeared the Neustadt's had tried to liven the exterior by painting the trim a light blue, or blue - gray.

As they approached the porch, Daniel's mind drifted back over forty years to their first summer at the Homestead. He noticed the frosted window in the front door. It was still there after all these years, the woman still greeting all visitors with her mournful smile. *Hello, Molina.* He could hear shouting inside; a young girl's voice shrieking, adult voices arguing.

Dean hesitated before ringing the doorbell, "Maybe we could come back later?"

"Oh no," Daniel insisted. "They're expecting us."

"We're used to this," Ruth added, in a comforting way.

Dean shrugged and pressed the doorbell. There was more shouting, then Becky Neustadt opened the door.

"Thank God you're here. Laurie's been throwing fits all day. She's worse now than ever before. She's been clawing at herself all day. Del's with her now. He had to take off work when she started. He's holding her down, keeping her from hurting herself. She tried to stab herself with her butter knife at breakfast this morning."

Daniel felt a surge rush through his body. Call it a thrill, a sensation, a quickening, whatever, but suddenly his senses were heightened, he was more - aware.

"Where is she?" he asked.

"This is Reverend Daniel Baumer and his wife, Ruth." Dean explained to her questioning look.

Daniel saw the mother's expression relax, "Upstairs, in her bedroom."

"The south bedroom?"

222

"Yes," embarrassed. "She refused to sleep anywhere else. She gave us fits..."

Who's in charge here, anyway? Daniel raged inside, *No wonder this family's in trouble. Calm yourself, Danny, don't give in to anger. It's the devil's game.*

"I'll show you-" she offered.

"DANNY? IS THAT YOU? OOOOH DANNY BOY..." came a hideous voice from upstairs.

Daniel smiled grimly. '*Nothing like coming home to friends and family.*

"I know the way." Daniel said, shortly, edging past her into the house. He turned and handed Ruth his briefcase for safekeeping. He was hit again by another rush of memories. The wood paneling his family had hung that first summer was still in place. Except for the furniture, nothing had changed. As he turned to enter the kitchen he looked at the bay windows and could almost see Brew sitting there, reading his paper. He blinked back tears. How he missed the old man. It was hard to believe he'd been dead for thirty years. Neighbors had found him dead on this very floor. He'd been dead for days... Suddenly, he saw him, lying face down on the kitchen floor beneath the bay windows.

Shake it off Daniel; stay focused. He blinked his eyes. Brew was gone. The problem was he didn't really know if this were the house trying to shake him up or just his memories assaulting him. Perhaps both. *Remember; don't give the enemy too much credit.*

He put his foot on the first step and paused, turning to look the couple in the eye, "One thing before we go up there – whatever you hear or see up there, please don't get involved or do anything unless I tell you. Don't speak to it or interfere with what is going on. The thing that has your daughter has one goal – that is to stay inside your daughter. It will do anything and everything it can to confuse us, distract us, or divide us if it can. If it can turn you against me or get me to doubt and back down it wins. Understand?"

The couple looked at him mutely.

"I need to know you understand and won't interfere. You're liable to see or hear anything up there. So do you understand?"

At about that time an inhuman howl rent the stillness, **"Daaaaaaanny... what's taking you so looooooong?"**

223

"Do you understand me?"

The two nodded.

"Good."

He turned back and ascended the steps. From behind him, he could hear Ruth, comforting Becky, "Don't take it personally. Daniel always gets like this when he's ministering deliverance..."

Thank God for Ruth.

He could feel the presence of the spirits much more strongly as he ascended the stairs. *You know I'm here. You've known I was coming. Well, I'm back. This time I'm armed and dangerous.* He began to feel a suffocating sensation in his head, his heart began to race, he felt his palms begin to sweat, and his mouth began to dry, tension coursed through his body. *My Lord, what am I walking into?* The thought raced through his mind. Then he caught himself. *God has not given us the spirit of fear, but of power, love, and a sound mind!*

"Get thee behind me, Satan!" he muttered under his breath. There was no use in the family thinking he was crazy - yet. "I rebuke you spirit of fear, in the Name of Jesus!"

It was gone, he felt his heart beat slow and his body relax. He was at the top of the steps. He could hear the girl making low animal growls now, hear her father trying to soothe her, reason with her.

As he passed through the middle bedroom, he caught himself automatically checking the closet doors to see if the shadows of the tree were still there. *Yep. Surprise, surprise!*

He broke through the feeling of dread that confronted him at the south bedroom door and burst through. Inside, he could see the little girl, slight, red-headed, on a bed in the near corner, her father and sisters pinning her arms and legs to the bed. When he entered the room, the girl kicked her arms and legs, throwing all three of them across the room. She looked at Daniel with large brown eyes, and smiled, sending a chill down Daniel's spine.

"Hello, Danny," she/it said in a voice that wasn't quite human. **"We've missed you."**

"I'll bet you have," Daniel said. It wasn't usually good practice to converse with the spirits; they would try to confuse you and shake your faith. This time, though, Daniel decided to play the game, for a little while at least. He was here, but as yet had no real leading from the Holy Spirit as to what to do. He wasn't worried, though, the Lord would let him know in due time.

He always did.

"You were stupid to come back. We'll destroy you like we destroy your brother and that slut Uta!" Daniel felt his blood rush at that. *Careful Daniel, don't play its game.*

"No, you won't," he said, as he moved closer to the bed. He was aware of the father and sisters getting to their feet, watching the whole thing in disbelief. Ruth, Dean, and the mother had entered the room behind him. He could hear Ruth praying intercession, soon Dean caught on and joined in. "And you're not going to hurt that little girl any more!"

He looked over at the two other girls in the room, while watching Laurie out of the corner of his eye. They were staring at their sister with wide, blue-eyed stares. He reached out to the oldest one, touched her on her blonde head, "Sweetheart, why don't you take your sister downstairs for awhile, okay?"

She nodded and scampered out of the room. *They could be twins, except for the difference in height,* he reflected. *Now that we have the non-combatants out of the line of fire...*

"Who's going to stop us? She's given herself to us!"

Daniel started to speak, but felt a check in his spirit. To his left front, over in the corner by the second twin bed in the room, he felt a heat. He smiled, "They are!" He pointed to the place from which came the heat. He couldn't see them but he *knew* there were two angels standing there, guardian angels. *Thank you, Lord! Where I am weak, He is strong.*

He saw the girl's eyes widen as she turned her head to where the presences were. The look of smug self-satisfaction was replaced by wide-eyed horror.

"I'm not going to play your game tonight, serpent. But I'll be back. In the meantime, my two friends there are going to keep you from hurting that little girl. Every time you try to inflict damage they're going to grab your arms and hold them up over her head as a sign to you and the world that Jesus is Lord! Do you hear me?" His emotions rose now, but it was okay, this was a righteous, holy indignation. "I serve notice on the hosts of hell who have ruled in this dominion that your stay here, your rule here is finished! I rebuke each and every demon from hell, every principality, every power, every ruler of darkness, every imp and unclean spirit in this house in the Name of Jesus Christ who is the I AM! Who is the Alpha and Omega! Who Was, and Is, and Is To Come! Amen!"

The girl's face contorted into an unholy rage, her eyes

225

narrowed to serpentine slits, *"You have no authority here! Murderers shall not inherit the kingdom of hea-"*

"Shut your lying mouth, serpent, in the Name of Jesus!"

The demon stopped in mid-sentence, leaving the girl's mouth open, her tongue hanging out of her mouth stupidly.

"I said shut it! In the Name of Jesus!"

The mouth closed so quickly it was almost comical.

There was confusion, fear for a moment in the eyes, then they narrowed again. Daniel knew what was coming next. Sure enough, he saw her hands jerk up in a clawing motion toward her face. Before they could get there, though, everyone in the room saw her arms get snatched away, as if by unseen hands. He heard her parents gasp as they saw their daughter being pulled up in the bed, her hands and arms held aloft above her. They watched as she was lifted up by her arms so that her body was suspended a few inches above the mattress.

Daniel wanted to giggle like a child. *The angels are showing off a bit,* he thought. *God wants to make sure there's no doubt Who's in charge around here.* He knew from the Bible and his experience that angels didn't show off out of pride or vanity, but to glorify God.

"Now, I speak peace over this house tonight so this family can get some rest!" He approached the girl, reaching out his hand. Her eyes widened in terror. He could still see the serpent there. He touched her forehead with his fingertips, "In the Name of Jesus!"

She fell back on her pillow as if she'd been shot. She lay deathly still. Her mother ran to her and touched her forehead tenderly. She looked up in amazement. "She's sound asleep!"

"Thank you, Jesus!" he whispered. *I don't care how long I serve Him,* he reflected. *He never ceases to amaze me with His awesome power. And His love, His awesome love.*

It was quiet now. He turned and saw Dean and the Neustadt family staring at him with a mixture of awe and fear. He'd seen this reaction before. "We serve an awesome God." He looked at the little girl, her face angelic now, sleeping softly. "Let's go downstairs and talk." He looked over to where he knew the angels were standing guard, "Thanks, guys."

He was about to leave, when he stopped, suddenly. Everyone turned, watching him. Daniel was looking around the room, his face contorted with a look of concentration for a moment. He relaxed and walked over to the dresser sitting against the wall between the beds. He reached behind it, felt around, and pulled out a *Ouija* board. *I knew it! Thanks again, Lord.*

"We need to burn this tonight."

"It's just a toy," Becky said. "We got it for the kids last Christmas."

"Burn it anyway. Come on downstairs, folks," Daniel said, tiredly. This wasn't the time to argue and he didn't feel like explaining – not about this. "We're done for the night. She's safe for now; she'll sleep. She needs it. It's been three weeks since she last slept well. We're exhausted. We'll get a good night's sleep and hit it again in the morning. We've got a lot of talking to do. Dean, I hope you told your wife to go ahead and feed the kids. We're going to be awhile."

It took about two hours for Daniel to explain to the Neustadts who he was and his experiences in the house. He didn't tell the whole story. Not yet. He could tell they weren't ready. But he told them enough to convince them he knew what he was up against. Still, in spite of what they had just witnessed in the bedroom, the parents, particularly Del, wanted to hold out that the CT scan they'd run on Laurie the previous week would turn up some sort of neurological disorder which would explain her odd behavior.

"Would it explain how she knew me tonight?" Daniel asked.

"Listen," Ruth said, gently, "did you tell Laurie we were coming?"

"No." Del said, "Pastor advised us not to like you said."

"Good." Daniel said.

"We didn't even know your name until you came here," Becky admitted.

"Then how did she know me?"

227

Silence.

"First, we're not telling you your house is haunted," Ruth joined in. "It's possessed."

"Possessed?" Del was incredulous. "That's even more unbelievable."

"Yes." Daniel said, "There is no such thing as a haunted house, as the world knows it, because there are no such things as ghosts, as the world understands them."

"The dead can't come back," Ruth interjected. "Doesn't Hebrews say 'It's given unto men once to die, and then the Judgment?'"

"Remember the story of the rich man and Lazarus?" Dean spoke up. "The rich man wanted to come back and warn his brothers and he was told he couldn't."

Daniel nodded gratefully. *Thanks, buddy.*

"So what's haunting or possessing our house, then?"

"The Bible calls them familiar spirits. Devils masquerading as dead people."

"That's kind of hard to swallow, preacher," Del said. "You're asking us to believe a lot, Brother Daniel. To believe our house is haunted. This is the twenty-first century."

"'My people are destroyed for lack of knowledge,'" Daniel said sadly.

"What?"

"Listen, Del," Daniel leaned forward now. "Do you believe the Bible is the Word of God?"

"I sure do!"

"Then what's your problem believing in demons, or devils, if you prefer? The Bible's full of stories and instruction about them."

"Well, it's just that- well that was a long time ago. People didn't know what we know now?"

"How about Jesus? Are you claiming Jesus didn't know better? He spent about one-fourth of His ministry either casting out devils or teaching how to fight the devil. Now, if He did that, that means He didn't know better, which means He couldn't be the Son of God.

"It could mean that He *did* know better but was pretending to cast out devils to please the people. That would make Him a fraud. Or, it could mean the gospel writers made up stories about Him to make Him seem greater than He was, or to fulfill a private agenda they had. If that's true, then we'd better

228

throw the whole Bible out, because you can't trust any of it. If they lied about that, then Jesus might never have lived at all or done anything they said he did. In my mind, the only answer is that demons are for real and they are with us."

Del remained silent, chewing over what he'd just heard. "It's kind of hard to swallow..." he finally drawled.

"That's why a *Ouija* Board is not just a toy, folks," Daniel said, softly now. "The Bible in the Old Testament strictly forbids anyone from even trying to speak with the dead. Remember Saul's final sin, the straw that broke the camel's back was when he approached the Witch of Endor, a medium, as the King James' Version of the Bible says, 'a woman who had a familiar spirit' to contact Samuel for advice. That was the final straw for God.

"Why? First, Saul wasn't relying on God. He was seeking another source for counsel. Second, trying to contact the dead was forbidden because God knows mediums can't really contact the dead. They speak with 'familiar spirits' who can pretend to be dead people."

"Why would they do that?" Del asked.

"The enemy comes but to steal, kill, and destroy," Ruth answered. "You see, the enemy wants to possess you body, soul, and spirit so he can take you to hell with him when the final judgment comes. Barring that, we think he'll settle for just leading you away from God's truth, which is there is a heaven to gain and a hell to shun."

"Think about it," Daniel said. "If there are ghosts roaming the world, then what happens to the idea of heaven and hell?"

"I saw a movie one time where a lady said ghosts were just spirits who'd lost their way after they died," Becky said.

"Yeah," Del added. "I watched a documentary about haunted houses on the educational channel. It said that the reason why many people who die tragically become ghosts is because their death came so suddenly they were unprepared and couldn't find their way to the other world. That's why mediums were needed to lead them toward the light."

Daniel couldn't help but snort his scorn for that idea. "I'm sorry," he apologized. "But that doesn't wash, either."

"Why not?"

"Where's God when these folks are getting 'lost'? It doesn't sound like an all-powerful, all-knowing God who's lost track of so many souls, does it? The whole idea of ghosts

229

undermines the Christian view of life after death."

"So how does a house get haunted?"

"I believe," Daniel said, "now, the Bible doesn't state this plainly, but from twenty years or so of experience, I've come to the conclusion that demons need a place to dwell. The Book of Jude states there are angels who've left their 'first estate.' Some of the more wicked ones are reserved in chains for the judgment. The Book of Revelation tells us that some of the really bad boys are imprisoned until the end time, when they'll be released to scourge the earth during the Great Tribulation.

"But we also see in the Book of Revelation, taken along with Ezekiel, Chapter 28 and Isaiah 14, that Lucifer, Satan, led a revolt in heaven. One-third of the stars (some read that angels) in heaven fell with him. That's a lot of angels. Some are bound, I call them P.O.W.s (Prisoners of War), excuse my military jargon. Others are loose as demons. These form Satan's army.

"Going back to Jude, when they rebelled, they left their 'first estate.' I believe they lost their spiritual bodies. Jesus in Luke 11 says, I'm paraphrasing here, 'that when the unclean spirit is gone from its house it roams the dry places seeking rest, and finding none, returns to its original house. Finding it swept and garnished, he goes out, finds seven spirits, more unclean than he and returns, thus the condition of the person is worse than it was originally.' I could preach all day on that, but for now let's concentrate on one part. It says the spirit, once cast out roams about seeking rest. Apparently, the disembodied spirits are uncomfortable when they're cast out. They have to have a host, a physical home, to know rest. Maybe the only way they can express themselves in the physical realm is through a host.

"Remember, the Gadarene demoniac? The demons begged Jesus to cast them into the herd of swine? They'll possess animals. That's the origin of the so-called witch's familiar, an animal possessed by the demon spirit that gave the witch her power. But demons apparently prefer to possess and destroy humans, created in God's own image."

Daniel paused, letting his words sink in. Del spoke out, "But how does that explain haunted houses?"

"Let me explain," Daniel said, glad to be back on subject. "These spirits, once they get a toehold on their victim, are able to cause harm to the victim or through the victim. If you study serial killers and mass murderers, and I have, you'll discover that many have a common thread. They heard "voices" telling them to do the terrible things they did.

"Charles Manson said he got his plan to kill Sharon Tate from listening to the Beatle's *White Album*. The music "spoke" to him.

"Richard Ramirez, the 'Night Stalker,' claimed to be influenced by the rock group AC/DC's music, he even took his name from one of their songs.

"David Berkowitz, the "Son of Sam," said his dog gave him orders to do the things he did. I could go on, but get the point?

"Now, let's say these men were demon driven and I believe they were. What happens when they've done their crimes and been arrested? What happens when they've murdered everyone dear to them?"

"I don't know," Del answered.

"It was a rhetorical question anyway," Daniel said, smiling. "If you're John Wilder, a sixteen year old kid who was into Satanism and who killed his mother and stepfather as a sacrifice to Satan, the demons deserted you to inhabit and destroy someone else. John, realizing he'd been betrayed, claimed to have given his heart to the Lord before he was executed last year."

"What's that got to do with haunted houses?" Del asked, getting impatient.

"I'll tell you." Daniel replied. *This is going to be more of a challenge than I first thought.* "You said you've seen a lot of movies and documentaries about haunted houses. What do most of them have in common?"

He watched Del's and Becky's faces as they searched their minds for the answer.

"Tragedies," Dean answered.

Thanks again, buddy. "You've got it. Terrible tragedies, crimes, murders, broken hearts, you name it. Most 'haunted' houses are places of great sorrow and tragedy. I believe that the familiar spirits either cause or are attracted by the suffering and sorrow. They appear to feed off it. Take the Dow family in New Hampshire. Do you remember them?"

Del's face brightened, "Oh yeah!" he almost shouted, "*The Gloucester House of Terror!* They made a movie about it! Some kid got into Satanism and killed his family, then committed suicide. Now no one can live there because the house is so haunted!"

"Possessed," Daniel corrected. "That one is supposed to

be based on a true story. It's obvious. Jerry Dow set up his own altar to Satan underneath the basement steps, praying to demons, sacrificing small animals to the Devil. He got himself possessed by a murderous spirit, killed his parents, then committed suicide. What do you think happened to all those demons inside that kid when their host died?"

There were shrugs.

"They had to live somewhere, possess something, so they possessed the house, staying there, reliving the awful things they had caused until they could find their next victim or victims. Maybe they get a kick out of deceiving gullible people into thinking they are the 'ghosts' of deceased persons. So those people will call on mediums, who are themselves possessed by familiar spirits to come and lead them to rest."

"Why?" Becky was confused.

"So they can lead other victims to hell, either by possessing them and forcing them to do terrible things, or by getting them to buy the lie, deny the existence of heaven and hell, or even the need for salvation. Remember, there is only one path to heaven and straight is the gate and narrow is the way that leads there."

"So you think that's what's happening here?"

"I'm pretty sure of it."

"You think all those stories about the house, the hanging and all that is true?"

This stopped Daniel in his tracks. Hadn't they seen or experienced anything in the house? He had to know what they knew. "Folks, pardon me, but have either of you seen or experienced anything unusual in this house?"

They shook their heads, "Brother Daniel," Becky said, almost apologetically, "the only things we know about this house are what Laurie told us about hearing voices and being held down when we first moved in."

"We thought she was letting her imagination run wild with her," Del added. "You know how kids can be. She never did mention it any more so we figured she was okay."

"We've heard stories, but that's all we thought they were – stories – until Pastor Dean, and now you've told us all these things."

"And you're not quite sure we're not crazy, either, are you?" Daniel said. He could tell the question caught them off guard. It was as if he knew their thoughts. It scared them. He was used to that.

She shook her head.

He had been flustered, but now it all began to make sense, why it was so easy for the spirits to get their little girl. He looked over at his wife who returned his look. He saw the sadness in her eyes. He knew they were a reflection of his own.

"So I'm the only one in this room who's seen the shadows on the wall, seen the ghostly figures at night, and heard the footsteps and the noises?"

"I have," Dean said, interrupting the silence, startling the others. They all looked to him, "When I was a kid, I snuck up there one time. It was easy to pick the lock. I didn't take anything. It was a dare. Some of the kids dared me to go up there and I told them I'd shine a flashlight from the window to prove I'd gone into the really haunted part of the house. I saw the shadows. And I saw - her. She was at the south window staring out. She looked at me and smiled. I dropped the flashlight and ran."

"Who?" it was Del.

"Molina." Daniel answered.

"Well, I ain't seen any shadows and I ain't seen no woman! Molina Felder's been dead for over thirty - five years!"

"No," Daniel said, grimly. "You probably haven't seen anything." He looked across at Dean. "But I bet Laurie has," he drew a breath, "and that thing roaming this house is not Molina Felder."

"You've got to understand, preacher," Del repeated, keeping his eyes averted, looking at the floor. It occurred to Daniel he always kept his eyes averted. *Secrets?*

"This all sounds crazy to me," Del continued still looking at the floor. "I believe in the Bible and all, but-"

"You haven't let it interfere too much with your perspective?" Daniel felt Ruth's hand on his arm. *Secrets.* "Listen, Mister Neustadt, with all due respect. My wife and I have taken time off work to travel almost seven hundred miles to help you. I am tired. I am hungry. I have been fasting all day to be prepared for what we need to do. I don't mind doing this. This is what God has called me to do. But if you don't feel you need our help, I'll be more than glad to get back in our car and drive home so we can see our kids and get on with our lives down there."

"It's not like we don't appreciate what you've done and all, Brother Daniel I mean this is all hard to digest so quick."

"I know," Daniel said understandingly. "I've given you a six week Bible study course in a couple of hours. I wish I could handle this differently. There just isn't time."

He thought of all the things he hadn't told the Neustadts; how he believed his mother, holding guilt, shame, and unforgiveness over her past had been lured into the house by the same demons who had destroyed Molina Felder's life. He thought of how the demons must have preyed on Roggie, playing on his sense of shame and inadequacy, leading him into mistaking sex for love, which ultimately led to Denise Fleischmann's possession and suicide and no telling how many other lives ruined; perhaps, even his death. Many times Daniel had wept thinking of his brother, killed while trying to escape the consequences of his actions in Vietnam.

He thought of Uta, an innocent victim, murdered in cold blood on Main Street. He thought of Brew who died in the house alone. Who knew what he saw or experienced in his last moments? No, there was much he couldn't tell them. They wouldn't understand.

Not now, at least; perhaps, never.

They were staring at him now as he mulled these things over in his mind. He finally nodded to himself. Maybe there was something they would understand.

He looked over at Ruth. "Honey, where's my briefcase?" *It's time for the heavy artillery.*

Ruth reached over the arm of the sofa and picked the briefcase from where she'd placed it. She handed it to Daniel.

Daniel placed the case on the coffee table and opened it. He took out the manila folder from inside. "This may help you."

He had two copies of the picture he'd taken of the house. He gave one copy to Dean, who was sitting in an armchair to his left. The other he gave to the Neustadts, who were sitting in the love seat on the right.

"This is a picture of the house I took a couple of years ago when we were here for my high school reunion." He watched them study the photo. "Take a look at the upstairs bedroom windows. Do you notice something strange?"

"One of the windows looks fuzzy, like there's something in there."

"But there's nothing in there, is there?"

"Could it be shadows?" Del asked.

"I wondered, so I had the picture blown up," he produced

234

two more copies of another shot, a close-up of the windows. "Look at these." He and Ruth studied their faces as they looked at the pictures. It was Dean who saw them first.

"Oh, my Lord..." he said, his eyes widening as he studied the images in the window.

"What?" Del asked, "What do you see?"

"How many faces are in there, do you reckon?" Dean asked.

"What faces?" Del asked, getting more flustered.

"I see them now!" Becky said, excitedly at first. The excitement faded to shock as she realized what she was seeing, "Oh, Lord..."

"What is it?" Del was getting angry, now.

"Faces, sweetheart, dozens of faces in the window there, see?" she pointed at the picture. "There. And there."

Del stared hard at the window in the picture. He could see light and dark shadows on the fuzzy spot on the window, but they were just that, shadows, not- wait a minute! There! That did look like a face of some sorts. No, call it a skull. It had horns. His mouth dropped open as other faces appeared before him, one after another, one on top of the other, overlapping. Hideous faces, like those on the gargoyles he'd seen in pictures of churches in Medieval Europe. It appeared the more he looked the more faces he saw.

"Dear, Sweet Jesus..." he whispered.

"That is what we are fighting," Daniel said from the sofa, across the room.

"It's like looking into the gates of hell," Dean whispered.

The air was hot and fetid in the night. All around the noises of the forest had stilled, the animals seemed to be waiting expectantly for something terrible to happen to the invaders in their domain. Daniel could barely make out the shoulder of the man in front of him. He could see the faint glow of the two fluorescent tabs sewed on to the back of the hat of the man in front bobbing up and down.

He was panting heavily, each breath stabbing his chest, but they couldn't stop. There were pursuers behind them. If they stopped for a moment the pursuers would catch up. It would be over.

He saw a clearing up ahead. They would have to charge right through it. That could be dangerous, he thought. They'd be in the open. Still, it was better than the alternative. The man in front entered the clearing. He disappeared.

Daniel strained his eyes to see where he went to. He halted suddenly. He was at the edge of a precipice of a wide gorge.

"Whew!" he whistled. "I almost lost it. Where's Tyrell? Oh no! He went over the edge."

Daniel edged back from the drop. It appeared bottomless. "I'm alone. All alone." Behind him he could hear the sounds of men shouting. "NVA!" Daniel looked to the left and right, trying to find a way across the gorge. There was none.

The voices were closer now. He turned, prepared to make a stand. He could feel his M16A1 in his hands, ready. He crouched, making as small a target as he could in the open. Now, a figure broke through the brush into the clearing.

Daniel choked back fear as he saw the face of the man. He'd seen it before in the jungle in 1975. The head was sitting crookedly on the neck. The man was smiling an evil grin. Daniel raised his weapon and took aim.

"You'll stay dead now," he whispered as he squeezed the trigger.

Nothing.

The man's grin grew wider as he walked slowly now toward Daniel, speaking Vietnamese.

Daniel reached in his flak vest and pulled out another magazine, locked and loaded, fired - nothing. The man charged Daniel. Daniel rose to meet the charge but lost his footing. Suddenly he was over the edge, falling, falling into the abyss. He tried to scream but terror choked any sound from coming out.

Now, something had caught him in the air, lifted him and was carrying him through the middle bedroom, helplessly. Again he felt such terror. Again he tried to scream but nothing would come out. He was helpless to fight. He was helpless to struggle. It had him.

Now, it was carrying him upstairs.

Oh, Jesus, *he thought,* help me before it's too late...

"Daniel! Daniel! Wake up!" it was Ruth.

Daniel woke with a start. *Another nightmare!* It was his fault. When Dean offered the guest speaker's cottage behind the church, he and Ruth had accepted gratefully. Daniel didn't know whether or not he'd make the twenty-mile drive to the nearest motel in Glen Haven.

He should have known to pray protection over himself, particularly considering the business he and Ruth were about. Even when things were "normal" he prayed a hedge of protection and applied the Blood of Jesus to his dreams. *People need to sleep, but Satan never rests, he* reminded himself.

Neither does God.

He'd goofed. He'd allowed fatigue to win. Instead of a heartfelt prayer, he'd mumbled a few words that had no meaning. He'd let his guard down. This was the first nightmare he'd had in years.

What really disturbed him was the part about being carried away down the steps. He hadn't had that dream since he was a kid. *'Living in the house. Welcome home.*

"Are you all right, honey?" Ruth asked. He looked over at her, found himself being bathed in her warmth,

"Now I am."

"What was it?"

"Same old war stuff," he said. He'd never told her about the dreams he had concerning the NVA soldier. It would mean having to tell her what happened. He told her the part about being carried away.

"It's the house," she said. "The spirits."

"Oh, sure." He looked at his watch, 3:00 a.m.. "Swell, we were going to get some rest."

"Well, you know the enemy isn't going to want us rested. Let's pray."

"Good idea."

There was a soft knock on the door. Daniel was awake instantly. For a moment he didn't know where he was. He reached for his M-16, didn't find it, and felt frantically at the empty bed beside him. He heard Ruth's voice, talking softly to someone. He heaved a sigh of relief. He knew where he was now. He was in Delphi. He was safe in the guest cottage. *Well, relatively safe.*

"Ruth?"

"In here, honey." she answered from the front room. "Pastor Dean is here."

Daniel looked at his watch, whistled softly, *Almost ten o'clock. Well, at least I got some sleep...* "I'll be out in a minute."

He dressed quickly. He'd shower later after he'd spoken

237

with Dean. As he walked into the room, he could tell something was wrong. It was a small room that served as a kitchen, dining, and living room. A small stove and sink sat in the corner, with some cabinets overhead. Daniel remembered thinking that with Delphi's choice of eateries, whatever they were calling the cafe downtown these days, a way to cook was a must for a visiting evangelist. A table with three chairs around it a few feet out from the kitchen served as the dining area. On his side of the room, by the bedroom door, was a small sofa, almost a loveseat. Ruth was sitting there. On the wall to his right, was an overstuffed chair. This is where Dean sat leaning slightly forward, with a pained expression on his face.

Daniel looked over at his wife and saw her expression, recognized it. It was the same expression he'd seen when the deacon board at the last church they'd pastored told them they were going to have to stop all this deliverance nonsense, it was scaring everyone. It was the same look she'd had when the District WHF Superintendent had told him that his teachings on spiritual warfare ran counter to WHF doctrine, that his style of worship was "too charismatic."

It was the same look she'd had on that last day in North Carolina, when the board finally ordered him to hand in his credentials. That was - after the scandal.

Let's get on with it. "What's up, Dean."

"Well, first off, the Neustadt girl woke up this morning her old self." Dean said, trying to put a good face on.

"She's not delivered," Daniel said flatly.

"I rebuke that," Dean said, weakly. "Remember the words-"

"-of our mouth contain life and death," Daniel finished for him wearily. "Yeah, I know that. I believe it. But the truth is the truth, Brother. To deny the truth is to play fool for the devil. The spirits are hiding for now, hoping to get us to leave them alone. They'll be back. We don't need to let up now. The house needs to be cleansed..."

"Well," Dean said, sadly, "the Neustadts said they'd prefer if you didn't come back..."

Oh Lord, Daniel thought. *Sometimes I wish I were wrong. Sometimes Your gifts don't seem like gifts."*

"It seems you scared them last night with all your talk of devils and angels," Dean said. Daniel felt an anger rising up within him. *Can they show me one thing I said last night that wasn't in the Bible?* He fought for control, though. It would do no good to show anger now. It would do more harm to an already deteriorating situation. It helped to look at Dean. Daniel was sorry for him. He obviously felt bad about having to deliver this message.

"It's all right, Dean," he said softly, placing a hand on his shoulder. He sat beside Ruth, who put her hand out. He took it. They sat together, holding hands, watching Dean, waiting for the rest of the news.

"He woke up this morning disturbed," Dean continued. "He called our district headquarters up in Chicago. He found out you were no longer a WHF minister, that you'd left the movement under a cloud."

What do you call a movement when it stops moving? Daniel asked himself. He stopped himself from thinking about the various names he had for it. He turned his attention back to Dean. "That didn't take long." *What cloud? I was cleared.*

"With Laurie's improvement, he said he'd feel better if you just went home. He thanked you for all your troubles and offered to pay you -"

"Forget it," Daniel said shortly.

"Well, you've been out some money getting here and it'll cost money to get back."

"Let's not forget the time we've lost from work." Daniel said.

"Dan-" Dean began.

"Forget it, Dean," Daniel said. "That's the one problem with this type of ministry. How do you charge for casting out demons? Do you charge by the hour or the demon?" He looked over at Ruth, "We'd chalk up if we ever ran into 'Legion.'" He turned back to Dean, "No, buddy, if you feel you have to do something for us, put the money in your benevolence fund for the poor."

"We don't-"

"Have one?" Daniel completed.

Dean shook his head sadly, "We just kind of help out as the need arises."

"So, has the superintendent called you yet about me?"

Dean nodded his head, again amazed at Daniel's perception. "About an hour ago."

"Are you in trouble?"

"Not if I close this matter immediately."

239

"That means get rid of me and Ruth and pretend nothing's happened?"

Dean dropped his head.

"Don't feel bad, brother," Daniel said kindly. "Ruth and I are getting used to it, aren't we, honey."

Ruth smiled ruefully. "Dean, we've been asked to leave some of the most popular churches in the southeast."

"Well, baby," Daniel said, rising. "I reckon we'd better pack up and get on the road. There's no sense in staying here."

"You don't have to leave so fast," Dean said, getting up from the chair. "I'm not running you out of town."

"No," Daniel said with a sad smile. "I know. 'No hard feelings buddy. We've just got to get home to our own lives and ministry. We've missed two days' work already and we're getting such a late start that even if we drive through, tomorrow will be shot. We're wasting time."

"I - I'm sorry."

"I know. It's not your fault. You've got to do what you've got to do. Remember, even Jesus couldn't do much in his home town because they rejected him."

"I wish there was something I could do or say-"

"Listen, it's all in God's hands. We have to trust Him. Don't sweat the small stuff, brother." Daniel turned to go into the bedroom and stopped, turned. "One thing, though."

"What?"

"What are you going to do when the spirits come back?"

Secrets...

It was a long, quiet drive home. Neither Daniel nor Ruth spoke much, nor did they feel like speaking. Ruth prayed quietly to herself, playing praise tape after praise tape, hoping to dispel the sadness she felt. Occasionally, she'd look over at her husband, seeing if he'd opened his gates to let her in. Eventually, she knew, whatever battle was raging in his soul between his flesh and spirit would end and his face would soften. She could come in. But not too far. There was always a small area in him where no one was allowed, not even her. She wondered if he let God in there. Could that be the wall they were up against?

She wondered why it was that people who needed help so much were so quick to refuse it. She thought of Jesus' words, *"They hated me, they'll hate you..."*

Daniel couldn't get the image of the little girl's face out of his mind. *Lord, please don't let her end up like the others.*

"There are none so blind as those who will not see." he said to himself.

"What, honey?"

"Just a quote." he said.

"Well, we did what we could."

"That's not going to help Laurie."

It was another hundred miles before either spoke again. Ruth had popped a praise tape into the car's stereo and was getting lost in the music.

"It's not over yet." Daniel said.

It took a moment for Ruth to realize Daniel had spoken. Then she had to process what he'd said. "What do you mean?" she asked, though she knew.

"We'll be hearing from them again."

Ruth nodded. She sighed. She somehow knew he was right. She suddenly felt sad, more than before.

They arrived home and found several urgent messages from Harriet Ross asking for prayer and for Daniel to contact her. *They'll wait.* There were two prayer requests from Nellie Foster, a little old lady from North Carolina who called once or twice a month for prayer when she was hit with any one of a number of aches and pains. Daniel called himself her spiritual "sugar pill." He'd pray for her and the pains would melt away. Ed Murphy wanted Daniel's opinion on what his pastor had been teaching last Sunday. Lillian needed prayer for her son. Edith wanted to know if it was sinful for her to buy new furniture or not. Rose had called to see if they had left for Illinois yet, then the next day to see if they were home.

Welcome home, Danny boy, he thought as the last message played. *My life and welcome to it.*

241

Chapter 15
June 15, 2010

And the evil spirit said, "Jesus I know, and Paul I know; but who are you?

Acts 19:15

Becky Neustadt clicked the phone off. She looked up at the ceiling anxiously. She could hear her daughter upstairs, holding a conversation with herself in two distinct voices. She tried to pray, but somehow found the words wouldn't come out quite right. She was so confused. Why couldn't she concentrate enough to speak to God?

She heard her daughter's voice, scared, plaintive. She couldn't quite make out the words; the tone made her heart break. *When will it end, God? It's been over a year. How long can I live in this nightmare?*

Then, there came the answer, a harsh, grating voice, cursing Laurie, uttering vile blasphemies, making dire threats against her safety and the safety of the family. Becky was glad she'd sent the other two girls to stay with her brother outside St. Louis.

She'd called Dr. Rollins earlier in the evening when the behavior first manifested. He'd diagnosed it as multiple personality disorder. He wanted to admit her to the hospital for "observation." Becky knew what that meant. They'd put Laurie on drugs to calm her. It would stop the symptoms, but Becky knew it wouldn't ultimately solve Laurie's problems. *What would?*

She'd begun praying, asking God for help. That's when Laurie really broke loose. She'd heard the sounds of a violent struggle upstairs in the room, before she could even react; Laurie came running downstairs screaming,

"Mama! Mama! Help me!" she'd screamed, "Johnny's after me!"

Becky had taken her little girl in her arms, holding her close, cradling her, protecting her, staring at the stairs, waiting for the unseen enemy to come. She would protect her baby. Laurie buried her head in her mother's breast, sobbing terribly. Becky soothed her, told her everything was going to be all right.

Then she felt the searing pain. Laurie had clamped her teeth on her breast. Becky'd screamed out in agony, pushing the child away, "Laurie!" she screamed, "What are you doing?"

"You stupid cow!" Laurie'd hissed in that terrible voice, *"Nurse me, Mama!"* A string of foul obscenities poured from the girl's lips. She charged Becky again, almost knocking her through the bay windows.

Becky'd fallen to the floor, rolled over on her back. Laurie was on her, sitting on her chest, digging her knee into Becky's injured breast and knowing the pain she was causing and enjoying it. She brought her face low, next to Becky's. Becky recoiled from the stench of her daughter's rancid breath. She felt as though she were about to vomit. Laurie licked her mother's cheek, and whispered, *"Mama, dear,"* it hissed. *"You tell Danny Baumer we're waiting for him. You tell that lily-livered Holy Roller if he doesn't come here, we'll kill this little slut and her entire family!"*

With that, Laurie had hopped up and ran upstairs. There had been sounds of arguing coming through the vent from the south bedroom since.

There was a knock on the back door. Becky pulled herself to her feet and answered it. It was Pastor Dean and his wife, Cindy.

"Thank the Lord you're here, Pastor," Becky said. "Thank you, Sister Cindy."

Cindy came forward, put her arms around Becky, and hugged her. She noticed Becky wince, "What is it, Becky?"

Becky explained what had happened. Cindy and Becky left to examine her wounds while Dean sat at the kitchen table, listening to Laurie upstairs. She was by the air vent, singing for him in an offbeat, tuneless melody.

"Blessed be the Child of God, the Child of God, the Child of God, Blessed be the child of God, the Holy Anointed One!" Dean was praying under his breath, *"Hey, preacher!"* it hissed, *"How come you keep saying the same thing over and over in tongues? 'You lost it? 'You doin' it from memory?"*

"Get thee behind me Satan!" Dean burst forth, "In the Name of Jesus!"

The thing burst out in hideous laughter! *"Come on up here and play, Preacher!"*

Angered, Dean almost got up from his seat. He checked

himself. No, this was over his head. He'd seen deliverances years ago, had even cast out spirits himself back when he first started out. But he'd never seen anything like this. He had to do something, though. There had to be someone who could help. There had to be someone who knew what to do. *Daniel Baumer?* No, the district would revoke his license if he had anything more to do with Daniel.

Brother Rider had become very upset when he'd called back last year. He'd called the Southeastern headquarters of the WHF and gotten Daniel's file faxed to him. Whatever was there had greatly upset Brother Rider. He had called within two hours of Dean's initial call for prayer and told him flatly to get Daniel Baumer out of town and to have no more to do with him. He was told Daniel Baumer was no longer a WHF member and to fellowship with him was to violate the WHF practices guide.

Dean had asked what Daniel had done, "I can't share that with you. It's confidential. Just know that Daniel Baumer is a dangerous man."

Still, Dean had to admit, Daniel had taken charge the one evening he'd been in the house and had calmed whatever it was that was tormenting Laurie Neustadt. He had kept Daniel's card, despite Brother Rider's urge – no command – to tear it up and throw it away.

Cindy and Becky re-entered the room. Dean looked at Cindy and saw the concerned frown on her face.

"It's pretty bad," Cindy said. "She needs to see a doctor. The bites actually broke the skin- through her clothes! She was bleeding. I don't like the way it's swelling, either, it looks like infection. It's spreading so fast – it's almost like venom!"

"I'll be all right. I can't leave Laurie home alone."

"One of us can stay here with her..." Dean inhaled deeply. "I can stay here while Cindy takes you in to Glen Haven."

"I don't know..."

"Listen," Dean said, sitting forward, "you're not going to do Laurie any good if you allow yourself to get sick." He paused, meaningfully, "Or worse."

Becky looked up at the ceiling, listening. Laurie was relatively silent. She was murmuring to herself. Becky strained to hear, but couldn't make out any words.

"All right," she said, though she still sounded unconvinced.

Dean saw them out the door. As soon as the car was

gone there was a loud thud upstairs, followed by a scream. It was Laurie's voice.

He rushed up the stairs, turned the corner and burst into the south bedroom. Laurie was sitting up in her bed in the corner of the room, laughing.

"Don't have a stroke, Preacher!" it rasped.

Dean felt foolish. Anger threatened to seep in. He caught himself, "Satan," he shouted, "I rebuke you in Jesus' Name!"

The demon shrieked in hilarious laughter. *"You don't have any authority over me, preacher!"*

Dean's face flushed red, "I said I rebuke you in Jesus' Name!"

"Rebuke yourself!" it said, laughing even louder, *"Jesus I know, Paul I know, but who in the hell are you? You bore me! Send me someone interesting "* It paused, as if in thought, *"Send me Danny Boy!"*

Why don't I have authority over the demons? Dean's mind raced over everything he'd learned in over twenty years of ministry.

"Oh Danny Boy, the pipes the pipes are calling-" the demon began singing, in a raspy, off-key voice.

Dear Lord, Dean thought. *What do I do now?*

"I wish you were hot or cold," the demon, tired of singing, began taunting the man of God, *"But because are neither hot or cold, but lukewarm, I'll spew you out of my mouth! You make God puke, preacher!"* It began making retching noises.

Dean backed out of the bedroom. He felt his face heat up with humiliation. He turned around and almost walked into the apparition of a man walking to the south bedroom doorway. He stepped aside quickly, watched it open the door and walk in, closing the door behind it. He heard what sounded like dozens of voices babbling in the room. *My God, my dear, sweet Jesus, what is going on in there?*

He moved toward the door as if to look, thought better of it. He turned around to go back downstairs, to think, to pray. As he turned he saw the shadow on the closet doors, saw the image of a man hanging from the branches of an oak tree that hadn't stood for Forty-three years.

He almost ran from the room and down the steps.

The minutes crept by. Dean sat at the kitchen table

praying, occasionally taking a sip of coffee with shaking hands. He was praying silently, his eyes clenched tightly against any further sights the house might throw at him.

Laurie was silent now. She had been for some time. The house, on the other hand, seemed to be alive. Dean could hear the sound of heavy footsteps from upstairs. Drawers and closet doors were constantly opening and shutting. Dean began praying harder, hoping to shut out the sounds that were assaulting him.

From the bathroom, Dean heard the sounds of a baby screaming. He put his hands over his ears, trying to stop the noise. He wanted to call on the Name of Jesus to help him, to make the noise stop. After the confrontation with Laurie in the south bedroom, he no longer had the confidence - the faith - to call upon His Name.

He thought about Laurie, upstairs in all that hell. He wanted to go up there, check on her. He didn't even know if she were alive, though something in his spirit told him she was fine physically. The devils still had plans for her.

The emergency room at Glen Haven Memorial Hospital was relatively quiet. There was a young boy in examination room one who'd fallen out of the top bunk bed. He was stoically receiving stitches to close the gash in his forehead. He kept asking if there'd be a "good" scar.

In exam room three two nurses were working with a young woman in labor. Cindy, sitting alone in the waiting room, wondered idly why they didn't go ahead and get her to the delivery room.

The doctors had taken Becky off to exam room four over an hour before. Cindy had been allowed to follow for the preliminary examination. Then the doctor ordered x-rays. She'd wondered why they had to x-ray a bite mark on the breast, and whisked Becky off to radiology. Cindy was left alone.

There were several old magazines lying around. Cindy glanced at the covers; one advertised an article, which promised to teach its readers how to please their partners. Another promised to tell men's love secrets. A third promised to reveal what men are really looking for in a woman. *So much for reading,* she reflected wryly.

The waiting room had a TV. A trash talk show was on. The topic was "Men Who Date Their Ex-wives' Mothers." Cindy was trying to ignore it. There was a sign over the set, which asked people to please leave the controls alone. Cindy read the sign for what must have been the hundredth time and contemplated ignoring it. She decided to obey the rules.

She looked down the hall for any sign of life. Nothing. A scream emitted from exam room 3, startling her. A fight erupted on the TV screen. A mother and her daughter were fighting over a man.

That was it. Cindy got up, switched the TV off.

She heard footsteps from down the hall. It was Becky, being led by a nurse. They went back into exam room four. Cindy decided to join them. Anything was better than the waiting room.

She saw the nurse leave the room. She entered. Becky looked up as she entered.

"Well?"

"The doctor said he was glad I came in, the wounds were getting terribly infected; almost - what was the word? Gang-"

"Gangrenous?"

"Yeah, that's it!"

"That's odd, gangrene setting in so soon."

"The doctor said it often happens with snake bites. Their teeth are so dirty, even if they're not poisonous-"

"*Snake*bite?" Cindy asked incredulously. "Didn't you tell them what happened?

"I told the nurse when we came in I got bit. I don't guess she wrote down what-who bit me. He looked at the bite, clucked his teeth together and said it was a strange place for a snakebite."

Cindy didn't know whether to be amused or not, "Did you tell him?"

"To be honest, Sister Cindy, I was too embarrassed to tell him my daughter did it, especially after he said it looked like snakebite. How do I explain... what's going on with Laurie."

Cindy nodded.

"I'm just worried he thinks I'm some sort of freak..." she shivered self-consciously. "He gives me these funny looks and grins. 'Makes me feel dirty..."

"I'm sure he's seen worse, honey."

"Not from me."

The doctor entered the room and seemed surprised to see Cindy there. Cindy was bemused. It was as if he hadn't noticed her before. "Oh, hello," he said, "I'm Doctor Norris." Cindy noticed he was about her age, mid thirties to early forties.

"I'm Cindy Grossman."

"'Relative?'"

"Friend, her pastor's wife."

"Oh," he said, she noticed the subtle change in his demeanor. He was less relaxed.

He turned to Becky, "Well, Mrs. Neustadt, I think you'll live. We've shot you up with anti-biotics; I have a prescription for some pills which will follow up on that. You should be all right. Just keep the dressing clean on those wounds."

"Thank you, doctor."

"Don't worry about it, Ma'am," he said with a grin. "That's what I get paid the big bucks for."

"Can I go?"

"Oh," he said, surprised by the question. "Sure. Call me in a few days at my office. Here's my card. We'll do a follow-up."

"Thank you, doctor." She got up to leave.

"Oh, Mrs. Neustadt," Dr. Norris, called as she left, "I'd be more careful with how I played with my snake."

I hate phones! Daniel reflected as he reached in the dark for the intruder into his dreams. He fumbled around the nightstand on which the bedroom telephone stood, knocked some items off onto the floor, finally found the phone. He glanced at his clock radio, *three a.m.; why doesn't anyone have an emergency at a decent time of the day?*

"Hello?" he mumbled into the mouthpiece.

"Brother Daniel?" it was a female voice, panicked. He recognized it from somewhere, struggled to place it.

"Yes." he said, trying to get his mind to function.

"Who is it?" Ruth rolled over toward him, coming out of her sleep.

"I don't know," Daniel said, cupping his hand over the mouthpiece, "some woman."

"Who?"

"I don't know!"

"Ask."

"I will, if you'll give me a chance."

"Brother Daniel?" the voice came over the phone.

"Yes." Daniel said again. *This is getting nowhere.*

"This is Becky Neustadt..."

Daniel's mind raced for a moment. He repeated the name, searching, "Becky - oh yes!" his heart jumped to his throat.

"Who?"

"Becky Neustadt from Delphi," he whispered.

Ruth was awake now. "What does she want?"

"Three guesses," Daniel said, cupping the mouthpiece again. "Yes, Mrs. Neustadt, what can I do for you?" He thought back; it had been almost a year since they'd been to Delphi. Laurie had never been far from his mind. "How's Laurie?"

"Pretty bad," Becky said, breaking down into sobs. "I don't know what to do, since Del died-"

Daniel was trying to catch up, "Del? Dead?"

"What?" Ruth was sitting up in bed now, straining to hear.

"Del's dead."

"What happened?" Ruth said.

"I don't know!" Daniel said, getting flustered at trying to hold two conversations.

"Brother Daniel?"

"Yes, Becky," Daniel said. "Listen, let me get on our other phone and I'll leave you here with Ruth, that way we can both talk and listen, okay?"

"I-I guess so."

"Good." He handed the phone to Ruth, "Here baby, talk away." He gave her a peck on the cheek and headed to the kitchen where the other phone was.

He treaded his way carefully through the dark, opening the bedroom door to the hallway. He tiptoed through the hall, trying to avoid any toy or other debris left by his youngest son, Joshua. Now he was at the dining room opening. He turned left to get to the kitchen and was confronted by a large, black, shadowy figure, blocking his way.

He felt anger rise up in him, checked it, and said, "What are you doing in my house, lizard? Get out of here in Jesus' Name! How dare you come into this home of the Holy Spirit?"

It was gone. *Yeah, the kimchi's about to hit the fan!** I should have known – I've been fasting. I guess we need to anoint the house again.*

He made it to the kitchen without further incident and picked up the phone.

"...what you have to do now is think about your children and their future," he heard Ruth's voice on the phone. "Danny, is

---

*A Korean dish, fermented cabbage, noted for its strong odor and spicy taste.

that you?"

"Yeah."

"Del passed away last March," Ruth told him.

"Yeah, Becky told me that," Daniel said, moving back toward the bedroom. "What happened?"

"It was a mining accident." Becky said, barely controlling her voice. "He was caught by a coal car-" she broke down.

"That's all right," Daniel tried to comfort her. "It's not important now." *Maybe no accident,* he thought. He felt the old familiar wave of frustration and anger begin to rise inside him. *I tried to warn him. O Lord, how long must it continue?* He took a deep breath. *No, this will do no good.* "I'm sorry, Mrs. Neustadt. What's going on with Laurie?"

"I don't know, Brother Daniel. She looks normal, but there's something - something *wrong* in there somewhere."

"Can you explain?"

"All during Del's funeral..."

"Yes?"

"She smiled, Brother Daniel. She smiled! When Brother Dean started preaching his eulogy she actually started giggling. My brother had to take her out of the church." She broke down crying again. "I don't know what to do. We had her tested and they all came back normal. We took her to a psychologist before, before, Del-" she swallowed.

"That's all right, go on."

"-and she was as normal as could be. The psychologist even suggested that *we* get some marriage counseling!"

Daniel smiled bitterly and shook his head at that. Why wasn't he surprised? "What has Pastor Grossman said about all this?"

"He's been praying and fasting for us, but he said this is all over his head. So I asked him if he'd get in touch with you."

"And?" he already knew the answer.

"He told me he couldn't contact you himself or he'd get in trouble with the District. He gave me your number."

"I see." *He's in a tough spot. At least he gave her my number.* "What made you think of me?"

"Laurie's been asking for you."

They sat at the kitchen table in silence, looking across at each other. There'd been no sleep after the phone call. There was

250

no question of what Daniel's response would be. Finally, Ruth broke the silence.

"You know, you don't have to go."

"I know."

"They've rejected your ministry once before. What's to stop them this time?"

"Nothing."

"It's a set up. The spirits are calling out to you."

"It could be the girl crying for help," Daniel countered, "If that's the case, I have no choice but to go."

Ruth nodded sadly. She understood.

"It's probably a trap," she said again, knowing the warning would fall on deaf ears.

"Yeah," Daniel sighed, "I know. I'm reminded of when Paul decided he had to go to Jerusalem. Old Agabus came up to him, took his belt and used it to bind Paul's arms, warning him that if Paul went to Jerusalem he'd be imprisoned."

"I know the story."

"I know. But you see, Paul knew what was going to happen to him when he went to Jerusalem. Agabus wasn't giving him any new revelation. Paul wasn't saying God wasn't speaking through Agabus. It was just Paul knew he had to go to Jerusalem to do God's work, even if it meant his death.

"There are some times God gives us a choice. He tells us, 'You don't have to walk through this fire. Or, you don't have to drink of this cup.'" He paused a moment, thinking, searching for words, "But you know you have to. Maybe it's a test. I don't know. I do know I feel I have to go up there and do what I can."

"Maybe," Ruth assented doubtfully, "I still worry..."

"Worry's a sin," Daniel teased, "it expresses doubt, which is the opposite of faith and whatever is not of faith is sin!'

"Daniel Baumer sermon number fifty-two, right?" she smiled. Her smile disappeared quickly. "Daniel, this is not something to joke about. Look at how much your family has suffered already."

"Do you think I'm not aware of it? Do you think there isn't a day that goes by that I don't think of Rog and Uta? Every time I look into Steve's eyes I see them." His voice cracked. He calmed himself, then, quietly, "That's why I have to go."

There was silence, while the two thought it over. Each lost in private thoughts.

Wait a minute, Daniel, what is all this about, anyway?

251

The Homestead

You know that greater is He that is in you than he that is in the world. God has not given us a spirit of fear, but of power, and love, and a sound mind.

But a chain is as strong as its weakest link, Danny Boy. God may be great, Jesus may be Lord, the Spirit may give power, but what about you, Dan? You are the weak link.

I can do all things through Christ who strengthens me!

Can you, Danny Boy? Will it be Christ who sends you, or some silly idea that the house is somehow responsible for Roggie and Uta's deaths? Roggie was in a combat zone; you know people get killed in combat zones. Uta was murdered. Stranger things have been known to happen. Remember, Danny Boy, your girdle is truth. If you're going up there on some fallacy your armor will fall apart, you'll be devoured...

Daniel contemplated that last thought a moment. He felt Ruth's eyes boring holes into his soul, watching him with loving concern. What if Rog and Uta's deaths were coincidences? *Could there be such a thing as a coincidence in a Universe ruled by an All-knowing, All-powerful God? What about Denise?*

She went crazy after her abortion. It happens often, Danny Boy, something the pro-choicers don't advertise, you've dealt with post abortion stress cases before.

"Daniel," Ruth interrupted the mental conversation, "I'm just concerned. All I know is what you told me, but how do we know that Roggie and Uta's deaths weren't just some sort of tragic coincidences? I'd hate to see you go up there and get devoured because you weren't girded with the truth."

Daniel's sat up in his chair, startling Ruth; she saw his eye's narrow and his jaw tense. She loved and trusted her husband, but felt a tinge of fear at the look in his eyes. It was a look she hadn't seen since his return from Vietnam so many years ago.

"What is it?" she asked.

Get thee behind me Satan! Daniel hissed angrily in his mind, *For thou savorest not the things of God! I rebuke you in Jesus' Name you slimy filth!*

"You know," he said finally. "I was just going over this thing in my mind, arguing with myself. And, in my mind, I just heard those words come at me, trying to talk me out of going."

Ruth's mouth dropped open. She nodded with understanding. She felt what the old timers called "Holy Ghost Goosebumps" all over her, confirming her conclusion. *Sometimes*

252

Satan's greatest weapons against us are those who love us most. As it was with Peter on that terrible night. "You need to go." She said with finality.

"You'll have to go alone. I can't get off during this inspection we're having. Not this week, maybe I can fly up on the weekend."

Daniel nodded. "Maybe it'll all be over by then. What is it, Tuesday? I'll have Wednesday, Thursday, and Friday, to do it. Who knows? I can be home for the weekend if all goes well."

"What about Stevie? Could he meet you up there?"

"No, he's counseling at the Summer Camp."

"How about David?"

Daniel thought about their oldest son in his senior year at Valdosta State. It would be good to have him.

"Oh yes," Ruth recollected. "He's with Steve. It's a shame your mother can't go...

He paused at that thought a moment. He'd worked with Rose several times in that area. He knew she'd be willing. She'd offered to go with them the previous year. He mulled it over, warming to the idea. Then, "No. I don't think it would work. I don't think she's up to it any more, besides I think she's still too vulnerable to the spirits in the house. "

"What about you?" Ruth asked. "You've been affected, too."

"I know," Daniel said, thoughtfully, "but somehow I believe it's different with me. I don't know... this may all be His idea anyway. It wouldn't be the first time the devil outsmarted himself.

"I guess I'm on my own until the weekend," he concluded. *Actually, I won't be alone; He's always with me.* "Don't worry, Love," he said, reaching across the table, taking her hand. "He's with me always. What more do I need."

"But even He told us to go by twos."

"Then he'll send me my partner."

Chapter 16
June 16, 2010

Finally, my brethren, be strong in the Lord, and in the power of His might. Put on the whole armor of God that ye may be able to stand against the wiles of the devil.
(Eph. 6: 10 & 11)

Daniel pulled his car up to the front of the house. He had made the fourteen hour drive in one day, getting up at four-thirty Georgia time and driving straight through. He had stopped only for gas and a bite to eat. It was now a little after six central time. He was physically tired, but spiritually refreshed.

He had spent the day with the Lord, playing his collection of praise and worship tapes on his car's cassette player and praying. All in all, it had been a pleasant drive, aside from a lunch hour traffic jam in Nashville. He had been halfway persuaded to pull over in Clarksville, perhaps visit the 101st Airborne Division Museum at Ft. Campbell. Approaching the exit for Ft. Campbell, he'd changed his mind, deciding to drive on through.

He'd tried to plan his strategy. Should he work on the girl first or cleanse the house? There was the problem of the two feeding off one another. It would be better if he could get her out of the house, get her delivered, and then cleanse the house. If that weren't possible, he'd go for the girl first. If he could get her cleaned up perhaps she could exert her own will to help him keep them out until he could cleanse the house.

He wished he had Ruth with him. It didn't seem right going into battle without her. He felt he was missing an important component to his arsenal, his rib. It helped to know she was praying intercession.

He hesitated getting out of the car. He didn't know whether or not to go in. He was tired to be sure. He would have to drive to Glen Haven for a motel room. This would make matters even more complicated. When he left to get rest, which he knew he'd have to do, he'd be at least thirty to forty minutes away if he were needed.

He hoped he could still get a motel room by the time he

got to Glen Haven. Being on the Interstate, he knew the place was going to fill up at this time of the year. That would be lovely, having to sleep in the car.

O Lord, this is going to be a real no-kidder. I'm really going to need your help on this one, more than the others.

He had just about made up his mind to drive off to Glen Haven and return in the morning. A terrible scream broke the silence. Daniel jumped in his seat. He was out of the car and running around to the back of the house before he even realized he was on his feet.

He stopped on the back porch, knocked on the back door. He heard more screaming, the sounds of things crashing from upstairs. He tried the door. It was unlocked. He paused, saying a short prayer of protection, and went in. He was still praying under his breath as he paused in the kitchen, getting his bearings. He heard the sounds of struggling upstairs, heard someone pleading, guessed it was Becky. *The south bedroom, of course!* There was laughing, unearthly, inhuman. He ran up the stairs.

He was halfway up the stairs before he noticed the apparition standing at the head of the stairs. *Molina.* "Get out of my way, demon, in the Name of Jesus!" He started up the steps again, saw the spirit hadn't moved.

"I said, *move!* By the Blood of Jesus!"

It was gone.

He rounded the corner. It was relatively quiet now. He heard quiet sobbing. *Becky. O Lord, please let her be all right.* He moved through the west bedroom, saw the door shut to the south bedroom. He sighed, tried the door, it wouldn't budge. *Of course, I should have known.*

He was getting tired of these little games. "I command this door to open!"

From behind the door, ***"You didn't say 'Simon says.'"*** Cackling.

"You know in Whose Name I come! Open the door now!"

The door flew open.

Daniel nodded and walked in. His senses were heightened to a fever pitch now. He was in combat. There was a figure lying on the floor sobbing – Becky. He saw the little girl, Laurie, out of the corner of his eye. She lay curled in the corner of her bed, glaring out at him, her tongue darting in and out of her mouth. She was grinning at him. She reminded him of a deadly

255

viper coiled for the strike. *The imagery is intended, no doubt.*

First priority, get Becky out of here. He moved toward Becky, keeping Laurie in the corner of his vision. He actually smiled when she sprang; he was ready. He turned quickly, "Stop! In Jesus' Name!"

The girl stopped short in midair, as though she'd hit a wall, and fell to the floor. He turned to face her squarely now. She recovered on all fours, animal - like, glancing up warily, as though afraid to look directly at him.

It was time to take control of the situation. Daniel looked down at her, cowering before him. He was softly praying in the spirit, *O Holy Spirit, guide and protect me, O Father, grant me Your wisdom, Lord Jesus, cover me with Your precious Blood.*

"Now I command you in the Name of Jesus to get back on that bed. Now!"

She scampered onto the bed, whimpering like a whipped puppy.

"Lord, I pray send angels to guard her and protect her while I'm gone." Speaking aloud to the demon forces he sensed at work, he commanded, "I forbid you to harm the girl Laurie in any way by the authority given me in Luke 10:19 and Mark 16: 16-20, and in the Name of Jesus Christ."

He felt a warmth in the room. Once more he knew the Lord had sent His guardian angels into the house. They'd probably never left. That was why the girl wasn't dead already.

"Nasty! Nasty! Nasty!" Daniel glanced over toward Laurie. He saw her tongue darting in and out of her mouth like a serpent's.

"In the Name of Jesus, I command you to be silent!"

He turned to the mother, "Becky?"

He turned her over gently; behind him he heard a growling. "I told you to stay put!" He didn't bother to turn around, knowing he was protected now.

"Becky?"

She was unconscious. He felt for a pulse, found it weak. There were bruises on her neck from where Laurie (or the demons) had choked her. There was a nasty cut and bruise over her left eye. It looked like a blow from a blunt object. He picked Becky up gently, not knowing if there were any internal injuries. He had to get her out of the south bedroom, though. He was trusting the Lord to guide his actions and thoughts.

He didn't feel there was a safe place for her anywhere

upstairs, either. He carried her downstairs and laid her on the sofa in the living room. He went into the kitchen, checked the refrigerator for ice, made an ice pack with a washrag and got her a glass of ice water.

She was coming to when he returned to her. She saw him; he noted the relief in her eyes.

"What happened?" she croaked as he handed her the water. She drank, grimaced with pain as she swallowed. "Thanks."

"I was hoping you'd be able to tell me."

"I was trying to feed Laurie." She remembered, "Oh, where-"

"She's upstairs under guard." Daniel said comfortingly.

"Who's guarding her?"

He smiled.

"That takes some getting used to, you know?"

"I've been told." Daniel smiled, "I don't see why. The Bible is full of stories of angels helping God's children."

"I know. It just seems weird- I mean it's one thing to read about angels in the Bible," her voice gave out at that point.

"Take it easy," he said. "I don't know how much damage has been done to your throat. Let me see it."

She leaned forward, pulling her collar down, "How bad is it?"

"It's pretty badly bruised." He paused a moment, "Here," he said finally, reaching out his hands. "Be healed, in Jesus' Name.

"I-it's amazing!" Becky exclaimed, her eyes wide with wonder.

"It's God." Daniel corrected. It always amazed him that Christians could be surprised when God did what the Bible said He would do – what *He* said He would do.

"Now, what happened?"

"Laurie was acting normal. I took her dinner. We were eating and talking, just like normal, like old times. Then she turned mean, angry, her face twisted. That's all I remember."

"When I came in she was on top of you, choking you. Have you been here alone?"

She nodded sadly.

"Don't you have anyone who could help you?"

"My mama and daddy are dead. The other kids are staying with my brother in St. Louis. My sister lives in Chicago.

There's no one."

"What about your in-laws?"

Becky dropped her head, "They- they don't have much to do with me- haven't since Del died. They don't approve of me."

"Is it Laurie?"

She looked up quickly, startled, a bit scared, "How did you know that? It isn't that psychic stuff is it?"

Daniel laughed, "No, it's like when Jesus spoke with the woman at the well?" He looked at her questioningly.

She nodded.

"He knew all there was to know about her. It's like Elisha knowing what the King of Syria was up to or Peter knowing that Ananias and Saphira were lying about their gift to the Church."

She was impressed, "That must be a neat gift."

"Sometimes it doesn't seem like much of a gift." Dan said sadly.

"What do you mean?"

"I dunno," he sighed. "Sometimes there are things you almost wish God hadn't shown you." He rebuked himself inwardly for that. *How dare I sound ungrateful for God's gifts?*

This is getting off track. "We were talking about Laurie," he said.

"Yes," Becky said, remembering. "What do you know?"

"Only what the Lord tells me," he paused again, checking a thought that flashed through his mind. "Was she Del's?" He saw her uneasiness at the question. He knew he'd hit a nerve. "This might be important to what's going on here," he explained.

"Well," she said, finally. "I guess it doesn't take the Great Skaramoosh to figure that out, does it?"

"No." He smiled, "I guess it doesn't."

"After all, Del and I both being blondes with blue eyes, Jennie and Rhonda both looking like us and then, there's Laurie, lookin' like the - milkman, or mailman, or- " she began crying.

Daniel felt awkward. He wanted to reach out and comfort her, knowing she needed someone to hold her. But he was a stranger. They were alone for all intents and purposes in the house. It might be misinterpreted. And the house had strange ways of affecting people.

He reached in his pocket, drew out a clean handkerchief, handed it to her. He put his hand over hers, squeezed. She straightened up, getting control, "Thanks," she said. "I'm sorry,

258

it's been-"

"No need to apologize," he said. "You've been through a lot."

"If it'll help Laurie, I guess I'd better share it. It's not like it's a big secret.

"Of all the places we had to come back to – Delphi – where everybody knows your name and history," She dabbed at her eyes. "I guess the only reason I agreed was the idea of moving back home."

"Delphi?"

"No, Brother Daniel, the house."

Daniel was stunned, "This house-"

"It's my family's home. My grandpa and great grandfather were born here," she noted the confused look on his face. "I'm a Felder. Johnny Felder was my grandpa. This was his house before he lost it in that lawsuit."   "Dear   Sweet   Lord," Daniel said. *Forgive me God; this is heavier than I thought.*

"What is it?"

"Everything makes sense now," Daniel said. "We're dealing with a family curse!"

"What?" she was doubtful.

"Let me explain as briefly as I can," Daniel said. "Do you remember in the Bible where God says 'I shall visit the sins of the fathers upon the sons unto the fourth generation'?"

She nodded.

"Now we know that God is just and he doesn't punish anyone for anyone else's sins. We are each accountable for our own failings, right? As a matter of fact He says elsewhere He won't punish a son for the father's sin. Is God contradicting Himself? Can He?"

She shook her head, trying to grasp every point.

"So what is God trying to say?" he continued without waiting for an answer. "Let me put it this way. Have you ever noticed how certain types of behaviors seem to run in certain families? You'll see several generations of alcoholics in the same family? Even psychologists talk about the children of child abusers becoming abusers themselves. All sorts of behaviors are passed down through families."

"I've read articles about that sort of thing."

"I believe this is what God was talking about. Some people call it a 'generational curse.' You see, scientists are searching about for genetic causes for these behaviors, and they may exist. However, if they find genetic evidence, it doesn't rule out a spiritual cause for such behaviors. There are spirits of lust, alcoholism, murder, suicide, and things like that. Remember, Ephesians 6:12 says, 'we wrestle not against flesh and blood but against principalities, powers,' spirits.

"You see, I've been trying to figure this out. Generally, when you're dealing with a certain type of spirit, there is a pattern of behavior they display. This helps you identify it. In so-called haunted houses, the 'ghosts' always follow a certain pattern, relive certain events, and walk certain paths. What's been happening with Laurie is totally against this house's M.O. It had me baffled unless there were new spirits in here I didn't know about. I didn't sense any new spirits in the house. But that's not unusual, they're often good at 'hiding.'"

There was a noise from upstairs.

"Laurie!" Becky was up and heading through the dining room; Daniel followed close behind her.

Becky halted at the bottom of the steps. It was dark upstairs.

"Do you have a flashlight?"

"Yes," she went to the kitchen counter, brought back two.

"Let me go first," he said, taking the first step. There was a definite drop in temperature as soon as he entered the stairwell. He began praying in the Spirit under his breath. *This is usual. What I can't get is how they can keep on. I thought I had them bound.*

At the top of the steps he paused, shadows appeared to dart back and forth in the edges of his peripheral vision. *Imps. They'll run until the big boys attack.*

He could feel Becky close behind him as they entered the west bedroom. Across the room he could see the door to Laurie's bedroom, opened. He stealthily made his way across the bedroom. *This is silly,* he rebuked himself. *They know I'm coming.* He straightened himself up as he entered the south bedroom, shining his light to his right to see if Laurie were still in bed.

He noticed a definite increase in temperature in the south bedroom, now. It was almost hot. It wasn't a physical heat. He looked at the little girl, sleeping peacefully. He smiled. He could almost see the guardian spirits standing over her bed. He nodded in their direction, could sense their nodding back. Goosebumps ran across his body.

"The angels are still here," he whispered to Becky, then

wondered why he was whispering. "The demons have left for a season. I guess they're bored. They're bound from showing out."

"So she's okay?"

"For now. They'll be back. We need to get her out of this room. This is the spiritual heart of the house."

"The sofa rolls out into a bed," Becky offered.

"Good."

Daniel picked the little girl up in his arms, cradling her as if she were fragile. He kissed her forehead tenderly and carried her out.

"Why don't you just go ahead and cast them out?" Becky asked as she carried them downstairs.

'I don't have permission yet."

"Permission?"

"From God," Daniel replied. "You can't do anything unless He gives you the 'green light'. Remember, even Jesus said He could only do what He saw the Father do."

"When will He do that?" Becky asked impatiently.

"I don't know," he said as Becky pulled the sofa out into a bed. "I don't have all the answers, Becky. I don't trust those that act as though they do. But, if you'll excuse me sounding sanctimonious, I know *The Answer*. He takes care of the rest."

"How will you know it's time?"

"I'll know."

"How?"

"I'll just *know*."

"You're in a mess." Ruth said, from over eight hundred miles away. Daniel had called to update her as soon as they'd gotten Laurie settled.

"Yeah," he agreed, "but the goo is at least starting to clear. Knowledge is power."

"Where are you staying?"

"I don't know yet," he said. "I was going to get a motel room in Glen Haven. I figured I'd better check in here first. It's a good thing I did."

"It sounds like you got there in the nick of time."

"Yeah, that's me, the Seventh Cavalry."

"Watch out, Custer. Listen," she said, changing the subject, "You'd better get some rest. You won't do them any good if you collapse. You'll only leave yourself open for the devil's attacks. I'm trying to get Friday off. If I can, I'll catch an afternoon flight and be in St. Louis Thursday night."

"Let me know so I can come get you."

"You know I will. Get some rest so you're around to come get me."

"Yes, Mother. I've just got some things to take care of here before I can rest, before I can leave here."

"All right. Well, I'll let you go so you can get done and get some rest. I love you."

"I love you, too. 'Bye Shug."

He hung the up the phone. He turned to Becky, who'd been sitting at the kitchen table sipping coffee, listening to Daniel's side of the conversation.

"You two love each other very much," she said wistfully.

"Yes," Daniel said. "I don't know what I'll do with her sometimes, but I sure don't know what I'd do without her. How about you and Del? You two appeared to love each other."

"We did, though we didn't always know it." She began to tear up, "I guess that's how I got Laurie."

"Yes," Daniel said. "Maybe you'd better tell me what happened. That is, if you're able."

"Oh, I guess I can handle it." She looked up at him, "Brother Daniel, I don't quite understand everything going on here, but if you think it might have some connection, it wouldn't be right to hold anything back. Especially after everything you've gone through and done to help us. After the way we treated you."

"Don't sweat the small stuff. What happened?"

"You probably have already figured it out."

"Maybe, but you need to tell me. Confession is good for the soul."

"Well, like I said, Del and I didn't always know how much we loved each other. We dated in high school. Everyone expected we were going to get married." Daniel had to shake his head at that one, "When I got pregnant it was settled.

"Del's family never forgave me for getting pregnant. Like I did it on my own!" she snorted. "Del was a big football player in high school. The University of Illinois was scouting him. Our marriage killed those plans. Gettin' an abortion was out of the question for both of us; we were both raised strict WHF. It was wrong enough what we done- did. An abortion would have made it worse. Besides, when I think of what a blessing Jennie has been- to have killed her- I couldn't."

Daniel nodded sympathetically.

262

"Well, Del went to work in the mines. We thought one day, when Jennie got a little older, when we got on our feet, I could get a job somewhere and Del could go to school. Of course, I got pregnant with Rhonda at about the time we began talking about making it happen. After that, we never talked about it again. We both knew we were in our slot - call it a rut.

"Then Del got laid off at the mines. We started having problems. I was able to get a job at the grocery store in Glen Haven. He stayed at home with the kids waiting for the mines to call him back. After a month he was going crazy sitting at home. I suggested he get a job somewhere else just to keep him busy until the mines re-opened. We had a terrible fight about that. He took it as an insult to his manhood or something.

"After that he started running with a bunch of the boys, leaving the kids with his mom. The only problem was the boys he was running with weren't all boys. I came home – we were living over by the park at the time – and caught him in bed with some girl who'd chased him during high school.

"Well, I whipped the tar out of that floozy and kicked him out. He didn't seem to mind too much. He started running around. I figured what was sauce for the goose was sauce for the gander. The manager of the store I was working at had made a couple offhand compliments toward me. One night he was flirting, I flirted back. That was all it took.

"When I found out I was carrying Laurie, I decided to take my kids and move to St. Louis. My sister-in-law got me a job as a receptionist in the lawyer's office she worked at. I figured I'd have my baby, save up money for a divorce and start all over on my own again with my kids. I didn't reckon anyone would want a woman with three kids. I'd raise them myself.

"I was about four months along when Del showed up. He'd heard I was pregnant. He asked me if it was his. I could have lied but didn't. I cared too much for him to do that. One of the toughest things I'd ever had to do, was confess to him what I'd done; what had happened. I guess it was then we both realized we'd grown up... what we were about to lose.

"He told me he still loved me and wanted me back. I told him I wasn't about to kill my baby. He told me he didn't expect me to. He said he figured if he hadn't cheated on me I wouldn't have cheated on him." Her voice began trembling with emotion, "He was such a *good* man.

"Brother Daniel, he raised Laurie as his own, never made

no difference between our kids. If anything I think he showed some partiality toward Laurie. She was his 'baby doll.' Whenever someone stupid would make a comment about Laurie's hair and eyes, he'd just make a joke about it. She was a real daddy's girl, always going off with him to town in his truck. The other girls would even get jealous.

"We lived in St. Louis for several years. Would have been happy there. Del took a job at the carburetor plant in St. Louis. He got on a good shift, working his way up. There was talk of a management position.

"Then he heard the mine was opening back up. He found out the company had wanted to call him back, offering a supervisor position. We moved home. When I saw your family had put our old house up for sale, I talked Del into buying it. He didn't want to. He remembered all the old stories about the place, the rumors. I talked him into it. Now he's dead. "

"The mine's a dangerous place. Do you really believe this house had anything to do with the accident that killed him?" Daniel asked.

"I don't know." Becky said. She shivered slightly, "Do you remember the last time you were here and you asked us if we'd seen anything unusual?"

"Yes."

"Right after you left, Del began seeing things. He didn't say nothing at first. Later, he said he was hoping I'd mention something. I didn't. I wasn't seeing anything."

"What did he see?"

"Oh, he said he ran into someone walking up the steps one night when he was going downstairs to the bathroom. He told me that one night, he was checking on the kids as they slept, he was coming out of Laurie's room and he saw the shadow of someone hanging from a tree on the wall where the closet's at." She paused, seeing the expression on his face, "You know about all this?"

"I've seen it all, too, when I was a kid."

"Pretty scary?"

He shrugged. "At first. After awhile, you get used to it. I figured they wouldn't hurt me, 'couldn't hurt me, for some reason."

"God had a plan for you."

"Maybe," he said, "I think they got to my brother Roggie."

264

"I remember you mentioning him."

"He gave in to the spirits here, I believe. They got him."

"What kind of spirits do you think are here?"

"Well," Daniel said, "Judging by what we know of the history of this place, there's a bunch, but that's not unusual. They often travel in packs anyway. You seem to find certain kinds of spirits together."

"For instance?"

"Well, you generally find lust and adultery together. Murder and suicide often like to hang around with spirits of guilt and shame. Understand, not everyone who commits murder is, quote, possessed by a spirit of murder, but they're often hanging around. If they don't cause the murder, they seem to feed off the misery somehow.

"I was talking about the spirits here. You've got spirits of lust, seducing spirits-"

"Seducing spirits?" she asked.

"Yeah, they tempt people into sexual sins. I think Bathsheba had one. I mean, what's she doing taking a bath on her roof when she knows the king often sleeps outside on his roof? Didn't she think someone would see her? David is responsible for what he did, but I believe he was set up. Like Joseph. Here's Potiphar's wife, standing naked in his quarters, another seducing spirit. But Joseph, unlike David, doesn't hang around. He splits."

"It didn't do him much good."

"No, sometimes it doesn't seem to do much good," he said, thoughtfully, reflecting on his own past. "But you have to trust God to straighten these things out. He does, eventually. As Joseph said, what his brothers and Potiphar's wife meant for evil, God brought about for the good."

"What else are we dealing with here?"

"I believe there's a spirit of abortion or murder at work here."

"Abortion?"

"My family had reason to believe there's a baby, your Great-great Aunt Molina's, buried on the property somewhere. It was dumped down the old well and covered over."

Becky's eyes widened, "How do you know that?"

"I'm sorry. I know this is your family and all, but we've done some research."

"No, I believe you," Becky said. "It all makes sense now."

265

"What?"

"Well, you know how families have secrets they never talk about in front of the kids. I don't remember Great Aunt Molina. She died before I was born. But I remember Daddy and the folks talking about her, how she was strange, living alone in this big house, with her ghosts and her 'baby,' that stuffed doll of hers. One night Daddy told us kids a ghost story about Aunt Molina's dead baby, how it was buried under the 'Old House' and its ghost would come get us if we were bad. Mama told us he was making it all up.

"For us it was all just a ghost story. But Daddy never would talk about the time he lived here as a boy."

There was quiet for a while, and then Becky sat up. "I know where the old well was!" she said. "It's under the old porch, where the bathroom is now!"

Dean glanced at the clock on the wall of his study. It was past midnight. He wondered if Daniel was still at the Neustadt's house. He'd passed by the house several hours before, saw the car with Georgia tags, assumed it was Daniel. He'd slowed his car, thought about stopping, then stepped on the gas and returned home.

Since coming home, he'd lifted up the receiver to the phone several times. He'd changed his mind, replaced it. Now he sat alone. Cindy and the kids were in bed. He'd been taking an account of his life. He didn't like the balance at the bottom of the ledger.

Where had all the years gone? He thought of his work in Delphi, his achievements or lack thereof. Almost twenty years as pastor, what was there to show for it?

Earlier in the evening, he'd gone to the office for a while; poured over the Church membership rolls since he'd been pastor. There had been fifty active members when he first took over the Church in 1981. Sunday school attendance had been sixty-three. He'd looked at last year's annual report. He'd found there were forty-six active members, if one didn't count the Bryant's, who were in a nursing home at Glen Haven. He visited them once a week, on Thursdays. Sunday school attendance last year averaged fifty.

Well, what did you expect, Dean? Delphi's population is down, too.

But could he say everyone in Delphi was in a church

266

somewhere?

He'd gone through his church registry. There hadn't been a baptism in two years, unless one counted the last revival where Ricky Butz came forward, rededicated his life to the Lord and asked to be re-baptized. He didn't even want to think about the last time someone had been baptized in the Holy Ghost when a guest evangelist hadn't been present.

He'd been telling himself he was doing the Lord's work all these years, bringing care and comfort to the congregation as they grew older and died. He comforted himself that these old saints in Delphi needed ministry, too.

Since his confrontation with Laurie Neustadt, though, he'd begun asking himself if he were copping out. These people needed ministry, to be sure. *Was this what I entered the ministry for?*

Why couldn't I exercise authority over the demon in Laurie Neustadt?

During this evening's service he'd had a strange thing happen to him. He'd held an altar call, as he did every service, asking people who wanted to get serious with the Lord to come up and dedicate their lives to Him. He asked anyone who wanted a fresh anointing of the Spirit to come forward. By the time he finished, everyone was at the altar. They'd be ashamed not to go.

He'd been enjoying the ministry at the altar, joining in with everyone shouting and praying in tongues. He'd thought the Lord was really moving.

Then a small voice in the back of his head spoke to him. *Dean, step back a minute. Watch.*

He'd ignored it at first. After all, he was feeling good, shouting and stomping his foot himself. Then the voice spoke again. *Dean, step back a minute and watch.*

Now he figured he'd better pay attention. He stepped back up to the pulpit and watched the twenty or so members of his congregation gathered at the front of the church.

There was Martha Hobbs, stretched out on the floor, her eyes closed, while Sally Reynolds and Rita Felder babbled over her. Norm Felder, Rita's husband (Becky's uncle) was stomping his foot, shouting the same words over and over again. Sister Hauser was running around the sanctuary howling. Her husband was lying on the floor kicking his feet, rolling back and forth in the center aisle shouting at the top of his voice. Bertha Henson was commanding a devil to come out of Nancy Schaub, while

267

The Homestead

Nancy cried and called on Jesus.

Dean felt nausea overwhelm him. Suddenly, he saw them as skeletons running, leaping, rolling around. He'd blinked his eyes in disbelief, but saw them just as plain.

Dear God, he thought, *they're dead and don't know it.*

He realized they were doing the same thing they did at every Sunday and Wednesday night prayer service. They were doing the same thing they'd been doing at every Sunday and Wednesday night prayer service for years. They were doing it from memory. It had become a ritual. They were dead.

He was hit with a terrible realization. It was his fault. He'd allowed them to die.

Chapter 17
June 17, 2010

After these things the Lord sent them appointed other seventy also, and sent them two by two before His face into every city and place, whither He Himself would come.
(Luke 10:1)

Daniel wakened suddenly. He'd been dreaming again, the same, tortured dreams about Roggie, Uta, and Nam. He opened his eyes and found himself staring into the face of Laurie Neustadt, who was sitting on the floor next to the love seat on which he had been sleeping. He stared into her big brown eyes. So innocent. So tortured.

"Mama told me to tell her when you woke up so she could cook you breakfast," she said.

He was at a loss for words. *I'm in the old house, the Homestead. Now I remember. It was late. Becky had me call ahead before I drove to Glen Haven. There were no rooms.* It hadn't taken much to persuade him to stay on the loveseat that evening. He'd also thought it would be a good idea to keep an eye on Laurie. Still, he'd best not spend another night alone in the house with the Neustadts.

"Are you ready for breakfast now?"

"Coffee," he mumbled.

"Okay," she said, "Black?"

He nodded.

"Just like my daddy liked it." She ran off to the kitchen, "Mama! The preacher's up!"

The preacher, he thought, *it's been a long time since I felt like a real preacher.* He stayed busy, ministering, counseling, teaching, discipling, but he missed getting in front of a congregation and "letting the hammer down." These other things were good and necessary, but it was in preaching that Daniel found life. *There'll be time for self-pity later, Baumer. Right now, you'd better stick with the problem at hand.*

He began to stand up. He groaned as his joints cracked and snapped as he exercised them for the first time that day.

"Ooooooh Lord," he moaned. "Help me get this body to

work!" *Well, that's one way to keep me in prayer, getting his legs, knees, and back to work without pain in the mornings.*

Don't blame God for your wasted youth, Baumer. God didn't make you volunteer for jump school – that was all your idea.

It had been quiet after the initial confrontation. Daniel figured the spirits were still hiding. Laurie appeared a normal ten-year-old girl on the surface. He had taken a good long look into her eyes, though. There was still something flickering in there, hidden deep, but occasionally peeking out.

It's a nasty secret, Lord. But it was going to have to come out. *You can't keep sin covered and expect the blessings of God.* It was going to be a delicate situation, peeling the scabs off these wounds without causing further damage.

He could hear the rattling of pots, pans, and dishes from the kitchen. He headed for the smell of fresh coffee and frying bacon. For a split second he was thrust back thirty years to his childhood. He half expected to see Brew and Roggie sitting at the table waiting for Rose to finish breakfast. He realized sadly that Brew and Roggie were gone. Rose's health was failing and in spite of Roger's denials, the family suspected the onset of Alzheimer's. Roger had just had knee replacement surgery. It was hard to think of his parents as being old.

"Laurie didn't wake you, did she?" Becky asked from the stove.

"No, I have my own alarm clocks," he replied cryptically.

"How do you like your eggs?"

"Over easy - listen, you don't have to do this-"

"I know," she said, without turning around. "Let me though. I miss cooking for a man."

"I really need to be getting along, finding a motel room..."

"I know," there was a hint of resignation in her voice. "It doesn't look right, you staying here. What will the neighbors think? Even though we slept on different ends of this big old house."

"Paul said-"

"Avoid the appearances of evil, I know," she finished his sentence." I understand. You don't have to explain. You're a man of God, you're married, I understand. It could hurt your ministry. But there was no way I was going to let you drive these country roads in the shape you were in last night - this morning. Besides,

I think your staying here was calming to Laurie."

"Maybe so," he conceded.

"Well, you've got to eat. There's no decent place until you hit Glen Haven. By then, breakfast will be over in most places."

"You've talked me into it."

She brought him his plate. He was about to eat his first bite when he heard a car pull up out front. A door closed. Becky looked out the window over the sink.

"It's Pastor Grossman."

Daniel continued eating. He winked at Laurie, who was eating a bowl of cereal across from him. She smiled back. He could hear Dean's footsteps outside the bay windows and on to the back porch steps. There was a knock at the door. Becky opened it. "Hello, Pastor, you're up and around early this morning."

"Well, I didn't get much sleep last night. I'm looking for Brother Daniel."

"Oh," she began, awkwardly. "He's here. Come on in."

"What's up, Dean?" Daniel said, rising and wiping his mouth.

"Don't get up, Daniel. Enjoy your breakfast. I'm glad you're here, I was afraid I was going to have to hunt you all over Glen Haven."

"Well, it was late by time we finished last night. I was exhausted. Becky offered me the love seat-"

"You don't have to explain it to me." He looked out the front window across the street to where Mrs. Schultz was pretending to be busy in her front yard. He grinned, "Now, Mrs. Schultz might want a written notarized statement that you two were good last night..."

There were smiles all around. The tension was broken.

"It might cause talk if you stayed here though." Dean said, "No, I know it will cause talk if you stay here. And you can't stay in Glen Haven, either, that's too far. You're needed here. That's why I'd like to offer you the cottage again. That is, if you'll take it. I wouldn't blame you if you didn't."

Daniel looked at his old friend. He was touched, "I appreciate that. What will your board say?"

"Let me worry about that. And I'll handle Chicago, too. God's been dealing with me. I've been praying all night."

"Pastor," Becky interrupted. "Before you get started,

271

would you like some coffee?"

He nodded. They waited until she'd brought him a cup and sat down.

Dean looked over at Laurie. He was surprised to see her behaving normally, "You seem to be doing well, Sweetheart."

Laurie nodded happily, "Can I go now, Mama?"

Becky nodded, "Just stay downstairs, Sweetie." She looked to Daniel, who nodded in confirmation. The three adults watched her scamper off into the living room. There was a moment of silence broken finally by Dean.

"I've failed, Daniel," he said, his voice choking. He didn't care that Becky was there. "All these years I've had my ministry on cruise control. I've gone to sleep at the wheel. My church has been stagnant for at least ten years. We've haven't grown, as a matter of fact, we're losing ground. There are only three families with children in the church. About eighty percent of my members are over fifty years old. I've been watching my church die of old age and content to let it happen.

"It's funny, when you think of it," he said sadly. "It took a demon to show me how much I've blown it for God. The other night when Laurie, or the demons, was acting out I commanded them to cease what they were doing. They told me I had no authority over them.

"It's put me to thinking about my walk with the Lord. If the devil isn't worried about me then I'm not doing much for the Lord."

I must be a real fireball, Daniel reflected sardonically.

"I've decided to do something about it," he said, "Danny – Daniel - I want to help you here. I need to help you. I was praying last night and I got the impression this was my last chance to - to - I don't know..."

"I understand," Daniel answered. "It's funny; Ruth was worried about me coming alone. I told her God would send me a partner if I needed one. But before you get into this you need to know what you're getting into." He paused a moment to let his words sink in.

"I heard it said once," he continued. "That salvation may be free, but the *anointing*, the ability to walk in the power of God, will cost you *everything*. Are you willing to pay the price?"

"I don't see as I have a choice, considering what's at stake here."

Daniel nodded, satisfied with the answer. He knew now

why Ruth hadn't been able to come with him. He also understood why he hadn't had permission to cast out the demons last night. God was waiting on Dean. He now understood that he wasn't the only one haunted by memories of this house. They would exorcise their personal demons together.

It was a few hours later. The men had left for the church so Daniel could get settled in to the guest cottage and clean up. Now they were sitting at the Grossman kitchen table having just finished up some tuna sandwiches Cindy Grossman had prepared for them and sipping iced tea.

He sipped his unsweetened tea and reflected on how much of a southerner he had become. The Grossman's had offered him sugar, but for a glass of sweetened iced tea to taste right, it had to be mixed while the tea was hot. *Oh well, when in Rome...*

"How'd you get into this ministry, Daniel?" Dean had patiently waited while Daniel cleaned up and ate. Now it was time to learn.

"I don't think anyone in their right mind wants to get in to a deliverance ministry," Daniel began as Cindy took his plate. He nodded thanks. She smiled back. It appeared she was genuinely pleased he was there. He continued. "I don't know if I got into it or it got into me. You know you don't 'choose' a ministry, 'it' - or He - chooses you.

"I had a kid one time, young in the Lord, all on fire. He told me he wanted to cast out a demon. He wanted to find a dragon to slay.' I told him not to worry. If God wanted him to cast out devils he wouldn't have to hunt them; they'd find him.

"We're all given the authority to cast out devils; it's everyone's job. I do believe there are those who are called to a ministry of deliverance. Some folks say there is no such thing, but the Books of Luke and Acts mentions several times that Jesus healed 'all who were oppressed of the devil.' Deliverance is spiritual healing.

"I guess God called me to it early... living in the Homestead (our name for the Felder Place) made me interested in the occult, from an intellectual point of view, of course. Then, when I answered my call, it seemed every time I turned around I was running into demoniacs. I started casting them out like the Bible describes. The next thing I know, every time I turn around there was a guy or gal with spiritual problems. One time I got

273

confronted in a restaurant in Myrtle Beach, South Carolina!

"I learned as I went. I made some mistakes on the way. I try not to think about those too often. You just learn and move on.

"I've had people break my heart after we've poured our lives into them. You know what the Bible says about a 'dog returning to his vomit?' I learned firsthand after working with a subject, just to see them go back into the sin that got them in trouble in the first place. It can get discouraging.

"Then, there's opposition from people who are supposed to be your brothers and sisters in Christ. Some folks just honestly don't understand what's going on. I think some might be in denial. Some are afraid they'll invite Satan in if they acknowledge him. And I think there are some who are jealous because their people come to me and not to them."

"Is that what happened with you and the denomination?"

Daniel nodded sadly. "You did your homework?"

"Yeah," Dean smiled. "After you left I called a few folks who knew a few folks. They said you had a run-in with the district superintendent over some 'doctrinal issues.'"

Daniel smiled sadly at that. "Yeah, they were getting complaints I was scaring people with all my talk of demons and warfare. I had one family in the church who was objecting to all the 'weirdoes' coming in to the church. Finally, I was given a choice – stop my practices or give up my credentials. You know the rest."

"What a choice, obey man or God."

"It seems a thankless ministry. It's one totally as unto God. It's definitely not a ministry to build a mega church with. It's kind of like a helps ministry. You find a family destitute, the dad unemployed or absent, no food in the fridge, about to be evicted, their electricity cut off, and you go in and help them. You pay their rent, bring in groceries, maybe even help dad find work. Usually, you'll never see them again once you get them on their feet. They'll go off to some other church, maybe even one that refused to help them.

"I used to think they were ungrateful, it hurt me. Then I realized they went to other churches because they were ashamed. They moved on to someplace where the folks didn't know how low they'd been.

"I realized it was the same with deliverance. Folks don't want to go to church and be reminded every time the pastor gets in the pulpit of the time they were rolling on the floor puking their guts out, and barking like a dog.

"You have to realize everything we do is unto God. The people we minister to don't belong to us, they belong to God. That helps me sometimes."

"It must be discouraging." Dean agreed.

"It can be. It comes with the turf. But, let me tell you, Dean; there is no other area of ministry I know of where you will experience the tangible presence and awesome power of God."

Both were quiet for a while after that.

Daniel interrupted the silence, "So, how'd you end up in Delphi, pastoring your home church?"

Dean leaned forward, "I just fell into it, I reckon. Cindy and I originally had planned on going into the missions' field. But the church helped pay my way through Bible College, the denomination required missionaries to have a few years' pastoral experience, and when I graduated the church needed a youth pastor... Then, about a year after I came on board, the former pastor, you probably remember him, Pastor Rosen? Well, he had to retire due to health problems - his heart - and the folks just felt I was the natural choice to succeed him

"It seemed right, you know? Here I was, pastoring the church I got saved in. Then the years passed, the kids came, and, well, its' been fifteen years."

"So what next?" Dean asked, changing the subject.

"The demons are hiding now, hoping they'll fool us into leaving them alone. First we pray. Then we go over and anoint the house with oil, cleansing it, reclaiming it. That should flush our enemy out so we can cast them out of Laurie."

"Remember," Daniel said, as Dean turned the corner, "the demon's tactics will be to confuse you, stall you, plant doubt in your mind. That's why it's usually a good practice not to get involved in conversations with them. They tried to argue with Jesus, remember, telling Him he was here 'before the time.'

"Satan is a legalist; he likes to adhere to the letter of the law while ignoring the spirit of it if he can. He'll quote or misquote scripture if he thinks he can confuse you. His demons use the same tricks."

"What do you want me to do?" Dean asked as he pulled up in front of the house.

"Again, intercede.   I'll be doing the direct conflict.

You'll be praying for me. Satan will attack you with all sorts of doubts and fears. Rebuke them in the Name of Jesus. You'll think they're your own thoughts, but actually they are the barbs of Satan trying to shake you and your confidence in Jesus and His Blood. He'll use guilt, shame, lust, any weapon or stronghold he can find against you. That's why Paul warned us to bring every thought into subjection to Christ."

Daniel looked at the house, then to Dean, "Ready?"

"'As I'll ever be."

"Good, let's go."

The two men got out of the car and walked toward the front porch. They could see Becky Neustadt's face in the window, watching them anxiously. They'd called ahead to warn her they were coming. Daniel checked his watch, it was 3:00 p.m., they'd been praying for hours at Dean's church. Dean's wife, Cindy, was on her way to St. Louis to pick up Ruth, who'd be arriving on the 6:00 p.m. flight from Atlanta.

Reinforcements.

They had discussed waiting until the morning, when all their forces were gathered and they'd had time to "pray up" more. Daniel had considered it. After thinking it over, he'd gotten uneasy in his spirit over waiting. He sensed the sooner they began the better now. He knew better than to doubt what he called his "gut feelings." Often, they were how the Holy Spirit spoke to him.

So they'd begin. If the thing wasn't finished by the time Ruth arrived, she'd spell him for rest, and so on. Cindy had signed on for intercession. They would have at least two teams. Daniel figured they could count on Becky for intercession as well. He would be careful in using Becky, though, as a mother, her closeness to Laurie would hinder her objectivity. At the same time, her authority as a mother would give them a bit of leverage over Satan's devices.

Daniel paused for a moment, gazing at the frosted glass pane on the front door. He was amazed it had survived all those years. He remembered how lovingly his mother had polished that window, her pride and joy. He felt sadness creep over him. How precious this house had once been to his family. How much sorrow they had experienced there. It seemed strange to him that in spite of it all, it was hard for him to not think of it as home.

Becky opened the door, "I'm glad you're here."

"How's Laurie?"

"She's upstairs in her room," Becky said, grimacing. "I went to take a shower, and when I came back she'd locked herself up there. She won't come out. I figured I'd wait for you to arrive."

"That's okay." Daniel smiled confidently. "When the time comes, we'll go in after her." He looked over at Dean, "As we used to say in the Army, 'let's rock and roll!'"

Dean smiled at Daniel. He was truly the most unusual minister he'd ever met. The three went into the kitchen.

"Let's pray." Daniel said quietly, as they joined hands.

From upstairs there was an animal growling and profanity, then, *"Oh, where have you been Danny Boy, Danny Boy? Oh where have you been Darling Danny? I've been running for my life, I've been with my neighbor's wife..."*

"Heavenly Father, in the Name of Jesus," Dean and Becky exchanged nervous glances as Daniel began, ignoring the singing, "we pronounce Your blessings upon this place and ask Your blessings upon ourselves, body, soul, and spirit..."

"I'll take you home again Eileen..." the girl's lips moved in song, but the voice was raw, grating, and the sound seemed to come from inside the listeners' heads rather than her mouth. Giggles interrupted the song as the demon, enjoying its own brand of humor carried on graphically detailing Daniel's alleged sins.

"...we ask that we be forgiven our sins, sanctified by the shed Blood of Jesus Christ and shielded from the attacks of Satan, our accuser and adversary..."

"Danny boy, come on up and let's play! I've got something for you, stud."

"...and command him to begone from this place by the authority given us in Luke 10:19 and Mark 16:16-20! O Lord, cover us with your armor, from the crown of our heads to the tips of our toes, that we might be protected from the fiery darts of Satan. We now take authority over this house and all who dwell herein..."

"Blessed be the child of God, the Lamb of God," came the mocking song from upstairs, *"the holy anointed one!"*

"...binding the power of the forces of hell from causing any more damage to the inhabitants of this place. We take authority over Becky Neustadt, over her children, over Laurie Neustadt, and command Satan to cease and desist all his attacks against this family. Furthermore, by the authority given us in

277

Matthew 29: 16-20, we bind these demons from assaulting our own families. We command you to leave these premises now, in the Name of Jesus Christ of Nazareth, Who Was, Who Is, and Who Is to Come!"

"I'll kill the little slut!"

"Furthermore, Lord, we request You send Your guardian angels to protect all those involved in this matter from any form of physical, emotional, or spiritual harm..."

There was a hideous scream of frustration from upstairs. Daniel smiled. It was the first physical reaction to their prayers. In his mind's eye he could see Laurie's arms being held above her head to prevent her from harming herself. He could sense the devil's frustration at being stopped.

There was thumping on the bedroom walls upstairs, Becky started and began to pull away. Daniel strengthened his grip on her hand, shook his head, smiled, while never missing a word of his prayer.

The thumping stopped, another frustrated scream, *"Leave my head alone you stinking..."* there followed a long line of filthy, if imaginatively descriptive insults of Laurie's guardian angels. Daniel smiled again. It was going well. So far.

"Now hear this!" Daniel intoned, "We now serve notice to the forces of darkness that your rule here is ended! We command you now, in the Name of Our Lord Jesus Christ to depart from this property in His Name and by the authority given us through His shed Blood! As we walk through this house, we reclaim it in the Name of Jesus Christ. As we anoint each doorpost and window, we mark them with oil as a sign of the Lordship and dwelling presence of the Holy Spirit in this house. Satan, you are defeated. We take authority over you and your demons, and call you accursed before our Lord God Almighty! Amen!"

The two men separated, taking bottles of olive oil out of their pockets, dabbing their fingers with it and making the sign of the cross over each window and doorpost. They prayed under their breath as they went through the house, Daniel taking the front part, through the dining room, Dean taking the back, through the old furnace room.

From upstairs, the rantings of the spirit grew louder, more intense, and even viler, more profane.

It was in the bathroom that Dean felt the oppressing presence of evil the most. He felt as though he were strangling as he struggled to anoint the window, "In the Name of Jesus!" he finally shouted, "Leave!" The presence left.

He met Daniel in the north room, the living room. They exchanged glances and, without a word they headed through the dining room toward the stairs.

As they made their way up the steps, the drastic drop in temperature once again struck Dean. He followed Daniel's lead, anointing the banister and each step on the way. At the top, Daniel motioned for him to anoint the windows on the landing, while he, Daniel, took the north bedroom. Having completed that, they met at the head of the steps. Daniel nodded; they entered the east, or middle bedroom.

Dean shuddered as he entered the room. The atmosphere was thick, pungent, smelled of death. He was almost afraid to breathe, lest he inhale something vile and unclean, which would contaminate him. He once more prayed the Blood of Jesus over him. He'd lost count of how many times he'd done that today, and plunged forward, behind Daniel who was already anointing the windows.

Dean moved toward the closet doors, touched the nearest, drew his hand back quickly.

"What is it?" Daniel asked, breaking his quiet praying.

"The door- it's vibrating!"

Daniel came over, touched the panel curiously, nodded, "This is one of the 'hearts,' or centers of the house." He poured a large amount of oil on his hand, which already was glistening from previous applications, and slapped his hand on the door, "In JESUS' NAME, LEAVE!"

Both Dean and Daniel were blown back by a wind as if from nowhere as the doors to the closet blew open. The wind blew through the room, past them. The door to the south bedroom flew open and stayed there, inviting them to follow. As if daring them to enter.

Dean checked his watch. It was six-thirty. It was hard to believe they'd been at the house an hour and a half. Outside the afternoon sun was beginning to cast the long shadows preceding its setting, but still cast enough brightness to cheer one's heart. He looked at the door to the south bedroom. He looked out the window again at the cheerful afternoon outside. He looked back at the entrance to the south bedroom. No light came from the opening.

He shuddered at the sight. He could make out the

279

furniture inside, but, it was hard to put into words, there was a pallor inside. It was as if the room and the things inside absorbed all light, all life, giving only a phantom image of what was inside. From inside there was only silence.

He looked at Daniel, who had paused a few seconds. Daniel returned his glance, nodded toward the door, and moved toward it with a determined mien. Dean saw Becky, standing at the doorway to the landing.

"Becky," Daniel called from the bedroom, "if you could, bring us some towels and a bucket."

Becky nodded and was off downstairs on her errand; she stopped, "What's the bucket for?"

"To save your carpet!" Daniel yelled back.

Dean followed him into the room. It was as if it were filled with fog. He looked on the beds for Laurie, didn't see her. He heard a hiss from the far corner, behind a dresser and saw that was where Daniel was staring. He saw the girl now, crouched in a corner, an eerie red glow from her eyes, her tongue darting in and out of her mouth, teeth bared at the three adults. He noted how strangely pointed her teeth appeared. Was it an illusion? This was not the little girl he'd known and hugged each Sunday morning and Wednesday night.

"Stay away from me, man of God!" she hissed.

Daniel moved forward with more boldness than Dean had to admit he felt. That voice. It seemed impossible it could come from the mouth of that little girl.

"Come out of her demon in the Name of Jesus Christ!"

"She wants me here and there isn't a thing you can do about it!"

"Becky, do you want your daughter possessed?"

Dean now noticed Becky in the doorway, standing with a bucket in her hand. She was staring at the thing, which her daughter had become.

"Becky!"

"Yes? I mean- no!"

"Then take your authority as mother and command the demon to leave."

"I command you to leave-"

"-in Jesus' Name."

"-in Jesus' Name-"

"-by your authority as Laurie's mother."

"-by my authority as Laurie's mother!"

There was a hideous scream as Laurie pitched forward, writhing on the floor. Daniel rushed forward to catch her. She continued her contortions in his arms, struggling as if in torment, screaming in pain, "They're hurting me!" she cried, "Stop them Mama!"

Becky and Dean rushed forward as if to help. Daniel held up his hand, stopping them, "Don't touch her unless I tell you!" he warned. He looked down at the girl, "Serpents, I command you to stop tearing at her. You will not harm her. I command this in Jesus' Name!"

The writhing stopped, Laurie's face relaxed. Then her stomach began convulsing.

"Bring the bucket, Dean!"

Becky moved just in time as Laurie began projectile vomiting.

"Is she all right?" Becky asked when the girl had stopped.

Daniel nodded.

"Is it over?" Dean asked, hopefully. Dean's nose curled at the foul odor of sulfur and rotted flesh, which filled the room. He couldn't bring himself to glance inside the bucket on the floor.

Daniel shook his head. He looked down at Laurie, apparently unconscious, and gently pulled back her eyelid with the fingers of his free hand. "I don't think so," he answered. "They usually like to do this, throw a few minor imps at you to fool you into thinking she's delivered. That way you'll leave them alone. The imps you cast out can come back and bring more buddies with them if you don't get the ruler and the gatekeeper." He stood up. "I wish it were going to be this easy. Let's get her out of here."

Daniel carried the girl out of the room. When they got to the head of the stairs, she suddenly came to life, kicking, scratching, and swearing, trying to get away. She leaned over and put her teeth into his shoulder, biting his left shoulder hard. He shouted with the sudden, unexpected pain, but fought the urge to drop her, holding more tightly. He could feel her teeth, unnaturally sharp, sinking into his flesh, grinding as she went, to do more damage. Dean rushed forward to help. Daniel urged him off, while rebuking the spirits. Finally, she stopped, going limp again.

He took her downstairs to the living room, where they placed her on the couch.

"Let me look at that," Becky said, motioning to his

281

shoulder.

Daniel pulled back his shirt to reveal a nasty ovular bruise developing on his upper bicep. Though his shirt had not been torn, she had broken the skin in several places. The punctures were swelling up, discoloring already. He knew he was in for a nasty infection or worse if it weren't cleansed, both spiritually and physically.

He was angry with himself for letting his guard down, letting it happened. He wondered at the same time how it had happened. He had applied the Blood over himself, had prayed up, had done all he knew to do to prepare for this. What had gone wrong?

You're the weak link in the chain. The accusation stung him. *But He is glorified in my weakness, for when I am weak He is stronger,* he replied.

You've never been up against spirits this powerful, Danny. You're outmatched. This house knows you. It has its hooks in you. It'll kill you like it did Roggie.

I am more than a conqueror through Christ Jesus!

Conqueror! A murderer like you? An image of a dying NVA soldier's face flashed before Daniel's eyes.

Nothing can separate us from the love of God. I am a new creature in Christ.

If that's the case, then why does it still hurt?

"Watch it now, this is going to burn." Becky startled him out of his thoughts. He was grateful. He saw she had a bottle of alcohol in her hands, "I'm sorry, but this is all I have. When you have kids, it's hard to stay stocked up on medical supplies."

He smiled wanly, "Let 'er rip. I've been through worse."

"I'll bet you have," she said, noting the strange, puckered scar on his shoulder. She knew it was a bullet wound. She poured the liquid on the wound.

It was like liquid fire, particularly on the open wounds. Daniel knew the alcohol would not be enough to clean this wound completely, though.

"Dean," he said, "I need you to anoint my arm with oil."

"Sure," Dean rose from the armchair and came over with his bottle of oil. "Do you think it was trying to infect you- er, transfer a spirit?"

"I know it was," Daniel answered. "Remember, these demons are clever, they've been around for ages. We're still casting out the demons Christ fought, Elijah fought. They seldom do anything unless they have a good (in their book) reason.

"No disrespect, Dean, but right now, they consider me to be their most serious threat here. If they could knock me out physically, they stand a much better chance of winning. If they can get me weakened enough physically, they might be able to destroy me. Remember, all the warnings of the Bible. 'Be sober, be vigilant, your adversary the devil roameth about like a raging lion,' 'don't let the sun set on your wrath, lest you give Satan advantage,' were written to born again, Spirit-filled believers." Daniel knew he had been sounding like a textbook, but he had a short time to feed a lot of information to Dean and Becky – ignorance wasn't bliss. He was also preaching to himself.

"It's kind of scary, when you think of it."

"Only if you let it scare you, brother," Daniel answered. "Remember, 'God has not given us a spirit of fear, but of power, of love, and of a sound mind.' He's also given us a spirit of adoption, whereby we can cry 'Abba', father. I like the literal translation of that word; 'Abba' is Aramaic for 'Daddy.' Also, remember what James said, 'You believe there is one God, you do well, for the devils also believe and tremble.'" He grinned, in spite of his pain, "I'm preaching to the choir, sorry."

"No," Dean said, "don't be. I've preached these words for years, but it's funny, I've never thought of them in the way you brought them out until now. If you'd told me this a few months ago, I'd accused you of being crazy, or worse. But after what I've seen today- it all makes sense." He held the bottle up. "Are you ready?"

"Yeah. Listen," Daniel warned, "don't be freaked out by what you may see when you pour the oil, okay?"

Dean stopped a moment, thought. "Okay," he said warily as he poured.

Daniel watched the oil ooze out of the bottle onto his torn skin. As the first drop hit the wound he felt a fire a thousand times hotter than the alcohol and he gritted his teeth. It was torture, but at the same time, felt good, cleansing. The oil hissed and steamed as it hit his skin.

Dean and Becky's eyes widened in disbelief when they saw the manifestation. Dean pulled back, as if to stop. "No! Don't!" Daniel ordered. Dean continued pouring until the entire arm was dripping with oil.

The pain lasted a few minutes, then was replaced by soothing coolness. The arm was being healed.

"Look!" Becky exclaimed, pointing at Daniel's wounds. Daniel opened his eyes, looked at his arm. The awful red and blue discolorations were receding before his eyes. The teeth marks were drying up, closing.

"Praise God!" he whispered. "We've got to get back to work," he said, standing up. He took the oil from Dean, dabbed some on his finger, and made the sign of the cross on his forehead, muttering a prayer of protection under his breath. He did the same for Becky. Then he gave the bottle back to Dean, who took it and anointed Daniel.

He turned to Laurie, who, he suspected, had been lying on the couch pretending to be asleep. He dabbed his fingers with oil and reached out to anoint her forehead. He was just about to touch her when she sprang up.

"Keep that away from me!" she hissed.

"Knock it off, in Jesus' Name!" Daniel commanded, "I bind your tongue."

It was almost comical to see the girl struggle to speak. Daniel reached out, touched her forehead with an oily finger. Laurie's face contorted with agony as she began writhing again, making inarticulate groans and moans.

"Come out of her now!" Daniel commanded.

"Mama, help me." Laurie cried, *"They're hurting me! Make them leave me alone."*

"Shut up, demon!" Daniel said sharply. He caught Dean's questioning look, "Another spirit, a new one. It didn't feel bound by my earlier command. I tell you, they're real legalists." He turned back to the girl; "You come out of her, too, now!"

"No!"

"What? You refuse me?" Daniel shook his head, "All right, I command you in the Name of Jesus! Come out of her!"

Another fit.

"How long will this go on?" Dean asked.

"Until we get them all." Daniel said, "Or I can find the ruler or gatekeeper."

"Ruler?"

"Yes," Daniel explained, without taking his eyes off the girl, "There can be thousands of spirits in her, but only one is in charge. Often, though, there is another spirit, a 'gatekeeper.' Usually, it is the first spirit to attack the victim. It allowed the others to get in. 'Get the ruler and the others must follow get the gatekeeper and they stay out."

284

"It sounds so confusing to me-"

"It can be; that's the point."

"Can't you just command them to come forth?"

"Sometimes," Daniel answered. "But I have to be led by the Spirit. Remember, there is no set formula in this, really. When confronting Satan directly you'd better be sure God is *completely* in control."

"How-" Daniel put up a hand, silencing him.

Laurie was sitting up on the sofa now, looking around as if examining her surroundings for the first time. She looked up at the three adults and smiled pleasantly, "Hello, Pastor Dean," she said sweetly. "Brother Daniel, how are you?"

"I'm fine," he answered, pulling up a footstool and sitting directly across from her.

"Danny," she said, pulling closer to him, "I'm so glad you're here."

She sounds so adult, Dean thought, *the way she's looking at him, my Lord, she's - she's sexy! God forgive me my thoughts!*

The girl was moving closer to Daniel, her face almost up to his. Becky's mouth opened in horror. Was this her little girl, acting like a tramp? Why didn't Daniel do anything, he was just sitting there.

"Come out of her Seducer, in the Name of the Most High God!"

Laurie fell back on the couch as if shot by a bolt.

Daniel shook himself. *That was close. It almost had me.*

So it went for hours. Spirit after spirit came out of the girl. Again and again, Daniel commanded the ruler to come forth. Still it was in there, hiding.

Daniel was tired; he looked at his watch, 8:30 p.m. The girl was lying on the couch, recovering from the last go around. He stood up, stretched. Outside, the neighborhood was being painted in shades of gray as the sun retreated behind the horizon.

Darkness, he thought. *For some reason they draw strength off the night. It'll be tougher.* He wondered where Ruth was. Had she made it in safely? He turned to the girl, who was watching him with a smug, self-satisfied look on her face. In the eyes, though, beneath the surface, he could see a boiling hatred, anger. *Rebellion,* he knew. He sensed it was waiting for him to speak to it so it could spout off. He went back to the stool across from Laurie and sat down.

"Rebellion," he said calmly, "I bind your tongue." He

saw her facial expression change from smugness to angry frustration. "Come out of her!"

Again, the routine. He was beginning to be concerned about the strain this was all putting on the girl. How much more could she take? The demons would like nothing more than to kill her, or better yet, have her die as the result of the deliverance session. It would destroy Daniel and Dean's ministries once and for all, probably put them all in prison for manslaughter, and make the entire Christian community look bad.

Ruth, show up. We need your expertise. Daniel was pretty good at gauging how far to take a person, but he still felt better with Ruth beside him. He realized he was incomplete without her.

He looked at Laurie again. There was something familiar about the spirit manifesting itself.

"I know you, don't I?"

The demon nodded, *"You cast me out of Mike Johnson."*

"Come out of her in Jesus' Name!" *Now I'm casting you out of Laurie Neustadt.*

The spirit came out. This time, it was nothing more than a slight cough. *Thank the Lord.*

Daniel sighed, "This is a good sign; there's less resistance now," he said to Dean, out of the side of his mouth. "I'm getting concerned about the women. If Ruth's flight was on time, they should be getting here by now." He muttered a short prayer under his breath for their safety. *We're being hit on all fronts, Lord.*

What else is new?

"Mama," it was Laurie.

Becky started to move toward her daughter, caught herself, and looked over at Daniel with a questioning glance. Daniel studied Laurie's eyes, detected nothing, and nodded for her to go to her daughter.

"That's good, isn't it?" Dean said, rising from his knees.

"I hope so. They may be in hiding for now." Daniel stood up, heard his knees crack. *Too many jumps when I was a kid.* The two men stretched and exercised their legs.

"I'm tired," Laurie said weakly.

"I know, baby." Becky said, cradling her daughter in her arms.

"How long will it go on?"

"I don't know, baby, just be brave."

"I'm scared."

"I know."

"Laurie," Daniel said, sitting back down on his stool, "can you help us?"

"I don't know..."

"We need your help, honey. It'll make it easier if you can help us."

"I'm scared."

"I know," he said comfortingly, "remember, Jesus loves you and is with you." When he mentioned the Name of Jesus, he saw the eyes harden slightly. *So, the demons aren't as far gone as they'd like me to think. Swell.* "Why don't you try to rest, now, honey, okay?"

She nodded.

Daniel motioned to Becky and Dean to join him in the kitchen. Before they left the room, Laurie was lying on the couch, sleeping. He looked down at her small form, watched her chest rise and fall smoothly in sleep. He reflected on her torment and hated Satan more than ever.

"There's something blocking her deliverance," Daniel said as they sat at the table. He took a sip of iced water. "There's something there - I can't put my finger on - holding us up."

"What do you mean?"

"Well, understand. Jesus gives us authority to cast out devils, but much still rides on the victim's free will."

Dean nodded, understanding.

"I don't get it," Becky said, "You'll have to excuse me I haven't been to Bible college."

Daniel studied her face, saw no trace of sarcasm, just a thirst to know, "Well, to be honest, what I'm about to tell you isn't normally taught at Bible College. If it were, we'd call it Spiritual Warfare 101. I'll try to make it brief."

"And simple." Becky suggested.

"And simple," Daniel agreed.

"First," he continued, "you've got to understand the nature of man, created in the image of God. God is one God in three persons. Man is one person with three parts, body, soul, and spirit. When you understand that, you begin to understand how Satan attacks people.

"There are three types of demonic attack, oppression, obsession, and possession. Christians cannot be possessed by the devil, but he can attack them. After all, who were all the warnings in the Bible written for?"

"I figured for everybody." Becky said.

"In a way, you're right." Daniel conceded, "But you've got to understand, the epistles, or letters in the New Testament, were originally written as letters of instruction and warning to the early Church - believers. It was only later, when the Church Fathers got together; they felt these letters were of enough importance and inspiration to include in our Bible. So Christians need to be aware of Satan's threat to them."

"Don't we always say that Satan isn't worried about the world, he has them, it's the Christians that are his focus." Dean added.

"That about sums it up," Daniel agreed. "So let's look at what we're up against. As I said, Satan attacks in three ways. The first is a physical attack, against the body, if you will which the Bible calls oppression. The Bible says in several places Jesus went about doing good and 'healing all those who were oppressed of the devil.' Much sickness is caused by direct demonic activity, though not all. Sometimes we're just sick because of the sin in the world caused by the fall.

"I believe people can be oppressed physically in other ways, through finances, personal failure, disaster, you name it."

"How do you know if your problems are caused by demons or not?" Becky asked plaintively.

"That's where you have to rely on the Lord."

"How?"

"That would be Spiritual Warfare 102." he smiled.

"Okay, professor, go on," Becky said, bravely managing a smile.

"Where was I? Oh, yes, the second avenue of demonic attack is through the mind, or soul, we call this obsession, an unclean desire - lust, or thought that overwhelms you. You've heard of people who are obsessed with an ambition, or a loved one? In a sense, that person or thing becomes an idol if it supplants God as being foremost in your heart. The door is open for the devil to come in and wreak havoc in your life. Satan will come in and rule your thought life, driving you insane. Then you're set up for the last step, which is possession.

"Possession is total Satanic control over you, body, soul, and spirit. I've run into a few cases of all out possession. The person has ceased to exist as an individual because the demons have total control. In less severe cases of possession, the people are subject to periods of "blackouts," It appears to be amnesia, but actually what has happened is that the demons are in charge and the person's soul is imprisoned inside, unable to communicate with the world."

Dean leaned forward, "Are you saying amnesiacs are demon possessed?"

"No, not all amnesiacs are demon possessed, but a demon possessed person will often exhibit symptoms similar to amnesia."

"You have to rely on the Lord to tell the difference, right?" Becky added.

"You got it."

"Now, involved in all this is free will. God gives us the right to choose whom we will serve. There was an old comedian who used to do a routine where the character would say, 'The devil made me do it!' It was funny listening to this wife explain how the devil forced her to buy a new dress her husband couldn't afford. But it wasn't really Biblical because when it all comes down to it, it's up to us to decide whom we're going to serve, God or the devil.

"The devil tempts us all. The Bible says even Jesus was tempted in all ways. It's not a sin to be tempted. What we do in the time of temptation is what determines whether we sin or not. Are we a Joseph, who runs from the temptation, or a David, who lets his eyes linger a bit on a sight they shouldn't behold and thus falls to the temptation?

"When we sin, we open ourselves up to the wiles of the devil. That's why Jesus warned us to make anything we had against our brothers right that very day. Paul says the same thing when he says not to let the sun set on our wrath, lest we fall into Satan's snares. I'm paraphrasing here, but the meaning is clear. These warnings, particularly Paul's, were for born-again, Spirit-filled believers.

"Often people get in trouble because they enjoy their sin more than they fear God. Some folks give in to demons because they're deceived. They believe the demon's lies that somehow the demons give them an edge, a power over others. I've even encountered people who didn't want deliverance."

"Why on earth not?"

"Like I said, they think the demons give them power. I had one guy come into my church one night, crawling with boogers. I wanted to cast those devils out so bad, but I never got the go-ahead. I couldn't figure it out. Then I finally got to talk to the guy, not the devils. I asked him if he wanted deliverance, he told me, 'no.' I couldn't believe my ears. He was a homeless drifter. He said the voices kept him company when he got lonely at night. I offered to take him to a shelter the churches in the area had set up. He didn't want any part of that.

"I could have cast the devils out. If I commanded them in the Name of Jesus they'd have to go, but it wouldn't do any good. He'd invite them right back in."

"I'd never thought of that." Dean shook his head.

"Remember in Matthew, even Jesus couldn't do many mighty works in His hometown because of their unbelief? Go back to the unclean spirit wandering the high and dry places seeking relief-"

"Then he goes back to his original home, finding it empty goes and gets seven spirits, more unclean than himself and the final condition is worse than at the beginning," Dean completed.

"Wait a minute!" Becky said, "Do you mean to tell me there are times you can't command the demons to leave?"

"No," Daniel answered. "The Lord gives me authority to cast out devils. I have that authority, but sometimes, you're better off letting a person go until they *want* help. Believe me, eventually, they will, most of the time."

"So why do you think you're having so much trouble with Laurie?"

Daniel looked over at Dean, their eyes met. *He knows, too, or suspects.* He thought, *Well, old friend, do you want to do it or should I?*

Dean received the message, took a deep breath, and leaned forward, "Becky," he began tenderly, tentatively, "this is going to be difficult -"

She knows too, Daniel said to himself, looking into her eyes, *or she suspects.*

"Well, pastor," she said, with a sigh, "then the best way is to just blast with both barrels." Her eyes teared up as her shoulders sagged. She reminded him of a beach toy when the plug was pulled and the air rushed out.

"Well, you know, when Laurie's behavior first manifested, there was a suspicion- I mean, often this behavior is an indication of, er-things."

"Do you mean, has Laurie ever been molested?" she

asked, her voice quivering with emotion. Her body heaved with sobs. Daniel wanted to reach out and hug her as he would a daughter. *Ladies, where are you?*

Dean's head dropped, "I-I'm sorry, Becky."

"Don't be, preacher," Becky said, getting up and heading for a cabinet. She opened it up, pulled out a fresh box of tissues, opened it, and began dabbing at her face, "You didn't do nothing wrong."

"How long have you known?" Daniel asked quietly.

"Not long enough!" Becky said, "Though the signs were there. Dear Lord, the signs were there! The shrinks asked us about that, you know? I was the one who pitched a fit. How dare they accuse my husband! Didn't they know what a good man he was? How many men would have done what he did, forgiving me and taking me back, raising my kid as his own?

"I was going to tear their eyes out. Del was the one holding me back. 'Now, now, honey, they're just doing their jobs, they gotta ask those questions. Oh, he was so good."

"How'd you find out?"

"It was right after he died. The girls crawled in bed with me one night, missing him. Laurie woke us up crying and moaning, twisting in her sleep, saying 'No daddy, please don't.'

"I watched her and couldn't believe what I heard and saw next. I asked Laurie about it the next morning. She didn't remember anything. Then I finally asked her the *right* question about her daddy. She told me the whole filthy story.

"I asked her why she hadn't said anything about it to me before. She told me she was afraid. Del, good old Del, had told her the truth about her birth to use as leverage to keep her quiet." She began shaking, "He told her if she caused trouble we'd give her away."

Daniel controlled the anger flowing through him. How many times had he seen this scenario in his ministry? How many more? *Is this the spirit of the age? The Lord said men would lack natural affection in the last days, was this part of what he meant?* As long as he lived, he didn't think he'd ever understand how a man could raise a child, even one not his own, and think of him or her in such a way.

"How long had it been going on, Becky?" Dean asked.

"A year – at least a year before he was killed," Becky began crying again. "I guess he was waiting for her to age a little!"

"Right before she began acting strange." Dean said, almost to himself.

"Wasn't that about the time you moved into this house?"

Becky nodded. Understanding began to dawn.

"Do you think the spirits here may have..." her voice began to trail off.

Daniel nodded sadly.

"Well, it's like you said," she concluded, "he still had to choose whether to give in to the urges or not."

"That's the hook," he answered. "Becky, I have to ask this question. Yesterday, we were talking and you didn't mention this, why not?"

"Del's dead. I didn't think it was important. I didn't see the point in dragging all this garbage out. Hasn't Laurie suffered enough?"

There was the sound of a car pulling up outside and doors slamming. It was the women.

"Reinforcements!"

Chapter 18
June 18, 2010

And he said, "Go and spy where he is, that I may send and fetch him."
And it was told him, saying, "Behold, he is in Dothan."
Therefore sent he thither horses, and chariots, and a great host; and they came by night, and compassed the city about. And when the servant of the man of God was risen early, and came forth, behold, an host compassed the city, both with horses and chariots. And his servant said unto him, "Alas, my master! What shall we do?"
And he answered, "Fear not; for they who are with us are more than they who are with them."
And Elisha prayed, and said, "Lord, I pray Thee, open his eyes, that he may see."
And the Lord opened the eyes of the young man, and he saw; and, behold, the mountain was full of horses and chariots of fire round about Elisha.
(2 Kings 6: 13 - 17)

It was a beautiful Illinois summer night. The stars glittered clearly in the heavens, reassuring the solitary figure standing on the porch that God was still in heaven and had everything in control. After all, if He could arrange the galaxies and solar systems, each in their place and hang them there in space, the problems we faced on earth were infinitesimal. If only we could have enough faith to put them in His Almighty Hands.

A cool breeze swept across Daniel Baumer's face, refreshing him. Call it a kiss from God. He'd forgotten how sweet the summers were in the Midwest. Actually, he'd never appreciated them until he'd moved to the Deep South. He thought of the temperatures they'd left, soaring into the hundreds during the day, cooling off to the luxurious high eighties at night. He sighed.

Then, he remembered the harsh winters he'd spent in this house, never quite fully prepared for the terrible snowstorms that hit in cold seasons. He remembered the frozen pipes, taking baths in melted snow water; remembered that terrible first winter when the furnace went out; remembered never feeling truly warm in the house from October to April.

There's a trade-off, isn't there, God? He asked. *The price we pay in the Deep South is our terrible summers. Illinois pays for its mild summers with its terrible winters.*

A flittering object caught the corner of his eye. Daniel focused his attention on it, watched it whirl its way to the earth. He walked over to where it landed, bent over and picked it up. He studied it carefully, holding it gingerly between his fingers.

A whirligig. The object brought a bittersweet mixture of thoughts, recollections, and emotions. It was a maple seed, often called "keys." Daniel remembered that Roggie and he had nicknamed them "whirligigs." He remembered Roggie showing him how, if you dropped them right, they would spiral to the ground. He remembered as a kid, playing with the seeds in springtime, picking the seeds up and dropping them again and again on the way home from school. He'd forgotten about the maple seeds, minor things lost in the more cataclysmic events of his life.

He wondered where it came from. It was normally too late in the season for the maples to drop their seeds. He looked for more on the ground, but found none. He remembered the nearest maple tree he could remember was in the Gardners' yard across the street.

He looked at the winged seed in his hand with wonder. He was swept by sadness at the sight of this object. The simple object, an example of God's ingenuity in ensuring the continuing of the maple tree was a reminder of all the things surrendered to the nomadic life of a professional soldier.

His children had never played with the whirligigs; they wouldn't know the joy of jumping in fall leaves or of eating snow ice cream. All these things he'd once taken for granted then forgotten. Now they rushed back in on him, things he'd given up - for what?

He thought of the times when people would ask him about the things he'd done, places he'd been. Sometimes, he noted the envy in their eyes, wishing they'd gone there, done that. Little did they realize he often envied them their stability. *That's coveting, isn't it, Lord?*

Tradeoffs. That's what it boils down to doesn't it, Lord? He asked again. There were times he longed for the stability and roots most people had. He thought it would have been nice to have grown up in the same town, met Ruth in high school, married her, raised their children where they had always been known, where their parents had always been known. Then he thought of what he would have missed, the places traveled to, the experiences, both good and bad. Would he have been the same man?

"Daniel?"

Ruth's soft voice startled him from his thoughts. He turned, his eyes filled with warmth as he beheld his wife standing in the door. *No, Lord, if I had it to do all over again, I guess the only change I'd make would be to get more serious about serving you sooner.*

"How's she doing?"

"I gave her as good a check-up as I could with her being asleep." Ruth answered. "The poor thing's so exhausted. She didn't even wake up when I took her blood pressure. But all her vitals are back to normal. She's just tired."

"Do you think it's safe to go on?"

"I don't know," Ruth said. "Physically, she appears to be all right, but it wouldn't hurt to let her rest, now that she's sleeping."

"I'd hate to give the enemy time to creep back in."

"I know," she agreed, "but we can always bind the spirits, pray a hedge around her."

"That seems to be having a limited effect, this time, baby," he said with a heavy sigh. "I don't know, but my authority over these demons seems to be limited somehow. I've never encountered such resistance before."

"Could they be more powerful demons than you've encountered before?"

"I don't know. I figured that high priest in Florida commanded some hefty goons."

Ruth nodded, "Perhaps, you're too close to this, then."

"Maybe," Daniel agreed. "Then, why would God have chosen me for this job? After all, what made Dean call me in the first place?"

"Maybe there are some things you have to deal with in this house before you can move on to the next step in your walk with God."

"Maybe," Daniel thought a moment. "I've come to that conclusion myself. Sometimes, it seems God has a funny way of using the devil to help his children discover the holes in their armor."

He looked at his watch. It was past midnight, "At least we've bought her another day. Maybe that's all God wanted for now. It's getting late. I reckon we'd better tell everyone to pack it in, so we can get some rest, 'hit it again tomor-later."

Daniel was back in Vietnam again. He was in the clearing in the jungle, looking down at the back of the NVA soldier's head. He knew what he had to do, swallowed hard, grabbed the man's head in his hands and twisted savagely, felt the resistance, heard the sickening snap, felt all resistance to his twist cease, felt the body go limp. He dropped the body. It fell to the ground. He looked down at his victim and recoiled in horror. It was Roggie.

He searched through Roggie's pocket; found the picture with his wife and child. He saw Uta and Stevie's face in the photo.

"Oh no!" he cried, "I've killed Roggie!"

"Daniel!" It was Ruth. "Daniel, wake up!"

He sat up in bed; he looked around wildly, trying to get a track on where he was. He saw Ruth, relaxed, "I was dreaming."

"Yes," Ruth said, gently, "again. You've been dreaming a lot lately."

"I know."

"Danny," she said, tenderly, "Maybe you'd better tell me what happened to you in Vietnam."

It happened on their first night on foot. The North Vietnamese had poured over the border invading the South in the spring of 1975. There was a full moon out, good for vision, bad for trying to stay unnoticed. Fortunately, they were in a wooded area, for the most part shielded from the moonlight. The major had decided to continue moving as long as they had cover. They'd pause for a few hours rest in the early morning hours, check their bearings before moving on. Moving at night was safer under the circumstances anyway.

The Major didn't need to explain that the last thing they needed was to be captured; what a propaganda coup it would be at this point in the peace process.

Tyrell was taking his turn at point. He would move a few

cautious steps at a time, searching for booby traps, listening for the slightest noise that didn't belong in the forest. They saw each other simultaneously.

A young North Vietnamese soldier was strolling down the trail as if it were a Sunday in the park. He was even humming a tune. Then he saw Tyrell and froze, as if trying to figure out who this was in the middle of his woods at night. His mistake. Tyrell didn't freeze, he moved immediately, tackling the much smaller man, placing his hand over the fellow's mouth and bringing him to the ground.

The other three members of the team rushed to the two struggling men. Daniel ran a few steps forward, his weapon at ready, watching for any others who might come along, the other sergeant, Scott, Daniel remembered his name now, had reached into one of his pockets and produced a roll of military duct tape (called "100 mile an hour" tape), used it to tape the Vietnamese's mouth shut. The major bound his arms and legs with some nylon cord.

"Anyone else?" the major asked of Daniel in a hissing whisper.

"No, sir," came the hushed reply. "All clear. I'll go ahead a bit and see what's ahead."

"Good." Daniel looked at the young man, trussed up and gagged, saw the terror in his eyes. A prisoner, he thought, the one thing we don't need now.

Daniel cautiously moved up the trail, again, listening for the slightest noise. About one hundred yards from where they'd seen the man, he heard noises. He tensed. Up ahead, he saw a slight glow along the trail. Moonlight. He inched his way along the trail, soon the noises became perceptible, voices. It's a camp. He backed against the brush at the side of the trail, tense, listening, torn between his curiosity to go ahead and see for himself, and the knowledge that it would be taking an undue risk in exposing himself, revealing the presence of his team to look. He knew enough, there was a sizable body of men in a clearing ahead they needed to avoid.

He backed away carefully, keeping his eyes on the slight glow up the trail until he could see it no more. Then he turned and ran back to where the team and the prisoner were waiting.

He knew he had to be approaching the place, but could see no one. Where'd they go? Into the brush. Good idea, but how will I find them?

297

The Homestead

"Pssst!" It was Tyrell, he signaled Daniel to follow.

The two made it through the brush, being careful to disturb the leaves and bushes as little as possible. Soon they came upon the major and Scott, hovering over the prisoner.

The major gave Daniel a questioning look, "There's a camp about two hundred meters ahead. Sounded like a sizable group. I didn't think it would be a good idea to see."

The major nodded, "There was a fork in the trail about half a mile back, let's backtrack to it and find a safe place we can get our bearings and figure out what we're going to do with him." He pointed to the prisoner.

All nodded. They rose. Tyrell removed the binding from his legs so he could walk, picked him up, put him on his feet. Daniel almost felt sorry for the guy; he was probably getting away from the camp to relieve himself in private when they ran into him. Tough break, he thought. It could have happened to anyone. That's why the Army taught its soldiers to use the "buddy system." Never go anywhere alone. Anywhere.

They moved about a mile from the campsite, found a small clearing back from the trail and held their council. They all knew what needed to be done. The question was who should do it. The major offered. Being in command, he felt it was his responsibility to do it. Tyrell disagreed. After all, he was the one who'd found the man and should have killed him outright. Daniel told him if he'd taken time to go for his knife, the kid would have screamed out and they'd all be dead or captured. No, Tyrell couldn't be faulted and, rank or no rank, the major shouldn't have to bear this burden.

"So what do you suggest, Sergeant?" the major asked, grateful at the generosity of these men. "Whatever we do, we've got to do quickly. Someone's bound to miss him soon."

"Why don't we draw straws?" Daniel said. "Short straw does it."

"Whatever we do, we'd better do quickly," Scott said, echoing the major, looking around warily. "They're going to be missing him soon and come looking for him."

"I've got some dice." Tyrell said, "We could roll. They're like my good luck charms." he explained.

Daniel always wondered at how in the almost total darkness of the jungle they could make out – barely – the number on the die.

"Sounds good to me," the major said sadly. Again, there

298

was no question what needed to be done. They couldn't release him. He'd give their position away. If they left him bound and gagged there was a chance someone would find him and he'd give them away. If no one found him he'd die a terrible slow death to starvation exposure - or worse, animals. It was a standard unspoken rule in this type of operation, no prisoners. Easily said, harder to do.

"I'll roll first," Tyrell said, blowing on the die, "One die, low man does it."

He let it roll, a six. He heaved a sigh of relief, handed the die to Daniel.

"Well, they're your die," he said rolling it, trying to sound lighter than he felt. He rolled, a two. How'd I know it was going to be bad for me?

The major rolled a four.

Scott rolled a six.

In the darkness, all looked sadly at Daniel. Without a word, Daniel rose and walked over to where the prisoner lay with his hands and feet bound together behind his back, his mouth still taped. He tried not to look into his eyes, which he could dimly see, even in the darkness.

How do I do this? He asked himself. He couldn't shoot him. It had to be quiet. His knife? No, he thought, too painful. It's bad enough I have to do this; I want him to suffer as little as possible. He thought of all the ways he'd learned to kill his fellow man, ruling one after the other out as too slow, too painful, or too noisy. What difference will it make? He'll be just as dead! He pulled out his knife, saw the prisoner's eyes widen at the sight. No. No knife. He'd used it before, but then it had been different, against a foe who could have defended himself.

It seemed he agonized forever, though he knew it couldn't have been long; otherwise the others would have come looking in on him.

The prisoner was bound hand and foot. He pulled the man to a sitting position, facing away from him. He could sense the prisoner's eyes darting from side to side, trying to see behind him. He knows what's coming. He must have known since we found him. It's the only way. He's a soldier; it's what he'd do in the same situation. That didn't make it easier.

He reached in the leg pocket of his jungle fatigues, felt the garrote he kept there. No. There's only one way to do this. He hoped he could do this properly. He knew the technique. He also

299

knew it looked easier in movies than it was in real life. But he'd practiced it in training; actually learned it in Jiu Jitsu classes.

He reached down and quickly put his arms around the prisoner's head and neck. The prisoner, who'd been sitting quietly, began to struggle and try to speak through the tape over his mouth. He gasped for breathes through his nostrils. Sweat rolled down both men's faces as they struggled in the dark. After what seemed an eternity, but in reality was only a few seconds, Daniel gave the head a violent jerk to the right. He heard a sickening snap as the vertebrae separated, felt the neck muscles relax, give way, as the head turned further to the right than it was supposed to. Then the body relaxed. Totally. He was dead.

He let go. He hadn't shed tears in years. Not since Uta's funeral. But now he cried silently. He'd been a soldier for over three years, had killed more men than he cared to think about during his two tours in Nam. This was the first time he'd ever felt like a murderer.

He had never told Ruth why he often paced the house late at night, sleepless. He never told her about the nights he relived killing that poor Vietnamese soldier in his dreams. He never told her about the photograph they found in his belongings of a young wife and baby. He never told her how he grieved for the little boy who grew up without a daddy.

Like Stevie.

Almost a year after his return from Nam and his marriage to Ruth, he had received an Oak Leaf Cluster and a "V" (for Valor) clasp for his Bronze Star. He had taken no pride in it; rather, he was ashamed to wear it. He knew why the major had recommended him for a higher medal. It did nothing to erase his sense of guilt over the young man.

As he spoke of things and emotions he'd suppressed for years, he cried again. And his wife, Ruth, held her man in her arms and stroked him gently, kissing his forehead and telling him it was going to be all right.

The phone rang from a far off place. Dean struggled to swim to the surface of a deep sleep. He blindly groped around his nightstand for the offending device. It stopped ringing before he found it. He heard Cindy speaking from the kitchen.

Thank you, honey. You're a good wife. He looked at the clock, 8:00 a.m. He needed to get up anyway.

"Dean?" she called from the kitchen, "It's Brother Kitchener, from Litchfield."

Swell. Brother Kitchener was pastor of the Litchfield WHF Church. He also served as Fifth Area, Illinois District Presbyter for the WHF conference. This could only be bad news.

He took a deep breath and picked up the phone, "Hello?"

"Brother Grossman," Kitchener's deep voice boomed across the phone. He always sounded as though he was preaching, "I hate to call you this early, but I've just gotten off the phone with a member of your congregation who is quite upset about some strange goings on-"

Well, this didn't take long. Whoever it was must have waited up all night to call him at the crack of dawn.

"-this person is concerned about a certain young widow, a Mrs. Neustadt?"

"Yes," Dean said resignedly, "I'm aware of Mrs. Neustadt's problems."

"This person also said you're hosting Daniel Baumer?"

"Yes," Dean said, getting defensive now, "Daniel is an old childhood friend of mine."

"Well, Brother Grossman," I suppose you are aware that Daniel Baumer lost his credentials with the WHF years ago?"

"I'm aware of that, Brother Kitchener."

"Then why are you are allowing him to minister to a member of your congregation."

"With all due respect, Brother Kitchener," Dean said, surprised at his own boldness, "I wasn't aware that God was a respecter of persons, much less denominations."

There was a pause, as Dean's words sunk in. "Is it true that this man spent the night in the Neustadt house alone with Mrs. Neustadt and her daughter?"

"Brother Kitchener, the man drove almost a thousand miles from Georgia to help a family in trouble. After driving almost a thousand miles he spent several hours praying and ministering to the Neustadt girl. As you know, the nearest motel is in Glen Haven twenty miles away. The man was exhausted; there were no rooms at the inn. Where was he going to stay?

"Also," he continued, "considering the fact that her daughter was still experiencing, er - problems- it wasn't advisable for Daniel to be too far away from the girl. She offered him her couch. It's a huge house, Brother Kitchener, there were extraordinary circumstances, believe me."

"Brother Grossman," Kitchener answered reasonably. "Please understand, I am concerned about appearances and your ministry. After all, a man of his reputation-"

"Brother Kitchener," Dean answered, fighting the anger that was rising, "any reputation, other than that of total honesty and integrity Daniel Baumer has is totally undeserved believe me. I've known him since we were kids. As I said, we're dealing with extremely extraordinary circumstances here. A young girl's life, her very soul, is at stake here. I have a good idea of what you may have heard - believe me, from what I've seen in the last twenty-four hours, anything Daniel Baumer has done was necessary and proper."

"I suppose you won't mind if I come down and investigate myself?"

"No, Brother Kitchener, feel free." he said. "We need all the help we can get. That is, if you come to help."

Dean hung up the phone. Cindy was standing in the doorway staring at him.

"What?" he asked.

"I can't believe that was you," she said.

"What do you mean?"

"I've been married to you nineteen years and I've never heard you stand up to anyone, much less a presbyter, like that."

"Was I wrong?" he asked, "You should have heard him."

"Oh, I can figure out his side of the conversation," she said. "No, I don't think you were wrong necessarily. I've just never seen you get this riled up before."

"I've never had a real cause to get riled up," Dean answered. "This might mean the end of my pastorate here."

"We've been here a long time."

"It might mean the end of my ministry with the WHF."

"If God wills it," she said, quietly. "Maybe it's time for a change. The kids are raised."

"You know, last night I dreamed we were in Thailand."

It was now 9:30. Dean had called Becky to check on Laurie and tell her they'd be running late. Becky reported that Laurie was awake but quiet.

"I may sound dense," Cindy was saying as they drove to the Neustadt house, "but what would her being sexually molested have to do with her hanging on to her demons?"

"They're her escape," Ruth explained.

302

"What do you mean?" Dean asked now.

"Well," Ruth began, "in our ministry we've come across cases like this. The child often retreats inside his or herself during the molestation incidents to escape the experience. Often, a spirit will come in and take over. The child actually welcomes this because when the spirit is in charge, they don't have to experience the trauma."

"We've also seen it in physically abusive relationships," Daniel answered. "Sometimes a spirit will 'take over' during the beatings, so the child doesn't feel the pain."

"So the devil's working both ends," Dean said.

"Yes," Daniel agreed. "There's often a spirit motivating a parent to behave in such a way as to abuse a child. It could be a spirit of rage, unnatural lust-"

"Do we have to know all this to cast the devils out?" Cindy asked.

"No," Daniel answered. "Not necessarily."

"It'll make our job easier, though." Ruth added, "After all, the devil is a legalist. If we have an idea of the type of spirit we're dealing with, if we can get a name..."

"They have names?" Cindy was skeptical.

"What do you think the ancient gods the people worshipped were?" Daniel asked, "Molech? Ashteroth? Dagon? Bel? Demon spirits."

"That's why God got so angry with Israel for worshipping them."

The car pulled in at the house. Once more there was the feeling of being watched from the upstairs windows as they exited. Dean looked over to Daniel to see if he too sensed it, Daniel glanced back and nodded slightly. Becky greeted them at the door.

"Laurie's in the living room," Becky said, as they filed in to the house. "She's been babbling to herself all morning. Sometimes it sounds like a convention in there."

"Hello, folks!" came the voice from the other room, *"Welcome to the party!"*

Daniel had to smile at that. Sometimes, he reflected, the demons could act so funny, so cute. One had to struggle to remember how evil they actually were. But, he reminded himself, that was their intention.

"How's Duc van Ho doing?"

Ruth saw Daniel's face blanch, she grabbed his arm,

"Whatever you do," she said, don't let it get to you. Don't let it know it's getting to you."

She saw him nod slightly, as he set his face. Daniel walked into the room.

"Oh Danny boy! We're so glad to have you back!"

"Quiet! Come out of her in the Name of Jesus."

Thus began the cycle all over again.

"What can I do?" Cindy asked after witnessing the first spirit leave.

"Pray." Ruth said quietly.

After an hour and several spirits had passed, Daniel sat back. "This is getting us nowhere."

The girl grinned at him. Her eyes were hard, serpentine, her tongue flickering in and out of her mouth again.

"The first one who blinks loses!"

Daniel began praying under his breath.

"Yabbadabbababbadabbayabbadabbablabba..." the spirit mocked him.

"I said be still, serpent! In the Name of Jesus I bind your tongue!"

The girl was silent.

"Listen," Daniel said, "I think we need to anoint the house again. I think we're dealing with what I was worried about. Somehow, the spirits are running back and forth. The house is acting as a sanctuary. Dean, why don't you and Cindy re-anoint the house while Ruth and I stay here with Laurie? You know what to do now, Brother."

Dean and Cindy took off through the house, praying over each doorpost and window, dabbing oil over each. Daniel and Ruth, meanwhile, stepped up their assault on the spirits in Laurie. There were more physical manifestations with the girl, which disgusted, shocked, and amazed Becky. She was mystified as to how the couple could ignore the display put before them and continue with their prayers and commands. She realized she, too, would need that concentration if she were to assist them. She would do her little girl no good if she collapsed. She bowed her head and prayed even more fervently.

Dean and Cindy returned, having anointed, in his words, "Every corner and crack in the place, even the toilet bowl."

"Good." Daniel nodded; he looked at Laurie, who was gazing at him with unmitigated hatred. Dean wondered if he detected a hint of fear.

"In the Name of Jesus," he intoned, "I command you ruling spirit to come forth, reveal yourself!"

A smile twisted the girl's lips, *"Somebody's gotta do it. We can't take prisoners!"*

Daniel winced, "Still your tongue, serpent! Again, I command you to come forth in the Name of Jesus!"

"No! No! Sil vous plait!"

"Stop it, demon!" Becky came forward.

"You can't have her! She's mine!"

Even Daniel was taken aback by the fierce savage voice emanating from the small mouth. Becky's mouth dropped open in horror. Was what she was looking at even her daughter? She could see Laurie's features, still, basically the same. The dark red hair, cut in bangs across the forehead, falling past the shoulders in back. There were her dark eyes, wide mouth, and a light sprinkle of freckles across the cheeks and nose, but the features were twisted into such a contortion.

We've flushed out the ruler!

Although Laurie's eyes were normally so dark as to be unable to distinguish the iris from the pupil, the entire iris appeared to be stretched vertically so as to present a slit. From the center of the pupil, again, barely discernible from the iris, came an unholy red glow. The skin of Laurie's face appeared to be pulled back across the bone to present a skull like appearance, flattening her nose to the point where it appeared to be two serpentine nostrils. Her lips, pulled back from the teeth, caused a skull like grin to appear where once had been Laurie's full red lips. This effect was broken only by the darting of her tongue in and out of her mouth like a pointed dagger.

Becky's temper flared. For over a year now, she had sat back helplessly and watched this thing- these - things, torment Laurie. She had discovered the terrible things done to her baby, so sweet and innocent. She had felt helpless to do anything to help her.

"You leave my baby alone you -" she screamed out an epithet. Both Dean and Cindy held out restraining hands, pulled her away.

"Come on Mama, let's play!" the demon mocked.

Daniel suddenly became detached from the situation. When the demon came forth, he'd been taken back by the appearance, by the raw power of the spirit he was seeing, both in the physical and spiritual realm. Indeed, this was the most

305

powerful demon spirit he ever remembered encountering.

Then he felt the overwhelming power of the Holy Spirit engulfing him, protecting him, and comforting him, taking him away from it all. Though he was still looking in the eyes of the little girl, confronting the spirit possessing her, he was somehow above the entire fray, looking down at the scene. It was not an "out of body experience" as he understood the term used by the modern pseudo-spiritualists, but he could see himself, sitting not a few feet away from the girl, holding her hands, vying for her soul. He could see his wife and friends, standing behind him, praying fervently for him and Laurie. He could also see the hundreds, perhaps thousands, of black shadowy spirits scrambling around them, waiting to attack his friends and him. They were being held back by a legion of angelic guards, standing in a circle around the group of humans, facing out calmly, assured of their power. Some relative few imps had made it through the ring and were attacking the humans, jumping on their backs, scrambling to climb up their legs, sitting on their heads. He recognized many of them, though he didn't know how. There were spirits of confusion, doubt, fear, anxiety, false religion, tradition, anger, lust, murder, suicide... The list grew. These were the ones they themselves had allowed through the heavenly guard God had given them. *God will do so much,* he reflected, *He is bound by His own Word and cannot lie. Some battles we have to fight ourselves.*

He saw a large dark spirit sitting off a short pace from him, glaring balefully at him. It was a furry creature with bat-like wings. He was reminded of the winged monkeys in the *Wizard of Oz*. He recognized it as his own spirit of guilt, the one he carried since that night in Vietnam. He realized it was no longer on his shoulders, weighing him down. He and Ruth had knocked him off earlier in the morning. It was only after he'd told her, recognized her acceptance of him in spite of his terrible secret that he could fully accept the forgiveness of Jesus. His confession was the final surrender of his sin on the altar. He now realized why the Bible told people to confess their sins to one another.

He was aware of so much now. Things were so much clearer in this frame of mind and spirit.

He realized he was "in the spirit" as the Apostle John had been on the Island of Patmos. He'd never experienced this closeness to God before. As he sat there, watching the conflict going on in the living room of the house, the Homestead, knowledge flooded his being. He realized that what they had encountered was what the Apostle Paul spoke of as a "Principality," or Prince. He was reminded of reading about the Angel Gabriel's struggle with the "Prince of Persia" in the Book of Daniel. He knew that what was being fought here was greater than a struggle for a little girl's soul, as important as that was in the eyes of God. It was greater than the struggle in his own heart to be the man of God he longed to be. He knew it was greater even than this house, the Homestead, which had hosted so much evil over its long history. He knew that just as the south bedroom was the spiritual heart of the Homestead, the Homestead was the spiritual heart of Delphi. The spirit that ruled the Homestead and tried to devour all who dwelt there, ruled Delphi, depriving its inhabitants of all hope. The mission was now clear – deliver the girl; deliver the house; deliver the town.

He saw in his spirit the terrible night when the town leaders, headed by Doc Felder had gathered in the very room in which they now contended and made the decision to "take care of Leon Folsom." He could see the look of righteous determination in their eyes as they allowed they would do the same thing had Molina been one of their daughters. He watched in terror as Leon fell into the trap they laid for him. He heard Molina scream as she watched her lover attacked by the mob of men beneath her own bedroom window. He almost felt the strangling sensation as Leon was lynched from the old oak tree in the front yard. He groaned inwardly as he watched Molina run away from home, only to be caught and brought back by the men her father sent. He saw the young girl go into premature labor, her father deliver his own grandson, then take it downstairs and throw the screaming infant in the old well, slamming the cover to the well shut, ordering the well to be sealed to keep its secret.

He watched Molina prepare the poisoned recipe, which nearly killed her with her father. He also knew her disappointment when she realized she'd survived. He saw her grow old in that house, carrying her baby doll, giving way to the spirits of bitterness, hatred, and insanity, which had come to dwell there. He watched a black veil, which he knew somehow was a curse of lust and murder fall over the town. He watched the town wither and die on the vine as the curse took its hold, killing the spirit of the people, without their knowing it. He sat as a silent witness as the town was stricken by tragedy after tragedy, the consequences of the town's sin. He knew there were few in the town alive at the time that didn't know what had happened to Folsom. Most suspected what had happened with Molina. No one raised a hand or spoke of it. To know to do good and refuse is to sin. The town suffered the consequences of their sin.

Now, his family's experiences in the house made sense. Rose and her family, as the offspring of a man of God and not part of the town's heritage had posed a threat to the demons' hold over the town. However, his mother's guilt and Roggie's insecurities made them prime targets for the particular spirits of the house. Daniel could now see the battle his older brother fought against the demon spirits at night, playing to his every insecurity and hang-up, alternately accusing him and feeding his ego, tempting him.

He bit back tears as he saw Roggie give in to the spirits with Denise, finally with Uta. *Be sure your sins will find you out.* Satan got Roggie out on a limb of promiscuity, and then sawed it off.

He saw Denise's father take her to St. Louis for her abortion, could see her face as she screamed with the pain of the procedure, the realization of what was happening to her, to her baby. He saw everything, even, and here his heart soared, Roggie give his heart to Jesus Christ as a buddy witnessed to him one night in their hooch in Vietnam. Daniel knew, somehow, it was two days before he was killed in the crash.

He saw the demons attack Del Neustadt, saw how much he hated himself after he'd done the things he did. He saw how Del's self-loathing and hatred actually led him to his death. In despair he'd actually prayed for death. He had grown careless, almost suicidal. Now, he could see how the demons were accusing little Laurie of being responsible for Del's death, to the point of convincing her she enjoyed what had been done to her. He could see the grotesque spirit possessing her. He knew it was the Prince of Delphi.

It was a large, cyclopic lizard like creature with a single horn jutting from the forehead above its single eye. Its shadow engulfed Laurie, choking her spirit.

Then he was "transported." He found himself lying on a hard stone floor, he could feel its rough surface scrape his skin. He opened his eyes and looked into the eyes of a man beaten so badly he could barely recognize Him for what He was. He stared into the swollen, bruised eyes; saw the broken nose, jagged broken teeth from a brutal beating. He was overwhelmed by pity for this creature. Then he saw the face being jerked away, as if several men were roughly picking up the Person.

There was some groaning and noises that he could not identify, followed by a whistling noise as if something was cutting the air; it was followed by a sickening crack and moan. *Somebody's being beaten.*

Then he recoiled as a searing blast of pain tore across his shoulders, ripping into his very soul. He searched around frantically and felt another blow. *Dear Lord,* he screamed inside himself, *I'm feeling your pain!*

No, Daniel – my Danny, came a reply from the depths of his spirit, *you cannot begin to feel My pain.*

Now he saw the face again, even more bloody and battered. This time it was as if it was being suspended in air. He heard words being spoken in a strange language, but somehow knew their meaning, *"It is finished!"*

Now he saw the Man's face again, beaten, bloody, tortured. He caught Daniel in His stare, through the battered eyelids, held His hands out, and showed the awful, jagged scars in His wrists. In his vision, Daniel reached out, took the hands. The Man was transformed. Daniel was blinded by the glow that emanated from the Man. When he could see again, he could see that a splendid robe of white linen had replaced the torn and bloody rags. The face was scarred, but healed, the eyes, opened now, were healed and glowed with a fiery holy glow. The hands with scarred wrists were still held out.

He saw the plan, the purpose, now. He knew what to do. If there had been no other purpose for his being born, it was enough that on this evening it was God's plan for him to defeat Satan's purpose in this girl, in this house, in this town, and proclaim God's redemption over Delphi, Illinois. *For the son shall not bear the iniquity of the father,* Ezekiel's words burned into Daniel's mind, *For Christ has redeemed us from the law of sin and death.* If he built no more churches, led no one else to the Lord, preached no more great sermons, it was enough to obey God on this day.

He was back. It had all taken but an instant. Ruth was still rebuking the demon for his sake. Daniel looked up, touched her arm gently, and smiled when she looked down at him.

"It's all right, honey," he said.

She gave him a questioning look.

"It's okay," he said. "We've won."

He saw her mind work, trying to figure out what he meant. She looked into his eyes, saw the light, which glowed through them, understood, and nodded.

"Demon," Daniel commanded, standing up. "Look at me!"

There was something in his voice that commanded everyone's attention. Dean, Cindy, and Becky stopped their praying, and paused, watching in expectation as Laurie stood up. The house itself was deathly still, as if in anticipation of what would happen next. They all noted there was fear in the girl's eyes where once had been scorn.

"Who do I serve?"

No answer.

"Answer me, in the Name of Jesus!" Daniel said, "Who do I serve?"

"Him!"

"Who?" He asked again, "Name Him!"

"Jesus!"

Daniel felt a great heat pouring over him.

"Look into my eyes, serpent! Who do you see in my eyes?" the demon hesitated, resisting. "I command you in the Name of Jesus Christ to look into my eyes!"

He watched the face look up. Their eyes met. He felt triumph as he saw a mixture of anger and fear flood its countenance. Laurie's mouth dropped open as if to scream.

"Who do you see?" Daniel demanded.

"Him!" It hissed, refusing to say the Name. Resisting until the end. But Daniel knew the "game" was over.

"Who?" He insisted, refusing to relent, "Say His Name!"

"You know Who!"

"Say His Name, I command it!"

"Jesus!"

"Most holy God!" it was Dean, almost simultaneously with the demon, as he dropped to his knees bowing his head to the floor.

Daniel started at Dean's outburst. He heard a thousand voices in unison speak in the back of his head, **"Remember your Father's business, Daniel!"** *I heard a voice as of many waters...*

"Now," he said, rising to stand, barely able to speak through the emotions. "Who commands you to leave?"

"Jesus!"

"Then what must you do?"

310

The demon nodded. The entire room was engulfed in a mighty wind; items were thrown off tables and stands. Sounds of doors opening and slamming shut came from upstairs. From the dining room came the sound of a window smashing. Daniel was dimly aware it was the frosted glass window in the front door.

Then silence.

Laurie slumped out of the chair to the floor.

"Danny," Dean said after a few moments passed. "Am I going crazy?"

"Dean," Daniel answered, "if we're crazy, then so is every man who helped write the Bible."

"Laurie!" Becky rushed to her daughter, who was stretched out in the middle of the floor. She picked her up in her arms. "Are you all right?"

Laurie moaned weakly, and then opened her eyes. For a moment her eyes struggled to focus, then fixed on her mother. She smiled a wide, toothy grin, "Oh Mama! Guess where I've been?"

"Where've you been, baby?"

"I've been with Jesus!" she said. "Isn't that neat?"

"That's neat, baby," Becky said, as tears rolled down her cheek.

"Why're you crying, Mama? Don't you believe me?"

"Oh yes, sweetheart, I believe you. If ever I believed you, I believe you now."

Chapter 19
June 19, 2010

*Then Nebuchadnezer, the king, was astonied, and rose up in
haste, and spoke,
and said unto his counselors, "Did not we cast three men, bound,
into the midst of the
fire?"
They answered, and said unto the king, "True, O king."
He answered, and said, "Lo, I see four men loose, walking in the
midst of the fire, and they have
not hurt; and the form of the fourth is like the Son of God."*
(Daniel 3: 24 & 25)

It was midnight. Off in the distance, Daniel could hear
the sound of a bobwhite, singing to the darkness. He looked out
at the porch through the empty window frame of the front door.
He started at a movement out of the left corner of his vision. He
looked directly at the source at the end of the porch. He smiled
when he saw a squirrel peek at him from the edge of the corner of
the porch. *What are you doing out this late, Rocky?* he asked,
mentally.

The squirrel eyed him warily for a moment, a treasure
clenched in his fists. Daniel tried to see what it was and gave up.
It was too dark.

"Hello, buddy," he finally spoke.

The squirrel started and took off around the corner of the
house. *Well,* he thought wryly, *I guess I ruined that magic
moment. 'Headed for the oak tree in back, I suppose,* Daniel
reflected absently, as he went back to studying the empty window
frame.

"That's something, ain't it?" Dean's voice came from
behind him.

"Yeah, that's something." Daniel agreed. There was no
sign of the shattered window. It was as if the glass had been
disintegrated.

"I've been upstairs all through the house. This is the only
window broken. Isn't that weird?"

"Yep," Daniel agreed, "that's weird."

He was just now coming down from the high of the battle. It was similar to being in a firefight, he'd often reflected. One's adrenalin is running full tide through one's system. The senses are all heightened. As he'd once read on a sign over the NCO Academy at Bad Tolz, one had never truly lived until one had faced death. Of course, he reflected, couple the natural, physical excitement with the presence of the Holy Spirit, not to mention what he- Who they all- had seen in that room, everyday life seemed bland.

He smiled inwardly at his friend, Dean. Dean, he knew, was giddy in the aftermath of the battle. Daniel had been that way after his first couple of jumps, after his first firefight. The joy of being alive had been overwhelming, beyond containment. He knew why birds sang in the morning. They were overwhelmed with the joy of having survived another night in the wild.

"Here," Daniel said, motioning to the window sill in the door. "Feel this."

He stepped aside as Dean moved toward the door. Dean reached out his hand, touched the wooden frame, "It's hot!" he said, astonished.

"'For our God is a consuming fire,'" Daniel said softly. "That's the power that destroyed Sodom."

"God's power."

"God's holiness."

The women were in the kitchen, talking quietly. Laurie was back in her room, again, now that it was safe. She was sleeping soundly. Daniel decided to go upstairs and check on her. He passed through the kitchen, nodding at Cindy and Becky, winking at Ruth, and climbed the darkened stairs, remembering the many times he'd bounded up and down them as a child. He rounded the corner to the east bedroom and remembered all the grand battles he'd fought on the floor.

He peeked in the south bedroom, smiled at Laurie, lying in bed, lit by a small lamp. *So innocent, Lord, please let her heal.* He turned around to go back downstairs and found himself staring at the closet door. There were no shadows.

Cleansed.

Something on the floor caught his eye. Trapped by the glare of the streetlight coming in through the window, it could hardly escape his attention. He stepped across the room for a closer look. He bent over, picked the object up and studied it, holding it up in the light with his fingers. It was a gray plastic toy soldier. A Civil War figure, depicting a Confederate general charging, sword raised in one hand, a pistol in the other; urging his troops forward. It had been one of his favorites. It was his General Armistead figure. He remembered its disappearance from this very room. He remembered the fight he'd had with Roggie over it. He wondered who'd found it and where.

He carried it downstairs, still looking at it. He couldn't believe it had turned up after all those years. He felt as though he'd found a long, lost friend.

"Becky," he said, when he reached the kitchen, "where'd you all find this soldier?" He had to make sure.

Becky looked up quizzically from her cup of coffee, "Brother Daniel, I've never seen that before. Where'd you find it?"

"Upstairs, in the east bedroom," Daniel said. "Could it have been Del's?"

"Naw, Del gave all his stuff to his kid brothers when he left the house. He never played with soldiers anyway. He always liked trucks and cars when he was a kid."

"I had one just like it when I was a kid. As a matter of fact I lost it when we moved here."

"I guess it's yours, then," she said. "Imagine finding it after all those years."

"Yeah," Daniel agreed. "Imagine." *God is good.* He clasped the figure in his hand tightly, and then opened his hand again to look at it. He put it in his pocket.

"Daniel!" it was Dean. They had spent an extra day in town resting at the church cottage. Daniel shrugged his shoulders inwardly. He'd hoped to slip out of town and avoid the awkward goodbyes. *I guess it wouldn't have been right,* he conceded.

"Hey, Dean," He had to smile at the grin on his friend's face.

"You weren't going to take off like that with out saying goodbye, were you?"

"I've never been too good at goodbyes, buddy."

"I'm glad I caught you then."

At that point, Ruth came out of the cottage with their last few personal effects, "Hello, Dean," she smiled.

"So, what are you two going to do now?" Dean asked.

"Well, neither of us has to be back at work till Monday. I

314

was figuring on spending the day and night in St. Louis. I figured I'd take Ruth up in the arch. She's never been in it."

"So you two have a day planned?" he sounded disappointed.

"I reckon so."

"What after that?"

Daniel shrugged, "'Go home, tomorrow. Hit it again." *The same old grind,* he started to say, but caught himself. Somehow, he knew it was going to be different, "What about you?"

"I figure I'm washed up in the WHF. I received a call from Brother Williamson himself this morning. Evidently, Brother Kitchener drove by the house last night while we were praying, heard some 'peculiar' noises coming from the house. They want a full report of what happened here."

"What are you going to tell them?" Daniel asked, knowing the answer.

"The truth, the whole truth, nothing but the truth."

"They won't believe you," Daniel said.

"Probably not. But that won't make it any less true."

"'...Having eyes and not seeing, possessing ears and not hearing...'" Daniel paraphrased.

"How has the church strayed so far from what Jesus and the apostles taught and preached?"

"Religion, tradition, rationalism," Ruth spoke from the passenger seat.

Daniel nodded, "Every denomination was founded on a rediscovered Biblical truth, you know. Their followers came along and built their tabernacles on those foundations and failed to move on to the next revelation. I've come to believe it's the height of conceit to be content in your relationship with God- to think you've got all of Him you need when there is so much of Him to have, when there is so much of Him we all need.

"There's a terrible war going on and the majority of the Church, girded in their armor, armed with the power of the Word and Spirit, are either blissfully unaware there's a war on or fighting the wrong enemy.

"So what do you do if they throw you out?" Daniel asked.

"I don't know. I've always been WHF. Maybe I should have concentrated on being a Christian."

Daniel laughed at that, "There's not necessarily a conflict

of interest there. In spite of everything and the way I sound, I'm not against denominations or fellowships, if you prefer. We belong to a fellowship. We all need accountability. I think an organization provides stability to the church –if it doesn't get in the way of God, or worse, become our God."

"I know," Dean admitted. "You know, I've seen other guys have falling outs with the powers-that-be and leave. I never thought it would happen to me. I never even dared imagined what I would do if it happened to me. To be honest, I figured I'd spend the rest of my life here, in the home church, keeping the garden hoed. Now that it looks like it's all gone and we're going to have to start over, I feel strangely at peace. Even Cindy is okay about it. She's the daughter of a WHF preacher."

"I guess that's the 'peace that passes all understanding' Paul spoke of.'"

"All I know is I've seen Jesus. Before, I don't know- I believed, but, since last night, He's more real to me than you are. I don't know what's going to happen to me now, but all I want is to go forward with Him. I figure He'll take care of me, you know?"

"I know."

"That's how we've been doing it all these years," Ruth said, smiling over at her husband.

Cindy came out of the house now, walked over to Dean, who put his arm around her. "Did you ask him?"

"Not yet," Dean said, "I was waiting for you." Dean met Daniel's questioning stare.

"We were thinking," he began, struggling for the words. "Cindy and I, that is, if things go the way we think they're going to go... there's nothing keeping us around here...well, we were wondering if you might need help down there in Georgia?"

"Do you mean you want to move down with us?"

"We were thinking, if the WHF doesn't want us, we could learn a lot from you two."

"We need help. Boy! Do we need help! We couldn't pay you anything, though, our ministry is so small, and the type of ministry we do... I mean, how would you charge?"

"Hourly rates?" Dean quipped. "Or by the demons cast out?"

They both laughed, remembering their conversation a year before.

"We've got money saved up over the years-"

"You've got money saved?" Daniel feigned surprise, "Man, you *have* had it soft!"

Dean and Cindy both blushed, and smiled. "It's not that much," she said defensively.

"We used to be pretty good street evangelists," Dean said.

"I'm teasing," Daniel said, getting a bit more serious. "If it comes down to it and you believe it's the Lord, come down. God will make a way. We'll throw another 'tater in the pot until you get settled."

They started to shake hands, thought better of it, hugged.

"Don't think the learning will be all one way, Dean," Daniel said as he got in the car. "I've a feeling there's a wealth of spiritual wisdom stored in you you're not even aware of. We could teach each other."

"Well," Ruth said, as they pulled off. "You've asked for ten. There's your first two."

"Yeah," Daniel said, grinning. "Actually, three. I talked to Stevie this morning. He wants to come work with us when he graduates."

"Praise the Lord."

"Yes, praise the Lord."

"Where're we going now, Baby?"

"The cemetery." Daniel said, turning off on Hillside Road. "There's some unfinished business there."

He stood staring at the faces in the picture for a long moment. There was still grief, but now there was hope. He knew now he would see them both again. He couldn't explain it, wouldn't try, but he knew they would all be together with God someday.

He fumbled in his pocket for a second, producing an object. It was the Armistead soldier. He studied it one last time, remembering the day he and Roggie had gotten their Civil War set for Christmas. It was one of his fondest Christmas memories, one of the few Christmases their dad had been allowed to spend with his family. He remembered spending the entire morning with his father and brother, setting up the soldiers, putting together the pieces of scenery and accessories. He remembered the sound effects record that came with the set, how it had started out playing Lincoln reciting the Gettysburg Address, ending with a few minutes of all-out battle sounds and bugles. Rose had been

317

taking the Christmas turkey out of the oven when the record switched themes. She had almost dropped it when the bugle blasted "Charge!"

Daniel laughed softly through the tears at the memory. He recalled the hours he and Roggie had spent with the soldiers, Roggie telling him everything he could remember from his history classes about the battles and wars that had been fought.

He reached out and dug a tiny hole in the ground beneath the headstone. He placed the figure in the hole and covered it carefully. *Perhaps, it won't be disturbed there.*

He stood and took one last look at the tombstone. Somehow he knew he wouldn't be back. His business here was over, the Delphi chapter of his life closed, all accounts settled. Rose had been speaking lately of moving Roggie and Uta's bodies to Alabama, where they'd purchased a family plot. She wanted them closer, so she could tend the graves. It would be nice to have the graves closer. He wondered whether it really made any difference? Those bones weren't Roggie and Uta anymore. He believed Roggie and Uta were in a much better place than here. At the same time, they were alive in his heart. When he wanted to see them all he had to do was close his eyes. One day though... *face to face...*

Now, as he looked out over the town, he wasn't sure moving the grave was a good idea. This had been the closest thing to a home either he or Roggie had known while they were growing up.

He looked back at the grave. Just bones and dust, he repeated. The real Roggie and Uta weren't there anymore.

He walked back to the car, took one last look at the town as he opened the door. It would always be home in a strange way. As he got in the car, he noticed Ruth waiting patiently for him. He looked into her warm green eyes, saw the love and compassion there, and found himself falling in love with her all over again as he had a thousand times before. He realized Delphi wasn't really his home anymore.

"Have I told you I love you recently?" he asked off-handedly.

Ruth hesitated a moment before speaking, as if she were thinking, "Not in a while."

"I'm messing up."

"What now, *Kimosabe?*"

"Let's take in the arch."

318

Epilogue
July 2012

Daniel opened the front door to the house, the impact of the dramatic rise in temperature and humidity from his climate controlled kitchen to the 95+ degree and 85% humidity waiting outside made him stop to catch his breath. He idly wondered how folks had ever survived without the conveniences most folks took for granted today, such as central air conditioning.

He knew from the times his family had been stationed in the Deep South when he was growing up folks survived it somehow.

He had about a fifty-yard walk down their drive to the mailbox on the road. By the time he reached it, his fresh shirt, just replaced after a shower, was already drenched with sweat. *Man, I must be getting out of shape.* Then, he reflected about half of the moisture on his back was probably condensation from the humidity.

He flinched at the heat from the mailbox lid as he opened it. It was scalding hot from sitting out in the hot sun all morning. He retrieved the mail from inside. The church building across the road caught his eye. He eyed the peeling paint and reminded himself of why he'd taken three days off this week. He sighed. In the heat it was an effort.

There would be time enough to get started after lunch. He should have started earlier, before the day's heat really set in, he scolded himself. So what if he had treated himself to an extra hour – or two – of sleep this morning?

He walked back to the house, thumbing through the mail on the way. He frowned at the electric bill. He knew it was going to be outrageous this month. It always was this time of the year with the heat. There were some letters from his fellowship; he'd look at those later. Then he noticed a personal envelope. He looked at the return address and postmark, Glen Haven, Illinois. Curiously, there was no name on the return. His curiosity was aroused.

He carefully opened the envelope. There was a newspaper article with a note attached.

He read the note:

Dear Brother Daniel,
        I hope this finds you and your family doing
well. We are all okay here. Laurie will be in
the seventh grade next year. It's hard to believe.
She did good in school, made the honor
roll. Anyway, I saw this in the paper and
thought you might be interested.

                    Thanks for everything.
                    Becky

Dan went on to read the article:

Bodies Found in Old Well Provide More Questions Than Answers

Glen Haven, Ill- The Warden County Sheriff's Department believes it has found the answers to a mystery uncovered two weeks ago when workers, clearing a vacant lot in the small town of Delphi, Illinois uncovered a well containing the skeletons of two people, one forensic specialists believe to have been a man in his mid- to late twenties, the other a very young, possibly newborn infant.

        The lot had been the site of an old town landmark, The Felder House, one of the earliest built and the largest houses in Delphi. For the past year the house had been uninhabited and up for sale by the previous owners until a fire destroyed the building in March of this year. The town then agreed to buy the property to make way for a small manufacturing plant to be built in the town next year.

        Authorities were stymied at first by the discovery of the bodies. "Delphi's a small town," Delphi Mayor Robert Grossman was quoted as saying, "No one could remember anyone disappearing, so the question was, who were they and how did they get in the well?"

320

Cahokia County Coroner Ed Brach determined the bodies must have been in the well at least fifty years. More exact dating was difficult due to the fact the bodies had probably been submerged in water several years.

"The water tables shifted during the mine cave-in back in thirty-seven," town resident and Delphi Water Board Chairman Cliff Beull said. "That probably exposed the bodies to air and started the deterioration. Unless we performed more extensive testing, which we don't have the facilities to do here, it would be impossible to get an exact date. It's a wonder anything survived under those conditions for that long."

"This makes it extremely difficult to get an ID," Cahokia County Sherriff Ned Kopf confirmed. "We'll probably never know for sure who they are or what happened to them."

Longtime Delphi resident, Wade Felder disagrees. Felder, who now resides in Oakside Manor Retirement Center, is a descendent of Jonathan Edwards Felder, who built the old mansion in the 1800s, claims the skeletons are the remains of a musician, Leon Folsom, who was lynched on the property after townspeople discovered his affair with Felder's aunt, Molina Felder. The skeleton of the baby can only be the remains of a child Ms. Felder allegedly gave birth to as the result of the relationship. "Rumor had it a baby had been born and done away with but it was something no one talked about except in whispers and only when they thought us kids couldn't hear."

"Aunt Molina lived in that house all her life- never married. She always carried around a baby doll. Folks said she was touched because of what happened to her."

Felder has requested, and authorities, reluctant to confirm the identity without firmer evidence, have informed the *Ledger* they are likely to agree, that the skeletons be given over

to his family to be buried in the family plot in
Delphi.

"We haven't been able to locate
Folsom's next-of-kin, if there are any. We don't
even know where to start looking. This crime, if
there was one, is so old, there's no point in
investigating further. Everyone involved is
dead." Sheriff Kopf concluded.

"It's only right," Felder insists. "We'll
bury Folsum next to Aunt Molina and the baby
with his mother."

Dan folded the note and article and began to slip it back
into the envelope. He noticed something in the envelope that had
escaped his notice before, he reached in and pulled it out, it
looked like a school picture.

"Dan," it was Ruth calling from the house "Phone!"

"Who is it?" Dan asked wearily.

"It's Emily. She's having a panic attack again. She needs
prayer.

"Has she called her pastor?"

Ruth made a face, "She's left a message on his answering
machine."

Dan sighed. He knew there were thousands of pastors
out there who were selflessly devoting themselves to their flocks.
For all he knew, Emily's pastor was out visiting the sick and the
shut-ins at that moment.

"Tell her I'll be there in a minute." Dan looked down at
the picture in his hand. The smiling face of Laurie Neustadt
beamed back at him. Dean and Cindy had done follow up
counseling with the girl after her deliverance. She appeared to be
doing fine.

Dan looked over at his peeling church building, wished
he had money to pay for it to be done. Then he looked up at the
clear skies, reflected on how beautiful God's earth was, and said
quietly, "Thanks, Lord, for giving us an occasional glimpse of the
harvest."

He turned and headed toward the house to answer his
phone.

322

Also by Wayne Wood

All the Way! And Then Some… A Cold Warrior's Journey

His memoir and testimony of his service in the US Army.

"If you ever get the chance to jump out of an aircraft from 800 feet carrying almost 150 pounds of equipment with 2500 other guys into a crosswind gusting to 75 knots – don't try it. It's not as much fun as it sounds…"

As a member of the elite 82nd Airborne Division in 1982, Wayne was assigned to participate in Gallant Eagle 82. What was to be the largest Airborne Operation since World War II, Gallant Eagle became the worst parachute disaster in 82nd history as high winds blew out of the surrounding mountains across the desert drop zone, wreaking havoc on the jumpers After being dragged over three-quarters of a mile, sustaining severe friction burns on his hands and arms, hitting a large boulder head first, and being left for dead by medics, Wayne recovered to be declared a fully fit paratrooper who would participate in the liberation of Grenada in 1983. In the process he found the God he had been running from for most of his life.

All the Way! is one soldier's story. In a time when America is gaining a new awareness of the sacrifices endured by our men and women in uniform, *All the Way!* tells a story of a forgotten generation, the "Cold Warriors." It is the story of "Army people," the soldiers who fight the battles and the families who wait for them. From Vietnam, to standing on a frozen hillside staring at the Iron Curtain in Germany, to the windswept desert of California, to the tiny island nation of Grenada, this story can only be told by one who has seen all facets of Army life.

COMING SOON!

Unhallowed

Another Daniel Baumer story

323

www.ingramcontent.com/pod-product-compliance
Lightning Source LLC
Chambersburg PA
CBHW070545260626
47161CB00002B/513